HER SCHEMES AND PLANS

BY DAVAJUAN

For my family—for loving me and always listening to,
laughing at, and believing all of my stories,
no matter how outlandish.

Detroit

The Woods --->

☐ Club Xanadu

Tyson D&D ☐ Dmitri Dav Freddy
              ■   CJ ■   ■
              ☐   ■   Wanda
           Embers Bar J&J Triplets

The Tracks

■ Mandy

The Park

☐ Pack Rat Pete's

Rouge Park

West Ridge

<----Crosstown

☐ Sears   ☐ Farmer John's

Rouge Park
Shopping
Center

Zane   ☐ Theater

<----Northgate

1
wrong Side of the Tracks

The haggard figure reappeared from the dark recesses of the concrete opening that led deep into the hillside. He glanced back at me just long enough to say, "None of it matters one bit, kid. Remember that. They'll tell you different, but it's a lie." He was dead wrong of course, but I didn't know it yet. It would take a handful of deaths and an entire summer for me to fully understand the truth that every little detail can be significant.

He was dressed in clothes that looked thick and rough, but warm enough. A golden gleam from one of his thin fingers caught my eye, standing out from the otherwise gray and brown aura he emitted. His face looked oddly familiar, but due to the grease smudges and thick beard, I couldn't quite place it. He seemed to have been living out there for some time. Some dirty blond tufts of hair peaked out from under a worn trucker's hat, with a light blue horse and rider logo on it.

He clutched at a green glass bottle with a peeling red and black label like his very life depended on it.

After his last cryptic statement, he turned and retreated once more into the culvert, which emitted a trickle of water from underneath the railroad tracks towering some twenty feet above him.

A minute later my companion returned. He had turned 14 already, a few months older than me, and was carrying a load of sticks that he'd scrounged from the ground in the woods in which we found ourselves. He was about my height, but much more muscular, and he had a crop of wild brown hair. A faint ring of acne traversed my friend's forehead, whereas I had none. It was a typical mid-May weekend in Michigan: sunny, with just a touch of chill to the air.

"I saw him again," I reported to him with an excited grin. "Do you think he's dangerous?"

"Probably not," shrugged Tyson. He was searching the ground for something. "OK, now where's that pan?"

I handed him one of the objects from my hastily cobbled-together backpack full of items I'd illicitly scrounged from around my house. He grabbed it from me and positioned it over the wisps of smoke now curling into the crisp air and slowly rising above the trees.

"Are you sure Skittles will really cook in this thing, Dav?" Tyson queried, calling me by my more palatable nickname. "The Cheez-Its might be more filling for our first meal." I had to chuckle at how odd his last sentence sounded.

"Sure, they'll cook up nicely," I said, guessing wildly. When planning a last-second escape from home, whatever can be grabbed without notice has to suffice. I stood warming my hands by the fire and continued with my previous rant.

"I'm literally just one problem away from expulsion at school," I complained. "And if that were to happen, there's really no point in going home ever again." I was being somewhat dramatic, but also slightly serious—I wasn't sure what my parents would do in reaction to yet another family embarrassment that centered around myself. I leaned against a massive tree, and studied an ancient carving that someone had etched into the trunk eons ago that appeared to read *R + N 4-Ever.*

I gazed over at Tyson Largo for a second and wondered why he had been so agreeable to the idea of running away. He seemed to have things much more together than I did: he was doing well in school, had lots of friends, was extremely athletic. It was hard to be jealous of him, though, because he was so humble and good-natured.

I knew deep down that this little escapade of ours wouldn't really last for long, but it was fun to pretend for the moment. I'd gotten in deep trouble again at school a few days prior, for leaving the school grounds without permission on a silly dare. It had earned me yet another suspension, as well as a torrent of criticism and lectures from my well-meaning, but exasperated, parents.

As the flames started to lick the sides of the pan and a colorful candy pancake of sorts began to form, I took a second to peer in all directions again, keeping a wary eye out for the hobo. The woods we were in weren't that large; they were a forgotten couple of acres butting up against a freeway, guarded on one side by railroad tracks, and on the other by an abandoned industrial plant that was literally standing on the city line between the southeast corner of Detroit and an inner ring suburb.

"Tell me again what you said to Crabb when you went to the office. Denny was laughing so hard he couldn't get it right," Tyson implored.

I smiled sadly, and repeated that I'd barely avoided expulsion on a technicality, since the building I'd ventured over to was owned by Crosstown Christian as well. My parents hadn't shared my friend

Denny's mirth at my quick thinking, however.

"Let's find out where that hobo went," I ventured calmly, but with a flutter of danger in my stomach. I hoped that Tyson would agree to my proposition. He was bigger and stronger than me by a mile, but often played the follower to my lead.

He pulled the pan away from the fire, and seconds later, we were consuming our hot and crusty candy concoction. The idea of leaving home permanently to scrape out an existence in these woods was losing its allure fast, if this was the type of food we'd be existing upon, I thought to myself between sticky bites.

He looked at the small camp we had set up, stamped the fire out with his foot, and—since everything appeared in order for the time being—he agreed. We set off back toward the tracks. They weren't far away. In a few dozen steps, the thick overgrown plants ended abruptly and trillions of bright limestone ballast rocks came into view, reflecting the morning sunshine vividly. Used to hold the railroad ties in place and allow for drainage, the rock system was well-designed; far below at the bottom of the ravine, there was a gaping drain hole that led horizontally into the rise.

"He went in there," I pointed to Tyson. Looking north and south, you could see a pattern repeating for miles: railroad tracks disappearing into the faint urban fog, the bright rocks on both sides of the man-made hill descending down like a waterfall, and drain pipes with small reflecting pools of runoff at their bases every thousand feet or so.

The mysterious sewer entrance reminded me of the Hardy Boys book I'd been reading as of late: *The Secret of the Lost Tunnel*. It was Number 29 in the series and I had been constantly scanning the shelves of the area thrift stores in search of the next volume.

Tyson picked up a smoldering cigarette butt he had found at the base of the tunnel entrance. He looked it over and took a huge drag from it, to my surprise. "Kent," he declared confidently. I wrinkled my nose at the name. I despised the smell of that brand, but secretly rather enjoyed whenever I got an illicit whiff of a Marlboro.

Inside the circular cement tunnel, the air was thick and rather unpleasant. It wasn't exactly a sewer smell; it was the smell of old things—metal and decay. The temperature fell almost immediately once we were inside, but the light extended in quite a long distance.

A thin ribbon of water lay below our sneakers as we moved forward, ducking down to avoid hitting our heads on the four-foot ceiling. It was certainly not a deluge by any means, as I'd often seen pouring forth during the wetter months earlier that spring.

As I stepped forward into the gloom, I bent over and picked up a tan plastic bag plastic bag with the word *Lynch's* printed on it in bright block yellow letters. I opened it up and found a generic receipt and some strands of plastic wrapping. We continued on hesitantly. A few steps before total darkness would have engulfed us, we came to a fork in the tunnel.

"Let's try this way first," I ventured, heading to the right. Tyson was right on my tail, his breath creating a faint puff of mist besides me. The chill was increasing every few yards, and you would never have guessed that the sun was shining just a few dozen yards behind us.

During our next segment forward, it began to get very dark. I could still sense Tyson behind me as close as could be, but there would have been no way to actually see him at this point. I began to wonder which of us would suggest we turn back first, and I vowed solemnly that it would not be me.

A left-hand turn at the next juncture forced us to rely only on our innate senses of direction, since complete darkness had overtaken us. Right when I feared we would never stop, a low unearthly howl began to echo through the tunnel from a distance ahead that seemed impossibly far away.

We both stopped dead in our tracks, cemented to the spot in the concrete tube we were crammed in. The cry grew louder, and reverberated through the endless maze of tunnels. At first it was unrecognizable, but soon a pattern emerged. It was a name being yelled over and over again in utter anguish. It eventually became crystal clear: *Nicolette.*

After what seemed to be several minutes, but in reality was just several seconds, Tyson and I simultaneously turned and broke into what could only be described as a crazy, crouching gallop. The adrenaline exploded through our veins, not unlike the torrents of rainwater that occasionally passed through those same hidden waterways.

A dime-size gleam of light finally appeared in front of us as we turned and hurtled down the initial stretch of tunnel, and grew exponentially as we approached the exit. Emerging from the entrance, both of us stopped, stunned by the sunlight, even though our subterranean adventure hadn't lasted very long.

For a split second, the sudden brightness caused the wooded scene around me to melt away, and I caught a glimpse of the boy's bathroom at the school I attended. I seemed to be transported back there all at once, without warning. The cool, humid air in the long room was punctuated by a slow, dripping sound. I could see the familiar shape of a young student down in the farthest stall, finishing up his business as he stood in front of the toilet. Just as I saw the light blue metal door swing open abruptly behind him, the scene melted away as mysteriously as it had just appeared, and I was back near the woods.

As soon as our vision had somewhat returned, both of us climbed pell-mell up the steep embankment, unconsciously heading toward civilization on the other side of the tracks and forgetting our brief excursion into the nearby woods entirely.

As our heads crested the top, we encountered the long waving grasses covering the opposite side of the railroad, and a new unexpected emergency greeted us.

"Get down!" I exclaimed and we both instinctively slid headfirst under the cover of the overgrowth. Several police cars with their lights ablaze silently dotted the aging parking lot that was located at the bottom of the hill. A handful of uniformed officers stood beside their squad cars, and one was making his way up toward where we were hiding at a steady clip.

Laying face down with my cheek against the dirt, doing everything in my power to remain motionless, I tried to will my chest to stop pounding.

I could sense Tyson a few feet to my left, and I hoped we were mentally on the same page. Kids were generally encouraged by the authorities to steer clear of these woods, and something told me the police would not look kindly on our presence.

"You two up there—stand up and come down here immediately!" the approaching officer commanded, revealing to me that our ploy to remain undetected had been completely in vain. After a couple seconds of useless internal reasoning, I slowly stood up straight where I was. Tyson did the same.

We glanced at each other with petrified expressions, and as I looked over Tyson's shoulder, I saw that we were about to be in a lot more trouble than I had originally imagined. Thick black smoke was now billowing upward directly from the spot in the woods where we had set up camp an hour or so earlier.

Trudging reluctantly down the hill toward the officer who had called up to us, I found my mind racing. *Had we not doused the fire? I could have sworn that we had done so. Were we somehow responsible? What would happen to us next? What would my parents say—or worse—do?*

Tyson looked rather calm as we arrived down at the police car nearest to our hiding place. I knew that he had been in small-time trouble before, but this was a new high-water mark for me personally. I could be a rude, impertinent brat when called for, but none of my offenses had ever approached the level of misdemeanor.

The officer opened up a notepad and made eye contact with us expectantly. His partner joined him. After an initial interrogation during which we danced around the pressing topic at hand, Officer Collier, as his badge revealed, finally addressed the elephant in the room.

"Let's get down to brass tacks. Did you boys set that fire?" He looked at us unflinchingly and calmly waited to hear our response.

For years, I had forged a pathway through life littered with half-truths, fibs, exaggerations, and outright lies. For example, I had feigned unconsciousness after a tricycle collision at a park in early elementary school. Two years later, I had embellished a stomach flu bout and rolled down the entry stairs of the bus on a class trip in front of dozens of students, and collapsed in a heap, horrifying the teacher and driver alike.

Not long after that, Jason and Johnny, the pair of sports-obsessed boys who lived across the street from me, had been playing a game of pickup football with my Dad. I had suffered an injury so unbearable that I was left rolling around and moaning in the grass, only to glance up to see their reactions. I was startled to find that the game had continued on without skipping a beat.

Undaunted by that humbling setback, I had continued to exhibit a pattern of a person whose stories and reactions needed to be taken with a very hefty grain of salt. However, Officer Collier didn't know any of this history of mine—so I knew immediately what had to be done.

As Tyson opened his mouth to answer, I jumped in first, hoping he would get the hint and follow my lead. "No, sir. But we think we know who did."

Tyson's eyes darted at me and he clammed up, seeming perfectly content to let me take this new theory as far as it could get us.

"Is that right?" the officer retorted. "And who might that be?"

"A hobo or tramp, sir. We just saw him out there in the woods a few minutes ago. He seemed really suspicious." I hoped my respectful manner would somehow lend credence to our tale.

Minutes later we were seated in the air-conditioned back seat of his patrol car. It was unnecessarily cold in the car for this type of weather and it left me shivering. Officer Collier and his partner, a dark-haired muscular man with a square jaw named Simmons, had gathered with the other officers in a semicircle with their backs to us, and they seemed engaged in some earnest discussions.

In the meantime, a fire truck had arrived, and its occupants were now scrambling to engage the roaring fire above us in the woods before things got even further out of hand.

A sense of dread and awe at our circumstances gradually set in. Tyson, for his part, sat motionless, gazing out the window at the small group of shoppers gathering to gawk at the proceedings upon exiting the big box department store located at the far end of the parking lot.

"What did this gentleman you mentioned seeing just now look like, exactly?" said a voice abruptly as the driver-side door was yanked open, jolting me back to reality. I loosely described the hobo, adding in a few extra embellishments to further bolster our story. Tyson confirmed my dramatic description and Officer Collier shut the door loudly.

Collier popped the door open again. "Names?" he demanded. Tyson answered obediently, and I used my entire name for once, which was probably just a knee-jerk reaction in light of the solemn occasion. The fireplug of a man looked at me oddly, then wrote it down as best he could, and shut the door once more.

Minutes later we were on the road, and a short trip of several blocks brought the official-looking vehicle to my front curb. My house was the nicest one on the street, its clean vinyl siding gleaming bright white in the sunlight, its lawn green and neatly manicured, making it stand out against the rest of the simple, aging frame bungalows that extended on both sides of the street as far as the eye could see. Most of them had seen better days a decade or two prior. I got out, and Tyson followed, explaining to the officer that he could walk home from there.

We stood on the grass easement under the beech tree planted squarely in the center of our property, which couldn't have measured more than ten yards wide from one side to the other. The car window rolled down once more, and Officer Collier stared at us from behind blue sunglasses as we stood facing him at attention.

"Stay out of those woods now, boys. Not a place for fooling around. Go inside and—play some video games or something. We'll keep an eye out for the man you described." With that, the window rolled up, and he and Simmons crept down the street in their car and eventually out of sight.

"Man, that was insane," exhaled a clearly relieved and anxious Tyson. "My dad will be wondering where I am. Oh wait—what about all of our stuff?" In the blur of the events, our gear had completely escaped my mind. The supplies were still strewn around the campfire in the woods, most likely now burnt to a crisp.

"We'll get to it later. Too soon to head back out there right now," I stated flatly. "See you tomorrow morning?" Tyson nodded his affirmation, and then he broke into a run west towards his own house located just a half mile away.

In 1987, there was a stark improvement in the quality of neighborhoods with every few hundred feet you got away from the Detroit city limits. My house was a stone's throw from the notorious border. Tyson's was further on, but his own home bucked the aforementioned trend. The Largos' small ranch looked perfectly normal on the outside, but the interior was a hoarder's dream.

I had been invited into the house by Tyson only a few times before, and I didn't have to wonder why, once I'd been inside for the first time. His dad was divorced, and the infrequent times he was actually at home after working one of his three demanding jobs, he clearly had better things to do than organize.

Heading even further west from Tyson's house, the structures transitioned quickly from simple sided bungalows to brick ranches, and then on to stately brick colonials. About a mile away from my own house stood a complex which was the center of my family's world: Crosstown Christian School and Church. Covering numerous acres, the sprawling campus was where my family attended religious services, and also where my dad was employed at the high school.

His job as a chemistry teacher at the college prep school, and the exhaustive education that had been required along the way to enable him to qualify for it, made us a bit of an oddity in comparatively-drab Rouge Park. While all the kids in my neighborhood attended the local public school in their crumpled Nickelodeon shirts and Z. Cavaricci jeans, I headed off to Crosstown Christian College Preparatory every day in a neatly pressed uniform consisting of khaki pants and a collared polo shirt.

It hadn't been lost on me that the acronym for the school was CCCP. I was amazed that they had overlooked the reference when brainstorming for school names twenty-five years prior. The familiar abbreviation and the jokes that went along with it made calling the place a Soviet gulag simply too easy.

As I stepped up the short segment of sidewalk in front of my house, I caught a glimpse of my dad inside just past the screen door. Before I could determine if he'd seen the police car dropping us off, a cringe-inducing yelp calling my name came from further down the street to the east, in the dead-end section of about a dozen cramped houses. I knew without turning around that the voice belonged to Friedrich Mann, known to the rest of the world as 'Freddy.'

After realizing it was too late to pretend I hadn't heard him, I turned half-heartedly and saw a short, thin boy with stringy light brown hair climb aboard his bike and take off toward me in a whir of pedals and wheels. He reached my front walk in seconds.

"Want to come over, Dav? We could build a fort in the backyard. Remember you said that next time we would–" Freddy implored before I cut him off. Freddy was just one grade behind me but significantly smaller and several orders more annoying.

"Not right now, Freddy. Dad has, um, some chores for me to do. I might come over later—or sometime tomorrow, OK?" I could see as the words came out of my mouth he was already thinking of his next move, but before he could even answer, I bounded up the stairs to my porch and disappeared inside our house.

Freddy was mildly tolerable at times, but his mother was definitely not. She seemed to be either drunk, or well on her way there, at all times of the day, and her incoherent screams at both Freddy and his ragtag younger sisters punctuated the air at random intervals both day and night. I hadn't seen his dad—a tall and lanky man with long hair and yellow highlights— around for quite some time, and I frankly was not empathetic enough to ask Freddy about him.

Most of my previous interactions with Mr. Mann had come in the form of grunts when I'd become bored enough to venture over there to see if Freddy was available. Single parents were the norm in this part of town; two-parent families like the two of ours stood out almost like a sore thumb.

Inside my own house, I found things were typically calm and pleasant. Mom sat on the couch in the front room of the house working on a crochet project. Dad was in the kitchen just to the right of that tiny room putting away the dishes. Our home was small, but always immaculately clean and spartan. Both of my parents greeted me cheerfully without looking up, and I slipped past them into the back of the house, where two tiny bedrooms contained both of my younger siblings.

Suzanne's door was ajar and against the hot pink glow of her walls, I caught a fleeting glance of her arranging some sort of soiree using her prized collection of Cabbage Patch dolls, their clothes all hand-sewn. Our fat, orange cat Muffin sat dutifully on the bedspread watching the ten-year-old girl at play.

Corbin, aged 5, was sitting cross-legged on the glossy hardwood floor of his light blue bedroom right next door, playing with Matchbox cars. He looked up, hoping I'd join him, but I swept past him without a word and headed to my own bedroom, located down a flight of stairs in the partly-finished basement. It was a hurriedly thrown together compilation of studs and drywall in one corner of the underground level—but it was totally mine. That alone made its value nearly incalculable.

I had barely crossed the threshold of my own room when a voice from upstairs demanded that I return back to the main floor immediately. A nervous twinge accompanied the fear that our fiery mishap in the woods had perhaps already somehow been discovered. However, as I reached the front room once again, I observed through the bay window what this line of parental questioning would actually be about.

Dad stood on the driveway with his arms crossed, hovering over a large black stain that contrasted sharply with the smooth light gray cement. He did not look pleased in the slightest. Just past him I could see Jason and Johnny playing pitch and catch alone in their front yard, like they did nearly every day.

I was kind of jealous of their inattentive parents, content to let them do whatever they wanted, whenever they pleased. My parents, on the other hand, never missed a beat. I had been hoping this next mishap would go unnoticed, but deep down I should have known better. The only surprising thing was that this offense had taken almost a full 24 hours to be discovered.

"What is this, Dav?" my dad asked in a frustrated, but even tone. As I walked out to meet him on the driveway, I contemplated making up yet another story. Then I considered the oft-repeated warning both he and my Mom would recite: "The truth has a strange way of wiggling itself out of the depths, both when—and how—you least expect it, Dav."

So instead, I went ahead and spilled the beans right away, which must have caught him somewhat by surprise. I couldn't help but notice at the same time that a black curtain of smoke still hung in the air in the distance over his shoulder, marking the location of my most recent escapade.

The afternoon before, my friend Denny McElfish from school had been over at my house. Denny had a wicked, sarcastic sense of humor, and the type of laugh that was irresistibly contagious and almost impossible to ignore. The two of us had come up with the brilliant plan of taking my birthday gift from the previous summer, which was a junior chemistry set, and seeing what might happen if you mixed all the chemicals together in one single large beaker. The resulting concoction had fizzed wildly to our mutual delight, but had eventually consolidated into a black tar that possessed an otherworldly scent.

For some odd reason, Denny had thought it humorous to dump

the entire contents of the beaker near the edge of our driveway. After panic had set in, we had made several frantic attempts to get it off—but they had all been completely futile. To my chagrin, Denny had headed home soon afterwards without a care in the world—and now I was going to be left holding the bag once again.

"Get this off of here completely, and never do it again. Oh—and you're stuck here at the house until that happens," Dad said with an unmistakable firmness, promptly walking back inside the house, leaving me alone to gaze at the black splotch helplessly. Grounded. This was exactly the type of situation that had worked me up enough to craft the plan with Tyson to leave home for good in the first place. I spent the rest of the afternoon grousing to myself as I scrubbed endlessly at the stubborn spot.

Later that evening, as the sun was finally fading in an orange-green glow over the lined trees to my left, I gave my aching knees a break and sat down with a sigh to admire my handiwork. The dark stain was now just slightly noticeable against the concrete. Freedom was now tantalizingly within reach—if only my Herculean efforts could meet my Dad's strict approval.

My basement was deathly cold at that time of year, and as I lay gathered up in a ball shivering under a thin, threadbare bedspread, I contemplated the day's events. The last thing I thought about as I faded off to sleep that night was the hollow look I'd seen in the hobo's eyes, and the name that we had heard echoing through the drain tunnels.

swiss cake Rolls

Two days later, I found myself reluctantly making my way back toward a classroom down a dimly-lit hallway. Passing in and out of shadows, I let my left pinky find the smooth groove between the endless cinder blocks, making it travel along them like an X-wing Fighter advancing through the Death Star's perilous troughs.

I often managed to make this activity a recurring diversion, inventing a trip to the boy's bathroom simply to break up the day's monotony. Scholastics came relatively easy to me—though you would have never guessed it by taking a peak at the grade books—and I needed the escape. I often used this alone time to hum a theme song I'd made up, to be used when a movie was eventually made about my life.

I recoiled as my nose detected a whiff of the sweet-smelling sawdust that teachers would dump onto pools of vomit. I wondered who the unfortunate kid was this time around, and hurried on.

Soon I crossed the classroom threshold and the bright lights inside of it snapped me back to reality. The room was square, painted light green, and had high ceilings and a solid bank of windows on the far side overlooking the street. In the center of the room, a neatly dressed slender woman was stooping down to look at another student's assignment, and she straightened when she saw me enter.

Darcy Townsend was the first teacher I'd ever had at Crosstown Christian that I simultaneously respected, feared and adored. Her combination of no-nonsense wit, patience and high expectations had quickly won me over. I usually made a conscious effort to cause no real trouble for her.

Violet Vereen—one of only a handful of black students in a school that was practically all white, like myself—made a face when she saw me, and continued to fight to get Mrs. Townsend's attention back to herself. I had found a way to get on the bad side of most of the girls in my grade over the years, a ploy that I was finally beginning to regret as we all hurtled toward adolescence. Violet and I had a surprising history, one that no other person in the world knew about, and neither of us was in any hurry to let on about it to anyone else.

Violet's family lived in a nearby wealthy subdivision. She was smart as a whip, and I knew she was on the fast track to an Ivy League school. Tyson was sitting in the second row, Denny was in the third row near the windows, and I was seated in the back, right next to Violet. My seat placement in such a remote location was a surprising gesture of trust from Mrs. Townsend, as the Crosstown faculty tended to keep the biggest troublemakers such as myself as close to their desks as possible.

A note arrived on my desk almost as soon as I could sit down. Hastily scrawled on a piece of notebook paper were the words, "New multi-stage bomb to test. Meet out back at recess for detonation." As I crumpled the evidence of the missive from Denny, Mrs. Townsend cleared her throat and announced the presence of a visitor to our 7th grade math class. Violet stared at the piece of paper in my hand, and implied with her eyes that it would be reported to the teacher as soon as it was feasible.

"Students, our new principal would like to have a quick word with you all. As you know, she has recently taken up this important post, and even though our school year ends in just a matter of weeks, she wants to get off to the best start possible with us. Ms. Stickler," Mrs. Townsend ended as she gestured and stepped back to yield the floor to a pale, middle-aged woman whom I had never seen before.

"Good morning, students," she purred in a sickly sweet tone, a questionably-genuine smile passing across her face. "Mrs. Townsend has told me all about this class that she is so very proud of." She was dressed in a dated business suit, her hair severely pulled back and above her head, and I saw that her right hand had a cast on it that ended just above the wrist.

"I know you are all very excited about the upcoming summer break, but I want to strongly encourage you to finish well. Make good choices. Your teacher told me something earlier, and I firmly believe it to be true. She said that our choices define us, and are solely what determines the trajectory of our future—for good or evil."

She glanced at Mrs. Townsend with a look I couldn't quite identify, and paused, seemingly to let that statement sink in, though most of the class had already tuned her out with recess impending. I, on the other hand, was surprisingly still very much engaged, and found Ms. Stickler's stare mesmerizing whenever it landed on me.

The previous principal had left in a cloud of scandal just a week earlier, though no one thought it necessary to share any of the sordid details with the students themselves. I had seen many looks of concern on the adults' faces as they hurried through the halls during those harrowing couple of days, and had heard bits of whispers, but nothing definitive.

Ms. Stickler had apparently been fast-tracked as his replacement and had arrived with a clear mandate to restore order quickly. She had appeared seemingly from thin air, the previous administrator Mr. Dustin Crabb already nearly forgotten. A single week in middle school can seem like a couple of months to those souls suffering through it.

At lunchtime, I sat down at the same table as always, with the same group of boys. Like every school day, the gymnasium had been transformed from a sporting venue into a cafeteria, with enough wooden folding tables and gray metal chairs to accommodate a couple hundred hungry kids. The throng was buzzing with pent-up energy from the first half of the school day.

There were a few exclusive tables in the lunchroom occupied by kids who had actually gotten up the nerve to experiment with being co-ed, but mine was certainly not one of them. My pals and I were a group of confirmed bachelors who were finally starting to admire the opposite sex, but still quite content to do so from afar.

Denny hopped down into the seat beside me and yanked out his lunch, which seldom varied. Amazingly, every item in it had an orange tint of some sort. He often theorized that it had contributed to the olive skin that he had actually inherited through his Italian lineage, along with his thick dark hair and brown eyes. Cheese puffs, orange Capri Sun, and an actual orange were usually included. My lunch was nearly as predictable, but much more boring.

I looked across the table and watched Trevor take out his own lunch. He was a short, pleasant-looking classmate with a flattop haircut, and his painstakingly-packed noon meal included a luxury item seldom seen in my brown bags: a Little Debbie chocolate Swiss roll. Trevor's lunch looked like it had been made for a Better Homes and Gardens photo shoot, with everything perfectly wrapped by his mom, every food group dutifully accounted for.

Every so often, he would deign to give me a morsel of the outer shell of chocolate from his dessert, almost as if he was Marie Antoinette handing out scraps of food to her begging populace. I tried to make eye contact with him to plead my case for a bite, but he was preoccupied, and my overtures went unnoticed.

As we ate, final plans were being solidified regarding the secret bomb detonation, and as we were doing so, a big hairy hand planted itself solidly on the table. Shadowing over me was the thick frame of Henry Hallas, recent college grad and alumni of Crosstown Christian, who also served as our middle school baseball coach. He was famous mostly for the false report of his untimely demise a few years earlier that had sent many in the student body into an emotional tailspin.

Supposedly his car had been crushed in a tragic rock slide on the way home from a tryout with the Knoxville Smokies farm team, but a day later the news surfaced that this had indeed been a different Henry. Crosstown's own Hallas was alive and well. No one had ever looked at him quite the same way since. I thought he had an unearthly, almost ghostly aura about him. "Baseball season is over guys, but—the fun has just gotten started," he said, obviously intending that statement to provoke a volley of follow-up questions, but he received none.

Baseball and I had a complex relationship. I loved to collect baseball cards, and I listened to the Detroit Tigers games on the radio often. However, my personal career batting average hovered around .025, and the highlight of my past season had occurred when I was lucky enough to get three straight walks in a game.

My dad loved the sport, and had coached our school's varsity team for over a dozen years. He was constantly trying to cajole me to put more effort into baseball, bringing me to the school on weekends to step inside the batting cage and face robotically-generated lasers that whizzed past my haplessly outstretched bat. I wondered if he sometimes secretly wished the athletic neighbors Jason and Johnny had been his actual sons instead. When the final strike of the past season had been called, I'd secretly celebrated inside.

When Tyson, who was a star hitter on the team, reminded Henry that the spring season was over, he happily explained that Crosstown Church was again fielding a Little League team over the summer, and that he'd love for us all to play on it. Somehow I doubted that my skills were the ones Henry was actually recruiting. Denny and Trevor were decent players in their own right, and they promised to consider coming out.

Finished with his mission at our table, Henry sauntered over to the next one. He stood behind Chester Wiggins, known to most everyone at Crosstown as Chet—a red-haired, sallow-skinned beast of a boy who was in the grade just above us. According to legend, Chet had once slapped a teacher right in the face in elementary, and then led the staff on a chase through the halls until he could be cornered and calmed down. Chet and I briefly made eye contact as Henry began his recruiting speech once more, but I pretended not to notice.

Chet leaned over and wrote on something in a hurried scrawl. Seconds later he held up a napkin displaying the phrase *YOU'RE A REJECT*, and laughed hysterically with his table mates. I didn't have much to do with the stocky punk, but I loathed him for a couple of specific reasons.

He annoyingly carried around a wallet gaudily stuffed with fresh crisp hundred dollar bills, which was bad enough on its own. But once, he had come over to observe our table while we were eating and, after taking a quick gander at all the items from my lunch, had quipped that "Dav would eat *crap* from a baggie."

Except, Chet didn't use the word crap; he had uttered a much more offensive version of the same word. The audacity of his burn had elicited gasps and hoots of uncontrollable laughter from my friends and enemies alike, and I was unable to cobble together an appropriate retort in time. At a typical middle school in the 1980s, that type of language wouldn't have been all that surprising; but at a religious school such as Crosstown, it was a shocking and suspendable offense. I had tried my best to steer clear of Chet and his unpredictable comments and behavior ever since.

Soon after lunch had concluded, a group of us huddled in front of a row of storage units located just beyond the imaginary boundary of acceptable recess activities. The dozen or so nondescript garage doors of the structure extended about a hundred yards along the rambling creek that cut its way through the church and school property.

At the end of the row, the structure remained uncompleted, a pile of bricks and other building supplies left stacked outside as if time had stopped right before the last unit had been finished. It had been that way for as long as I could remember. I'd arranged the abandoned bricks into interesting structures and towers several times before when I had been bored while there on a Sunday afternoon.

Tyson, Denny, Trevor, and I peered excitedly down at a small contraption made of paper, cardboard and packaging tape that lay on the ground between us. A fuse protruded from the top of it, and Denny produced a black matchbook with green printing on it from somewhere on his person. All boys love fire—and all boys love explosives of a mysterious nature even more. I glanced down and saw the matchbook had the words *Club Xanadu* printed on it in a cheap, flowery script. I recognized the place as a seedy gentlemen's club that was a few blocks from my house.

We were all alone in the alley that accessed the storage units, except for a single vehicle—a wood-paneled Ford station wagon that was parked at the far end of the passageway, its wheels half on the concrete and half on the grass. A pay phone stood there as well, leaning slightly as if it had been struck by several cars in the past.

This was not our first detonation of a homemade explosive on school property. The incendiary device in question had to have been at least Model 4 or 5, and Denny had become somewhat of an expert. This revision had been created to have several stages, each consisting of a layer of paper laced with the scraped-off dust from handheld holiday sparklers. I glanced over at Denny as he lit the fuse, and his eyes reflected back an almost maniacal glow of anticipation. We all took a few cautionary steps backwards and waited.

The first blast was a satisfying one, sending flames and cylindrical shoots of smoke a few yards into the air with a loud bang. After nervously peering around to be sure our antics were still going on undetected, we enjoyed the next few stages with awe and muffled adolescent yelps. After the paper package had finally stopped erupting, we congratulated ourselves on a successful exploit and stood chattering to one another, reliving every aspect of the event.

Just then, movement from within the abandoned station wagon attracted my attention and I squinted down the alleyway to see a familiar face behind the steering wheel. Dustin Crabb and his unmistakable mop of tousled black hair, with gray streaks around the temples, had fixed his beady black eyes on us. The disgraced administrator was passively observing us, though he made no motion to jump out and stop us.

Affixed to the front of the vehicle was a blue license plate reading *PRTYBOY*. I wondered if it had been meant to signify "party boy," or "pretty boy." Both seemed almost equally ridiculous and out of place.

Even from that distance, I could tell he was wearing one of his classic white button-down shirts, half untucked and most likely covered with traces of cheese dust at the fringes like usual. What the recently-fired leader could possibly be doing lurking around on school property, I hadn't a clue. But, as the other boys noticed his presence as well, it had the effect of making us vacate the premises in a hurry.

We hightailed it back up the alley, but in the middle of our escape, Denny realized we had left the remains of the bomb out in plain view. He stopped on a dime and sprinted back to retrieve what was left of the package. Trevor, whose worst offense ever recorded had been to scratch out key letters on the hand dryer so they spelled *Push Butt. Stops Atomically*, didn't even bother to look back. Tyson and I stopped and watched to ensure Denny successfully acquired the smoldering evidence. At the exact moment he leaned over to grab the paper contraption, we sadly learned that unfortunately one explosive stage had still remained.

Not long afterwards, our three slouching figures could be seen sitting in a row of chairs against the wall that was just across from the new principal's office. Trevor had successfully avoided capture. Tyson looked concerned. I stared down at the floor, and occasionally stole a look over at Denny to reassure myself that I wasn't imagining things; his eyebrows had been nearly burned off by the bomb's unexpected finale.

His only solace was that school pictures were already in the books for the year, and his shame would not be documented for posterity. He kept muttering to himself something about what his mom would do. He'd pulled the red fire alarm handle in the gym down a year prior after Tyson had dared him to, resulting in a serious stint in detention, but he'd managed to stay out of trouble ever since.

The outside world was visible through plate glass windows, and Violet Vereen passed by several more times than necessary, her head held high, with her hair pulled into big thick loops of braids and mounted neatly on top of her head. She smiled at us, but it was obviously a smile of satisfaction, not necessarily friendliness or sympathy.

A few more students loitered near the office as well, probably trying to confirm or deny the awful truth that was spreading like wildfire through the school about Denny's tragic lack of eyebrows.

I listened as a weeping and frazzled girl tried to explain to the secretary that she had been saying "shush it," to her noisy classmates, not swearing at them, as they had all breathlessly and gleefully accused her of.

Darcy Townsend came into the office just then, and I saw a flicker of disappointment pass across her face, with a scarce hint of sympathy mixed in. She said nothing to us, but left a stack of papers on the green island countertop that divided the free from the doomed, and soon retreated back to class where life continued on without us.

The sound of the school secretary's typing from across the room droned on and on in a seemingly endless loop. I was growing increasingly impatient to get on with the proceedings and learn my fate. There was no doubt that, whatever punishment lay in store for me there at Crosstown, the consequences at home would easily trump it. The heavy wooden and windowless door in front of us still had the name Principal Dustin Crabb displayed, but inside I knew the cold, emotionless figure of Joyce Stickler awaited us instead.

No doubt she would be salivating to make an early example of us, and simultaneously strike fear into the rest of the student body. *What could be taking her so long?* I wondered. After a short consideration, and realizing no adults were looking, I dashed up next to her door and put my ear against it.

The agitated voice of Joyce Stickler was chattering quickly in a low tone. There were several outbursts and long pauses as she listened to the person on the other end of the line. I was unable to discern what was being said for a stretch of time. I crammed my ear even further into the corner of the door frame nearest the silver handle. Soon I could hear Ms. Stickler clearly once again, and her voice hissed with intensity and fury along with a hint of fear.

"What I want, Nicolette, is justice! Where is justice now?"

That seemed to be the exclamation point on the conversation, and she slammed the phone handle down onto its cradle. A slight ruffling of papers and the sound of swift, determined footsteps alerted me of her impending approach, and I darted back to my seat with the others.

What Stickler had said reminded me of the slogan I'd heard a lot over the previous summer, during the investigation into the murder of a Trinidadian immigrant by three white teens in Queens, New York. Demonstrators had chanted, "No justice, no peace." I wondered what specific injustice our new principal could be referring to.

Soon afterward we were all dutifully standing at attention in front of Ms. Stickler's desk. Instead of a double barrel blast though, she surprised me and expressed her significant disappointment in our choices, using the same sickly-sweet tone she'd employed earlier.

Her words faded quickly into white noise in the background as I attempted to process what I had overheard. *Justice for who? And that name again—Nicolette. Was it just a coincidence? Probably,* I thought. But it was rather odd. The adult world usually seemed dull to me, full of mundane and repetitious duty. This little plot presented me with an interesting change of perspective.

I suddenly heard Tyson utter a meager, "Yes, ma'am," right beside me. Denny recited the same phrase one second later. I immediately felt that I had returned to the center of attention and that the background noise had stopped. Ms. Stickler looked at me expectantly, but I did not know what to say in reply, other than to parrot the same lame response as my friends. At that exact moment, Dustin Crabb and his *PRTYBOY* station wagon shot by the window over Joyce Stickler's shoulder, and was quickly out of sight in a cloud of billowing dust.

field Day ribbons

3

The school year was drawing to a merciful close. Memorial Day weekend had come and gone in a blur, and with it, the tantalizing finish line that meant summer break was finally visible on the horizon. The first Monday in June was usually warm and sunny in Metro Detroit, making it perfectly timed for an event that brought out the best and worst in every single 7th-grade boy at Crosstown Christian College Prep: Field Day.

I was slightly above average in height as a middle school kid, but a tad scrawny, and relatively useless at all of the skilled sports. However, I prided myself on the fact that I was among the fastest runners in my grade. Along with a smattering of colored ribbons I'd earned for some pencil drawings, my only other tangible claims to fame were the first place awards I'd earned as the winner of the 100-yard dash, an honor I'd secured for the past three straight years.

That morning, I was awake earlier than usual. I stumbled upstairs into the light, nearly crushing our poor cat Muffin, and headed straight to the kitchen. Through eyes that resisted being opened, I poured myself a heaping bowl of Honey Smacks. As I squinted at the box looking for details on a possible prize inside, I became vaguely aware of a neatly-dressed boy sitting on the couch in the living room, located just through the arched entryway and not a dozen feet away from me.

I had forgotten that this morning we were all on Gregory Watch. That was what my entire family had dubbed them—the mornings once or twice a week when one of the other boys in my grade was dropped off on our front porch before the crack of dawn, so both of his parents could head off to their wearying factory jobs in southwest Detroit.

Gregory Bassford was a quiet, spectacled, excellent student who was perfectly content to sit silently on our couch with his hands folded, while the rest of the household swirled around him in a hectic blur of preparation. Pushing his glasses higher up the bridge of his nose was his trademark gesture. He was the kind of kid that you knew would someday be successful, managing the same group of people that had teased him about his looks during childhood.

He always appeared in our living room mysteriously, like an apparition, and we all went about our business like he wasn't even there. There was only one bathroom in our cozy bungalow, with five people getting ready all at the same time. This led to lots of drama, loud demands, and frenzied conversations about the upcoming day's plans, with the occasional trickle of toothpaste oozing out the corners of mouths. Gregory simply sat and observed it all.

My dad was like clockwork when there was a deadline of any kind. He wanted us in the vehicle at very specific times—for example, 7:22 am if we had to be somewhere by 7:30. Being late was not even a conceivable option in his mind. Ranking staff members at Crosstown

Christian were afforded the luxury of borrowing one of the numerous vans from the church's fleet. It accommodated a dozen behinds if necessary, so when our family drove in ours, each of us got our own row to spread out.

This arrangement made the mundane five-minute commute—from my own city of Rouge Park to the sprawling school and church complex just across the border into West Ridge—much more enjoyable. That morning, we piled once again into the dark purple van with clean gray cloth seats along with Gregory, who continued his silent repose in the van as we headed off, sitting up as straight as an arrow.

"Field Day today, right Dav?" Dad asked out of nowhere, as we roared down the side street that led away from Rouge Park toward the school. I hadn't mentioned it to my family the previous evening at all, for fear of jinxing my chances at a four-peat in the dash.

"Yeah," I confirmed, glancing over at Gregory, who was dressed in his usual uniform, as if that day were any other day. He either didn't seem to connect the dots on that fact—or was perfectly comfortable wearing the clothes he was in, despite the athletic nature of the upcoming school day.

"Great morning for it," Dad commented. As I was finding out the older I became, pithy observations about the weather were a terrific go-to for adults to cap off a conversation. He glanced over his shoulder at me quickly, and added with a smile, "Good luck, son. I hope you win." I forced a grimace in return.

We turned right and pulled onto the smooth black asphalt that covered all the main thoroughfares throughout the Crosstown campus. The van soon emptied, and we each headed our various directions. As I approached the entrance to the middle school, I spied a haggard-looking figure marching from the direction of the small creek that wound its way through the school grounds.

The creek was skirted by a thin line of trees, and led eventually behind the same storage garages that had been the site of our improvised explosive detonation. Two other youths that looked strangely exultant bounded up and down on either side of the dejected boy, who I could see as he drew even closer, was soaking wet from head to toe.

Grangeford Ballanger was by far the best athlete in our class, and to make matters worse, he was also from one of the richest families at Crosstown. The pinnacle of my outrage was that he also happened to be a well-behaved and respectful kid who volunteered to pray at almost every group assembly, making him a darling of teachers and administration alike. Leadership had nearly fainted as a collective group when he had recently been selected to preach in front of the entire student body at our weekly chapel session.

So it was with some surprise that I realized the soaking wet and filthy young man walking in my direction was Grangeford himself. Denny and Tyson were his mirthful companions, and they were lending him about as much moral support as Job's friends had for the suffering Biblical character. All three boys were dressed in their best sports clothes and expensive sneakers. Tyson wore a new black Nike headband I'd never seen before, and Denny's new Reebok shoes literally gleamed in the dawn light. By now I was pretty much used to seeing Denny's fledgling eyebrows that were now struggling to return to their original bushy glory.

Grangeford's family had arrived at Crosstown near the beginning of that school year, when his dad had been named CEO of Downriver Bank and Trust. Rumor was Grangeford was struggling in a few specific classes; special "extra credit" assignments had been added to his ledger at the insistence of his coaches, to ensure his grades stayed high enough for him to qualify to play middle school sports. He would be going for his first Field Day ribbons today, and I grudgingly had to admit that had a terrific shot at taking in a huge haul.

"What happened?" I asked, while barely suppressing my happiness. It was already dawning on me that if, for some reason, Grangeford was unable to participate in the day's athletic endeavors, my own chances at retaining the sprinting title were exponentially greater.

There was a rickety wooden bridge leading across the creek to additional property that the Crosstown organization owned. As if that wasn't an easy enough way to gain access to the other side, an intrepid youth from a long-past era had shimmied up an aging tree that hung over the creek and attached a frayed yellow rope to one of the outstretched limbs.

This legendary rope swing had evolved into a sort of rite of passage for the male student body. The administration had made it abundantly clear that the tantalizing challenge was strictly off-limits. Several versions of the rope swing had been cut down, only to miraculously appear again in a slightly different form soon after. Only an adolescent of significant strength and gumption could pull off a journey to the other embankment and remain dry.

Grangeford had now apparently joined the illustrious ranks of those boys who had bravely battled the rope—and lost. He was wet from head to toe, and smears of mud had completely sullied his new running shoes and outfit. He left a wet path of forlornness as he trudged toward the main door to the school and subsequently disappeared.

He loved to brag that he'd assembled a collection of every badge and award the Scouts had offered thus far. I wondered what his troop master would think of this shortfall. Even someone of Grangeford's stature wouldn't be allowed to be caught in this type of rebellious act and remain unpunished, and he knew it as well as we did. I relished the thought more than I knew I should have.

Soon the sun had climbed higher in the sky, and the last vestiges of dew had been burned off the blades of grass that covered the athletic field on the near side of the creek. Hordes of eager, chattering kids spilled out of the side doors onto the field, awaiting instructions from frazzled teachers holding bullhorns. Stakes with colorful ribbons attached to them marked off the events' boundaries, and several rows of tables were erected, complete with snacks, sign-up sheets and orange sports drinks in Dixie cups.

Before long, the announcement was made for the running of the 100-yard dash. Whether it actually was an advantage or not, I'll never really know, but I had gotten it into my head at some point in the past that I ran faster bare-footed. A minute or so before the first whistle, I removed my socks and shoes, vaguely conscious of the curious looks from the other kids around me, and relished the feel of the grass between my toes.

There were several preliminary heats designed to weed out the stragglers. I lined up next to Joey Cobb, a spindly youth with large ears who had broken his arms so many times it was more common to see him in a cast than out of one. I wondered again about the one I'd seen Stickler wearing, but the impending events pushed it out of my mind.

I breezed through my initial heat as the winner, and was soon through to the finals without much trouble. Tyson and Denny were among the winners in their respective rounds, and before long the eight fastest boys in the school were lined up just behind a bright white line awaiting the whistle. Grangeford was nowhere to be seen, and I knew with an internal jolt of excitement that this was going to be an even easier victory than usual.

I looked ahead and saw the finish line, which was another strip of white paint, a mere hundred yards ahead. A small collection of teachers, bitter previously-eliminated boys, and a couple of preening parents stood near to it. My feet felt right at home in the soft grass, and my legs had a slight tingle in them. In my own mind, the tension was palpable and my ears started to detect a warm buzz, like when a microphone gets too close to a speaker. I knew the starting whistle was approaching. I was in the zone, and I knew that somehow, this moment had been curated just for me.

Suddenly, from directly behind me, a commotion of some sort began. I blocked it out as long as I could, but seconds later, there was no more ignoring the kerfuffle. Annoyed at the break in my concentration, I turned around to see what it was all about.

A triumphant Grangeford Ballanger had marched out of the side gym doors, with Ms. Stickler on one flank, along with his father, who was dressed smartly in a flashy business suit and silk tie, accompanying him on the other.

Mr. "Bah-lawn-shay," as the family all insisted their last name be pronounced to anyone who would listen, flashed me a nasty grin. Grangeford stretched for a moment for the effect, and then took his ill-gotten place right alongside us on the starting line. The other boys turned and resumed their own mental preparations, but I stood staring back in disbelief.

"What about the first heat? What about the semi-finals?" I objected. Ms. Stickler shook her head quickly with an upraised hand and a silent smirk, and headed off to a different event nearby in a demure strut. I turned back to Grangeford, who now wore a completely different outfit from head to toe, the mud and water evidence of his earlier unfortunate escapades down by the creek gone right up in smoke. As an only child, Grangeford was used to having the best. The expected disciplinary consequences for his flagrant disobedience were nowhere to be seen either.

Before I was able to even form an additional thought about the unfair travesty, the countdown for the final sprint began. As more students gathered along every side of the painted lanes to watch the proceedings, I bent slightly at the knees, crouched, and got ready to spring into action.

I looked sideways down the line at the row of legs ready to launch, and was shocked to see how many of the boys now had thick hair growing on them. *How have I not noticed this disturbing development until now?* I wondered. My own gangly legs were solid peach in color and nearly hairless.

The whistle blew and we all thundered down the field as a group. I felt confident for the first five seconds, as the wind streamed through my hair and my legs felt like they were barely touching the turf. The cheers around us faded into a low hum.

As if time was nearly at a standstill, I observed that Tyson, Denny, Grangeford and myself were beginning to pull away from the other runners. Then, at about the fifty-yard mark, to my horror, the other three began to inch ahead of me slowly but surely. I gasped, begging my body for one last superhuman burst, but there was nothing left for it to give.

For the last ten yards, I stared ahead blankly, the three other boys shoulder-to-shoulder in front of me, blocking my view to the finish line. It was over. I had failed. My momentum carried me past the celebrating mob, where I eventually crashed in a heap to my knees.

Fourth place. The words sounded incomprehensible and completely foreign in my own head. They didn't even make a ribbon for fourth place. My name would not be called from the awards ceremony podium this time. Past wins would quickly become old news tossed in the dustbin of CCCP history. The thoughts came on me like waves, and I struggled to process them. I got up from my knees robotically and wandered forward, aimlessly.

A sympathetic Gregory Bassford made a move in my general direction, probably hoping to express his condolences. But I continued walking away from the crowd, so he quickly abandoned the effort. Without even a murmur of acknowledgment or congratulations to my fellow competitors, I headed off the field.

After resisting the temptation for as long as I could, I finally looked back. One glance revealed all that I had feared: Grangeford with both hands held high, thanking some adoring onlookers. His beaming father stood nearby, shaking hands with another parent. How he'd managed to enter Grangeford in the race at the last second, I couldn't know for sure. But I had a pretty good guess.

"I'll slit the idiot's throat!" I thought, as rage pulsed through my entire body. The words scared me as soon as they had formed. I shuddered and immediately regretted them as I looked back in Grangeford's direction again.

Tyson and Denny were close by him now as well, reveling in their good results, and a faint thought of happiness for their good fortune flitted through my mind, but left as abruptly as it had arrived.

I found myself sitting alone on the hard gym floor later that afternoon, separated from the rest of the dozens of huddling, sweaty youngsters. The sound of a film projector cranking to life brought cheers from the throng, and after a few technical mishaps, the familiar and reassuring tones of Glenn Yarborough singing "The Greatest Adventure" announced that we would once again be watching *The Hobbit*, which drew even more applause.

Tyson, Denny, and Grangeford sat together, ignoring the movie, exchanging their own animated versions of both the day's tragedies and heroics. As cartoon Bilbo Baggins began his amazing quest of discovery and danger up on the massive screen, I realized things would be different for me from then on. The world seemed to be moving on without me.

When the film finally ended with a series of rapid clicks, the overhead gym lights came back on slowly and the students scattered. I walked alone up to Mrs. Townsend's classroom at a turtle's pace and, as I'd hoped, found it abandoned by the time I finally arrived there. Grabbing my belongings, I stopped by my dad's empty office on the way out of the school and left him a short note written on a scrap of construction paper. It said, "I'm walking—Dav."

I took a different route toward home that afternoon just for the heck of it. The one-mile walk provided lots of time for frustrated reflection. *Why had Grangeford been allowed to race? I had beaten my other two friends by several yards the previous year—what had changed? Had Tyson and Denny been secretly training without me? Had I doomed myself by running barefoot?* I had so many questions, but few answers.

The brilliant afternoon sun was high in the sky, which was a deep gorgeous blue. The reflection off the sidewalks and cars lining the side streets back to back was nearly blinding. As I walked by an old Dodge, the sun caught me square in the eyes and everything else around me faded—just like had happened in the woods days earlier.

I was transported back to the bathroom at school once more. A figure standing in front of the toilet came into focus, as the veiny, tanned hands of an adult appeared behind him through the open stall door. They slowly reached out toward the unsuspecting young man's neck. One menacing hand seemed to be missing a pinky above the knuckle.

The monotonous sound of water dripping every few seconds or so was the only sound, echoing off the baby blue cinder block walls which had been painted over so many times throughout the decades they were now rounded at the edges. Just as the boy abruptly turned his head toward his assailant in alarm, the vision faded back into the recesses of my mind. I stopped to catch my breath in the present world, considering what it could possibly mean, before moving on.

Even though this neighborhood I was walking through extended miles in every direction—an endless grid of houses that looked more or less the same—there was really no way for someone to get lost, as long as you just kept going the same way.

At some point, every street in the neighborhood ended at a large grassy park, beyond which—over a ten-foot-high chain link fence meant to keep people like me out—was the railroad and ribbon of forest that ringed it in from the rest of the city. Somewhere out there, I imagined, the hobo we'd seen was probably still lurking.

When I was just a stone's throw from where this particular street ended abruptly, I came back to the real world. I was now on a quiet, shaded avenue that was a bit more obscure to me, several blocks south of my usual haunts. Right in the midst of a row of twenty cookie-cutter houses—all of which looked as if they could have lined a crowded store shelf—loomed one that seemed completely out of place. It seemed to have appeared there almost as if by magic.

It was made entirely of red brick, and towered a full three stories high, which was completely foreign in this working-class collective of vinyl-sided bungalows. Elaborate stone flourishes that arched over the wide porch, as well as along the sides of the house separating the multiple floors from each other, gave it an austere, sophisticated look. I wasn't sure how I'd never noticed the place. But it wasn't the impressive house itself that caught my attention. It was a girl.

video games & jolt Cola

Maybe a lot of families went out to eat in the 1980s, but mine did not. Going to a restaurant of any kind was a pretty big deal. So, when the call would come from out of nowhere to grab some shoes and hop into the van, we didn't ask a lot of questions. Suzanne, Corbin and myself would be out the door in a flash, bickering mildly over who sat in which seat, but excitedly awaiting to discover the delicious destination.

Quite often the restaurant was that haven of cigarette smoke, pumping music and tantalizing smells, all housed under one slanted red roof, also known as Pizza Hut. Besides serving up scrumptious pizza pies, visits there also served to expose me to all the music industry's current hits. At the front of the place, near the registers and bathrooms, a glowing jukebox hungrily munched the quarters of guests waiting to be seated.

Nearly every time before exiting our vehicle, my mom would warn us once again about the melodious heresy we might possibly be exposed to once inside. Most kids of that era were well-versed in the hits of Prince and Michael Jackson, while at our house we knew every line of the complete works of Christian musician Patch the Pirate.

And so it was that I was pleased to actually know the lyrics to the song that was pleasantly wafting across the yard toward me, emitted from a boombox on the porch of the sprawling house. It was positioned just a couple of feet away from the most beautiful girl I had ever seen in my life.

The song had just begun and U2's Bono was singing:

I have climbed the highest mountains,
I have run through the fields,
Only to be with you.

And bizarrely, though I had just laid eyes on her a second or two before, I could completely relate to his words. She was wearing a bright yellow MTV shirt, the large logo appearing in all the colors of the rainbow, and she had perfectly smooth skin the color of caramels, and hair so dark brown it was almost black.

I continued on straight as an arrow down the sidewalk, but I slowed imperceptibly to make sure my time in front of her towering house stretched out as long as possible. She was fiddling with something at her feet on the porch, then rose to walk down the cement steps toward me. The walkway curved away to her left, spilling out onto the driveway a few feet from where I now walked.

She passed from the shade of the house out into the direct sunlight and I noticed her piercing green eyes for the first time, which seemed to contrast unusually with the rest of her complexion. I made eye contact with her for a split second, and she performed an obligatory short nod. She appeared to be a year or two older than me.

A brand new green Mustang GT was parked in the driveway, and it had been backed in, apparently in quite a hurry. A classic blue Michigan vanity license plate was affixed to the front of it that read XANADU. I had loved license plates ever since I could remember and always seemed to take notice of them more than most people I knew.

On a road trip years earlier, my parents had suggested that I keep a tally of all the states' plates that we saw along the highway, most likely to just keep me from agitating my siblings—but the simple diversion had stuck. After decades of issuing new and colorful plates each year, the Great Lake State had now settled into a rut of royal blue beauties with white letters and numbers stamped into them.

I'd never encountered this specific plate, car, or girl before in my life. How all their existences had eluded me up until that day, I couldn't figure out. I prided myself on my encyclopedic knowledge of the surrounding square mile.

A few more steps took me past her house, and I managed to not look back, which I figured would have looked quite ridiculous. *One thing is for sure*, I told myself. I would be going to great lengths to find excuses to be back on the 800 block of Paris Street as often as I could manage.

Closer to home, I walked opposite a rundown, tiny corner house occupied by the Vietnamese triplets, three kids who were one year younger than myself. They all attended Rouge Park Public, and when their parents weren't hollering at each other, they were working long hours. Their screen door was open and was hanging from one less hinge than recommended, like it always did.

Besides being some of the only Asians in the neighborhood, the

Ly trio also roamed the streets at all hours, and were often left to fend for themselves for meals using whatever loose change they could round up.

Another feature of the family that fascinated me was the nature of the triplets' first and middle names, which were simply three combinations of the same four: Dai Din, Din Duong, and Duong Dai. It had taken me some time to get them all figured out, but I was ninety-percent sure that it was now Dai who saw me from his window and called for me to come over.

"Dav, come in here and see what we got!" he called and then disappeared from the screen. It had clouded up considerably and the warm sunny day now threatened to unleash an unexpected downpour. Socializing was the last thing I felt like doing after the day's disappointing events, but I reluctantly darted across the street, up the front steps and into their house.

The place smelled of dog food and grease. It was a mess in the main living area like it often was, and as I passed through it, everything turned considerably darker inside and out as the first rolls of thunder grumbled discontentedly. The lights were off in the triplets' bedroom and they were gathered around a small black and white television placed on the floor, surrounded by candy wrappers and empty pop cans.

A large box with the Styrofoam and cardboard inserts still hanging gaudily out from the top of it was just to the right of them. Din and Duong each gripped a plastic remote that snaked towards a brand new Nintendo Entertainment System, hastily positioned on top of a couple of empty pizza boxes.

"Check it out!" Dai squealed. "A Nintendo! It came with Mario and Duck Hunt—and it's totally rad." I was duly impressed, and a sharp pang of jealousy struck, almost in conjunction with the bolts of lightning now appearing at regular intervals outside. I looked around for a clear space to sit, which wasn't an easy task. I finally found a spot farther back in the room, but well within range of taking in the action, as Mario attempted to traverse a difficult span from one stack of blocks to another.

Nintendo systems were still quite the luxury item in 1987, though they had been available in stores for a couple of years. A few of my friends, like Denny for example, were lucky enough to have one, but I did not. To find the triplets playing one of their own, when I knew for a fact that sometimes there wasn't enough food to go around, was rather baffling.

Outside, their dog Queen started to bark ferociously as the rain poured down from an angry sky. "Should you bring in the dog?" I asked rhetorically, but received no response.

A couple of minutes later, while realizing it might be a long time before one of them would relinquish a remote, I noticed a disgusting-looking object on the floor next to me and laughed out loud.

"Oh, cool—you got one of those fake dog poop toys?" They were a popular plastic gag at the time, available at convenience stores on the same aisle as Whoopee Cushions and electric hand buzzers. Without looking away from the TV screen, Din said, "We don't have one of those."

The awkward realization of what I'd unwittingly discovered told me it was probably time to head home. Queen's barking hadn't let up for a second, but the rain had tapered off as quickly as it had begun, and it seemed a good time to make an exit. "Very cool that you guys got a Nintendo," I said, carefully searching around the dim room for my shoes. "How'd you score it?"

The boys looked at one another and Dai finally said, "We got jobs. Delivering stuff."

Davajuan

This was a surprising revelation. The triplets were known around the neighborhood for many things, but hitting the streets to earn large amounts of hard-earned cash wasn't among them.

"How long have you been doing that?" I asked, somewhat skeptically. "Started last week. Already earned enough to get this NES, and as much of this junk as we want," Duong said, gesturing proudly toward a towering pile of licorice packs, Jolt Cola cans, and other various convenience store products that possessed dubious health value.

Probably picked them up from D and D Market, I thought, which was the party store owned by Yugoslavian immigrants found at the far end of my block. They had arrived sometime within the past couple of years from their balkanized homeland, which seemed to be careening toward inevitable war.

"Nice," I said. I wasn't quite sure if I completely believed their story yet, but as I got up to leave, I promised to come back soon and try my hand at Duck Hunt. From the living room, I could hear tension building between the triplets' parents.

"I know, I know! That *chó chết* gutter's overflowing again. It's leaking down the foundation into the basement," their dad barked. After an unintelligible retort from their mom somewhere else in the house, he replied back with an irritable edge in his voice. "I'll try talking to Justus again and get him over to take a look at it. But I haven't seen him in weeks. Shut that dog up, Dai! That beast never stops barking and carrying on!"

I slipped out through the hall unnoticed and jetted out the front door. My house was just around the corner, three houses in. I cut across Jason and Johnny's lawn and took the most direct route to my house. Though the rain had mostly stopped, I figured there was little point in getting more wet than necessary.

I glanced down the street toward the dead end right in time to see Freddy's mom stomping down the sidewalk away from me, literally dragging one of her mangy girls by the collar like an animal.

Her cursing reverberated off the standing puddles up and down the street as she splashed through her own muddy front lawn, and up the crumbling front steps into her house. I shuddered to think of what would happen within those walls next, and the thankful glow I suddenly felt for my own family matched the lights coming out of my house as I arrived. There was a red Volkswagen Bug parked out front.

I entered the house and kicked off my shoes, right around the same time my mom called from the kitchen to remind me to do just that. Dad was in the living room, and he was drinking a can of Vernors with a fellow teacher, Mr. Asperat. He was a bachelor who taught French and German, coached the chess team at the high school, and was also known to be quite handy with tools. They both greeted me, and after waving a polite hello, I made my way towards the hallway.

"Dav, Mr. Asperat was just reminding me about how you used to wow our guests with your geographic knowledge," my dad smiled.

"Ah yes, the famous red atlas!" Asperat recalled with a smile. "You and your wife would invite all of us young teachers over here to your house back in the day, and then sit young Dav on your lap and he'd recite the states, their capitals and even identify the flags of every country in the world. It was really quite remarkable. You must have been what, Dav—three or four?" Mr. Asperat asked admirably.

"Sounds about right," I nodded uncomfortably, and then shifted toward the door again. This was a story that I had heard repeated many times over the years, in many different settings.

"Are you also keeping up with your drawing? Your mother and father have always prided themselves on that as well," our guest continued.

"Doing my best, sir," I dutifully replied, and before the interrogation could continue even further, I darted towards the basement.

After dinner, I finally got around to taking a shower to remove the sweat and grime of the failed Field Day. With only the one bathroom between the five of us, getting uninterrupted time in there was a challenge. I liked my showers as long and as hot as tolerable.

Suzanne whined outside the door that she had to use the toilet, but I completely ignored her repeated pleas. As the nearly-scalding water sprayed onto my head, I bitterly refused to look down at the rest of my body. I already knew what I'd find there: the body of a boy. The rest of my classmates were quickly becoming men, and I was being left in the dust. It was a bitter pill to swallow.

Late that night I tried to fall asleep, replaying the sequence of my discovery of the girl in the yellow shirt. The image of her was burned into my mind and I analyzed it further now in the darkness. It was amazing what I could recall about her. Yellow hoop earrings, bubblegum-colored pink lipstick, a black decorative cord of some kind wrapped tightly around one wrist, her hair curling slightly under at the shoulders, a few stray wisps across her face. Fingernails painted a pale orange, slightly chipped in one spot. I had her house number memorized as well: 862. I made plans to find my way back there the following day.

The next morning, Tuesday, was cloudy and cool, the sky still appearing grumpy from the previous afternoon's pounding storm. *Just one last half-day to suffer through*, I muttered to myself as I pulled on the Crosstown uniform that lay crumpled next to my bed. Running my hands down over the wrinkles, I hurriedly grabbed my backpack, then put it back on the floor, as I remembered there would be no actual learning that day. It was simply a placeholder, tacked on to the schedule to ensure there were enough days on record for it to count as a full school year.

By mid-morning, I was standing next to a long, cushioned pew just a few rows from the front of a cavernous, frigid chamber. The church often served to house big events for the connected school. The entire student body had all walked down the long, echoing halls that spilled out into a foyer and from there, into an auditorium with vaulted ceilings, that could seat at least a thousand souls when necessary.

The stained glass, in every color of the rainbow, reached at least fifty feet into the air, and depicted various Biblical scenes. A towering angel, constructed of geometric panels in cream, green and purple, looked at me stoically with a mix of piety and pity. The moody sky outside gave the glassy scenes a somber appearance.

As the ceremony was coming to order, I whispered to both Tyson and Denny, asking if they would be over in my neck of the woods in the morning to figure out how to best kick off the impending summer break. Denny glowingly reported that he and the family were off to a beach house in Hawaii for three weeks. I was crestfallen and turned hopefully to Tyson.

He shrugged and notified me that he had to report for work first thing in the morning at the aluminum factory job his dad had snagged for him. He said he'd have to see how many hours a week they had slated for him and would let me know. We all hurried to our seats as the moderator cleared her throat.

High above the pulpit, around which several teachers and staff were now scurrying, was the baptismal, where I'd demonstrated my commitment to God a year or so earlier. I remembered looking out from the heights, standing in lukewarm water that reached up past my waist, down at the hundreds of onlookers gazing up at me from far below.

I had known beyond a shadow of a doubt since the early dawning of my consciousness that God was real, but was He really living in me, I wondered? The venerable white-haired pastor of Crosstown Church had worked through a series of late-night fire and brimstone sermons that had left me wide-eyed, frantic, and eager to guarantee that He was. But still, I wasn't completely sure yet of all the implications that went along with my nascent belief.

Awards were now being handed out, bland speeches made, and platitudes spoken. I sat like a statue as the Field Day ribbons were distributed. Endless names were called out aloud and my beaming peers shuffled out of their seats, returning with their valuables in tow. I tried to count down the seconds until the unpleasantness was over.

Grangeford Ballanger was invited up to the podium to say the final prayer to close out the school year, which was quite an honor. His parents were in the back, snapping Polaroids, eager to witness this event and gloat over the stack of certificates and ribbons that dangled gaudily from his arm.

I broke protocol and took a glance around the auditorium during the prayer. Most eyes were closed and heads were bowed, except for a few fellow reprobates such as myself scattered in various rows. My eyes fell on Ms. Stickler, in the row closest to the front, and her eyes seemed closed in earnest contemplation. She was motionless for the entire prayer except for a brief moment, when she appeared to mouth the words, "Forgive me." I noticed with interest that the cast she'd had on her right arm previously had now mysteriously disappeared.

And as Grangeford closed his banal rehearsed performance with an ending flourish, it dawned on me that summer had officially arrived. I was completely and utterly free. *But*—I thought gloomily as I watched Tyson, Denny and the others be dismissed row by row out through the glass double doors and into a procession of idling cars—*free to do what?*

BMX bikes

The answer to my question was not long in coming. Early the next morning, my mom summoned me to the kitchen table and invited me to sit down while she continued to work.

"Exciting news, Dav!" she began as she turned to put away the sparklingly-clean dishes from the previous night's homemade dinner. I'd learned from past experience to reserve judgment on whether the news was truly exciting until hearing my parents out completely.

"Mr. Asperat was telling other teachers in the staff room about your drawing skills last week. Mrs. Townsend spoke up and seconded his opinion. She absolutely adores you, Dav," Mom said as she turned from the refrigerator and smiled at me.

I knew this to be the case, though I wasn't sure why. I had been an absolute terror for her early in the year, but after she'd laid down the law with me in a kind, but firm fashion, we had definitely grown on each other over the ensuing months.

She went on to explain that since I was heading into the 8th grade, I was now eligible to be an assistant at the yearly program run by Crosstown Church—and thousands of other places of worship across the country for that matter—known as Vacation Bible School, or VBS for short. The pieces were beginning to come together as she continued speaking, and this clearly was going to be one of her pronouncements that was more dreadful than exhilarating.

Having discovered the existence of my artistic abilities, the program director had called our house to inquire whether or not I would help illustrate some large-format pieces for the week-long children's event. My mom had accepted the honor for me on the spot, of course—no questions asked.

The main piece was to be a ten-foot high replica of the ancient Philistine soldier named Goliath, the giant slain by young David and one of his five smooth stones. The director hoped that it would embody the size, strength and evil demeanor of the actual character. When I was not occupied with creating wall props to disturb the children, I was to be assisting the various VBS staff with odd jobs and other errands.

I protested uselessly to Mom for a minute or two, and was met with a calm but determined brick wall. Truthfully, the longer I thought about it, creating the Goliath drawing was starting to sound like an interesting challenge to me. I secretly loved any attention I could get for my artwork, while at the same time often attempting to play it off as no big deal. This would be a centerpiece display on the church campus that could attract a lot of admirers, I slowly realized.

"OK, that sounds pretty cool," I eventually agreed. "When does VBS start?" I asked her, as I swung the TV around on its wheeled stand to face the breakfast table. I poured myself a massive bowl of Golden

Grahams, a rare name-brand treat of a cereal for our household, and shook up the jug of orange juice made from concentrate until it formed a frothy head.

She told me that the program began the following Monday. That information put me in a better mood, seeing that I still had several days of clear sailing ahead of me with no responsibilities other than entertaining myself.

"There will be lots of things to do this summer, Dav," she continued. "Swimming lessons start at the Community Center in a couple weeks, Youth League baseball after that, the trip to the ocean with my side of the family, and—" she paused for effect.

"You also did say you'd like to get a job this summer," she reminded me. It was true. I'd complained so much about not having my own money to blow on nonsense for the past year that she and my dad had gotten me to commit to finding some work once the school year ended. I begrudgingly nodded, and rinsed my dishes in the sink before stacking them on a towel on the postage-stamp-sized counter. Our kitchen was small, but decorated smartly and arranged efficiently to maximize its usefulness.

Just as Corbin and Suzanne were stirring, I bounded out the door into the bright sunshine and turned the corner toward the backyard. Dad was already gone for the day, back at the school once again to close down his classroom and wrap things up for the year. I crossed our small grassy backyard to the shed, which housed all the family's bikes and yard equipment. Garages, especially attached ones, were rare on this side of town, and storage sheds were the next best option, unless you belonged to a family like the triplets'. With nowhere to store yard equipment and kids' toys, some of the neighbors had resorted to simply leaving their belongings strewn all about the yard wherever they wanted, content for them to rust.

I pulled my bike from the shed, and examined it again with a judgmental eye. During those years, bikes were of the utmost importance to the kids in my neighborhood. Mine was serviceable, and not a complete embarrassment by any means, but it was far from ideal.

It was a 24-inch yellow and black Huffy brand bike, with padded sleeves reading *BMX Racing* on both the top tube and the handlebars.

It lacked two absolutely necessary components, however: pegs, and a freecoaster hub. Pegs were small posts that attached to the rear axle, allowing the rider to stand on them and perform stunts. A freecoaster permitted the rear wheel to roll backwards without engaging the hub and forcing the cranks to rotate backwards, as they would on a normal freewheel or cassette style hub.

Even though my bike somewhat looked the part, any true street BMX aficionado would look at it and know in an instant that it was sorely lacking. This fact was a constant source of stress for me, as the neighborhood at large was overrun with a horde of rowdy teenage boys just chomping at the bit to point out these embarrassing anomalies.

I didn't know any of them personally, but rumor had it the roving band of thugs called themselves the Biker Scouts. The name had probably been borrowed from the popular villains in Return of the Jedi, who were known for zooming around the forest moon of Endor on speeders somehow suspended a few feet above the ground.

My parents had presented the bike to me as a gift at Christmas. It was a major purchase for them on a shoestring budget, and their eyes had lit up expectantly as I tore the sheets of wrapping paper off the contraption. I had been overjoyed to upgrade from a child's bike to what felt like a fine piece of machinery. After I proudly took it for an initial spin up and down the sidewalks in the freezing rain, several neighbor boys had huddled around me to examine it.

I had claimed matter-of-factly that it was an official BMX bike, and I referenced the graphics on the pads to prove it. The other boys weren't so easily convinced and happily pointed out the lacking features. I lied without missing a beat, and said the pegs and hub upgrade had been back-ordered and were in the mail. Four to six weeks was the standard turnaround time for shipping back then, if you were lucky. I'd figured that delay, along with the drifting snow banks, would buy me some time to concoct another story. Of course, the upgrades had never arrived, and I had avoided the subject at all costs going forward.

That morning, though, the streets were empty; the teenage ruffians were most likely still fast asleep, enjoying the onset of summer break, I figured. I told my mom I was leaving with a yell over my shoulder as I took off like a shot down the driveway, the comfortable breeze whooshing through my hair and bringing a smile to my face. With Tyson and Denny unavailable, I knew I'd have to get creative if I wanted to have someone to hang out with.

As I zigzagged up and down the streets in the immediate vicinity of my house, I brainstormed my various options. There was a kid one grade below me at Crosstown a few streets away who had a swimming pool, a luxury of staggering proportions. I had spent a good part of the previous summer over at Zane Turley's house, and still felt the occasional tingle of the plantar warts I'd regrettably picked up on the wooden deck there.

I'd picked away at them for months thinking they were just splinters, trying in vain to get them out. Before long, there were a dozen of them scattered across both soles of my feet. They'd finally gone away on their own somehow during the winter months. For most of the past summer we had enjoyed a generally raucous time at Zane's suburban chlorinated oasis.

I considered heading off in that direction, but then I remembered that his dad was probably still furious with me. I'd convinced Zane to drag his younger brother Zack's mattress into the water to use it as a diving platform on one of the last days of the season. We'd struggled to pull the inundated mattress right back out in front of his livid father once he'd discovered it.

I could still remember the red-faced glare his dad gave me from over the wooden privacy fence as he'd watched me speed away from the house. The mattress had taken days to dry out even in the brutal summer sunshine. There was another uncomfortable reason I wasn't in a huge hurry to get over to Zane's place, but I pushed the unpleasant thought out of my mind.

So, I kept on riding, and soon pedaled by a favorite destination of mine called Pack Rat Pete's. The nondescript brick building on a busy street corner contained the largest collection of sports cards and other random ephemera I'd ever seen. I had been building my own baseball card collection for the past several years, and whenever I was lucky enough to come into a few bucks, I'd usually head there straight away.

Gleaming boxes containing the new wood-grained editions for 1987 had just appeared on the shelves at Pete's a couple of weeks beforehand, and I'd already purchased several. For just 40 cents, the wax packs offered 15 crisp new cards and a stick of pink chewing gum that was as hard as granite. I had decided to keep these newly-acquired cards in perfect condition, and had found a narrow white cardboard box in the basement that worked perfectly for the purpose.

Today though, I passed right by the card-collecting establishment without stopping, seeing that I was dead broke. I began to rack my brain for new ways to earn money over the summer to fund my interests. Earlier that morning, my mom had mentioned a few potential ideas for how I could earn some extra cash, and I ruminated over them as I pedaled.

Perhaps subconsciously, by this time I was back on the yellow-shirted girl's street. My heart jumped a bit as the imposing house came into view and I could once again see her, this time wearing a light blue tank top. As I approached, she headed off the porch and back behind her house. I slowed my bike to a crawl, and then finally came to a complete stop in her driveway. I leaned over and fiddled at an imaginary problem with my bike chain and peered down the driveway after where she had gone.

This time the garage doors were raised, and the green Mustang GT was nowhere in sight. The inside of the two and a half car garage was lit up brilliantly with several bright spotlights, and I could see that the entire interior was covered with hundreds of colorful old license plates from floor to ceiling. Most of them appeared to be from Michigan, Ohio and Illinois. I happened to know that all three states had a long history of issuing plates in different and interesting colors almost annually.

Some vintage gas station signs were peppered in here and there among the plates, and a genuine-looking Sinclair Oil Corporation gasoline pump stood against one wall. I'd seen the iconic green dinosaur logo with the red lettering before, but that had been on a trip out West years prior. I took one step away from my bike, momentarily awestruck at the dazzling sight. Then, I put down the kickstand, and curiosity led me a couple steps even closer to get a better view of the intriguing collection.

"Oh, hey," said the girl as she rounded the corner of the house again, with a pile of short wood planks in her arms. "What are you doing?"

Her green eyes flashed fiercely in the sunlight, and I realized in amazement that she was even more attractive up close. She was about an inch taller than me, her slender limbs tanned and athletic-looking. I stammered for a second, then spit out something about the garage decor. She smiled in an odd way, with her eyebrows raised as she looked off to the side.

"Yes," she said in a slightly annoyed manner. "They're pretty cool. My step-dad collects them. Or, he used to—back when he had time for hobbies." Then she made clear with her body language that she had no intention of discussing it any further, and moved past me with the wood planks back toward the porch.

This put me in the odd position of being farther onto her property than she was, and uninvited at that. Hesitantly, I moved back in the direction of my bike to leave. She turned back to me.

"Anyone ever tell you that you look just like Dave Coulier?" she asked. I looked back at her blankly. "C'mon... Full House?" she prompted, and as I stammered for a response, I noticed another person approaching on a bicycle. I sensed trouble and mounted my own ride quickly.

The teenage boy cruised in and hopped the curb belligerently, coming to an abrupt stop on the grassy easement. He was about 15 or 16, with sharp features, and a smirk on his face. His glossy Mohawk pointed high into the air and his scalp revealed a complicated mix of twisting tattoos.

He wore a sleeveless blue jean jacket, his lean but muscular arms gripping the custom handlebars of his bicycle with enough force to make the veins stand out. Walkman earbuds dangled from the sides of his head down to his waist, and heavy metal music was playing loud enough for me to hear even while I stood frozen about ten feet away from him.

"Wow, who's your new friend here, Mandy?" he asked with a grin. She looked up to see who he was, and then back down at whatever she was doing on the porch, ignoring the question entirely.

"Isn't it just about nap time, little guy?" the teen punk asked me in a falsetto-like whine. "Why don't you just keep on pedaling, if you can make it down the street without training wheels." He turned back towards Mandy.

"Where's Enrique?" he demanded. She once again acted like she didn't even hear the question. He got off his bike and let it fall in a heap on the grass. He was clearly not the kind of person who utilized kickstands very often. I gazed at his expensive ride and noticed there wasn't one installed anyway.

"Did you hear me, Airhead Barbie?" He marched with a purpose toward the porch. I considered escaping down the street, but something kept me bolted into place. Mandy looked up this time with disdain, and fidgeted slightly in the porch swing. He approached the ornate steps and it was clear he wasn't going to stop there. As if through a fog, I heard someone call out a high-pitched voice.

"Leave her alone!" the voice commanded, and then I realized with utter alarm that the speaker had been myself. The bully stopped mid-step and whirled toward me, trying to process the situation. "What did you just say, dweeb?" he finally asked, in outrage.

Mandy stopped what she was doing and looked straight at me, suddenly intrigued. Apparently this twist in the exchange had finally gotten her attention, when it seemed nothing else would. The punk's shocked expression slowly transformed into an evil smile.

"Oh, so you're a feisty one, eh? I get it." He nodded. "You think I'm here to cause trouble and that you're going to save the princess or something. News flash, kid: Mandy here's my girlfriend. And, I work for her old man to boot. So, I'd advise you get out of here before you lose any baby teeth."

He took a couple steps closer to me and I could see he had a small scar on the left side of his face running down from his cheek to his chin. He clenched his fist and slammed it into the other, and I noticed he wore black arm cuffs with small silver metal spikes embedded. I assumed he had fulfilled that threat on many a helpless neighborhood kid in the past. Behind him, Mandy pursed her lips and motioned with a quick tilt of her head that I would be wise to scram as soon as possible.

After a moment's hesitation, I did just that. "You're so mean, Ryne," I heard Mandy say as I picked up speed. He laughed and said something sharply back at her, but I was quickly well out of hearing range. I felt the red flush into my cheeks as I pedaled furiously. She pitied me. What an idiot I was. It would be a cold day in hell before I was caught back in front of that house, I swore to myself.

6

dead yellowjackets

I walked straight through the propped-open glass double doors of Crosstown Church on the first morning of VBS and immediately entered a maelstrom of staggering noise. Several hundred children were screaming a chorus in unison, egged on by a sweaty man stomping back and forth on the stage, waving his arms wildly as if he were directing traffic in a busy intersection.

He was the program director, a slightly rotund, tall and friendly man. I knew him well from our time spent together for private trumpet lessons. Shannon Worthy was well-known around the Crosstown campus, famous for his constantly ruddy cheeks and propensity to walk the halls at top speed while conducting an imaginary symphony orchestra in his own little world.

One side of the church auditorium was shouting, "Halle-Loo,

Halle-Loo, Halle-Loo, Halle-loo-yah!" The other side would retort at a volume many decibels above a jet airplane's with the phrase, "Praise – Ye – The – Lord." They would counter each other several times before switching roles.

If there ever was a perfect illustration of making a joyful noise, this was it. Several kids appeared to be close to unconsciousness from over-exertion. There's not a shadow of a doubt that God heard it, but I wasn't quite sure how He'd feel about the display. He hadn't accepted Cain's gift, and this seemed kind of along the same lines to me.

Over the course of the several days that had passed since the embarrassing incident with Ryne, I'd had little to do, so the arrival of the kickoff event for Vacation Bible School on this cloudy Monday morning wasn't a complete disappointment. I'd called up Zane to see if he'd be interested in starting a lawn-cutting service with me. He had promised to get back to me with an answer after checking with his dad about borrowing the lawnmower.

Impatiently, I'd racked my brain for other profitable money-making schemes that had reaped benefits in the past. Wanda Kogan, a spry chain-smoking widow with brilliantly white hair, lived in the house directly behind Freddy Mann. I'd shoveled snow off her walk for a few bucks one frigid winter morning, and she'd invited me back again on a couple of occasions to help move a piece of furniture, or paint something, and had paid me decently for the trouble.

Every year the school conducted a fundraiser, called the Walkathon, and dispatched hundreds of students throughout Metro Detroit to seek willing sponsors. The actual event spanned ten miles on a pre-selected day every fall. Typical ways to support the cause were to sponsor a walker for a flat amount, or for a certain amount per mile walked. Anyone raising over one hundred dollars in funds would receive a special prize from the school, often twenty bucks in cash to keep for themselves. I always made that threshold a goal, but had never successfully reached it myself.

I remembered that Wanda had agreed to sponsor me the previous year. "I'll do two dollars," she had stated matter-of-factly, and my heart had jumped, thinking that it was a commitment per mile. *Twenty percent of the way in just one house call,* I had thought with glee. It turned out that she had meant it as a flat amount. Still, it seemed to be worth a try to visit her once again and inquire about some work.

When I had bounded up the front walk to her house and lifted my hand to knock on the storm door, she had seen me through the screen.

"Don't need you now, young man," she had rasped, reading my mind. "I've got someone helping me clean out the basement for the next few days." I had sullenly thanked her, and trudged back home, my mind heading back to the drawing board.

Seeing now that the VBS kids were currently occupied with their singing in the auditorium, I started looking around for one of the leaders, hoping to receive some initial direction on the Goliath project. I headed down an adjacent tiled hallway. It was odd seeing the teachers, who usually wore dress clothes and nylons, in comfortable jeans and T-shirts now. Somehow, it made them seem more human.

The sound of sneakers instead of clicking dress shoes tapping down the shiny hallway floor was a stark contrast to the school year. I saw Mrs. Townsend walking toward me, and she greeted me with a quick hello and a warm smile. Right on her heels was Principal Stickler, who glared at me as she passed by but said nothing.

Reaching the end of the passageway, I climbed the stairs to the elementary school wing and entered it. The entire floor seemed deserted and was nearly dark. This surprised me, since I knew that these classrooms would soon be teeming with children once they were dismissed into smaller groups to begin work on the day's craft. Not finding anyone around, I decided to search for the art supplies I'd need. I started in a cluttered storage balcony overlooking the elementary gymnasium. Long ago it had served as a second floor viewing area for sporting events, but sometime in the past a massive drapery had been erected to completely block it off from view from the gym floor below.

I rifled through some boxes near the top of the stacks, and after a minute or two uncovered an amazing find. Special collector baseball card sets encased in plastic were neatly arranged in a banker's box. *Future prizes for some church event,* I thought. I could already glimpse Mark McGuire, Jose Canseco and Barry Bonds cards visible at the top of the packs. *These must be worth a fortune,* I thought, as the greedy wheels in my mind began to turn. I chastised myself, but the seed for a possible heist in the future had already been planted.

Just then, from the gym floor below, I heard a door open and a couple of hasty footsteps walk several strides inside and then stop abruptly. Two people were talking in hushed tones. One was clearly Ms. Stickler, who said in an agitated voice, "I am positive that terrible woman knows something about what happened to Justus! He's been missing now for weeks. I'm concerned she's done something."

"Have you gotten the police involved?" asked a voice that I recognized immediately as Mr. Asperat's.

"Of course we have. They performed a welfare check a couple of days ago and didn't come up with anything." Ms. Stickler paused. "Justus has been, well... It's unfortunate, but he's started hanging out with Dustin again. How he ever got into a position of authority around here, I'll never know. " She sounded bitter, and her allusion had apparently meant something significant to Asperat, but it meant little to me. *Could she possibly mean Dustin Crabb, the disgraced principal?* I wondered.

"Oh, I see. Joyce, I'm so sorry," Asperat said with a heartfelt and reassuring tone. "Dustin's still got friends in high places here; you know that as well as anyone." She sighed at that assertion and continued.

"Because of that renewed relationship, the police say there's no telling where Justus could be. But, I know that something awful has happened. I'm well aware that you have complicated feelings regarding everyone involved. The things that have gone on in that house of his…" her voice trailed off.

Her tone of voice changed again, growing colder. "But, one thing's for sure: whatever will be, will be." Her steely facade seemed to return in an instant. "There's no changing other people and their choices, Rene—you know that. Once someone starts down a certain path…"

The door to the balcony closet unexpectedly opened behind me, and I turned from my eavesdropping to see a startled Mrs. Townsend staring at me. I was still holding several of the packaged baseball card sets, and I realized that I looked very much like a deer caught in the headlights.

"What exactly are you looking for out here?" she asked calmly. Below us, I heard Asperat and Stickler walk out of the far end of the gym quickly without speaking another word to each other. I explained to her that I had been looking for art supplies to begin the Goliath portrait, and that straightforward statement distracted her long enough for me to put the cards down, as if I'd been in the process of clearing out some space to search. *I have precious few allies here at Crosstown, and it would be a pity to lose one as kind as Mrs. Townsend*, I chastised myself.

She suddenly looked forlorn and explained she had to get back to her own VBS duties. I hesitated, then asked her if everything was OK. She paused in the door frame, and smiled a sad smile. "Just pray for my siblings. One of them has made some negative choices in life, and those are coming back now to haunt her. But God can intervene, I do most certainly believe that." She thanked me for my concern, and wiping what appeared to be a tear from one eye, left and hurried back down the hallway.

A while later, after finally finding the teacher in charge of decor, and getting some firm details on her vision for the biblical giant, I walked back toward the auditorium. The morning's events were wrapping up, and on the stage, Program Director Worthy was overseeing the dramatic weighing of the offering.

There was a gigantic scale that looked like a teeter-totter of some sort, and kids from either side of the aisle were taking turns dumping in their collected coins to see which group had donated the most raw material. In the background, a pianist was playing a jaunty rendition of another VBS favorite. The spectacle held the kids' attention as raptly as a live WrestleMania event might have.

"Shannon," I repeated to myself as I walked out the church doors, my day's duties complete and my mission now clear. "Shannon. What an odd name for a man." I had always been intrigued by parents who chose to name their children something relatively unexpected, when there were thousands of perfectly normal names available. Outside, the clouds had now abated, and the impending walk home seemed much more inviting.

About halfway there, I became aware of a bike approaching from behind me, and turned just in time to see the nasty, grinning face of red-haired bully Chet Wiggins nearly running me down. He blew past me at top speed, whizzing within inches of my arm. He wasn't necessarily a tall kid, just stocky—and mean enough to intimidate someone more than simply his overall size could have.

"Don't like my driving? Get off the sidewalk!" he called back to me as he crossed the next street without looking either way. As he gradually disappeared, I wondered what Wiggins was doing over in Rouge Park. I was surprised to see him and his sleek, expensive bike in this neck of the woods.

Nearing home, I abandoned my hastily-made vow and brazenly passed in front of Mandy's house again, hoping for a glimpse of the current object of my affections. I looked around nervously, keeping my antennae out for Ryne. Her house looked empty, but the green Mustang sat parked rather crookedly directly in front of the house. As I passed by it, I peered inside the sports car. In the driver's seat, fully reclined and nearly horizontal, sat a man fast asleep.

Several beer cans were strewn on his lap and all across the passenger's seat. He wore an expensive-looking black leather jacket and his hair was slicked straight back close to his head. He had a thick mustache, and the rest of his face appeared to have not been shaved in several days. His dark eyebrows were furrowed, and in his sleep he suddenly jerked his head in my direction. His piercing eyes opened and locked onto mine. I didn't like the looks of him, so I continued walking quickly, without looking back at him again.

At home, I greeted my family without stopping to chat and made my way straight for the hallway telephone. It was hidden inside a wooden box hanging on the wall, and from the outside it looked like an antique device, complete with a hand crank on the right side and an earpiece dangling from a cord on the left. My mom thought it looked quaint, and I'd always enjoyed revealing its more modern contents to my friends when they came over. I had arranged to give Zane a call that day, to confirm our plan to cut lawns in the afternoon. After a couple of rings he answered, and sullenly told me he had been grounded, and the work would have to wait.

I hung up the phone and sat down on the landing across from Corbin's room. He was inside tinkering around pointlessly with some Weebles. He was in his own little world, just a few feet away, blissfully ignorant of the pressures awaiting him as a teenager. It was hard to explain, but even though I desperately wanted to grow up as soon as possible, I also was scared of losing once and for all the complete lack of responsibility that childhood offered. The privilege of simply getting on a bicycle and riding in no certain direction—with no fallout to deal with later—was a considerable one.

He was almost old enough for me to play with without it being a constant annoyance. Lacking anything else to do, I reluctantly peered inside and asked him if he wanted to kick the soccer ball around with me in the back yard. We had invented a sort of game where he was the goalie and I simulated the remaining players of both sides. He usually seemed to enjoy playing the game with me. He jumped up with a smile on his face and we headed outside together.

The afternoon was warm and the smell of burgers grilling nearby wafted over from an adjoining yard. We had only just begun playing, using the red wooden picnic table in the middle of our yard as an obstacle, when Corbin yelled out in pain. I stopped dribbling the ball with my feet and left it where it stood in the grass. I walked over and saw him gingerly rubbing the sole of his bare foot, and I quickly yanked a stinger out of it for him. *Yellowjackets again,* I knew immediately. There had been a slew of them in the backyard for years, and we had never discovered a nest or how exactly to get rid of them.

"That's it," I declared dramatically. "The Yellowjacket Reign of Terror has come to an end." Corbin stopped bellowing in an instant, curious at the nature of my brash statement. I marched over to the side of the house and found the kinked green garden hose lying in a haphazard pile. I attached it to the spigot that protruded out from just under where the white vinyl siding began. After twisting on the spray attachment, I solemnly returned to the scene of the sting.

I hated the things with a passion, for good reason. On a previous family vacation hike, my cousin had stirred up a massive nest. Both of us had been stung, though I'd received the brunt of their punishment. I'd iced my wounds in the background and tried to take it like a man as the rest of the clan hovered over and tended to my younger cousin's angry welts.

Over the next hour, we hunted down the yellowjackets buzzing around the backyard one by one, like hired guns. Whenever he spied one, Corbin would call for me, and with an initial mist, I'd knock the insect out of the air. Once it was helplessly squirming in the grass, I'd unleash the full force of the water pressure onto my quarry. We had no mercy. I lost count of how many we stalked down and eliminated, but I know they numbered in the dozens. For some odd reason, spraying each enemy into oblivion was cathartic for me. With every blast I thought of Grangeford, Ryne, Chet and everything else that had been weighing on me recently.

When our sadistic mission was finally complete, fully-recovered Corbin scampered back inside to get a snack. I aimlessly walked around to the front of the house to see if anything interesting was happening on that lazy early summer afternoon. I expected to find Jason and Johnny taking turns pretending to be Alan Trammell or Jack Morris, but they weren't outside. I did spot their scary German shepherd Damian staring me down from their backyard, though.

The massive and muscular dog stood as still as stone, a black and red Beware of Dog sign affixed to the fence just under his snout. Damian resembled a small horse as much as he did a dog. I gave a slight shudder and continued to wander down the sidewalk in the general direction of Freddy Mann's.

The sun was starting to descend from its peak, but the air was still warm and seemed to be getting even more humid. I heard the faint twinkling music of an ice cream truck a block or two away, the first one I'd heard that season. I usually had to let it pass by due to lack of funds, but once or twice a year my mom or dad would let us splurge. I'd tried the most expensive treat on the menu only once—a $2.00 delight called the Pink Panther. It was a pastel-colored ice cream concoction made in the iconic shape of the popular cartoon character's head, complete with two yellow gumballs for eyes.

I heard a voice call my name and knew immediately it was Freddy's. A fleeting thought of turning around and ignoring him quickly passed, as there wasn't anything else to do at the moment. I answered him, and continued down the street into the dead end. His was the second to last house on the street, which butted up against a double-height chain link fence. This barrier separated the neighborhood from the abandoned park.

The park in question had been owned at one time by one of the Big Three, but it had passed out of that company's consciousness decades earlier. A lone steel play structure stood roughly in the middle of that field, its rusty poles and swing-less crossbeams off limits to all but the most ragtag youths in the neighborhood, simply for safety reasons. Several hundred yards further on was another high metal fence that marked the extreme boundaries of the park, beyond which were the railroad tracks and my infamous wooded haunt.

When I was one house away from Freddy's, I was startled to see two girls suddenly appear on a sagging front porch of a rather rundown neighboring house. They were talking excitedly to one another, and descended the three rickety wooden steps without noticing my presence.

One of the girls was Roxy, a neighborhood tart with a bad reputation who seemed to believe she was a younger version of Madonna. She was wearing a black miniskirt, tight white tank top and black lace tights. She was quite pale and had applied a generous amount of bright red lipstick. I was surprised to see that the girl walking next to her was Mandy.

I'd avoided Roxy like the plague for several years, ever since she'd cornered me in my own backyard and attempted to coerce me into an erotic game of truth or dare. The most daring feat I'd been willing to undertake was pulling up my shirt. She had done the same without even a blush—and it had made me feel completely uncomfortable around her ever since.

"Do you really think Pete will let you sell these things in his store?" Roxy asked Mandy skeptically. Mandy was carrying something wooden and bulky in her arms as they turned off the house walk and onto the general sidewalk, now heading in my direction. I racked my brain for something to say during the impending exchange, but came up with nothing.

"Totally," Mandy said. "I told him what I was making and he thought people would buy them for sure. He's a little creepy but, what else is new," she added with a knowing glance in Roxy's direction. I kept walking toward the pair, a sense of dread hitting the pit of my stomach.

Mandy looked amazing as always, and at the same time seemed completely unaware of the fact. This was in total contrast to her current companion, who clearly thought about her appearance at all times of the day and night. Roxy had been linked romantically to every disreputable teen in the neighborhood at one point or another. She was in the same grade as Mandy, but her taste in young men extended all the way up through the senior class and beyond.

"Oh hey," Mandy nodded, as we came face to face on the sidewalk. "You live close to here?"

"You know this kid?" Roxy asked, crinkling her nose. "This moron is one of Freddy's friends." Mandy's expression changed to something I couldn't clearly identify, but it wasn't necessarily a pleasant look.

With the recent theatrical release of A Nightmare on Elm Street, Freddy's stature in the neighborhood had risen a surprising rung or two, due to his shared moniker with the horror flick's iconic villain. But, he was still avoided by most of the older kids.

"I'm Dav," I blurted out, immediately thinking it sounded immature and oddly delivered. Mandy nodded politely and smiled.

"I'm not exactly *friends* with Freddy," I started to explain in a lower tone. From just over the girls' shoulders, Freddy called for me again loudly, this time in more of his typical, annoying tone of voice.

"Uh-huh," said Roxy with a sarcastic tone, and she was clearly ready for this brief conversation to be over. She pushed forward to resume walking, but I kept talking anyway.

"What is that you're working on?" I asked Mandy, motioning to the stack of curious objects she was carrying. I was frankly surprised at the steadiness of my voice, and that I had even been able to spit out anything, for that matter.

Mandy stopped and her expression changed to a more friendly one again. She opened her mouth to reply when Roxy spat, "It's none of your business. You don't have to show him, Mandy. Let's get going." She wrapped her arm tightly around Mandy's and tugged at her. Mandy shrugged, but leaned forward slightly so I could see the top item of the stack.

A rough wood plank about 18 inches long had been stained, and letters from assorted colorful license plates had been cut up one by one and reattached, to spell out the words ROUGE PARK. I could see another one that read WEST RIDGE right below it, but the half dozen other pieces she was hauling were obscured.

"That's an awesome idea," I said, and she smiled at me as the girls swept by and kept on walking, Roxy's wishes finally winning out.

"Thanks, Dav," she said over her shoulder and in a moment, they rounded the corner and headed in the direction of Pack Rat Pete's. I heard Roxy say something to her in a negative tone, but the words were unintelligible. I was genuinely impressed at Mandy's idea, and especially her industriousness, and the thought lingered for a moment until Freddy's plaintive pleas finally snapped me out of my reverie.

I sulkily completed the short walk to Freddy's house, observing the general state of disarray of his property as I got closer. The lawn—or what was left of it anyway—hadn't been cut yet that season. The roof was half covered with a blue tarp, which was crudely attached, apparently in an attempt to postpone the inevitable. I felt a pang of pity for Freddy and the state in which his family was existing. He beckoned me into the backyard.

I look around warily. "Are your parents around?" I asked. My reluctance was partly from being trained by my own folks to only play at people's houses when adults were present, but in this case it was mostly because I had no desire to have any interaction with Freddy's erratic mother.

"No. Mom's out with the girls doing something or other," he called back over his shoulder. So I followed him to the backyard, which was in no better shape than the front. The cement driveway, crumbling here and there from general neglect, led straight back to a single car garage.

A massive oak tree dominated the entire rear portion of the property, its endless branches creating a canopy over several adjacent yards in addition to Freddy's. A trunk of epic proportions jutted out from the dirt, and large branches extended over the garage and actually touched it in some places. It had created an amazing natural playscape of sorts.

Wiry Freddy was up to the garage roof in seconds, and I scrambled up alongside him, using the tree as a ladder. We immediately resumed a game of make-believe we'd invented weeks earlier, the last time I'd begrudgingly visited.

Freddy was currently obsessed with a band called The Pet Shop Boys, and their song *West End Girls* in particular. He had a strange fixation for the line:

Sometimes you're better off dead,
There's a gun in your hand
And it's pointing at your head.

He would repeat it at random times during our games, and it made me feel slightly uneasy.

He convinced me to pretend that we were in our own band, and together we cobbled together some lyrics set to the same catchy beat. We choreographed our own music video, and took turns telling each other that it would air on MTV once we were finally discovered. *Two kids swinging on vines from the roof of a dilapidated garage; stranger things have made it onto television before,* I reasoned.

It was getting hot. "Freddy, do you have anything to drink?" I asked, sweatily. "Sure, there's some Sunny Ds in the fridge inside. Grab one for me, too," he requested breathlessly, as he sat down in the shade. I felt relatively comfortable venturing inside the house, knowing there was no one else from his family around.

As I headed inside, more lyrics from the song played through my head.

In a West End town, a dead-end world;
The East End boys and West End girls.
In a West End town, a dead-end world;
The East End boys and West End girls.

I'd never even heard the real version of the song with my own ears. Freddy's performance of it had become my personal rendition of the popular tune.

Inside, the Mann house smelled of stale beer and cigarettes. The dishes had not been done in ages, and were stacked stinking in the sink. I stepped over random objects that had never made it back to where they belonged, and eventually arrived at the refrigerator. It was filled to the brim with random items, but the Sunny Delights were there, true to Freddy's word. I grabbed one and twisted off the top, downing it all in one, almost continuous draught.

On one counter I saw a mountainous stack of rumpled papers, junk mail, final notices, legal threats and other correspondence. I casually picked up the top letter, feeling free to snoop for a second or two. I stopped short as I read the addressees on the front of the envelope: Justus and Nicolette Mann.

7

goliath of Gath

The following morning as I mashed up a new container of orange juice on the kitchen counter, I thought over what I had discovered inside the Mann house. I could still hear the voice shouting Nicolette's name through the dark drain system. *Had the voice sounded angry, sad or even outraged?* I racked my brain to decipher its tone, and waffled between multiple options.

What was the connection to Principal Joyce Stickler? She had said 'Justus' not 'justice' when I'd overheard her on the telephone, that at least was clear to me finally. How was she associated with this dysfunctional mess of a family? And on top of that, how did the disheveled and disgraced Dustin Crabb figure into things? I couldn't make any sense of it all.

Upon arriving at Crosstown for the second day of VBS, I hurried straight to a classroom on the second floor that had been designated for me to create Goliath. I had been supplied with a massive cylindrical ream of white paper about four feet wide, and I proceeded to roll it out on the tile floor to begin work. I measured off a ten-foot length with the classroom yardstick, and started with a rough pencil drawing as I consulted a reference photo from an illustrated Bible I'd acquired.

I worked hard on the sketch for half an hour or so, slowly becoming more and more frustrated at the overwhelming scale. Every few minutes I'd step back, or stand on a desk chair to get a better perspective, but it was becoming clear I'd bitten off more than I could chew artistically. The legs were too big for the rest of the body, and the head was too small for the rest of the drawing. I erased and adjusted it several times, but to no avail.

I felt the presence of an observer behind me, and glanced back to see the familiar face of Violet Vereen. She had also been cajoled into assisting at VBS, and was dressed in jeans, a pink top and had her hair artfully done in a braided style down her back that I hadn't seen before, which I thought looked kind of nice. *It's too bad her attitude doesn't usually match the rest of her cute appearance,* I thought ruefully.

"What is wrong with him?" she asked flatly, staring at my drawing. I ignored her question and dug my eraser into the paper a little bit harder. "I think his hands look weird," she added after another minute. I hadn't even considered that particular flaw, and it made my blood pressure rise. "And his feet are pointing sideways," she added. "If you look at how I'm standing, you can see that in real life, your feet point—"

I finally stood up and looked at her, with my hands on my hips, turning my back on the drawing. "Thank you ever so much, Violet," I said snidely. "As hard as it is to believe, this isn't quite as easy as it looks to an amateur. Now, if you'll leave me alone, I can—"

She cut me off. "I was just going to suggest," she retorted with a sweet smile, "that you borrow an overhead projector. You could display your reference image, blown up to the correct size, right onto the wall and then simply trace over it." She handed me a roll of tape from the jumbled pile of supplies at my feet. "Use this to hang the paper on the wall. I could help you, you know." She smiled at me pleasantly.

My frustration eased, and I had to admit it was a good solution to the scaling problem. We searched the rest of the second floor together for a projector, but couldn't come up with one.

"My dad uses one in his classroom all the time," I recalled as the bell rang, alerting the children that it was time to leave again for the morning. "I'll see if he can get one for me. Meet me back here tomorrow, Violet, and we can, um—work together. That is, if you want to," I said cautiously.

She beamed at me. "Of course. You clearly need all the help you can get. See you then!" With that, she turned and left, leaving me to think about how oddly and unexpectedly positive our interaction had turned out to be.

At home, I downed a quick lunch around the table with Corbin and Suzanne, and jumped up to answer the phone as soon as it rang. It was Zane, and he told me his imprisonment had come to an end, and he was free to mow lawns with me for the afternoon. I held my hand over the receiver and confirmed with Mom that the plan would work. She agreed happily, most likely pleased to see me finally able to earn some money.

Zane, my mother, and I all shared quite an interesting history when it came to lawnmowers. The summer before, at the end of the very first day of our lawn-mowing partnership, Zane and I had strained to load his family's mower into the back of my mom's maroon station wagon to transport it back to his place. It had been hot, and we were exhausted after successfully completing a number of jobs.

The back hatch wouldn't quite close because of the mower handle, so Zane and I had sat with our legs dangling out the back as we headed over to his house a few short blocks away. I had been sweating so profusely that I had taken off my shoes, and set them on the grass. As we drained a pair of Capri Suns, Mom had slowly backed the wagon down the driveway, into the street, and then back up the driveway facing our house. That's when things had started to go quite badly.

As the station wagon continued backwards and up the opposite driveway, my feet were unexpectedly pulled down under and pinned against the cement, and subsequently dragged. I had yelled for Mom to stop the vehicle, but she thought I was talking about grabbing my shoes, and said we would get them in a second.

My yells had turned to screams as the tops of my feet slowly ground against the rough pavement, tearing away my tube socks along with the top layers of flesh from both feet. The whole scene reminded me of the terrible way that the Thuggee guard had died in Indiana Jones and the Temple of Doom, which I'd seen for the first time recently.

By the time my mom had finally understood the gravity of the situation and stopped the car, the damage had already been done. I had slid down to the ground from my seat in the back of the wagon and pried my legs loose from underneath. With both feet bleeding profusely, I had hopped around in the middle of the street in a painful panic, not knowing what else to do. I had looked down with horror and noticed several toenails were completely gone.

My mom had sprinted to grab the garden hose and had begun spraying my feet down like she was putting out a raging house fire. Zane had stood watching in disbelief, his only response to finally ask me if he should get me some pain medication.

"Bring me the entire bottle!" I had sputtered to him between sobs. Zane had bounded into my house and managed to find some pills. There had been no denying the severity of this mishap. It had been one of the rare occasions when my reaction matched the actual situation at hand.

An hour or so after the gruesome incident, I had been propped up comfortably in the living room recliner, feet cleaned and soaked in iodine. Eating Cookies 'N Cream ice cream straight from a half-gallon carton, and watching a rerun episode of G.I. Joe, I had begun to feel human again.

Over the next few weeks, the toenails had slowly returned. All that was left now were a few scars on the tops of my feet, along with the strong conviction to never again ride with my feet dangling out the back of a vehicle. As Snake Eyes would often say, "Knowing is half the battle."

I now said goodbye to my family and bounced out the door, heading to meet Zane at a halfway point a block or so away. Zane was a large kid for his age, and was already red-faced and out of breath when I met him a few minutes later. Since I was rail-thin, the two of us formed an unlikely pair as we headed down the street together.

If anyone was ever tempted to needle Zane about his pudginess, one only had to remember his older brother Zeus, who had sprouted into a 6' 8" monster and headed off to play basketball on an athletic scholarship. He attended a strict religious school in the South that had finally decided to dip its toe into the unholy waters of intercollegiate sports.

Whenever I saw Zane for the first time in a while, I felt awkward, and I hated myself for it. At the end of the previous summer, Zane's younger brother Zack had gone missing while at camp up north with the church. After days of exhaustive searching, the authorities had finally given up. None of us kids knew quite how to handle the situation, so we basically ignored it. Zane's dad hadn't darkened the doors of Crosstown since the tragic event. I couldn't say I completely blamed him.

The two of us now started knocking on doors asking permission to cut people's grass. We focused mainly on the houses with overgrown lawns, which were numerous, thinking our odds were best at those locations. After a dozen potential clients declined our services, I walked up the sidewalk to a house with a particularly mangy-looking lawn. Out back I could see the grass was over a foot high. I knocked on the door, and an unkempt man in a tank top came to the door.

"Do you need your lawn cut, sir?" I asked.

"Sir!" he laughed with a smoker's cough, and called back over his shoulder. "He called me sir!" he repeated as a couple of muffled chuckles could be heard from a back room. "Sure kid, I'll pay you a couple bucks."

I turned and nodded at Zane, who started up the engine in a few pulls. While he began on the first few passes, I did a quick walk-through and removed numerous sticks, beer bottles, and other assorted garbage from the front yard. As I waded through the grass in the back, I wondered if the mower would even be able to get through the overgrowth without choking out.

I returned to the front and decided to let Zane handle it before giving him a breather. I squinted through the heat radiating off the sidewalk to see one of the Ly triplets approaching. It was Dai, and he was riding on one of their old rusty bicycles with a basket affixed to it. He had a couple of brown paper bags resting neatly in the front. To my surprise he came to a stop right in front of the house we were working at, and jumped off, grabbing one of the bags.

"Oh—hi," he said, looking a bit uncomfortable. He walked to the side of the house and knocked on the screen door. An arm reached out momentarily and took the bag from him roughly without a word. He returned to his bike, gave me a little tight-lipped wave without making eye contact, and then took off in a flash.

He continued riding down the street in the same direction. His whole visit lasted less than thirty seconds. The noise of the lawnmower was substantial, but I could still detect that inside the house, the man with the scratchy voice was now yelling.

"Special delivery! The candy has arrived!" Several cheers could be heard in response. I stood there trying to figure out what had just happened. The triplets had told me about a delivery job—was this it? *What exactly are they delivering?* I wondered. It didn't look on the up and up to me. I peered down the street and in the distance, I saw Dai get off his bike again and perform the same sequence.

Zane was done mowing the front. I motioned for him to switch with me and he gladly obliged, twisting the top off the huge plastic bottle of Hi-C his mother had sent with him. I rolled the mower around back and cut off the engine to empty the bulging bag of clippings. I was only a few feet from the open side window. I could hear two of the occupants talking to each other in low voices.

"There was a note inside the bag of jelly beans this time. Enrique says this is the last delivery before we pay up in full. Or, things could get real nasty for us," the first man said. His companion grunted and said something unintelligible with an edge to it, but underneath his brashness there seemed to be genuine concern.

Zane's mower nearly faltered, but managed to cut through the immense growth in the backyard after some serious effort. When we were finally finished and drenched in sweat, I went back around front and Zane knocked on the door while I reclined against a tree for a breather. The man who hired us tossed a wad of singles to Zane and vanished. This was a typical experience for us; you never knew just how much you might get paid for a yard job. It could be three bucks, it could be fifteen.

We managed to find our second wind and scored a few other jobs that same afternoon. A couple of them were easier and paid better, and one lady asked us to return every week all summer. I jotted down the address jubilantly and told Zane the excellent news. Noticing the time, he said he had to leave, and we split up our earnings. Seventeen bucks apiece. I was happy with the take. Zane headed home and we promised to reconnect the next day.

As he pushed the mower down the street, I remembered the terrible day that past November when the teachers had summoned everyone into the frigid gymnasium. They solemnly announced that Zack's body had been found in the lake at camp after dragging the bottom several additional times. I had looked around for Zane that day but he was nowhere to be seen. I'd wanted to say something to make it better, but I knew there were no words that could accomplish any such thing.

I was absolutely parched and realized that D and D Market was just a short walk away from where we'd finished. Soon after, I was inside the freezer-like convenience store, and weaved my way back through the maze-like towers of 12-packs and 2-liters to the line of refrigerators. I initially grabbed a Yoo-hoo, then reminded myself that I needed some hydration on such a hot day, and selected an ice-cold orange Gatorade instead.

At the register, standing in front of an endless display of glossy magazines featuring scantily-clad women, I waited to be helped. Dagmar, the owner's wife, soon appeared from the mysterious back of the store and nonchalantly rang up my purchase, while staring up at the miniature television above her which was noisily playing a daytime soap.

"My friend," she cooed in an exotic accent, "you've been working very hard today, I can see." She looked me over from head to toe. "My friend," as she liked to repeat often, "hard work will determine your fate. We are all in control of our own destiny, as I always say. And I see good things for your future, if you stay on the right path." She smiled and handed me a few coins in change. I thanked her for the cold drink and left.

The blast of heat outside was startling. I had already decided to stop inside Pack Rat Pete's as well and pick up a few packs of baseball cards with my recently-acquired wealth. It was another couple of blocks' walk. Pete's place, in contrast to the Yugoslavians' store, was not air-conditioned, and he had cranked up a couple of huge metal standing fans for the first time of the season. Every window along one side of the store was propped wide open by various creative means. The loud whirring noise dominated the entire interior, but it created an amazing breeze.

The inside of his shop smelled of old paper, and it was a strangely pleasant scent. Glass display tables lined the center of the shop showcasing valuable selections, with several rows of shelves surrounding that area containing organized boxes of sports cards and assorted memorabilia from the past eight decades.

Pete himself was a rather plain looking middle-aged man with a mustache and neatly-combed dark brown hair. He usually wore clothes that merged with the brown and gray interior and exterior of his shop, making him seem like simply an extension of the place.

He slowly walked out from the back office as I entered and greeted me with a half-hearted nod. One other kid was in the store gazing down at a collection of 1958 Topps stars encased in plastic protectors, screwed down to prevent any damage being done by inexperienced or clumsy hands. Card grading was a brand new phenomenon, and the hobby was really starting to take off for kids and adults alike.

I'd learned a good bit about the business in my chats with Pete. He had explained card grade conditions, pointing out flaws in my own cards such as gum stains, off-centered printing, and the infamous flaw of being "dog-eared." Cards possessing anything but crisp corners earned this negative moniker, driving down their values.

I had determined that my new collection of 1987 Topps, in particular, would stay pristine. Previously, when I had shown my dad an early copy of Beckett Baseball Price Guide and pointed out the value of my existing cards, he had been extremely skeptical.

"Something is only worth what someone else will pay for it, Dav," he advised, and pointed at a page in the price guide. "How much will collectors pay you for this card—the one that it says is worth three bucks, in near-mint condition?" I hesitated and considered the question.

"Probably nothing. They have most of them all already."

"Then that's about what it's worth. Sorry to be the bearer of bad news." I had been irritated at him as I left the room, but I knew he had a valid point. It had done little to reduce my voracious appetite for card collecting, though.

I grabbed five packs from the box on the counter nearest the register. It came to an even two dollars. As I pulled out a couple of bills to pay him, I noticed that nearly a dozen of Mandy's signs made from license plates had been hung on the wall, stacked vertically from floor to ceiling just to the right of Pete's office door.

"Oh cool. I actually know the girl that made these," I said to Pete, handing him the money.

"Do you now?" he said, eyebrows raised. "Mandy is a very talented girl. I like to help her out in any way I can. Tough situation."

"What do you mean?" I asked. He considered the question for a moment, and weighed what to share with me. "Well," he started and then finally added, "Have you met Mandy's stepfather?" I admitted I had not.

Her Schemes and Plans

"He's trouble. Stay away from them, kid. You don't want to be involved. Getting on Enrique Willow's bad side is about the last place you'd ever want to be." Just then two more customers entered as the bell on the door jingled. He quickly stood up from resting his elbows on the counter, and headed over to help them. It was clear that I wouldn't be getting any more information out of him regarding Mandy on this visit.

"How much are the license plate signs?" I asked him. He turned back toward me as I stared at the designs. I noticed the two I'd already seen, plus several more commemorating surrounding suburbs and attractions, such as Northgate, Lakeview, Brownsville, and Tiger Stadium.

"Ten bucks," he replied with a warm smile. "I'll take that one then," I said, pointing at the one that read DETROIT.

8
old Haunts

"Come on, Dav. Get in the car, then," my dad called wearily down the stairs after dinner that night. I had convinced him to take me over to the high school so we could find an overhead projector for me to use with Violet.

"It's for VBS, dear," my mom had gently coaxed him. The Detroit Tigers, off to a rough start in early June and sitting at just a .500 record, were on national TV that night against the Boston Red Sox. I knew that Dad had planned a quiet evening of baseball, relaxing with some Better Made potato chips and an ice-cold New Coke on the big recliner. I came up the stairs two at a time, thanked him, and he joined me in the station wagon half-heartedly instead.

The gigantic parking lot at the Crosstown complex was completely empty. It must have contained nearly a thousand spaces. The black asphalt was still hot from the sun it had absorbed during the heat of the day. We got out of the car and Dad unlocked the front door of the silent building.

The carpeted hallways of the high school made almost no sound as we walked toward the AV room. Once there, Dad flipped on the lights, which flickered momentarily, then came on with a yellow-tinted brilliance. He found the sought-after projector in less than a minute. It was heavy, and the two of us supported it on either side and carried it back out to the lobby.

"As long as we're here, I have some last-second things to wrap up. Why don't you go shoot some baskets in the gym or something? I shouldn't be too long," Dad suggested. This type of delay was not an uncommon occurrence.

Many Sunday afternoons, my siblings and I would come over for a couple hours of diversion, especially during the icy and dull winter months. I was also keenly aware that Dad was always on the lookout for an opportunity for me to focus on my athletic skills. I had little interest in basketball, but I headed in the general direction of the gym anyway.

The gymnasium was dark, except for a few beams of sunlight streaming in from the side doors to the west. They were the same doors that I'd watched Grangeford emerge triumphantly from just a few days earlier, primed to snatch my title of sprinting champion right from under my nose. Every squeaky footstep I took across the shiny floor echoed in a hundred directions, and it was strangely pleasant to be alone in such a huge space.

In one corner stood a humming milk machine. It had been there as long as I could remember. Every time I found myself alone in the gym like this, I loved to check for forgotten change underneath it, and perhaps score a free drink of thick chocolate milk. I reached into the change slot and was ecstatic to feel a quarter and dime. In a flash I had deposited both and heard the familiar clunk of a Borden paper milk carton tumble through the system and land in the bottom drawer. I grabbed it and tore the top open greedily.

As I enjoyed the first cool sip, I remembered all the times on the other side of the gym when Dad would bring me to this place to face the dreaded batting cage. I would climb under the hanging net and position myself around the rubber home plate, my jaw clenched in grim determination. Dad would fiddle with the settings to get the right pitch speed, and then the balls would start to fly.

"You're still just a little late, Dav," he would offer after a couple of strikes whizzed by me. Every time I swung the bat, it looked like the ball simply passed right through it. The pitches looked like the streaks of white light that came rushing toward the Millennium Falcon whenever Han Solo was lucky enough to get the ship's warp speed working.

"Don't swing upwards like that. A nice even swing," he'd call out, motioning with his empty hands from just outside the net. "Not every one has to be a home run." *A home run?* I'd secretly have settled for making contact just once and dribbling it along the ground.

These sessions would usually end in the same way: after dozens of pitches, I'd abruptly tear the smelly varsity batting helmet off my head and drop the bat in disgust. Dad would try to be positive with me, but I could see he was often as frustrated as I was.

It had now been quite a while since we'd attempted the batting cage scenario again. That was a relief to me in one way, but it also left a nagging pang of disappointment. *Why couldn't I just hit a baseball?* I racked my brain for an answer as I exited the gym, and entered a long, thin storage room.

The smell of chalky gymnastic powder and ancient leather

basketballs filled the stale air. Evidence of past generations of gym classes had piled up over the decades. I dug around the room for a bit, looking for anything of interest, and eventually pushed some equipment away from on top of an aging cabinet to reach its contents.

Among other things inside, I was happy to find a tall stack of black Michigan license plates—dated 1979—in a yellowing paper bag. The top one was a slightly-rusty twin of the one I'd seen on Dustin's station wagon: *PRTYBOY*. Surprised, I studied it for a second or two and wondered how it had arrived in this place. A few other random plates from various states were in there as well.

I found a cool green 1973 Ohio plate that read *Seat Belts Fastened* on the top in raised letters. A red plate from Indiana that had been issued in the 1960s was another. *They must have been removed from a preceding fleet of church vans and school buses and then forgotten,* I figured. I had an instant epiphany, and I grabbed them. Continuing on in the peaceful darkness, I wandered on toward the administrative office wing.

Dad was still in his own office on the far side of the building I knew, so I decided to avail myself of a prime snooping opportunity. Amazingly, the side door to that particular wing had been left unlocked, probably as a result of the relaxed structure during the vacant summer months. I left the bag of plates in the hallway and went inside. A few of the staff had been known to come in from time to time, but other than that, the place was generally deserted for the entire summer break.

Joyce Stickler's office door was cracked open slightly, and I tiptoed in somewhat reverently. In the dim light I could see a few pieces of random wall art, and a handsomely-framed diploma announcing that she'd been awarded a degree in education from Eastern Michigan University in 1969. I hadn't been in her office since the immediate aftermath of Denny burning his eyebrows off. I thought back and remembered that after she had dismissed both of them, our conversation had taken on a vastly different tone.

"Wait here a minute, young man," she'd interjected as I got up to leave along with them. I had sat back down as she closed the door behind them. She had returned to her desk and looked at me coolly, unblinking. It was an uncomfortable gaze to fall under. She had pursed her lips in thought and her eyes narrowed behind her glasses.

"Denny simply received the just reward for his folly," she had lectured, referring undoubtedly to his singed eyebrows. "And Tyson, well…" she had paused. "I'm new here as you know, but from what I've been told, one could hardly be surprised regarding his poor choices," she had added, and I wondered if she was referring to his difficult situation at home.

"But you," she had said pointedly, clicking her tongue to the roof of her mouth several times. "What will your parents think? You have quite a history of pushing the boundaries set in front of you, don't you?" She had let that question hang in the air a bit for effect.

Her next exhortation echoed now in my mind: "During my upcoming tenure here, I want the student body to come to grips with this reality: Who we choose to associate with will completely determine our fates. You can see the truth in this already, can't you?" She had seemed to be almost pleading with me all of the sudden.

"Will you find yourself alone in the gutter someday, every last chip gambled away? Or will you rise to the challenges of life and greet them victoriously? It's entirely up to you. Trust me, I've seen this played out in my own life, very close to home." Her last words had seemed to leave a bitter taste in her mouth, and she had become lost in thought. Shortly afterward, I had been dismissed.

I'd found her brazen implications about my friends bothersome, so it gave me a small sense of satisfaction to now be invading her personal sanctum on my own terms. I turned her small desk lamp on and surveyed the landscape. In the top drawer of her desk, I found a stack of meaningless files, and a folded up five dollar bill, which I immediately pocketed with a grin. The second drawer below it yielded nothing of interest.

The bottom drawer contained a box of Kleenex, and a manila envelope which was unmarked on the outside. I pulled it out and opened the top metal tab to reveal the contents. Inside I found three sheets of paper, and a business card. The business card was for Officer Collier of the Rouge Park Police Department. His phone number was highlighted in yellow, and paper-clipped to one of the loose pages.

I looked at that page first, and scanned it quickly, seeing immediately that it was a police report, apparently filled out hastily by Collier himself. It detailed a visit to the Mann home a week previously, in a futile attempt to locate Justus. It was devoid of additional details, except for a brief summary at the bottom, stating that no additional information could be determined at that time.

The second piece of paper seemed to be the minutes of a school board meeting, dated about a month earlier than the police report. The words CONFIDENTIAL were typed in a large font at the top of the summary. One paragraph caught my attention. It read that Dustin Crabb had been terminated, effective immediately, due to "significant lapses in moral judgment requiring reprimand and removal."

The board had strongly recommended finding a replacement as soon as humanly possible, in order to allow the new hire adequate time to adjust at the end of the school year, and then hit the ground running the following fall semester. That helped explain Stickler's almost miraculous appearance.

The last page contained handwritten notes, and I assumed by the neatness of the cursive that they were Joyce Stickler's herself. I scanned down the page, speed-reading them and storing them away for future reference. Snippets like "Nicolette's criminal record, public intoxication, etc.," "Enrique Willows, arrest warrant in Illinois," and "Club Xanadu?" were written neatly in rows. A couple of phone numbers were included, and I began to memorize them, but at the same instant, a light turned on in the main office lobby, and I heard the terrible sound of keys jangling.

Something inside alerted me it was not my dad. I quickly tossed the manila folder and the loose pages back into the bottom desk drawer and slid it closed silently. I prayed under my breath that the person wouldn't continue on toward Stickler's office, but I realized with a jolt of terror that the footsteps were indeed heading my way. Turning the desk lamp back off, I slid into the coat closet, pulled the door closed, and then held my breath.

Mr. Asperat entered Stickler's office without turning on the lights. He approached her desk, crouched down, and opened the drawers one by one, just as I had mere moments earlier. He rifled through its contents for a second, then stood up abruptly, seeming to find what he had been looking for. He glanced around for a second, then departed as quickly as he had arrived.

I exhaled, and when the lights to the main office lobby had been turned off once again, I exited my hiding place and stood still, trying to catch my breath. *Why did Stickler have Asperat running her errands,* I wondered? *Or had he been there on his own personal mission?* I pondered the revelation about Crabb, and wondered again at what connection Joyce could possibly have to the missing, enigmatic Justus Mann.

The fact that Nicolette Mann, so often observed to be a dangerously-loose cannon, could have a criminal record was hardly surprising to me. But what could Club Xanadu, the seedy nightclub located just blocks from my house over in Rouge Park, have anything to do with this strange collection of people? And how were they all connected to

Enrique Willows?

I exited the office area from the same door I had entered, picking up the bag of license plates in stride. Thinking for a second, I darted out to our station wagon and deposited the plates in the back seat, returning back into the school through the door I'd propped open.

Soon afterward, I heard my dad heading down the darkened hallway in my direction, boisterously whistling a hymn. He locked the extending gate behind him, and then we closed up the school for the night and left, with the overhead projector successfully in the back of the wagon.

The next morning, Violet came bouncing down the stairs to the back of the church, and helped me haul the projector up to the classroom, where Goliath was dutifully waiting. After getting it in position, she ran over to the door and turned off the lights, and a perfect representation of the giant appeared up on the roll of paper, which was now hanging from the dropped ceiling tiles with the help of two strips of tape.

"See!" she said, nodding approvingly. "Easy as pie. Now, you get tracing and I'll start searching for the right color crayons to match his outfit."

It took several minutes to get the outline drawn, and then to go over the pencil marking with a black permanent marker, but it was clear from the outset that the result would be a terrific one. Violet laid out greens, reds, and browns of various tints and hues, organizing them by color and arranging sticky notes detailing what region of the drawing they would eventually fill. I was growing impressed with her design skills, and found it slightly intriguing as our relationship seemed to be heading in a positive direction once again.

We joked back and forth about my previous attempt at the giant, and her teasing didn't annoy me as much as it often had in the past.

She looked very pretty again, dressed in jeans and a blue ruffled top. Her eyes danced in the reflection of the projector, and the fact that we were entirely alone in the upper wing—while at the other end of the complex kids screamed their choruses and weighed the day's hefty offering—gave me a strange pleasant feeling. *The totally unpredictable Violet Vereen,* I thought to myself. I was starting to appreciate her again in a way I hadn't for a long time.

Several years earlier, an object had fallen behind a tall filing cabinet leaning against a classroom wall. We'd both attempted to grab for it from opposite sides. Our fingers had unexpectedly brushed one another's, and I was rather shocked to discover that she proceeded to grab my hand and refuse to let go.

Hand-holding of any kind was a big deal in early elementary, and I remembered well the new, electric feelings that had shot up my arm, making me feel warm all over. We had often silently sneaked back to that spot and repeated the same secret practice. The next year, we had been placed into separate classes, and the unique ritual faded into the past. Neither of us had ever spoken about it to each other out loud since.

I wasn't actually sure what the church would even think about a possible attraction, much less the members of my own family. Things had changed a lot in the world in the previous twenty years, but in 1987, an interracial couple out in public was still a pretty unusual sight, and often taboo.

I recalled how earlier that year in Mrs. Townsend's class, I had been staring ahead at the map of the United States displayed at the front of each classroom, lost in thought. It was a large political map of the entire country, with each state outlined and filled in with a different pastel color, while also displaying the largest cities and capitals.

I had traced around the map in my mind again and again,

wondering if I would be able to draw the entire thing from memory if I'd wanted to. The iconic and familiar shape of Michigan's mitten, the protruding peninsula of Florida, the sharp southern tip of Texas, the boring stacked squares of Colorado and Wyoming. My eyes had just been rounding the far north tip of Maine when I'd heard an authoritative voice, coming from what seemed like a mile away, asking a pointed question and then pausing expectantly.

Mrs. Townsend had repeated the question and I'd looked back at her dumbly. She had stared at me, her eyebrows frozen in a raised position. She was kind, but always reserved the intangible ability to make any student a bit frightened.

"Forty-five," Violet had whispered in a barely audible voice. "Forty-five," I'd repeated out loud, robotically. Mrs. Townsend had looked a bit surprised at my correct answer, but had forged ahead with the next math problem. "Thank you," I'd whispered at Violet without looking at her. She could be unexpectedly nice like that if she wanted to be.

"Dav, what exactly are you doing?" she asked now, snapping me back into the present once again. "This drawing has to be done by the time the groups break up. You promised the leaders it would be ready, remember? Now get coloring with me!" she commanded. Our eyes met and we both smiled briefly, but then we awkwardly looked back down at the illustration and continued our work.

About half an hour later, I was supremely satisfied to hear the admiration of passing kids as they noticed the finished Goliath for the first time on their way out of the day's session. Mrs. Townsend stood beside it, proudly explaining the armor and weaponry and confirming that the villain had actually been that tall to anyone who stopped to ask. She shot me a look of approval as I stood against a wall not far from our creation, perfectly positioned to absorb all the compliments.

Violet stood next to me, and as she adjusted her stance against the wall, our hands inadvertently brushed each other. She suddenly saw that her ride had arrived, so she grabbed her backpack from the floor, and ran off without saying anything else to me. It had been an unexpectedly good morning.

heavy Lifting

    That afternoon, I was lying shirtless on the rough surface of my own front porch, enjoying the quiet privilege of having absolutely nothing in the world to do. The sun had heated the concrete up to a scalding temperature, and I could feel the gravel leaving temporary pink pockmarks in the skin of my back, but for some reason, it felt oddly comforting. The sun high overhead felt hot on my face as I closed my eyes and took in the smells of summer. A wave of nostalgia, thankfulness and contentment swept over me, and I lingered for a long while and drank it in. I had the vague realization that it would be one of those iconic memories I could conjure up in moments of quiet reflection throughout the rest of my life.

    Life will never be this simple again, the voice in my head reminded me. *Enjoy it while it lasts. Sear moments like this on your consciousness, so you can recall them when the going gets rough. Because it will.* The voice sounded different than the one I usually heard in my mind. It seemed older and wiser somehow, and almost prophetic.

I sat still listening to the wind blow through the branches of the large beech tree in our front yard. A good number of the older trees in my neighborhood had been felled during a derecho in the early 80s, but somehow this one had been spared the destruction. It was the only American Beech on the block, and I had loved climbing up into its heights ever since I could remember. On especially daring climbs, I could get high enough to see the Crosstown campus in one direction, and the distant towers of the Renaissance Center in downtown Detroit in the other.

The silence was broken by Corbin, and after resisting as long as possible, I finally sighed and gave in to his incessant whining and agreed to take him on a bike ride. My parents shared an older red girl's bicycle, complete with a bright yellow child seat affixed firmly to the back of it. Corbin was a pretty big kid for five, and certainly could have ridden a bike on his own if he'd wanted. But he loved to squeeze himself into the seat behind me whenever I'd agree, and pretend we were traveling around the world. We would enter a land of make-believe, which allowed me to utilize my encyclopedic knowledge of geography, and every new block we happened upon would become another exotic country to visit and explore.

On one such ride about a year or so prior, we had arrived at a stoplight ready to cross the main road dividing Rouge Park from West Ridge. Hauling Corbin around was no easy task, as the seat was designed for kids half his size, and gaining momentum again after coming to a stop was really the only challenge to the whole endeavor. We had waited patiently at the edge of the curb until the *Walk* signal had become illuminated. When the light had turned green, I had laboriously started up again, and we had nearly gotten to the other side when a car had slammed into us broadside, coming to a stop in the middle of the crosswalk.

The bicycle, with Corbin strapped into it, but helmet-less as all kids were in those days, slid across the pavement and I tumbled, stunned, in the other direction. After a few seconds, I had looked up, expecting the driver to emerge frantically from her vehicle to check on our well-being. I had been amazed to find her gesturing and yelling noiselessly from inside the car, acting like the collision had somehow been my fault.

In an instant, I had been on my feet rushing over to check on Corbin. I was sure after a collision of that intensity he would be crying, and perhaps even injured—but he was just looking straight ahead, with glassy eyes. I had brushed his light brown locks out of his face to check for tears.

Not knowing what else to do, I mustered every ounce of energy I had and righted the bike again, walked it gingerly the rest of the way to the other side of the busy thoroughfare. We stood there together as I attempted to catch my breath. The lights had changed back again, and traffic had resumed, streaming by as if the whole harrowing event had happened only in my imagination.

In light of this disturbing history, I always found it a bit surprising that Corbin was still so enthusiastic about heading out on yet another one of our tandem adventures. I pulled the red bike loose from the shed, just as Suzanne came running outside announcing her intention to come along with us on her yellow scooter. She was wearing her olive green stretch pants like she did at least five days a week, rain or shine.

I tried to convince her not to tag along, but she wouldn't listen to me. After getting Corbin situated, I pushed out into the street and callously left her in the dust by the time one block had passed. Her pleas for me to slow down and wait for her gradually faded into the distance as I turned the corner to head along the main road, in the general direction of our previous misadventure.

"Where are we going this time, Dav?" Corbin asked from behind me. It was another warm afternoon, but the breeze we felt as I pedaled strenuously was refreshing. "Let's see," I replied, looking up at a street sign. "Paris, Corbin."

"Oh cool, France!" he smiled.

"Nope, not France. Good guess, though," I replied, cryptically. "We have just entered the official city limits of Paris, Texas! Welcome to the Lone Star State, Corbin. Whoa—see that sprawling ranch over there?" I asked him, laughing and pointing.

I continued to embellish on our imaginary surroundings, pointing out the cowboys, the huge expanse of empty plains, and the oil derricks looming in the distance. Corbin lapped it all up in silence. I didn't even have to turn around to know that he was smiling at every word of my grandiose descriptions.

As we reached the next corner, I swung out wide and made an exaggerated turn onto the side street perpendicular to us. I looked up to see a huge group of boys on bikes, at least 15 of them, heading directly toward us. They were a giant mass of gleaming spokes, black outfits and spiked hair in various formats. Turning around at this point was absolutely impossible, I realized.

The group spotted me and sped up. Like a deep cut that happens so suddenly the wound gapes open for a second before the blood finally and terribly catches up and gushes out, the distance between us closed in mere seconds. Their rides surrounded us, and came to a halt with squealing tires, forcing us to do the same. Several boys stopped to admire the ugly black marks they had made on the pavement. I immediately saw that the boy in the center was Ryne. My heart dropped.

"Well, isn't this the cutest thing you've ever seen?" he laughed, gesturing at my parents' bike, the child seat, Corbin, and myself. The group laughed heartily at the hilarious sight. I scanned the crowd for any other faces I knew, and spotted the sneering Chet Wiggins just to the right of Ryne. The rest looked vaguely familiar but I knew none of them personally. Pretty much all of them were older than me, and the ones around the fringes drew their bikes in close to see what was going to happen next.

"What's your name kid?" someone called from near the back. I didn't volunteer any information, preferring instead to just stare ahead, wracking my brain in vain for what to do next.

"Didn't you hear him, jackweed?" asked another punk close to me. "When a Biker Scout asks you a question, you answer it! What's the name?" He slapped the back of my head very hard. Several more of them laughed. Another fist came in from out of nowhere and slammed my temple. Though I was dazed, I stood my ground and refused to back down.

Corbin finally spoke up and told them my name, and then commanded them to leave us alone. Unfortunately, he didn't use my nickname, but my full name in all of its unusual glory. The Biker Scouts nearest the front of the mob emitted sputtering laughs of incredulity, and proceeded to punch each other in the arms and back, almost to confirm that it hadn't been a mass hallucination.

They repeated my name gleefully to one another over and over again. Someone called out, "What in all holy hell kind of name is that— Norwegian or something?" I could feel my face turning a deep hot pink. I could also sense tears close at hand, but I somehow managed to keep them at bay, just barely. Ryne attempted to quiet the group once more with a raised hand.

"Pretty sad that your kid brother has to do all the talking for you. Almost as sad as this sorry excuse for a bike. Clearance rack at Kmart,

Davajuan

apparently." He kicked the front tire so hard I thought it might burst. "Bluelight Special, no doubt. By the way, does anyone actually know this turd?" Ryne asked, now directing his inquiry to the general audience.

Chet Wiggins spoke up. "He's a Crosstown brat, I know that," he contributed, leaving out the important and potentially embarrassing tidbit that he happened to be one as well. I considered pointing it out right then and there, but I knew that would only lead to even more trouble for Corbin and I. Low mocking whistles rose up from the group.

"Whoa dudes, we are in the presence of greatness," Ryne snarled. "He must be loaded, someone search his pockets," another Scout suggested from the back.

"Take me home now, Dav," Corbin whispered in my ear. "We've got to get out of here!" I gave him an impatient nod, but I couldn't see any way through the wall of delinquents in front of us.

Two girls came marching down the sidewalk, which the inquisition had now spilled over onto, and they pushed their way through the rowdy group to the center. Roxy and Mandy, apparently on their way home from one of their routine visits to D and D Market, each carried a Mountain Dew and a half-eaten Twizzlers package.

"Leave them alone, you scoundrels," Mandy said to Ryne in a playful voice, but I thought I could detect a tinge of earnestness just below the surface. "What did these two kids ever do to you? Haven't you guys got anything better to do?" she asked, looking around. "No deliveries ready yet for tonight?"

"Hey Ryne, don't let your little girlfriend boss you around. Soon she'll be calling all the shots," someone yelled out, drawing a few nervous laughs from the group, and visibly irritating Ryne.

"Guys—she already *does* call the shots—you know who her dad is!" someone else on the other side of the throng added.

Her Schemes and Plans

"Shouldn't you be running back to the kitchen and cooking up something for us with *baking soda* right about now?" Ryne spat back, eliciting raucous laughter from the other boys, but the drug reference completely escaped me. He was starting to look even angrier.

"Enrique told me to keep you in line, girl. Never forget that. And he said absolutely no talking about business out in public!" Ryne yelled at her, his temper rising to a crescendo.

"I'll talk about whatever I want. You know I can't stand what you guys do," she shot back, crossing her arms. "And that goes for Enrique too. Taking advantage of hurting people who can't help themselves—" she stopped short, remembering that Corbin and I were standing there, and thought better of finishing her sentence.

"Wow. He'll be pretty upset to hear that's what you think. And I'll make sure he does," Ryne glared. "You know what? Let's blow this joint, guys. Mandy needs to get back to running this glorified preschool. We have important stuff to do."

"And you, kid?" He returned his condescending gaze to me. "Don't ever let me see you alone, or I'll finish what I started." He turned and motioned to the others to mount their rides. He contemplated something for a moment. "Hey Roxy," he called, without looking back at her. "Come on with me, babe."

Roxy, surprised, blushed a bit and giggled. "Really?" She glanced at Mandy, who rolled her eyes but said nothing. Impulsively, Roxy adjusted her leather skirt, skipped over and hopped onto Ryne's bike, and he took off, pedaling while standing up so she could sit on the molded seat. Whoops and cussing proceeded out from the entourage, as the mass of BMX bikes and their rag-tag riders left the scene. Roxy looked back once, smiled at Mandy and shrugged. She made a gesture for Mandy to call her later on the phone and quickly turned back around, looking as happy as a lark to be counted worthy to ride with Ryne.

"He's not my boyfriend, you know," Mandy stated flatly as she watched them disappear. I was happy and surprised to hear it, but said nothing back. She turned to me, as if she had abruptly remembered we were still there.

"Is your head OK? It looks a bit red near your ear." I nodded nonchalantly, even though it was still throbbing uncontrollably. Corbin looked her over from head to toe, and then blurted his own name out to her. She politely introduced herself to him, and stood standing on the curb staring blankly again after where the posse had gone. She looked gorgeous as usual, even though she was perturbed.

"Enrique's not my dad. A while after my real dad left, Mom got into trouble, and Enrique was right there, as if on cue," she said bitterly. "He can smell vulnerability like a hound dog. Before I knew it, he'd taken over our lives." She paused, and I waited to hear what else she might share about herself.

"Then Mom got sick. His kind side, if there ever was one, disappeared as fast as her health did. All the sudden his facade was gone, in a poof of smoke. I began to realize what a monster he truly is. And the second I am old enough and have enough money saved up, I'll disappear from here for good, too."

"Sorry if I'm wrong in saying this, but he seems to take pretty good care of you. You have a nice house, nice clothes…" I offered.

She smiled smugly. "Sure, he buys me whatever I want, and I can basically go wherever and do whatever I want to. But you'll find out someday it's not the same." She continued to stew, apparently relieved to have a listening and sympathetic ear for once.

"He's nothing like my real dad. The day my mom finally drove Dad away was the worst day of my life. Why she treated him the way she did I'll never understand. He's out in California somewhere now, I've heard. Redondo Beach. Someday I know I'll see him again." Her determined face formed a frown once again.

"For now, Enrique's all I've got left. But why am I bothering you with all this?" she added, becoming agitated at herself.

"Look, I've got to go. Please stay away from those guys. They're nothing but trouble, and you're not cut out for that crowd. For that matter, I could be trouble for you, too. You don't really know me." She looked at me sadly.

I wanted to tell her it was no bother at all to hear about her struggles. I wanted to puff out my chest, contradict her and say I could handle them all—but I knew that would sound ridiculous. Of course she was correct. I was completely out of my depth. Ryne could toss me around like a rag doll. I imagined that I might actually manage to get a few shots in on Chet Wiggins if I ever got the chance, though, before I went down fighting. She started to walk away. I finally thought of something pertinent to say.

"I saw your signs at Pack Rat Pete's. Have any sold yet?" I asked, knowing at least one had, since it had been propped up against a pile of books on my dresser for an entire day already. She turned around and her delightful face brightened considerably.

"Yeah! How did you know about them? Oh, yeah—Roxy," she nodded, and rolled her eyes again, recalling our previous meeting. "Two of them have sold. Pete says he thinks they will do pretty well. He might even show them to a friend of his who has a gallery downtown." She smiled and obviously thought that last tidbit was quite an impressive one.

I remembered the plates I had stolen from the storage room at Crosstown the night before. I had hoped they might possibly lead to an interaction such as this, but I couldn't have imagined it would come this soon.

"I have some plates you could use," I offered. "You know, for your crafts. Want me to bring them over some time?" I asked casually, but every muscle tensed in anticipation of her answer, ready to discover whether or not she thought this was an unnecessary or ridiculous offer.

"Really? That's super nice of you!" She looked at me oddly. "Are you sure? Where did you get them? In your garage or something? That's where most people store them."

"Around," I said vaguely. "I have nothing else to do with them. Thought you might like them. They have a lot of character," I said, then thought it sounded nerdy. My mouth was starting to get dry.

"Character, eh? Nice. OK, sounds good. See you later." She turned and walked away. "It was nice to meet you, Corbin," she said turning her head a few seconds later. He beamed at me.

Suzanne appeared at the end of the street we were standing on, and when she saw us, she flew toward us on her scooter. Her mass of thick and wild blonde hair fluttered freely behind her as she pushed vigorously. She came to a stop right in front of us.

"Meanie!" she scolded me. "Don't leave me again. I've been looking for you all over the neighborhood!" Even though she could be annoying, I loved her as much as anyone else in the world. I was surprised she seemed to still feel the same way about me, even after I'd tossed her down the basement steps a few years earlier, knocking both front teeth loose in the process. I knew she looked up to me, so I was glad that she had not witnessed our humiliating exchange with the Biker Scouts.

"Wait till you hear what happened to us!" Corbin began. I hoped he'd leave Mandy out of his tale. His reports almost always found their way into a discussion around the dinner table at the most inopportune times.

We rode straight home all together at once. I was putting on a brave face, but I absolutely did not want to risk any additional confrontations with Biker Scout punks while riding my parents' bicycle. Dad was home from work and in the front yard, playing a pick-up game of football with Jason and Johnny again. I wasn't sure why, but it bothered me.

They didn't skip a beat as my siblings and I turned and headed up the driveway on the way back to the shed. Jason made a great diving catch and Dad praised him effusively. He ran over and shook him by the shoulders laughing. Johnny ran over and put a firm tackle on them both and they all fell to the grass wrestling around. I avoided them and slipped in by the side door and headed down to my room.

In the basement, I reclined on my bed for a long while and contemplated recent events. I thought about Ryne, the angry veins on his biceps stuck fast in my mind. I stared at my own arms, and to me they might as well have been the long shafts of Tinker Toys, with knobby connectors acting as my shoulders, elbows and wrists. *Something has to be done,* I said to myself. I determined right then and there that I'd start working out. *Before too many months I'll be able to squeeze Ryne's head like a grape between my huge arms,* I imagined. I knew deep down that Chet Wiggins' head might have been a more realistic goal.

Out in one corner of the unfinished portion of the basement, Dad had a dusty weight bench. I cleared some random boxes off the bench, and put some twenty-five-pound plates on each side of the bar. After one last swipe to remove some remaining grime, I looked up at the bar above me, and took a deep breath. *Ninety-five pounds. Not much less than my current weight. I can do this,* I told myself.

With my hands spread wide, I heaved the load straight up, and then let it lower down to my chest. I was horrified to realize there was going to be no way it was getting back up to its initial spot. With the bar resting on my chest, I frantically tried to decide whether or not to yell for help.

I could hear Dad and the neighbor boys celebrating another amazing football play outside, and I vowed not to go that route. With a desperate heave that sapped every last ounce of my strength, I got the bar halfway up, and then—arms shaking—let it come crashing down backwards onto the floor as I contorted myself to avoid getting my head crushed.

"What was that?" I heard my Mom ask loudly from upstairs with a concerned tone, and then heard her small footsteps hurrying down the landing to the basement. "Oh my!" she emitted with a cry of alarm, as she rounded the corner and came down the remaining steps.

"What happened, Dav?" she asked. She must have been busy baking something, because she was wearing her checkered blue apron, and wrung her hands into it now to get the flour off them.

I hunched motionless at the end of the bench. Despite my best efforts, tears were finally welling up in my eyes. She walked over to me and tried to pick up the weights, but she was petite, and they were nearly immovable to her as well. After a couple of awkward attempts, she eventually sat down on the bench beside me and tried to make eye contact.

"What's going on, son?" she asked, more as a statement than a question. The evidence was pretty obvious. I hadn't cried in front of anyone for over a year, shattering all previous personal records. I briefly considered clamming up and blowing the whole thing off, but the recent string of frustrating events was simply too much.

"Mom?" I started slowly, considering every word carefully. "How much longer am I going to be—like this?" I looked away from her searching eyes. She sat in thought for a moment.

"You have a perfectly fine body for a young man. But I have a strong feeling you are going to have, well—a growing up summer, for lack of a better phrase." I could sense her smiling at me, and I ventured a sheepish glance back at her.

"I want you to always remember something: you can do absolutely anything you put your mind to, Dav. I truly believe that. For you, son, the sky will always be the limit." It was, in a sappy but completely genuine sort of way, exactly what I needed to hear.

Dad came in the side door loudly just then, huffing a bit from the rigorous activity. "Oh, Dav, there you are. Working out, eh?" He came down the steps quickly. "Good news! There's a couple fun things I want to share with you." He glanced at my mom, who nodded that it was fine to reveal the news.

"Jason and Johnny have been wanting to get to a Tigers game really badly for a while, but it hasn't worked out for their own family to take them yet this year. I was able to get us some really nice box seats from a businessman at Crosstown. The game is tomorrow afternoon!" he beamed. I responded happily. It did sound fun, though I'd frankly rather have gone with him alone.

"And, secondly," he continued excitedly, "Your Mom and I have been thinking it is long overdue for you to get a new room over on the other side of the basement. One with a closet, some natural light, a little more space," he added as he ticked off the benefits on his fingers.

This was tremendous news to me. I'd loved the solitude of the basement ever since moving down to the lower floor when Corbin came along, but these new amenities really sounded great. "Asperat is going to come over and help me. He's got some experience from framing in houses as a teenager, and he has all the tools we'll need to do it right."

"When will you start?" I asked, eagerly. "Next week, most likely," Dad responded with a smile. Without thinking, I ran over and gave him a hug, then pulled back just a little, thinking that the level of enthusiasm was a bit juvenile.

But, he pulled me in close and made it seem completely natural, which I appreciated. Now in a much better mood, I told them I was heading upstairs for a quick snack. Mom told me to stay out of the cereal, which was always off-limits between meals.

I already had other ideas. My first clumsy attempt at protein-packing was to crack a half dozen eggs into a tall glass, stir them up with a fork, and gulp the mixture down while barely managing to repress my gag reflex.

Then, I grabbed a piece of loose-leaf paper and a pen, set up at the kitchen table, and started planning out my first week of workouts as best I knew how. My days of living as a scrawny kid that the Biker Scouts could embarrass and pick on at will were numbered.

10

michigan + Trumbull

I hadn't seen the Ly triplets around the neighborhood very much lately, so the next morning I walked over to their house, went up to the drooping screen door, and knocked. There was no noise at all on the entire property except for Queen, who barked relentlessly in a high-pitched yelp, as she always did whenever a stranger was even close to the house. A couple of doors down, Wanda was on her porch sweeping off something with a broom, puffing on yet another cigarette. She waved hello to me and continued on with her chore.

"Shut up, Queen!" an angry adult's voice yelled from somewhere in the jumbled interior. After a moment, a tired-looking Duong came to the door.

"Hey, Dav. We're not really doing much today," he said sullenly. His left eye looked swollen. I noticed it, but said nothing. I wondered if he'd received it from a member of the Biker Scouts. My own head still hurt from the thump I'd gotten myself from them. He said goodbye abruptly, turned and disappeared back into the shadows of the house. I heard a couple of other low voices inside, but what exactly they said was unintelligible to me.

That was strange, I said to myself, then realized that it really wasn't that odd, to be honest. My life seemed amazingly structured, mundane and routine compared to most of the other families in this section of Rouge Park. It made me feel blessed and somewhat boring at the same time. I walked back along their side fence toward my own street.

Dai was taking something out to the backyard, and saw me. I could tell he was contemplating pretending not to notice me, but it quickly became an absurd charade, so he eventually turned and nodded at me. One of his nostrils was crusted with blood, and he looked as if he'd seen a ghost.

"OK, Dai, what happened to you guys? What's going on?" I stopped and demanded. He immediately cringed, and gestured with his hands to let me know he wanted me to lower my voice. "Fine, OK," I acquiesced. "Now can you tell me what happened to you?" I implored.

He looked doubtful, and glanced back toward the house. "I can't right now. I'll tell you later. Now, get out of here before they hear you," he urged. He continued on his way to the garage, and frantically waved for me to make myself scarce. After trying to come up with something else to say and drawing a blank, I complied, nodding my agreement, and continued on back to my own house.

At home, Dad was busy making sketches and plans for my new room in the basement. He had made markings on the existing walls and floor, and was standing with a tape measure and a pencil in his mouth. "Mr. Asperat is free for dinner on Monday, and I want to be ready to hit the ground running," he said with the yellow pencil between his teeth. "I'll get the studs, drywall, and other supplies tomorrow after church. You'll be in your brand new digs in no time!"

I excitedly thanked him and hopped over to my old room to get ready for the afternoon Tigers game. I had an old blue and orange t-shirt that still fit decently, and I planned to take my glove and a ball left over from last year's Youth League season in case I got close enough for an autograph from Alan Trammell or Chet Lemon.

I'd gotten Larry Herndon and Lance Parrish's signature the season before on a couple of ticket stubs after observing batting practice, and they were both displayed close to Mandy's sign on my dresser. My mom liked to call my clothes dresser an *armoire*, perhaps since that made it sound much more cosmopolitan and expensive than it actually was. She had found it cheaply unfinished, and had then stained it herself to match the rest of my hand-me-down furniture.

Mom yelled down to say that I had a visitor. I popped up the stairs and was happy to see Tyson outside. I ran out to greet him on the front lawn. I hadn't seen him for a week since he had been working nearly full-time down at the aluminum factory.

"Hey, how's it going?" I asked him, slapping him five as he sat straddling his bike on the sidewalk. "What's the name of the place you're at again?"

"Revere Enterprises Aluminum," he recited proudly with an official voice. "It's tough work down there, but the money is insane. They have me pulling 10-hour shifts 5 days a week, and the last ten hours are time and a half."

"What do they have you doing?" I asked in wonder.

"Sweeping up the grease, emptying trash cans, loading finished boxes onto trucks, that sort of thing. Anything the union guys refuse to do, really," he shrugged.

I asked him to remind me of where it was again, thinking I might ride down and take a look. He recited two crossroads much farther south than I typically ventured.

"They're really shorthanded right now, too, because a couple guys left and apparently haven't come back. They can't keep up with the orders because so many people want new gutters installed this year. It's pretty stressful." It was good to see him. Tyson already seemed even older and more mature than when school had let out, for some intangible reason. He was pretty proud to be gainfully employed. He also appeared to have grown an inch since the last time I had seen him, which I both admired and despised simultaneously.

What a change a few months can make, I said silently to myself. Only the previous December, Tyson and I had been messing around during the final Christmas performance rehearsal over at Crosstown. Every student in the school had been gathered in the high school gym. The teachers were on high alert, and any murmurings or distractions were being clamped down upon swiftly. As our grade had shuffled onto the risers after being summoned, the two of us broke out in raucous laughter over a shared joke. The disturbance had echoed throughout the entire gym.

Rather than Mrs. Townsend, I had been surprised to see Principal Dustin Crabb come marching with a purpose toward the two of us. He had grabbed us both roughly by the collar and dragged us to the side of the gym away from the center of the action. He pulled us close to his face, and I could smell the lingering stench of cigarettes he enjoyed, sneaking out secretly between meetings to inhale behind the school. I was so close to him that I could see he had something crusty left over from a Danish or donut clinging to the corner of his mouth.

"I'm going to make an example of you two this time," he hissed, and reached for a Ping Pong paddle conveniently located on a chair along the gymnasium wall. Despite the rehearsal continuing on unabated right next to us, many students couldn't resist stealing sideways glances to witness the spectacle.

"You first," Crabb had growled at Tyson under his breath. In those days, spanking in private schools hadn't been entirely phased out, and Tyson knew what to do. Quivering from both apprehension and embarrassment, he had bent over and received three massive wallops to the rear end. He had tried to contain his anguish, but eventually failed. That more sensitive version of Tyson was a far cry from the young man standing next to me now.

I had been up next. Spanking was no new experience for me, both at school and at home. I had vowed in the preceding seconds to find a way to stifle my reaction to it. Too many people were watching for me to let Crabb win. I took my position where Tyson had stood a moment earlier and waited. The pain never arrived.

What I heard instead was a whooshing of wind, and then the splintering of wood as the Ping Pong paddle had broken in two right at the top of the handle. Roars of surprise and laughter bubbled up from the nearest half of the observing student body. I stood up enough to peer back and see the look of frozen shock on Dustin Crabb's face. There was literally nothing else he could do.

I saw the confusion proceed across his face as obviously as if I had been watching a Commodore 64 computer's terminal display. Finally, at a loss, he turned and stormed off right out of the gym, exasperated. The other teachers managed to eventually quiet down the roiling crowd of kids, but the damage was already done. I liked to imagine that humiliation had marked the beginning of the end for the reviled Principal Crabb.

Tyson continued talking with me in the front yard for a bit, and then I had to scramble to finish getting ready for the Tigers game. About the time he pedaled away and headed back home, Jason and

Johnny ran out of their own house, in full Tigers regalia, gloves and gleaming new baseballs in tow. Jason looked like he was struggling to manage an entire packet of Big League Chew that he'd stuffed into his mouth. They both looked incredibly excited, having heard about the close seats. I'd never seen two kids more geeked about baseball—or sports in general, for that matter.

A short time later, all four of us were settled in the station wagon. As Dad backed out, he leaned out the window and looked over at Jason and Johnny's house to wave goodbye, but no one even made an attempt to come to the door or a window, so he put it into drive and we headed downtown. I was proudly ensconced in my usual spot in the front seat, with the two boys in the back. Even though they could both quote the current batting average of every player in the entire Tigers lineup, it was important for me to put them in their rightful places every once in a while.

With the windows rolled all the way down, we sped down the on-ramp onto the interstate, and Dad hit the power to the radio and fiddled with the dial. He let it come to rest on the local Top 40, and I waited for him to turn to another station, but strangely, he didn't. This was unusual, but not entirely unexpected.

Dad had grown up as a quintessential Midwest kid in the 60s—so pretty much a heathen. He'd had an All-American childhood, complete with the popular music of the day as its background soundtrack. Then he'd met Mom, a straight-laced young lady from a devout and well-to-do east coast family, at a Bible college in the deep south. Contemporary music of any kind was shunned both there and within my mom's strict upbringing, so it was a rare day when the radio in our family car played anything other than the news or sports.

A sultry voice on the radio sang:

When you see her, say a prayer
And kiss your heart goodbye
She's trouble, in a word get closer to the fire
Run faster, her laughter burns you up inside
You're spinning 'round and 'round
You can't get up, you try but you can't.

If I'd ever heard a perfect description of my feelings for another person, Madonna's latest smash hit nailed my current impressions of Mandy. I pictured her, and her life so different, more interesting and dangerous than mine, and wondered what, if anything, we could ever have in common.

The home team still played at iconic Tiger Stadium, which stood proudly at the corner of Michigan and Trumbull Avenue. There were paid parking lots that fit neatly into nooks and crannies all around surrounding Corktown, but my dad liked to hunt for free spots along lonely streets in random sketchy neighborhoods half a mile or so away to save some money. Even though we lived mere blocks from the actual Detroit city line, it was still a twenty-minute drive to the stadium, and we passed through a stunningly wide range of neighborhoods as we got closer to our destination.

Grand, massive brick homes once owned by wealthy merchants and aristocrats would line one street, only to be followed a few blocks later by rows and rows of burned out, abandoned husks. I was still too young to know much about the real history of Detroit, and the complex tale of how racial injustice, devastating riots and the subsequent fallout had forever transformed this Paris of the West into the declining metropolis we were driving through now. Soon, Dad began looking around for a suitable place to park.

I was excited to watch the Milwaukee Brewers in person. They'd started out a red-hot 13-0 that season, led by All-Stars such as Paul Molitor and Robin Yount. Even though they'd cooled off a bit as the campaign had progressed, it would be a meeting of two baseball clubs very much in contention for the pennant. After a few minutes, Dad pulled off a minor parallel-parking miracle and squeezed in tightly against a side street curb between two other cars.

A brief distance away from our locked vehicle, Tiger Stadium came into view. The massive white structure with a ring of light blue around the top rim was an impressive sight to me every time. The intense sunshine bounced off it with a dazzling and overwhelming brightness, and it made my head hurt to even look at it as we approached on foot.

I closed my eyes and to my horror, my bizarre vision had resumed once more. The hands I'd previously seen reaching into the bathroom stall now latched onto the helpless young man's throat like a powerful vise. I could somehow feel the ashy breath of the abuser on my own neck as the young man's eyes began to bulge in desperation. Just as a stern voice joined the lonely sound of droplets as they echoed along the tiny square tiles of the damp floor, the figment faded once again.

I turned my head away from the brightness reflecting off the stadium's facade as we kept walking at a strenuous pace. Dad looked around every so often to make sure all three of us boys were still with him as he pushed ahead.

As we drew closer to the ballpark, various vendors and panhandlers pressed up against us, along with the throngs of other fans convening on the ballpark, hawking their wares. I saw an old black veteran amputee sitting in his wheelchair, holding small American flags for sale. His sad eyes met mine for an instant and I looked away.

We stopped for a moment and Dad bought us each a paper bag full of fresh roasted peanuts, and a can of ice-cold Faygo Red Pop, which the vendor produced from a massive cooler after receiving the correct cash. His stand was in the shade, tucked onto the last bit of turf before the endless swath of concrete began. As we approached, I looked up and saw the towering banks of lights a hundred feet above us, passing from view as we entered the stadium.

The stadium was absolutely abuzz that afternoon, the crowd of 40,000 plus Detroiters filing in happily to find their seats. Humongous green girders held up the stands, and we weaved through them once inside to find our own section, which was near home plate. Instead of going up the stairs as we typically did when we had general admission seats in the outfield, we headed down from the concourse toward the vibrant grass of the playing field, my excitement building with every subsequent row we descended.

"I must be in the front row," quipped Dad turning to us, quoting Bob Uecker and his iconic Miller Lite television commercials that had been playing recently. "Here we are," he said, gesturing to four empty seats impossibly close to the impending action. Jason and Johnny beamed ecstatically, and scrambled over each other to get situated.

I squinted and looked at the players running out to warm up, and my head throbbed. Their crisp white uniforms—that I'd seen so often on our grainy television, with blue piping around the chest and collar, complete with the Old English D placed right over the heart—seemed almost surreal. The noise of the crowd, the loud music playing, and a suddenly churning stomach were beginning to alarm me. Becoming ill was the last thing I wanted to happen on this special occasion. I tried to shake it off and focus on something else.

"Anyone want a hot dog?" Dad asked looking down the row at the three of us. Jason and Johnny accepted immediately, but I shook my head. The very mention of it made me want to gag. Dad flagged down the vendor and promptly scored three steaming franks, topped with enormous dollops of ketchup and mustard. As organ music began to play, we all stood for the National Anthem. Halfway through the rendition, I felt absolutely nauseous. I looked down at Dad with his hat off and hand over his heart, and suddenly bolted up the stairs toward the bathroom.

I hunched over a filthy toilet, racking my brain as to why I had become so quickly and violently ill. Suddenly, I remembered that I had hurriedly downed another mixture of a half dozen raw eggs again that afternoon after I'd lifted weights. *Could that be the source of this misery?* I wondered. My mom had warned me about the danger of uncooked eggs. *I should have listened to her,* I chided myself.

The pain of the migraine headache and my violently contorting bowels soon compelled me to rock back and forth over the porcelain, moaning audibly. I heard someone else enter the bathroom. It was Dad.

"Oh, Dad—Oh, Dad!" I moaned repeatedly, despite hating myself for doing so. He crouched beside me. "What is going on, Dav?" he asked, looking quite concerned. I kept chanting his name over and over again, desperately hoping to vomit quickly and perhaps find some temporary relief.

He stood up and paced outside the stall. "I'm sure you feel pretty rotten, Dav—but you need to calm down, son," he implored. He stood looking into the bank of mirrors contemplating what he would do next.

As I began to feel even more intensely ill, my moans increased. As they did, so did Dad's impatience. "I have to go check on Jason and Johnny," he said, somewhat exasperated. "It's not safe for me to leave them out in that crowd alone for long." He started to walk toward the bathroom exit. Two security officers walked in just then, on a mission to determine the source of the dramatic commotion I had been creating.

"Sir, what's going on in here?" one of them asked Dad. He

stammered something about that I was feeling sick to my stomach. "Young man—everything OK in there?" the other officer asked with a serious tone. "He's not doing anything to you against your will, is he?" The officer stared at Dad with an emotionless expression, waiting to assess my response. "I'm sorry, but we have to ask," he shrugged.

I sheepishly confirmed to the officers that I was indeed very sick, and he was not mistreating me in any way whatsoever. Dad's face flushed with anger as he realized what they seemed to be insinuating.

"You'd be surprised what we have to deal with in here. Kid, do you need medical attention? We could take you to the First Aid Station," the first officer offered. After hearing I had a pounding headache, one of them handed my Dad some Ibuprofen and suggested that I take it with some water from the drinking fountain just outside the door.

I thanked them and did as they said, moving from spot to spot nearly doubled over as the officers looked on. By the time they left, Dad had calmed down somewhat and took a couple of deep breaths. "OK, Dav, I'll be back. I have to check in on the other boys really quick," he sighed. After he left, I sat leaning against the clammy commode with my eyes closed, waiting for relief to come in one form or another. Tears welled up as I realized that this debacle had ruined everyone's outing. I was mad too— but what I was actually mad at, I didn't quite know for sure.

Rain started to fall in the fifth inning, and by the seventh, the other three were ready to leave. The Brewers were ahead, and some of the rest of the crowd agreed with us, as the field crew pulled tarps over the infield to wait out the deluge. My pounding headache and sensitivity to light had faded, but the racking cramps still made walking all the way to the car a challenge.

We trudged through the rain all the way back to our parking spot, flanked by hundreds of other departing fans. The boys were silent on the way home, as was my dad. I tried to gauge his face, and he looked disappointed, but there was another emotion present as well that I couldn't yet identify.

"We'll try to get to another game soon, guys," he finally offered to the brothers in the back seat. They nodded politely. I was curled up in the front seat, without a seatbelt on, trying in vain to find a position that felt tolerable. By the time we pulled into the driveway back at our place, the rain had stopped, and the sun was peeking out once more, teasing us that back at the stadium, the baseball game was about to resume. The rain sizzled on the sidewalk as the boys ran across the street, saying thank you and goodbye. Dad departed in the direction of our house, leaving me to sit in the car alone for a moment to collect myself.

When I finally did go in, the house seemed empty. Corbin and Suzanne must have been playing in their rooms with the doors closed. As I passed the landing to the upstairs on the way to the basement, I heard low voices. I held completely still to try to discern what they were saying.

"I just don't know what to do. The boy is so tough to read."

"Maybe he really was that sick. You know, he could be telling the truth. Embellishing a little maybe, but still feeling pretty awful."

"It's not just that. This incident is just the icing on the cake. You know he has a history of things like this!" Dad fumed.

"I'm sorry, dear. I'm sure it's frustrating. Hopefully the other boys had fun?" Mom queried.

"I'm not sure. I hope that they did in spite of it all. But I just don't know if I can believe anything he says anymore. It's sad, but it's true."

His words stung with more intensity than an entire nest of angry, stirred-up yellowjackets. I headed to my room dejectedly, without making a sound. Deep down I knew that I had made this bed for myself—and it was, unfortunately, time for me to lie in it.

11

holes and hot pockets

Mom spent all of Monday morning scurrying around the kitchen, preparing an authentically European meal for Mr. Asperat's impending visit later that evening. Dad was up early as well, laying out the tools and raw materials that would be used to construct my new room in the basement. I heard them both while I was still lying in bed, debating how to spend the day.

During the night I'd had an epiphany, the kind that could only be explained by understanding and appreciating the awesome capability of the human brain to solve problems while you are unconscious and sleeping. I'd stumbled upon an idea that would give me the perfect excuse to see Mandy again, while utilizing my geography skills, and the tricks I'd learned with Violet while using the overhead projector. I could hardly contain my excitement

As I stretched my arms above my head, I felt that pleasant soreness of a successful workout. I could see through the slightly-opened door that sunshine was gloriously streaming in through the glass block windows, signaling that the storms of the weekend were a thing of the past. I was also relieved to realize that my aching stomach and pounding head seemed to have completely recovered since Saturday's baseball game debacle.

The day before had been a typical summer Sunday, with three services, three meals, and not much else exciting. I'd spent the lazy, quiet afternoon alone in my room, listening to Corbin's metal cars scrape playfully along the wooden floor of his room directly above me. It had given me plenty of time to think.

How sick had I actually been? I had asked myself, the confidence in my own recollections slipping by the minute. *Was it all psychological? How can a person know that the thoughts in their own mind are based in reality?* I had shaken off the doubts, reminding myself of the lingering aches that had traveled into the next day along with me.

No matter what, I knew I had to maintain my steadfast belief in the truth of what I knew to be real. Whether or not anyone else believed me, I had to believe myself when push came to shove. I was sure that anything else would lead down a path to paralysis, or maybe even insanity.

I sat up in bed and returned to the present, and assessed my options for the day. I knew Denny was still enjoying the sand and surf nearly halfway around the globe, and Tyson had gone camping up north with his dad for the next couple of days. Zane had informed me at church the morning before that he was somehow grounded again, and I didn't have most of my other school friends' phone numbers. *I'll have to get creative today,* I thought to myself.

"Good morning," I said as I entered the kitchen, taking in the smells of the interesting dishes my mom was preparing. She turned and looked at me, a bit frazzled.

"Hello, Dav. Sorry, I can't talk right now. I'm making wiener schnitzel and crepes for Mr. Asperat tonight. I've never made either one, probably biting off more than I can chew—no pun intended," she laughed dryly.

"He teaches French and German at Crosstown, as you know, and I really want to impress him with some traditional cuisine. Now, how long do these cutlets need to soak in the egg mixture?" she asked herself, retreating back to her own world.

"Oh," she suddenly interjected, "Freddy stopped by a bit ago. I told him it was a bit early, but that you would head over there later. You don't have anything else going on, do you?" she asked. I dejectedly had to admit that I did not. I ate quickly, threw on some play clothes, and walked outside into the warm morning sun. It was going to be a humid June day, I could already tell.

"Just make sure you get back in plenty of time to clean up for dinner," she called out the front kitchen window as I left the yard. "And Dad may want your help working on the project downstairs!" I agreed to check in regularly.

Almost without thinking, I scanned both my own block and the cross street in all four directions, searching for any sign of approaching Biker Scouts. I realized what I was doing in an instant, and tried to shake off the cowardly notion. *You can't live like a prisoner in your own neighborhood*, I scolded myself.

I walked into Freddy's backyard apprehensively, hoping that for some reason or another his mom was absent again. Freddy popped out from the side door, almost as if he possessed a tracking device that announced my arrival. He greeted me excitedly. I heard his words, but got distracted by his unwashed face and gazed at his sunken eyes with a sort of disdainful pity.

"I have an idea!" he said, nearly hopping around with energy from an unknown source. "You know how sometimes you're not allowed to come over, and sometimes I'm not allowed at your place?" I couldn't tell exactly where his line of thought was heading, but I played along anyway. "Yes," I concurred cautiously.

"Let's make a tunnel from my house to yours, right under the street!" he exclaimed proudly. I thought it over, and gazed diagonally to where my house stood a couple hundred yards away. Though of course totally impossible to complete, pretending to do so seemed to have some potential entertainment value, I admitted to myself. Plus, it was another chance to live out the Hardy Boys' underground adventures in real life. "Sounds kind of cool," I agreed.

I looked down the driveway and saw a couple of Biker Scouts pass in front of Freddy's house, make a gradual turn at the dead end, and cruise by once again slowly. They stared into the backyard at us menacingly, and I didn't like the looks of them. Freddy noticed, and scrunched his face.

"Chet Wiggins," he said with disgust. "You know Chet?" I shot back at him, slightly surprised. I looked up just in time to confirm that it was indeed the red-haired jerk. "Yes—believe it or not, we actually used to be friends," Freddy explained.

"He lived a couple streets over and his parents knew mine really well. We used to have sleepovers here. Then, out of nowhere his dad got a huge promotion over at the bank, and they moved into that super fancy part of West Ridge." He stopped digging and looked at me squarely. "Money changes everything, doesn't it Dav?"

We got back to planning our epic tunnel project as I chewed over what he'd said. Freddy was concerned that the effort would be discovered and shut down by his mother before we could complete it,

Her Schemes and Plans

and I agreed. We decided on a spot behind his garage, butting up to Wanda's backyard. The ground there was already devoid of grass, and the soil seemed loose and good for some easy digging.

We went into the garage, which was a dizzying assortment of old gaudy plastic toys and broken-down bikes, to find some useful digging implements. It took a good while for us to sift through things and uncover an ancient shovel, and a forgotten hand spade. When we emerged from the garage with these, I noticed the Biker Scouts were now parked down on the apron of Freddy's driveway. They were watching us closely, and now Ryne had joined them.

"This is trouble," I murmured to Freddy. He nodded, and tried not to make eye contact. "Let's just keep working," he suggested under his breath. "Maybe they'll get bored and leave us alone." I thought that was a good idea, so we both turned and headed down the side of the garage along the fence toward the rear.

"This spot seems as good as any," I said cheerfully, attempting to forget the presence of the observing Biker Scouts. "Let's get digging!" Freddy seemed to appreciate the upbeat take, and we both started moving earth.

As we dug, we discussed some of the challenges we'd meet along the way: possible gas lines, buried electric wires, sewage systems, large boulders, even perhaps hitting the water table. I began to think of where the exit should be on my own property and how we could possibly gauge where we were at once underground.

Just ten minutes in, we were already sweating. I took a break and peered around the corner to see if the intruders were still staked out in the driveway. They were. Ryne saw me and catcalled to me. Chet lurked in the background, along with a handful of others. *What could we possibly be doing that's so interesting to these punks?* I thought. Chet called out to Freddy, asking him to come and have a quick chat, but I stared at him and shook my head fervently.

"Don't go out there," I advised. "If you do, you're liable to get a few teeth punched in. I can speak from experience," I warned him. So we continued to work on the entrance to our tunnel without addressing them further.

"Quit that awful digging!" a voice hollered from behind us. I stood up to see Wanda on her backyard deck, arranging a few plastic storage bins. "You'll make a terrible mess," she continued. "Plus, when Nicolette sees that? Whew, boy," she whistled dramatically.

"Someone else was digging right there awhile back and I yelled at them, too. They scampered off like the rats they were," she smirked. "I think I know who it was, but that's my little secret," she added wryly.

She turned and opened up the back door to her cluttered little bungalow. "Hold on, Mandy, I'm coming! That girl needs to chill out, and I need a smoke," she grumbled to herself. My heart skipped a beat. *So Mandy is the person helping Wanda organize her basement,* I realized. I longed to catch a glimpse of her.

From inside Wanda's house, I could hear her singing huskily along with the radio. Freddy informed me it was the newest single by Smokey Robinson.

If I could feel her warm embrace,
See her smiling face,
Can't find anyone to take her place,
I've got to see her again.
I would do anything,
I would go anywhere,
There's nothing I wouldn't do.

Her Schemes and Plans

Isn't that the truth, I said to myself sappily. I wanted to see her just like the song said, but Mandy did not appear. She had been on my mind for days, and I was working hard on my scheme to get myself over to her place, but it still needed more time to ferment.

"Let's take a break," I suggested to Freddy, standing up. "We'll have to keep digging later when we aren't being watched so closely." Wanda peered out the window at us, checking to see if we had complied with her request. Freddy got my drift and we arranged our digging implements up against the moss-stained siding and headed toward the house.

As we did, the Biker Scouts silently mounted their bikes and dispersed, which I found confusing. Freddy grabbed two Solo cups filled with cold water and we sat on the dingy back stoop and continued to plan our ambitious project.

I heard my name being called faintly from the general direction of my house. I reluctantly stood up and told Freddy I was being summoned, but that I would return as soon as possible to continue our mission. I jogged home, surveying the horizon for Ryne and the gang, but the coast was now completely clear.

"Yes?" I huffed, as I entered the front screen door. Mom poked her head out the kitchen entryway, hands full of dishes. "Dad wants your help with the basement project. He has some long studs to bring in from the van."

"But first, make a quick phone call to Mr. Asperat and tell him dinner will be a bit later than I thought," she requested. "Let me see if I can find it—oh yes, here it is—easy one to remember: 382-2228. This Viennese potato salad is taking a lot longer than I'd hoped!" She continued to bang around in the kitchen noisily as I did so.

The rest of the afternoon was spent hauling in all the supplies from the hardware store, and doing odd jobs like holding open the back door, and positioning the measuring tape while Dad jotted down dimensions. Along the way I received an impromptu lesson on general construction. He clearly wanted to have gotten a good head start before Asperat joined us. It was oddly satisfying work, I had to admit, as the afternoon grew late and dinner time approached.

A sharp rapping on the aluminum frame of the front door eventually announced Mr. Asperat's arrival. Dad and I washed our faces and hands quickly in the basement utility sink next to the washer and dryer, and then I bounded up the steps, and joined Corbin and Suzanne in the living room. Mom had trained us well on how to be gracious and cordial hosts. Dad arrived upstairs with us a minute later, and shook Asperat's hand firmly with a smile.

"Thanks again for coming over. I really appreciate the help. My wife has been slaving in the kitchen all day to make some of your favorite dishes," Dad said. Mom poked her head out and said it was almost ready.

The table was set with our nicest flatware, including cups made out of actual glass instead of our daily plain plastic. I wondered where the things were actually stored during the months between their occasional use.

After a few pleasantries, we surrounded the table and Dad prayed. The dining room, such as it was, barely fit all six of us. There were only inches to spare at every elbow. Corbin sat on a stool since the dining set had only come with five chairs. We had used the same suite ever since I could remember.

Mom's German and French concoctions were a hit with Mr. Asperat, and Dad and I tolerated them. Corbin and Suzanne wrinkled their noses, and just picked at their plates, but neither of them verbally disparaged the food—they knew better than to do that.

"What have you been doing to entertain yourself lately?" Asperat asked me with a smile. He studied me intently and waited for an answer.

"Well today, Freddy and I have been digging a tunnel that will reach all the way over here to my own backyard," I shared. Asperat looked genuinely shocked to hear about it. Mom lectured me to be sure to clean up any mess we'd made, and also to confirm that the Manns were OK with such an activity. I agreed heartily, but knew there was no chance of me actually following through on that directive with the likes of someone like Nicolette.

Before long, Dad pushed his seat back with a contented sigh, signaling that the time to start work in the basement had finally arrived. Asperat thanked Mom many times over and stood up as well. Mom asked all three of the kids to stay and help clean up. I resisted, saying my services were needed downstairs more urgently.

"You can join the men in a minute. It won't take long with all of us helping!" she said cheerily. Suzanne got right to work while Corbin insolently sat in the middle of the floor, getting annoyingly underfoot in our tiny cramped kitchen. He had learned that infamous youngest-child tactic quite well: the one where you make yourself of such little use that you are eventually excused from assisting altogether.

Soon after, I was heading down to the basement to help, and as I reached the landing, I heard Asperat's voice and stopped short to listen. Ernie Harwell's dulcet tones were announcing the evening's starting lineup for the Tigers on a nearby portable radio, but our dinner guest's words were still clearly audible above the crackle.

"I have to admit, I was getting very nervous about the whole situation," he said to my dad. "The Ballangers are pretty important over there, and when I refused to fudge Grangeford's grade, his parents threatened me several times. A failing mark in my class would mean a season spent not playing sports for Crosstown. They have big plans for that kid. Those people think they can get away with murder. I was sure I'd be sent packing."

"I had no idea," Dad replied. "Hopefully the school is going to stand behind you?"

"No one would tell me directly. Thankfully, I found out another way that the board is actually going to back me up," Asperat said with an upbeat tone. I recalled seeing him rifle through Stickler's desk. *He must have seen the school board meeting notes and gotten the answer he was seeking,* I reasoned. I realized he had not been there on directions from Stickler as I had originally guessed, but on a clandestine mission of his own.

"Did you find out through Joyce?" Dad asked. "Never mind—I shouldn't have asked that. You don't have to tell me," Dad apologized.

"It's fine. Not directly. Joyce and I are indeed close friends, have been for a very long time. I put in a good word for her when Crabb was dismissed. She has walked a tough road, I can tell you. Grew up close to here in fact, but left for many years. She made specific choices in her life that led her to any success she's had. Some others in her circle weren't so lucky," Asperat said with a tinge of regret.

With a pause in the discussion, I continued down the stairs to the work area, now ablaze with several floor stand lights which Asperat had brought with him. He rose to greet me.

"I brought a little surprise for you and your siblings!" he smiled. "I just remembered. I will get it for you when we're done. It's something I've had for a while and don't use anymore."

"What is it?" I asked excitedly. "You'll find out soon enough," he laughed in response. I nodded and we got to work. After a couple of hours, the studs were successfully in place, and the sheets of drywall were cut and nailed up. For the first time, you could see the actual footprint of my new space, complete with a closet and an opening left for a small upper window to the outside world. I stood in the center of the partially-completed project and found the sight exhilarating.

"Dav, we're wrapping up for tonight. Thanks for your help, son," Dad said warmly. "And thank you so very much, Asperat. Got time for a coffee and dessert?" Asperat agreed happily, and we all headed back upstairs.

"You can make it up to me by helping me move next month. I finally bought a house in West Ridge and will be leaving the old Rouge Park apartment for good. Can't start a family in that cramped space!" he beamed. My parents congratulated him on the news of the purchase and pressed him to reveal who the mysterious lucky lady might be. They continued to discuss the development as I told them I was heading back to Freddy's for a bit and wouldn't be gone long.

The sun had set, and Freddy's house was pitch dark. I looked to the right and saw the triplets zoom into their overgrown backyard and drop their bikes in a heap. They looked in my direction, but continued on and scampered inside their own house, its lights ablaze.

As I approached Freddy's, I could see him in the dim light sitting on the porch alone, eating a Hot Pocket. "What flavor?" I asked him. "Pizza," he replied proudly. Though they'd been around a few years, I'd never actually eaten one myself.

I didn't mention my own elaborate dinner, and thankfully he didn't ask, because it would have seemed awkward to even try to explain what it had consisted of. He informed me there'd been no sightings of either Biker Scouts or Wanda the rest of the evening, so we decided it was safe to get back to work on the tunnel.

As I followed him into the backyard, dodging random objects in the driveway, I stared at him from behind with a feeling of disgust and pity. As the thoughts took shape, I immediately regretted them. Who was I to think more highly of myself because I had just been served a delicious, lovingly-prepared meal? I would wager I was the only kid on the block so fortunate, but that didn't make me any better than any of them.

What difference was there really between Freddy—with his tan, but scrawny limbs nurtured mainly by junk food—and Chet Wiggins, for example, brashly flashing his wealth from inside his wallet while constantly showcasing his gleaming white teeth? Choices, and fate perhaps; but not Freddy's or Chet's. Maybe those of their parents. *Why do some kids feel entitled to flaunt the spoils of their parents' good fortune,* I wondered?

Looking around, and seeing and hearing no one, we got back to work on the hole, which was now a couple of feet deep. The Hardys would have been proud, I thought. The soil was soft and we made quick progress as the sky grew completely dark. The moon made random appearances every so often, whenever the fast-moving clouds revealed it—huge and pale and yellow. The only noise was the buzzing of street lights and the thudding of moving earth. I began to think ahead and attempted to do the math on the distance underground all the way over to my own house.

"Freddy, walk over to my place and count your strides," I commanded. "Each one should be around three feet. We need to know exactly just how far this tunnel has to go," I explained. He set down his tool and obliged.

My shovel hit something soft as he scampered off, and I carefully began to remove the dirt from around it, preparing to dislodge the impediment. I thought it must be a deflated ball, or something wrapped in matted cloth. A couple of more shovelfuls showed that it was attached to something bigger, that extended deeper into the ground. Frustrated, I sent the shovel farther down on all sides of the object, determined to wrench it out. I knelt to investigate what I was dealing with.

With my bare hands, I cleaned off the top of it, revealing stringy stands of something dark yellow. Intrigued, I brushed the dirt off the sides, my fingers slowly exposing protrusions and recesses that seemed vaguely familiar. With growing horror, I began to realize that what I was cleaning off was not a soccer ball, but a human head—its mouth agape and open eyes nearly choked with dirt.

A jagged cut, just beneath the chin, had splayed the throat wide open, and dried blood was caked all around what must have been a mortal wound. I recoiled in complete terror, just as the moon came out again in full intensity.

I stared down into what appeared to be the decomposing face of Justus Mann.

12

a messy situation

I heard Freddy's bare feet running back toward where I was kneeling. After remaining frozen for a brief moment, I shook off the initial shock of the grisly discovery, and shoveled several quick handfuls of dirt back on top of the protruding head. *There's no way I can let Freddy find out the fate of his father like this—not here, not now,* I thought. The faint but unmistakable smell of death and decay reached my nostrils for an instant before mercifully receding.

I wavered on my feet for a moment, feeling faint. I tried to focus on a dirt stain on the garage siding, to steady myself, and ensure that this was indeed really happening, and that I was not trapped inside a terrible dream or another one of my bizarre visions. I struggled, but managed to maintain a clear head and command of my thoughts. *The next few minutes will be very important,* I told myself. I had opened my mouth to redirect Freddy away from the hole, but he beat me to the punch.

"Mom's about to pull in the drive!" he warned me. "You should leave. She said didn't want anyone over here tonight. Go over the fence and through Wanda's yard. Hurry! I've got to get inside. We can dig more tomorrow!" he urged, and then disappeared through the back door. The headlights of Nicolette's aging sedan bathed the driveway and garage in light, casting long and strange shadows that nearly reached me as I crouched just out of view.

I silently tossed several more frantic shovelfuls of dirt into the hole, but when I heard an angry woman's voice shouting epithets and heading my way, I placed the shovel carefully on the ground and scaled Wanda's fence. It made a metallic twang that was slightly louder than I had hoped, so I rolled to the ground and came to rest next to a row of bramble bushes.

I glanced into the back of Wanda's house and it was dark except for one small light somewhere deep within. I stayed exactly where I'd come to rest, completely still. I wasn't sure if I was more immobilized by the general dread I held for Nicolette, or by the shock of what I'd just discovered in her yard.

The shadowy figure of a woman came into view. She paced around the hole, and looked several times in all directions, cursing all the while. I couldn't see her face, but her speech was slurred and she seemed unsteady.

"Oh, that is the final straw," she raged. "He's messed with the wrong person this time. There's gonna be hell to pay. No one does this to Nicolette Mann and lives to tell about it. People think they can do whatever they want to me, and not suffer consequences. Well, I've done it once, and I'll do it again if I have to." She continued to rant in a delirious tone as she returned to the house and slammed the back door shut behind her.

When it finally felt safe to move, I sprinted like a doe through Wanda's side gate out onto the adjacent darkened street. I skirted around the corner house and back onto my own block, avoiding the eerie yellow circles cast by the street lights. Queen howled out like a crazed prison inmate as I passed the triplets' place.

I burst into my own house, and ran straight into the brightly-lit living room, and found Mom and Dad sitting on the couch and big recliner sipping hot drinks pleasantly. Asperat entered the room once more from the darkened hallway soon after, and excused himself for what had been an apparently brief absence. All three of them then looked at me simultaneously and smiled. Mom realized something was wrong with me in an instant.

"Dav!" she exclaimed. "You look as white as a sheet. Is everything OK?" Asperat and Dad looked at me curiously as well. I considered spilling the entire story right then and there, but when I opened my mouth, nothing came out. I didn't know how to start.

I paused, and tried to imagine their reactions at being told I'd found a body in our neighbor's backyard while digging a tunnel behind a garage. It would be seen as the capstone in the series of my fantastic—and often imaginary—tales, I knew for a fact. I could picture the polite, nervous laughter from Asperat as he tried to figure out if I was actually serious or not. That would be followed immediately by irate and disappointed looks from my parents.

No—there is no way I can tell them now. Later tonight, I told myself. *But, someone has to be told!* a voice inside my head screamed. *Someone has to do something! But, what could actually be done,* I asked myself?

Nothing for poor Justus, I reasoned. His sightless eyes stared up at me from the grimy pit again in my mind. I argued with myself for what seemed like minutes, but in reality was likely only a matter of seconds.

It was, however, starting to become an awkward pause as the adults calmly awaited my answer. I opened my mouth again, determined to reveal all the gory details, but instead I found myself saying, "It's nothing. I'm fine. Just tired out from running around."

"Well, go grab yourself an ice water, young man!" Mom instructed as she looked nervously from Dad to Asperat. "Don't want anyone getting dehydrated around here." Dad jumped right back into recounting the time when one of his star players, Henry Hallas, had done just that one hot afternoon a decade earlier, right before an important double-header, and they all started to laugh again together.

Robotically, I grabbed a cup from the kitchen cabinet and filled it to the top with water from the tap. As I pulled it close to my face, I noticed my hand was shaking almost imperceptibly. I slammed the cup down and marched downstairs to my room.

I sat in the dark on my bed staring forward into the blackness, a thousand thoughts running through my head. *Who had killed Justus? And why?* I remembered Wanda mentioning someone digging in that exact spot previously. Had she witnessed the crude burial and the perpetrator without even realizing it?

I considered the raging temper of Nicolette. She was definitely capable of doing something this heinous under the right circumstances. And, what about the phone call between Joyce Stickler and Nicolette? Had that been a veiled accusation of some sort? What connection did Stickler have to Justus, anyway? My unanswered questions were beginning to pile up.

Suddenly, a sharp knock on my bedroom door brought me back to reality. It opened before I could even answer, and I was surprised to see Asperat lean in and smile at me. "You forgot something," he teased. *There is no way on earth he could know what I saw, could he?* I wondered frantically. I sifted through my brain for clues to what he could be referring to.

"The surprise, remember?" he reminded me. "Are you sure you're OK? You look like you've seen a ghost." He waited to see if I'd reveal anything else to him, but I sat there in stunned silence.

"It's fine—come on upstairs and check it out. Corbin and Suzanne are already playing." He turned and led the way. I followed him obediently, walking almost on auto-pilot. "It's a bit old, but it's still a fun system," he continued. "I have no more use for it in my apartment, so you and your family can have it for as long as you like," he explained in a friendly tone, as we mounted the stairs and entered the living room once more.

My siblings and Dad were gathered around the small black and white television, playing a video game. I looked down at the floor and observed wires protruding from an Atari 2600. At that point in time, Atari systems like these were already around a decade old, but considering we'd never had a gaming console of any kind in the house, it was a major upgrade.

Corbin turned to me excitedly. "Space Invaders, Breakout, Pong and some other alien attack game!" he nearly squealed. Suzanne tugged at the controller, attempting to wrestle it from Corbin's iron grip. "It's my turn, Corbin! I want to play Breakout next. That one looks really cool," she demanded.

"I pushed the button!" Corbin yelled as his spaceship crashed in a cascade of blocky pixels. I smiled woodenly at Mr. Asperat, and thanked him for the thoughtful gift. All eyes returned to the flickering screen, and soon I silently slipped back out of the room. Asperat inserted the Breakout cartridge as Suzanne had requested, and then explained the details of how the game was played as I descended the stairs.

"This one's my favorite. Always has been," I heard him say with child-like glee. "See the layer of bricks across the top third of the screen? The ultimate goal is to get rid of every single one. The ball moves around the screen, bouncing off the top and the two sides. When you hit a brick, the ball bounces back and the brick is destroyed. Don't let the ball get past you at the bottom! There's eight layers of bricks, and after a few hits, the ball starts to go faster and faster. Let's give it a go."

Playing video games was the last thing on my mind at the moment. Yells, congratulatory exclamations, groans, and other outbursts continued to filter down the stairs toward me for a long time, but I paid them little attention. My brain was consumed with what to do next as I gradually drifted off to an unsettled sleep.

Soon after, I opened my eyes and found myself at school once more, as Mrs. Townsend silently paced the front of our old classroom, during what was apparently an important test. I looked at the endless lines of writing on the paper, and was frantic to find it was in a language I couldn't even read. I looked over at Violet, who was finishing her test with ease. She ventured a smile at me, and then a look of confusion and worry crossed her face. She motioned for me to look down.

When I did, I realized with horror that I was completely naked. The bright white skin of my body shone like a blinding light, and I couldn't fathom how I'd gotten there in that state without noticing. Beads of sweat started to drop onto the desk, making unusually loud splashing sounds.

Out in the hallway, something caught my attention. Biker Scouts were streaming by the open door, their hollering and epithets echoing down the hallway as they raced by, one after another. Suddenly, Mandy stood at the doorway. She gazed at me but I averted my eyes and pretended to work harder on the test.

When I glanced up again, Ryne was behind her now, smiling

menacingly, and stroking her shoulder. Mandy pretended to make a phone with her hand, held it up to her ear and mouthed, "Why didn't you call me?" I could think of nothing else to mouth back except, "Sorry." *How utterly pathetic was that response?* I chided myself. I foolishly hoped that somehow she had not noticed that I was wearing nothing.

When I looked up again, the dirty corpse of Justus Mann was standing behind them both, his arms sagging lifelessly at his sides. Enrique, Dustin Crabb and Nicolette joined him, laughing maniacally about a shared joke. Nicolette produced a gun and casually unloaded a slug into Justus' temple, and he dropped to the tile floor in the hallway outside the classroom like a sack of potatoes.

Sometimes you're better off dead
There's a gun in your hand
And it's pointing at your head

As Freddy's eerie singing voice faded, I saw Joyce Stickler run up and kneel down next to him, screaming. I feverishly looked back down at the test again, not wanting to witness any more of it. The drops of my sweat had somehow turned to blood, and they splattered in bright red droplets onto my paper, obscuring the already unintelligible words. Soon the single drops turned into trickles—and then to my horror—they became solid streams of pouring liquid. I was bleeding to death, right in front of everyone, in the middle of my classroom.

Pounding footsteps made me bolt upright in my bed. It took a moment, but like often happens, what seemed completely real one second had evaporated into an obvious farce the next. *Of course it was just a dream,* I scolded myself. *But what is happening to me?*

Tears seemed to be at the ready. Giant sweat beads had formed on my forehead during the vivid nightmare, and I found the morning air was so humid that even the basement felt stifling. I heard my mother run past my bedroom door and stop in front of the washer and dryer.

"Argh! Not again! This thing—" she yelled above the sound of rushing water. "The hose came off again. Dav! Can you come help me please? Everything is getting soaked!" I got up and groggily walked out into the open area of the basement, rubbing my eyes.

The bare concrete floor in this area felt cooler, and rivulets of water from the washing machine were already snaking their way toward the round drain grate several yards away. Together we were able to get the gushing hose mounted back where it belonged within a minute or two. Mom sat down in a metal folding chair next to the dryer, huffing and frustrated.

She thanked me for my help in between caustic complaints directed at the faulty laundry appliance. In the brief moment of silence that followed, I considered confiding in Mom regarding my grisly discovery. I looked at her irritated expression as she caught her breath, clearly deep in thought about all the other tasks the upcoming day held for her. She was a hard worker, and poured everything she had into our family, and I admired her for it. I was just about to begin telling her when she stood up abruptly.

"No rest for the weary, Dav," she smiled weakly. "I was just coming down to get you up. Today is the first day of the swimming program over at the community center. Get something to eat, grab your suit and let's hit the road."

"What about Corbin and Suzanne? Are they coming too?" I thought perhaps a solitary car ride might work perfectly to reveal the previous night's events.

"They're both enrolled this year as well," she replied. "And they've been up for an hour already. Come on, let's go!" She used that familiar tone that all parents eventually have to employ to get their teenagers moving. I followed her as she jogged up the stairs. "We have to stop at Lynch's later to get a costume for Suzanne for a birthday party. She's dressing up as a mime!" The name of the store caught my attention.

"Where's Dad?" I asked, ignoring that line of thought for the moment. I felt an insatiable need to share my burden with someone.

"Off to the hardware store again for some more of those special screws. Not long till your new room is all set! Are you excited?" she asked expectantly. It was hard to be excited about anything right at the moment. The story I needed to tell was weighing heavier on my psyche seemingly by the minute.

Mom was helping Corbin as he got ready, and hollered for Suzanne to grab a few beach towels from the hall closet. There was an unexpected angry knock at the front door just then. Mom jumped up, startled. We both looked up at the same time to see the flushed and livid face of Nicolette Mann.

Her eyes were bloodshot and they had a slightly wild look to them. She was clearly about to burst with outrage. I realized with alarm that this was not going to be a friendly visit. *Could she possibly already know that I had discovered her secret?*

"This is not really a good time, I'm afraid," said Mom with a slight air of annoyance as she struggled to jam one of Corbin's feet into a rubber swim shoe. "Is this important or can it wait till later today?" she asked Nicolette without looking through the screen window.

"You. You did this!" Nicolette barked out in my general direction. I froze, waiting on pins and needles to hear what she was about to say. *Maybe she is going to try to frame me for Justus' death,* I thought frantically. That novel thought struck me with a new and deeper strain of terror.

Mom finished with Corbin's feet and stood up wearily. It was clear Nicolette was not going to wait for a better time. Mom walked to the screen and faced the seething woman directly for the first time. She opened her mouth to begin but Nicolette cut her off. I braced myself to hear what wild accusations she might come up with, and prayed my parents would side with me on this one.

"Your son has completely dug up the area behind my garage!" she seethed. "He tossed the dirt against the siding which now has to be washed. It's an absolute mess back there." She stopped to take in one quivering breath, and then continued.

"I've told Freddy to stay away from your troublemaker of a son, but up until now he hasn't listened. Well, this was the breaking point! I pride myself on keeping that backyard looking nice, whenever possible," she continued to rage, and I knew both Mom and I were rolling our eyes internally at that last statement. The Mann property existed in a perpetual state of disarray.

I kept waiting throughout her diatribe for the other shoe to drop, but amazingly, it never did. If she knew about the body buried back there, she was a pretty good actress. She seemed consumed with the filth created by our tunnel project, and not so much that I had been back there in the first place. After a while, the actual details of what she was ranting about faded into a rambling, irritated continuum of white noise.

I was pretty sure she made it clear that I was never to set foot on their property again. On the other hand, I considered as I stood there, maybe this was all just a ploy to redirect us from the real issue. Maybe she was indeed fully aware of the presence of Justus' corpse, and this was simply the most reasonable way to guarantee there would be no more prying eyes or digging hands, I reasoned.

Finally, her protestations came to a stop, and Nicolette stood there silently, panting. She wore an oversized and stained Led Zeppelin tee that had probably originally been bright red and was now a sad pink after countless washings. Her greasy hair was tied up in a haphazard fashion and mounted on the top of her head. A couple faint streaks of gray started at her temples and gradually faded into the pile. Her reddened eyes darted back and forth between the two of us. I wondered what possible chain of events had caused Nicolette Mann to arrive in that state, at that hour, chewing out a kid and his bewildered mother for digging in her backyard, which now doubled as an impromptu burial ground.

"Well?" she demanded, clearly expecting a response. I stood silently, not even knowing how to begin.

"I'm very sorry to hear about this," Mom said sympathetically. "I can promise you that Dav will never go digging in your backyard again," she said solemnly, glancing back at me at that point to elicit my complete cooperation. I nodded. "In fact, when we get back home later this morning, he can come over and help—"

"Absolutely not. Out of the question. I don't want to see your son on my property ever again!" she shouted, turning on her heel and storming down the walk. Across the street, Jason and Johnny stopped playing catch long enough to stare at us for a few seconds before resuming play.

No issues with that on my end, I said to myself silently. The woman was clearly deranged, and I imagined what she was capable of doing to me if I were to ever reveal the truth. *Not just to me,* I gulped. *My entire family as well.* I would have to think long and hard about all the implications of revealing her secret.

We both watched her stomp all the way back to her own front yard, where she kicked at a stray plastic riding toy of some sort, and cursed vehemently before disappearing. Mom looked back at me with raised eyebrows, and she said nothing else about the matter for the moment. She herded all three kids into the station wagon and sped off to try to make it on time to swimming lessons, in spite of the unexpected confrontation.

The black imitation leather seats were hot enough to melt crayons, which had happened many times before, and Corbin cried out as his thigh accidentally touched a blistering-hot seat belt receptacle. I spent the entire subsequent ride to the community center with my front seat window rolled all the way down, letting the hot wind blast my face.

I closed my eyes as we sped south, and tried to get the disgusting details of what I'd seen out of my head. The sickeningly-yellow strands of hair, the dirt-caked eye sockets, the swollen lips. I tried to focus on an image of the smiling, pretty face of Mandy Willows instead, but whenever I did, the bizarre sequence from my dream would replay itself again, ending with Justus lying dead in a pool of blood on the school hallway floor.

Lessons in Lifesaving

    The first thing anyone noticed when walking into the Rouge Park Community Center during summer swim season was the invisible wall of chlorine, walking into which brought tears to the eyes and singed the nose hairs. I always felt that I could almost see a green mist hanging in the air, it was so heavy.

    Once I had grown accustomed to its presence once again, I reluctantly headed toward what was currently one of my least favorite places on earth: the men's locker room. Suzanne and Mom went through the ladies' entrance, and Corbin and his Spiderman onesie of a swimsuit disappeared into the men's side ahead of me.

    Few 13-year-olds look forward to changing into a swimsuit in a public place, and the format of this locker room left nowhere for anyone to hide. Two long wooden benches reached from one end of the room to the other, in between banks of lockers. A twin version of this was just on the other side of a cinder block wall that ran the length of the chamber, with several feet of open space above and below for a bare minimum of privacy from the opposite sex.

I was ecstatic to find the locker room completely empty that day. In the hectic moments before leaving, as I was being excoriated by Nicolette Mann, I'd forgotten to perform one of my more ingenious tricks: wearing my swimming suit underneath my play shorts to avoid any moments of complete nudity. There in the solitude, I was free to change without fear of prying eyes from other teenage boys eager to point out my lack of body hair or other developments. The only sounds were coming from the shower area, as drips of water echoed in the damp recesses nearest the entrance to the outdoor pool.

As I pulled off my terry cloth shorts and reached for my swim trunks from a duffel bag, I heard a girl's voice over the wall in the adjoining locker room, and a male voice join it just afterwards.

"Ryne! You perv. Get out of the girl's side!" I immediately recognized the bubbly voice as belonging to Roxy.

"Ha! Thought I might find you in here. Perfect chance for me to check out the future stars of Club Xanadu," Ryne said crudely. Roxy made a sound of feigned outrage, but it was clear she took the comment as some sort of compliment.

"That's so wrong!" she squealed. "Someone is going to see you in here. Get out so I can change—I have to lifeguard a lesson and I'm late for it already!"

"No one's listening. Calm down. And don't bother waiting to change on account of little old me. Seriously though, I can put in a good word for you with Enrique. He's always on the lookout for the next generation of talent," he said with a lusty edge.

"I can't believe you! But—seriously? Do you really know Enrique

Her Schemes and Plans

that well?" she asked somewhat admiringly.

"Enrique runs this town. But I have so much dirt on him that I can get away with anything. Before long, that place will be mine. And if you think I've got money now," he paused and I heard some rustling sounds. "This is nothing. I've almost got enough saved for a Mustang of my own, and when I get one, the Biker Scouts will be yesterday's news," he bragged.

"And what does Mandy think of all these big plans of yours?" Roxy asked, with a tinge of resentment.

"Mandy? Ha! She talks a big game, but she'll do whatever Enrique tells her to do at the end of the day. No one crosses him without paying a price. Her whole future is already all planned out and she doesn't even realize it yet. And I'm pretty sure it includes a prominent spot over at Xanadu," he said snidely.

"She'll never go for that. She's not the type," Roxy stated, implying that she, on the other hand, might be. "You'd be surprised," Ryne responded slyly. "She knows where her bread is buttered."

Now that my suit was on, I was pulling off my tube socks one at a time, and taking as long as possible to get ready in order to catch as much of this putrid conversation as I could stand. Ryne continued to brag about his influence and conquests since he had a willing and listening ear, and Roxy continued to do her part by giggling repeatedly and flattering him.

My blood boiled at the idea of Mandy wasting her life away in such a place as Club Xanadu against her will. She was so much better than that. She had the potential to do anything she wanted, I thought. *Why am I so confident of that, though?* I asked myself. Was it simply because I'd seen her creativity on display with the wooden license plates signs? Or was it something else more intangible—a look in her fiery eyes, the way she held her head high among the immoral rabble she found around her?

"Alright, I'm out of here. Really big things going on tonight at the club, and I've got to go strike the fear of God into those uppity Yugo party store owners, too. Have to keep the proletariat in line," said Ryne, obviously using a word he'd heard used by the real brains of the operation. *He seems blissfully unaware that he is just a replaceable cog like the rest of them,* I thought.

"You're going to strike what in who? Are you really that tough deep down, Mr. Ryne Daulton?" she asked in a syrupy voice. Her voice lowered and it sounded like she drew closer to him.

"No one messes with Enrique—or me for that matter," he retorted, ignoring her advances. "If you don't believe me, ask those filthy Manns sometime," he replied in defiant tone. I caught my breath at the sound of that not-so-veiled threat, and wondered what he could mean by it. She whispered something that I couldn't hear and he laughed evilly in response.

"So glad I was able to sneak in a little visit, Roxy. See you around town," he said as he walked out, to which she responded with a cloying laugh and farewell.

Swimming lessons went about as expected. Corbin danced around the edge, and right when the instructor thought he might actually get into the water, he'd run away to the high fence surrounding the pool and beseech my mom to let him out. Mom didn't budge, and simply continued to work on her current crochet project, comfortably perched in the shade on a set of metal bleachers overlooking the pool. Suzanne was in Intermediate class, and she performed very well, as she always did at whatever she put her mind to.

I was in Lifesaving Class, the most advanced class the Center offered, and I was a bit wistful that this course would mark the end of many enjoyable years of training for me there. After an hour of alternating between dragging heavy dummies in distress out of the deep end, and then treading water for long lengths of time to build up our stamina, we were done for the day. I saw Roxy perched high above the water on a stand as I walked out, but she looked the other way.

I was quiet the entire ride home, wrapped in my towel to avoid soaking the car seat. Mom spent most of the trip reassuring Corbin that the pool was relatively safe, especially when there were lifeguards close by. In between making logical points and having them summarily dismissed, she noticed my silence and asked if there was anything wrong. I denied that there was. I had determined during a long spell of treading water that I had to tell my parents the entire thing somehow later that afternoon. I just hadn't figured out how to begin yet.

Zane wasn't available to cut lawns that afternoon, so I wolfed down a quick lunch, and headed out into the neighborhood on my bike. I'd grabbed a few dollars before departing and had determined to treat myself to some more baseball cards, and then maybe some mindless junky snacks at D and D Market.

The open air and freedom I felt as I pedaled away from the house was refreshing, and made my terrible discovery of the previous evening seem like a quickly-fading memory. At every street corner, I stopped briefly to check if there were any Biker Scouts on the horizon, but the broiling streets were surprisingly empty and quiet, save for the hum of air conditioning units in the homes of the families privileged enough to have them. We did not, and my house absolutely roasted on afternoons like this, until the house fan in the stairwell of our bungalow was able to catch up around an hour after the sun set.

I entered Pack Rat Pete's and walked straight to the counter. I noticed that none of Mandy's signs were there. The vertical series of nails protruding from the wood paneling were now empty. *Have they all sold?* I wondered. *Or has she decided to stop selling them?* A few other younger boys I didn't recognize were just finishing up with their purchases, and once they left, I was the only patron left. Pete looked at me with a thin smile.

"Back for more Topps, eh? You've got quite the addiction. I'd thought you'd have the complete set by now," he winked. "How many of them do you have?" I told him, and he nodded, impressed. "Keep them mint, they might be worth something someday," he smiled, and fiddled with his mustache. He looked stressed and tired.

I glanced down and saw that there were only two packs left in the display box. Disappointed, I started to ask him if he had more, but he read my mind. "I think I just got another case this morning—I'll go have a look," he volunteered and went through the open door frame into the back.

I gazed at the wall behind the counter, observing some of the knick-knacks Pete valued enough to put on display. There was a shelf full of bowling trophies, including two from events hosted at Lightning Lanes, the sprawling complex located right next to Crosstown Church and School. A signed Kirk Gibson jersey was folded and showcased handsomely behind glass in a wooden shadow box. On a hanger hung Pete's own Rouge Park High varsity jacket, with a puffy embroidered baseball logo. "Class of 1965" was displayed on the side of the black jacket in smaller orange type.

I did some quick math, remembering that Asperat said Joyce Stickler had attended Rouge Park High School as well. If she graduated from Eastern Michigan in 1969 as her diploma had said, I wondered if she and Pete had been high school classmates back in '65. He walked back up to the counter with a new unopened box. I ignored the cards for the moment and asked him bluntly about it. He stopped and looked at me curiously.

"Joyce Stickler? Doesn't sound familiar. But, we had huge classes back then. I didn't know everyone by name. Rouge Park was a really booming place back in those days, and all of us Baby Boomers came through school all at once, or so it seemed. Hard to believe it's already been more than 20 years," his voice trailed off and he looked into the distance. I wondered if owning his own sports collectibles joint had been the master plan all along, or if life's winding road had led him there despite other intentions.

"Only one way to know for sure. I think I can dig up my yearbook in the back. Let's take a look!" His eyes gleamed, apparently stimulated by the unexpected break in the monotony. He invited me to the back room and I watched him sift through a pile of boxes and trunks.

He cleared off the largest one at the bottom of the pile, asking me to transfer a few items to other shelves. He blew the dust off and opened the creaky charcoal gray trunk. He spied the yearbook seconds later. It was entitled "Kaleidoscope"—the cover of which was embossed with a funky font, the whole thing made to resemble a medieval, bound volume.

"OK... senior class... 1965," he said, flipping pages rapidly. "Hmm. No Joyce under the Ss." He looked at me. "But, she might have had a different last name in 1965, right?" *Of course*, I nodded, annoyed that I hadn't thought of that obvious fact myself. I had never met or even heard about her husband, but it seemed very possible that she had been married at some point. He started at the beginning of the Seniors section, and with his finger, scanned down the pages, examining each name in succession.

Halfway through, his finger stopped abruptly. It came to rest next to a photo of a blonde-haired, slim girl with a bouffant haircut. It stood out next to the other girls in the class, who seemed to have already begun converting to the new trend of long, straight, ironed-hair in the mid-60s. She didn't smile, and had a forlorn, but determined look on her face. I glanced at the text next to her picture, and was stunned to read it, but it all came together quickly and made complete sense in an instant. The name of the girl looking back at us from the yearbook page was Joyce Mann.

A short while later I entered D and D Market with a jingle. As the door closed behind me, I turned to examine the glass pane that had apparently been knocked out. Shards lay sparkling all over the floor around the entrance. The store was empty, but there was a commotion of some sort happening in the back, out of my view.

Dagmar and her husband Dmitri were arguing in loud and frantic tones. As I walked to the refrigerated section, I realized they were speaking Croatian, with some English profanity and exclamations thrown in for good measure. I selected a cold Dr. Pepper, and made my way to the register. They continued arguing for some time, until I cleared my throat. The banter stopped abruptly, and a flustered Dmitri appeared almost instantly.

"Oh, hello my friend. I apologize for the wait, my friend. Just this? Do you need a bag today?" He seemed in a rush to get the transaction complete so he could return to the fray. Just below his red headband, a ring of gleaming sweat had formed. He was wearing a white tracksuit. He could have stood to lose a few pounds, and that was more evident now even more than usual, as his chest with a red Adidas logo emblazoned on it heaved as he tried in vain to catch his breath.

In addition to running this store, he was also known as the neighborhood handyman, and could fix almost anything. Dagmar remained hidden from view, continuing to issue the occasional epithet just loudly enough to reach my ears. She was roughly stacking boxes of some kind, and it sounded like she eventually kicked them over on purpose in exasperation.

"I don't need a bag, Dmitri. Thanks. But—is everything OK?"

I asked, surprisingly myself. I remembered what Ryne had said in the locker room, and assumed that he had something to do with this situation. I was growing increasingly tired of Ryne—and all the Biker Scouts for that matter—getting away with whatever he wanted.

I felt completely powerless to stop him, so I thought perhaps commiserating with someone else might be therapeutic. I stood silently waiting to see if he would answer me. Dmitri seemed to consider it, assessing me quietly. His breathing slowed, but eventually he shrugged and simply smiled opaquely.

"He won't say a thing to you!" hollered Dagmar's indignant voice from the back of the store. "Will you, Dmitri?" She finally appeared, her eyes flashing as she hauled a few stacks of two-liters in her arms. "And do you know why? I will tell you, my friend. He is a coward."

This unleashed a torrent of Croatian again from my irritated neighbor, interlaced with sporadic English. "How dare you, woman! I came all the way to this country to escape this type of thing. And now, we are in a worse place than we were back in Split. Can you believe it—kickbacks to these young punks!"

Most of the rest of what he spat out was unintelligible to me. She matched his fervor with every response and I began to feel helplessly stuck in the middle.

"What young punks? Ryne? The Biker Scouts?" I finally asked loudly. Dagmar and Dmitri stopped arguing and looked at me. "How do you know that, my friend?" Dagmar asked. "You have your own trouble with those ruffians too, I wonder?"

"Be quiet, woman!" Dmitri scolded. He turned back at me. "Look, my boy," he pleaded, "We are having enough trouble from these scoundrels already. The last thing we need is to poke the bear, so to speak. We're not the only shop in Rouge Park that is facing these threats. We will all have to deal with it in our own way. And—not through the police," he emphasized in a friendly but firm tone. "My advice? Stay as far away from these people as possible. Do not get entangled with them if it can be at all avoided."

"And why would he take your advice? It's working out so well for you and I!" Dagmar shouted from the back of the store to which she had returned for another load of pop.

"Someone needs to do something," I said emphatically, realizing that getting Ryne and the Biker Scouts off the scene would benefit my own interests tremendously as well. I didn't want to watch them drag Mandy down any further, and I was concerned at whatever they were forcing the triplets to do. Dmitri recoiled and shook his head, then motioned for me to follow him to the front glass doors.

"Look, do not take offense, but you're still just a kid. See all those shops, Embers Bar, restaurants, salons?" he asked in a softer voice, sweeping his hand from the left to the right, all the way to the steamy horizon. "Every single one of these places is allowed to run at the pleasure of one solitary man. He has everyone in his pocket, and spies everywhere. And he rules from that den of iniquity called Xanadu." He spit out the last words as if they were poison, now pointing left to the extreme north end of Rouge Park, mere yards from the Detroit city limits.

"Enrique?" I replied, already knowing the answer.

"You got it. Things changed when he moved in a couple years back. And they won't ever be the same until he's gone," he said in a distant voice as he carefully ran his fingers along the jagged edges of glass.

Soon after, I walked slowly home, passing by the nondescript brick edifice of Embers Bar, home of the World's Best Corned Beef. I had never doubted the title, judging by the amazing smells that it emitted. I'd never actually been inside, but had peered in several times when the door had been open. In the past when I'd done so, the unfortunate smell of stale beer had occasionally mingled with the fantastic corned beef and turned my stomach.

The thick steel door was open again as I passed by, and the disheveled figure of Dustin Crabb emerged, shielding his eyes and staggering along the sidewalk behind me. Tires screeched as a car came to a stop perilously close to Crabb. Through the lowered passenger window, I heard a woman's voice eviscerating Dustin, but I could not hear her exact words. Dustin ranted and raved right back at her.

"I told you! I have no idea where he is. Why won't you leave me alone, woman? Ask that crazed sister-in-law of yours again if you really want to get somewhere! He was last seen at his own house. Now get out of here before I put you in a cast again!" he screamed, slurring some of the words.

The light blue sedan squealed its tires and continued down the street as abruptly as it had arrived. I could only guess that the irate driver was Joyce Stickler. I wanted to sprint after her, flag down the car and put an end to her misery with the truth about her brother. But she was already far away in the distance, and I saw her turn left wildly at an intersection heading back toward West Ridge.

I watched Dustin long enough to see him glare at me, a mix of anger and embarrassment on his face. He then continued on his way with a hurried but unbalanced gait in the direction of Xanadu. I turned away from him and continued on toward home with a more determined stride.

I didn't know how yet, but I vowed that I was going to be part of the solution to this dysfunctional neighborhood. And I was going to start by shining the light on poor Justus' fate. I arrived at the porch in time to hear Mom ask me to grab the mail from the mailbox, which had just been delivered, on my way into the house. I did so, and glanced down at the smattering of bills and junk mail.

An envelope with my name on it caught my attention. It was scrawled quickly on the front, and had no stamp or return address included. I was slightly disappointed to see no other mail addressed to me. I had quietly sent out requests to a few relatives in other states around the country asking for them to send me their old expired license plates, but none had arrived as of yet.

I dropped the rest of the mail on the arm of the couch and went straight to the basement, greeting my mom through the kitchen entryway as I passed. Dad was hard at work putting the finishing touches on my new room. He had hung the new door, and installed a wooden pole in the closet to hang clothes from, along with a small shelf just above that. It was really beginning to come together.

"Dad?" I asked him as I walked into the room, stepping carefully over some stray tools and trying to stay out the drywall dust that had been swept into a pile. "Can I talk to you for a second about something?"

"Sure, son. Give me just a minute," he said, with two screws clenched between his teeth. He was attempting to install the new door handle while down on his hands and knees. In a minute or two he was successful, and set down the screwdriver and turned to give me his full attention.

"Looking pretty awesome in here, eh? You'll be sleeping in here soon! Now what is it you wanted to discuss?" he asked with a smile.

"Nothing, Dad. Sorry—it wasn't important," I said blandly without looking up at him. I was staring at the contents of the envelope addressed to me. On a single piece of paper, words had been written hastily in black marker—the key words in all capital letters—reading:

"*I KNOW that you know. Don't even THINK about telling a soul, or that cute little kid brother of yours may find himself with his THROAT SLIT.*"

14

a surprise inside

The rest of the week passed by in a blur, uneventfully. At times it felt like I was sleepwalking through the hot summer days, moving numbly from the kitchen to the car, through the locker room, into the pool, back into the car, and then down to my own room again. I spent hours on my bed staring up at the ceiling in the dark.

I didn't have the slightest idea what to do about my nagging secret, or how to move on from it. The horrible thought of my innocent brother being hurt by someone was enough to immobilize even the bravest person. Whenever I began to seriously think about finally sharing the story with my mom or dad, the image of Corbin laying on the floor in a pool of blood was simply too big of a hurdle to overcome.

I thought about the threatening note often, which I'd hidden in the dropped ceiling panel directly above my bed. *Whose writing was it? Had I ever seen it before?* I wondered if it was Nicolette's. I had a pretty good idea of how to find out for sure, but I didn't dare enter the Mann house again after her visit the morning after my discovery. I tried to consider who else might have a reason to do Justus harm besides Nicolette. The only other person that kept coming back to my mind was Dustin Crabb.

I remembered overhearing the conversation between Joyce Stickler and Asperat at Crosstown, mentioning that Justus had been associating with Dustin again, and that it had happened for a stretch of time in the past as well. *Had the two men argued over something, and then fought?* I wondered. It seemed a perfectly reasonable explanation after observing Dustin's recent erratic behavior.

He had lost his job—and much more, most likely—in the fallout from whatever his "moral failings," as the school board minutes had generically described them, had been. Alcohol and drug use of any kind were strictly forbidden for all students and staff at Crosstown. Perhaps both Justus and Dustin were involved in whatever shenanigans were going on within the neighborhood drug trade as well. If so, those paths all led eventually back to Enrique, and by extension, Ryne. It was a lot to think about.

I jumped out of bed on Saturday morning, and finally decided to follow through on what I'd been planning to do for some time. After a quick workout of push-ups, sit-ups and arm curls, I caught my breath as I sat on the bottom basement stair and opened a grocery store bag.

Three separate packages from various aunts and uncles had arrived in the last couple of days containing generously-donated license plates. An old white plate from Tennessee with the state outline on it, an old red plate from the 70s from South Carolina, and a light blue plate from New Jersey. That one utilized the outline of the Garden State as the dash, placed between the identifying letters and numbers, which I liked and thought was clever.

My collection of colorful license plates had now grown to span over a dozen states, and I was excited to use them as the catalyst for my grand plan with Mandy. I stacked them in my school backpack, swung it over one shoulder, and headed away from my house on my Huffy bike.

It was cloudy and cooler than normal for a morning in the middle of June. It was a relief after the past sweltering week, which had been perfect for swimming lessons, but little else. I had been awarded my Lifesaving certificate, handed to me by a member of the staff, as Roxy looked on from the back of the group with a look of extreme boredom. I'd attended my very last lesson at the community center pool, having completed everything they had to offer.

I came to a stop outside the triplets' house. I had seen little of them during the past couple of weeks, and I was growing concerned for their well-being. I set down my bike on their front lawn and knocked at the front door.

Their mom, a small and sullen-looking woman, eventually made her way to the door and looked out at me dully. "The triplets aren't here. They're working," she said flatly.

"Working for who?" I asked audaciously. She stared at me. "Not sure," she said evasively. "They're delivering stuff for a company or something." I tilted my head and waited, looking for an additional reaction but getting none. I asked her to tell them I'd stopped by, and she woodenly agreed and disappeared. A couple of doors down, Wanda, who was sweeping off her front porch again, nodded at me and waved as I continued on my way to my intended destination.

Minutes later I drew close to 862 Paris Street. I stopped a few houses down to collect myself and get a lay of the land. Enrique's green Mustang was thankfully nowhere in sight, and there wasn't a trace of Ryne and his high-end bike or intimidating mohawk. Mandy wasn't visible on the porch or in the yard, and the house was completely still. My confidence was beginning to rise, so I parked my bike on her front walk, took a deep breath and headed up the driveway toward the garage, my backpack in tow.

From a boombox sitting on a table in the garage, the sound of piano keys and a woman's voice came belting forth at top volume. I was surprised I hadn't heard it earlier when I was drawing near to her house. I caught sight of Mandy with her back to me, holding a hammer as a microphone and dancing, and then heard these lyrics as the electric guitar and bass joined in for the swelling chorus.

You don't know how long I have wanted
To touch your lips and hold you tight, oh
You don't know how long I have waited
And I was going to tell you tonight
But the secret is still my own
And my love for you is still unknown
Alone

In front of her was a table, and she had set up an impromptu assembly line of some sort. She was kind of a mess, in dirty jeans and a loose white t-shirt, paint spilling down the side of the table which she'd covered with a gray tarp. I stood still and watched her work, hammering away to the beat of the song.

It appeared she was making another batch of her lettering signs. After every letter was successfully driven into the wood, she would segue into another dance sequence. It was slightly embarrassing but totally mesmerizing to silently watch her. I briefly considered following the advice of the song to leave her alone, but I had come too far, and

I finally got up the nerve to walk up beside her.

"Ah!" she yelled, jumping, her eyes flashing angrily. "You can't do that!" She reached over and lowered the volume on her boombox, which had a thin mist of red paint speckling it. "What are you doing here? Were you watching me?" She asked the last sentence suggestively, and I knew I had turned as red as the paint she was using.

I changed the subject and peered over her shoulder at her latest handiwork. She had around a dozen more signs in various stages of production, and they looked neater and more polished than the first batch I'd seen. She had expanded the city names to cover a good portion of the municipalities of the county.

"I wanted to see what you were up to. I noticed that Pete didn't have any of your signs up. Did they all sell?" I asked.

"Of course," she beamed. "And, he commissioned me to create a second collection." She gestured to the pieces in front of her, and was obviously proud of her accomplishment. I was impressed as well. I took one last breath and laid it all out there.

"I want to work on a project with you, too." I waited to gauge her reaction. She looked at me dubiously and thought for a moment. "I'm not sure I need a partner," she replied and turned back to what she was doing. "I kind of work best when I'm on my own."

"Alone, eh? Kind of like your taste in music?" I joked as the chorus, much lower than before but still audible, repeated the very word. She turned back to me. "What—don't you like Heart? They're the best."

I admitted that I hadn't ever heard of them. She looked at me flabbergasted. "You've got to broaden your horizons, kid." She was hammering another letter onto a reddish wood plank a second later, and turned the volume on the boombox higher once more.

The 'kid' label stung a little, but I pressed on regardless. I pulled my backpack off my shoulder and lowered it to the garage floor. It was

Davajuan

a JanSport, navy blue with leather trim, and I was pretty proud of it. It had taken me an hour standing in the aisle at Sears to convince my mom to spring for one that pricey the previous fall.

I unzipped the backpack and pulled out my stack of license plates. She peeked at them out of the corner of her eye, but kept working. Now that I was finally up close to the impressive garage display, I remembered that most of Enrique's extensive wall collection were from a few nearby states. I held my own plates one at a time in front of her, and shuffled the states she must have already seen plenty of times before to the back of the stack. At the sight of the old red South Carolina plate, she finally gave in.

"Look," she sighed. "These are really cool. But if you look around, you can see I've got a good pool to choose from already. Enrique doesn't want me touching the ones he has on the walls, but there are stacks and stacks in boxes in the back that I can use for whatever I want."

I was not going to be deterred. "But what," I said grandly, pausing every few words for the effect, "if we wanted to make something other than just signs out of the letters?" She paused and looked skeptical. I was dying for her to ask me to explain my cryptic suggestion further, but she still didn't take the bait. She stared at me with her arms crossed. Finally I couldn't contain myself any longer.

"Fine, here it is, Mandy. I'm going for broke here. Let's cut out plates into shapes of all fifty states and make a big map of the entire United St—" I gushed all at once, but Mandy cut me off. A car was roaring up the driveway, and she grabbed my arm instinctively and pulled me out of view. I nearly lost my balance, but recovered and hovered in the shadow of the house waiting for an explanation.

"You've got to get out of here. Enrique absolutely hates it if I have anyone over here without his permission. Especially guys—unless it's Ryne of course," she clarified as she frowned. "Hide over there behind the air conditioner," she hissed.

Enrique yelled at someone else in the car as they idled halfway up the driveway. The brand new and perfectly-tuned 5.0 liter engine growled with a rich low tone, keeping me from hearing exactly what was said. He suddenly cut the engine, got out in a huff, and slammed the door. I could hear the passenger meekly do the same.

"And don't even dream of smoking in there again, you animal," Enrique commanded. "Let me put it to you it this way: I don't need to know. I don't want to know. But you'd better get your loose ends cleaned up real quick. Your little minions riding around the neighborhood peddling my wares are your concern. Any trouble they run into, you run into. If you think owing me 50k is trouble, just see what happens if your problems ever become my problems!"

He pounded up the steps to the front door and noisily went inside, tossing things out of his way. I heard the muffled sounds of glass shattering, followed by a string of profanity. I peered around the corner to see the pacing figure of Dustin Crabb, and he seemed to be wearing the same soiled outfit as he had been the last time I'd seen him outside of Embers Bar.

He looked more flustered than usual, and was saying something to himself repeatedly. He cut a pitiful figure, and I almost felt sorry for him for a moment. "Get in here and make the call!" Enrique screamed out the front window at him. Dustin jumped a little and hurried inside obediently.

"Mandy!" Enrique bellowed through a back window. "I'm hungry, get in here and make something for me. It's been one of those days already, and it's just getting started, apparently." His voice trailed off as he walked to the front of the house, and Mandy looked back over at me apologetically and shrugged. She nodded toward the fence, which was partially obscured by a manicured hedgerow, and I understood that she wanted me to leave quickly and without being seen.

She walked calmly around the corner of the house and disappeared. I waited about a minute, and then darted to the fence and scaled it. Only then did I remember my backpack, which was sitting in plain view in the mouth of the garage back on the other side of the fence. I hesitated, then continued making my escape through the neighbor's yard crouched low, and decided it would have to be retrieved later once the coast was clear.

At the front corner of Mandy's house, I leaned against the brick wall and listened. Inside it had gotten quiet again. I braced myself, then sprinted for my bike which I'd left on the front sidewalk, mounting it and pedaling away for all I was worth in one smooth motion. I was relieved to have escaped Enrique's detection, but when I thought of how my plans with Mandy had been interrupted when I had finally been so close, I sighed dejectedly.

The sky was gray and gloomy as I wheeled back onto my own street. I was happy to see Tyson in front of my house, straddling his bike, and he was jawing back and forth across the street with Jason and Johnny, and another boy from the neighborhood, as they played pickle with a baseball and gloves.

CJ and his sister Rochelle lived across the street from me, and two houses down from the sports-obsessed brothers, and they were both bossy and irritating. CJ was a good bit younger than the rest of us, and played with my brother from time to time when Corbin could tolerate it. When Corbin had been a toddler, he'd referred to him as "CJ Cross da street," and the name had permanently stuck in our household, since his actual last name was a mystery to us.

CJ Crossdastreet was one of the most mouthy and snotty children I'd ever met, and he had a favorite phrase he'd often use as a taunt directed at me. "You're not mans," he would say, his incorrect grammar taking some of the bite out of the attempted affront to my masculinity.

The first time he'd used it, I'd stupidly taken the bait, and angrily sent his basketball rolling down the street, only to see it destroyed in dramatic fashion by the wheels of a passing truck. His cries of injustice had brought my parents outside, and I'd ended up having to spend fifteen hard-earned dollars to pay for the ball's replacement. His churlish look when I handed him the brand new ball had bothered me more than the work required to pay for it.

Like most of the other kids in my neighborhood, CJ and Rochelle did basically whatever they pleased. They were rather spoiled from my limited perspective, judging by the name brand shoes and plastic tchotchkes they were always toting around. But their property was rundown and neglected, and there was an ancient vehicle of some sort permanently ensconced in their driveway, surrounded by waist high weeds that were gradually reclaiming it back to nature.

CJ kept getting tagged out in pickle, and Tyson was taking the opportunity to let him have it from his vantage point in my front yard. Jason and Johnny simply smiled and continued to send missiles from one base to the other with such terrific zip their gloves popped satisfactorily. There was no denying they were quite good at any sport they chose to play. Every time CJ was caught stealing, he would moan and claim some sort of conspiracy. As I pulled up next to Tyson to enjoy the spectacle, CJ had finally had enough.

"OK, you two wise guys. If you're so great, I dare you to come over here and see if you can get me out. Word on the street is you both throw like girls. And Jason said you can't catch a ball if your life depended on it." Jason shook his head denying the charge, but he looked slightly guilty. CJ had directed his last taunt at me, but continued to glare at us both while standing between the two other boys, waiting to see if his challenge would reap any dividends.

Tyson and I grinned at each other and walked across to the spotty grass of Jason and Johnny's front lawn, worn thin like a bad haircut in numerous places by their endless athletic endeavors. As I crossed over, I gazed down into the dead end and saw forlorn-looking Freddy sitting alone on his front porch.

I waved weakly, and he nodded back at me, but didn't budge from where he sat. He clearly had firm instructions from his unhinged mother to give me a permanently wide berth. I shuddered at the thought of her, as well as the horror of what lay hidden in their backyard—still completely unknown to downcast Freddy, as far as I could tell.

Once on the other side, both Tyson and I accepted the mitts tossed to us by the brothers, and took up our positions at the two imaginary bases. Rochelle, nicknamed Roach, a large girl with burnt orange hair that matched the car rotting on her property, walked up to observe what would happen while holding a half-eaten neon green Push Pop.

I took the ball first, and CJ stood next to Tyson across the yard from me at the other base with a determined look plastered on his smudged and smarmy face. I sailed one down to Tyson just as CJ took off toward me in a dead sprint. He was a relatively fast runner for his age, but the ball from Tyson arrived back to my glove in plenty of time to tag him out.

Somehow though, it glanced off the end of my mitt, and CJ slid into the base safely, cackling with glee. I turned and ran for the ball, which continued to bounce on the sidewalk all the way to CJ and Rochelle's house. I chastised myself under my breath as the ball disappeared into the weeds around the rusty car in their driveway. I knew I would never hear the end of it.

I pushed the weeds aside and crawled toward the rusting edifice. There was no obvious sign of the ball, and I leaned over and looked underneath the decrepit car without finding it. It was dark and cool beneath the overgrowth, and it smelled like the soil after a hard rain. Both front doors of the old coupe were missing, and now I could see the dirty brown cloth seats and floor, which were covered with trash of every imaginable color. I searched the interior of the vehicle on my hands and knees without getting inside, but no ball could be seen.

After another few seconds, red stitching against scuffed white cowhide caught my eye, and I stretched my arm down to the floor below the crumbling steering wheel to grab it. My hand brushed against something else metallic and heavy. Curious, I ignored the baseball and slowly retrieved the object carefully between two fingers. It was a hunting knife, with a brown wooden handle, which had an intricate logo carved into it.

The symbol, about the size of a dime, was a vintage fleur de lis, with an eagle cleverly intertwined. As I pulled it closer to me, I could see for the first time that the blade, from tip to hilt, was almost completely covered in blood.

15

"what is Truth?"

Startled, I dropped the knife the same instant. It slid back down close to where I'd found it. Frozen momentarily by yet another morbid discovery, I snapped back to reality when Tyson called out for me again.

"What's taking so long? It was bad enough that you blew the catch!" The other kids, including Roach laughed rudely at Tyson's comment and bantered amongst themselves. I grabbed the ball, and emerged from the tall weeds. Jason had already taken my spot, and when I threw him the ball, the game continued on without me.

CJ returned to being mowed down between the bases, Roach continued working on her Push Pop, and Johnny watched the proceedings with amusement. I sat down against a tree in their front yard and considered what I'd found, and thought of what I could possibly do about it.

Could that somehow be the weapon used to dispatch Justus? I wondered. The evidence on the knife blade meant a crime of some sort had definitely been committed. No small scrape or minor injury could produce that much blood. But in this neighborhood, that didn't mean anything definitive, I realized. Crimes were committed daily within the few square miles that comprised Rouge Park. And the frequency and violence of those crimes seemed to be increasing at an alarming rate.

Tyson announced he had to get going. He put down the baseball glove and ball and exchanged fives with the other boys, except for CJ, who took a pouting seat in the dirt and moped about his most recent base-running faux pas. I got up from my spot next to the tree and walked with Tyson back across the street to his bike.

"Duty calls," he said with a smile. "They're really working me like a dog down there at Revere. Check this out," he said, pulling a crumpled piece of paper from his back pocket. He unfolded a check and showed it to me proudly. "My first payday!"

The check was in the amount of several hundred dollars, which was extremely impressive. I'd never had so much money in my life. But the thing that caught my eye was an image in the upper left corner of the check. It was a blue horse and rider logo, with the name Revere Enterprises underneath in blue script. I immediately knew I'd seen it somewhere recently, but couldn't remember where. I congratulated Tyson on his windfall, then he said goodbye and sped off back toward his house near the West Ridge city line.

He stopped a handful of houses down and called back to me. "Hey! Don't forget baseball starts Monday. Henry Hallas will be expecting you!" he teased. With all the excitement, I had forgotten about the upcoming summer Youth League season, and a pang of anxiety hit my stomach. Dad had volunteered to help out again as assistant coach, and I could already visualize his dejected face from down the third base line as I struck out on three pitches once again.

As Tyson continued on his way and disappeared from view, it suddenly hit me. I'd seen that Revere logo one of the last times we'd hung out together in the woods. *It was imprinted on the hat on that hobo,* I reminded myself. As I walked aimlessly down the block away from my house, I examined the seared image of his haunted look, and the faded trucker hat, in my mind's eye again. *What connection could he possibly have to the aluminum factory,* I wondered? The hobo could have found the hat anywhere, discarded in the woods for example, I knew. Still, it was a strange coincidence.

I looked up and was startled to see two uniformed officers descending the front walk of the house right before mine, and then turning up the pathway to my own front door. They soon both stood on my porch looking quite official, and the bigger one knocked on the metallic screen door. As I drew closer I could see it was Officers Collier and Simmons.

Mom came to the door just as I arrived back on my front lawn. "Ma'am, one of your neighbors, Justus Mann, has been missing for several weeks," Collier explained. "We are canvassing the neighborhood today looking for anyone who might have any information, no matter how trivial, that could lead us to him."

"Is he in trouble for something?" Mom asked. Simmons shook his head. "We are simply trying to confirm his whereabouts and safety, ma'am. Have you or anyone in your family seen Justus recently?" She said she had not, and then noticed me standing on the grass.

"Have you seen Freddy's dad recently, son?" she asked innocuously, almost as a formality. I stood frozen, frantically considering my options. Here was the perfect chance to unload my terrible secret, to the proper authorities, and send them over to Freddy's backyard to dig up the horrible truth once and for all. Then, sickening images of Corbin's innocent face flooded my mind, along with awful thoughts about the threatening letter. Anyone capable of nearly sawing off Justus' head would be able and willing to follow through on hurting my little brother as well. It was a price too high to risk, I decided.

"No, sir. Haven't seen Mr. Mann in weeks. I really don't associate with them very much any more, or them with me," I added. *At least the last part was true,* I consoled myself. The officers thanked us both and continued on down the block. I exhaled and prayed that my story had been believable.

The next day was Sunday, and per my dad's typical firm requests, we were all in the purple church van by exactly 9:22 am. Sunday School started at 9:30 sharp. My dad was a very precise man who had calculated the total time the trip to Crosstown Christian took to within seconds. That included stoplights, random delays, and the long walk all the way from the parking lot behind the church to our seats in the sprawling sanctuary near the front of the property. Mom had already examined and approved everyone's outfit, though she had frowned at me briefly and mentioned that I'd worn the same striped short-sleeved shirt three Sundays in a row.

The two morning services proceeded without incident, except for a brief chance to catch up with Violet between them while standing in the church lobby. Our eyes connected as she took a long drink from the fountain outside the ladies' room, and my stomach fluttered just a bit when she made the surprising move to walk over and have a chat with me. She asked what I had been doing recently, and I shared the major highlights, including swimming lessons and some anecdotes about cutting lawns.

"What have you been up to so far this summer?" I asked. She

told me about her summer job babysitting, and that her family was planning a trip to Disney World during July. As she talked, I quietly admired her smooth brown skin, perfect teeth that gleamed bright white, a hint of pink lipstick and makeup, and above all her dark brown eyes that flashed with nearly every word. *When did she transform from the tattling teacher's pet I'd known for years into the beautiful girl standing here now?* I wondered.

"Violet," a deep voice said firmly. We both looked up to see her father standing near the double doors into the sanctuary. He was flanked by Violet's two younger brothers. Leon was one grade below me, and played on the summer Youth League baseball team as well. The only thing I really knew about Leon was a story that had become school legend, involving his private parts and an unfortunate incident with a zipper, which had culminated with him running down the hallway exposed and screaming for help from any source available.

All three of the Vereen men were dressed in suits and ties, and looked quite put together. The two boys were distracted by other things going on around them in the busy corridor, but her father seemed to intentionally frown at me for a split second, and then motioned for Violet to follow him to their customary pew.

The tinkling piano and muffled sound of stilted conversations soon died down as the enthusiastic music minister Shannon Worthy stepped up to the pulpit. After a few hymns, the announcements were read, and I lost focus until it was announced that the summer Wednesday and Sunday night youth program would resume that very week, during the same time slot as the adult prayer meeting. This pleased me immensely, because it meant less sermons to endure while squirming in one of the hard wooden pews. And, it would give me a chance to reconnect with some of my school friends that I hardly saw during the summer break, not the least of whom was Violet.

We always sat about halfway back on the left side of the auditorium, and Violet and her family had their own regular spot that they preferred all the way on the opposite side. I tried unsuccessfully for a few moments to make eye contact with her across the massive throng, but she had her eyes lowered and was reading either her Bible, the bulletin—or perhaps even the song hymnal, which I sometimes resorted to myself, if the sermon was especially dull.

Behind her sat Mrs. Townsend, smiling quietly with her hands folded, and next to her was her husband, a tall, lanky and serious man with dark, slicked-back hair and thick-rimmed glasses. Denny had breathlessly revealed to me once that Alan Townsend was rumored to be packing heat at all times. I wondered with awe if he actually had a firearm somewhere on his person that very moment.

One row farther back sat Joyce Stickler, wearing a severe-looking avocado suit, her face solemn and drawn. In the last row, where the older singles liked to gather, sat Mr. Asperat. Somehow he noticed me, and he gave me a quick, polite nod. Just then, the Ballanger family entered, running late as usual, and made quite a commotion getting to their seats.

Both parents flashed plastic grins at the congregants around them, and Grangeford, clutching a massive Bible and wearing exactly what you'd expect a young man to wear to brunch at a fine country club in the Hamptons, followed dutifully behind them.

I had grabbed a blue-bound volume from its shelf in front of me when the venerable, white-haired Senior Pastor Shay, an imposing man who was in terrific shape even though he must have been well into his eighties, took his place behind the pulpit and opened the Word.

"What is truth?" he asked the congregation, as his rich booming voice echoed throughout the vast room. He let the question hang in the air. The smallest cough at that moment would have seemed like an atomic bomb being detonated.

"That is the question that Pontius Pilate asked Jesus when confronted with the very Truth of all creation, in the form of a person. He asked it sarcastically, as if there was no way for a man to actually ascertain it. But I am here today to tell you that we are all confronted with the Truth, and what we do with it will define our lives, and even our fate into eternity."

He paused for a moment, but I had already lowered the hymnal I had been mindlessly browsing, and was now hanging on his every word.

"Turn with me to Psalms 5," he instructed, and the high-pitched crinkling sound of hundreds of King James Bibles rapidly turning in unison broke the temporary silence from the crowd.

"Here, the Psalmist warns us all: Thou shalt destroy them that speak lies; the LORD will abhor a bloody and deceitful man." He looked up from the text and his piercing blue eyes panned the parishioners. "King David, a man very familiar with the consequences of lies, issues a dire warning to us all." I thought the pastor made eye contact with me for just a fleeting moment, and it made my blood run cold.

I'm not lying about it—am I? I asked myself. By not telling anyone about the body of Justus, I was actually protecting Corbin from an unknown and very real threat. Plus, no one could help Justus now. His fate had been sealed. It was far shrewder for me to work to shield others, and not get involved in that messy situation any more than I already was, I thought.

A bloody and deceitful man, I repeated from the passage, and the vision of the stained hunting knife hidden in the rusted-out car reappeared in my mind. *It must have been tossed there by Justus' killer, as he or she hurried from the scene,* I imagined. It was a frantic move, made by someone who had not planned beforehand and simply reacted to a set of circumstances. A crime committed on a whim, in the heat of the moment. Did that point to Nicolette? Or someone else?

The idea of someone desperate enough to kill Justus, hurriedly bury the body, and discard the weapon, all while living in my own neighborhood was terrifying. *Yes,* I nodded imperceptibly. *Better to stay as far from the situation as possible at this point,* I thought to myself. Pastor Shay's voice then asked us all to turn to Proverbs and I was jolted back to the present.

"David's wise son Solomon takes his father's negative instruction even a step further. Instead of simply warning us that lying will bring about our own destruction, in Proverbs 14 he counsels us that: A truthful witness saves more lives." The pastor let his thunderous voice emphasizing that final phrase reverberate through the entire auditorium. "Our duties to the ones around us do not stop at just not lying. We must tell the truth! Or more people may die."

I shook my head in disbelief. I studied the tanned and craggy face of the pastor, contorted with emotion as he laid out his case for truth to the congregation, and wondered how he had gotten so deep inside my head. *More lives.* But had the author actually said the word *more?* Or had I just imagined it?

I looked down at the text again, rereading Verse 25 several times, and I did not see it printed there. I had subconsciously added the word *more* myself, I realized solemnly. I knew what I had to do. The question remained: Would I be able, and willing, to do it?

During the short van ride home after the service, I sat silently and alone back in the third row, deep in thought. Dad pulled into the packed parking lot of a 7-Eleven at the biggest intersection in Rouge Park, as he typically did on Sundays at around noon, and I jumped out robotically. Mom rolled down her window and handed me a couple of dollars, as the sounds of Corbin saying he was hungry and Suzanne asking him repeatedly to be quiet so she could continue reading wafted out of the van for public consumption.

Inside the store, I grabbed a thick Sunday paper, a gallon of Vitamin D milk, and then perused the shelves for my own personal prize. I was allowed to pick between an Atomic Fireball, a piece of Bazooka Joe chewing gum, or a Wonka's Everlasting Gobstopper as a reward for this minor weekly chore. I grabbed a yellow Gobstopper, visible through the cellophane wrapper, and stood in line at the cash register.

While I waited to check out, Enrique's green Mustang swerved into the lot and parked haphazardly in the only open spot. The top was down, and Enrique was dressed entirely in black, wearing stylish sunglasses. He threw a cigarette butt down to the asphalt, strode with purpose into the convenience store and went straight up to the register next to mine.

"Tigers play at one?" he asked the attendant, as he pointed to a box of cigarettes and nodded when the right one was acquired. The attendant confirmed it. "That fool out there just bet me triple or nothing they won't win the pennant this year. I'll take his money again—and then some!"

The attendant reminded Enrique that the Tigers were currently mired in third place. "The Blue Jays are unbelievable this year. Seventeen games over .500 already. Your friend may be right," the worker stated. Enrique retorted with a huff and some more statistics just as it was finally time for me to pay for my items.

Two blondes wearing sunglasses, thick makeup and pastel-colored blouses with the collars folded skyward were crammed into the back seat of the Mustang, cackling at something. Dustin was in the passenger seat, wearing sunglasses as well, and that same white filthy shirt he seemed to have on at all times. He wasn't sharing in the ladies' mirth.

He appeared to become aware of our van's markings in the adjacent spot and slumped down in his seat to avoid detection by my parents.

Enrique brazenly walked out a minute later without paying, jumped in the car and peeled out of the lot in front of me as I walked to the van with my purchases. Dustin looked the other way in a pathetic attempt to pretend he hadn't noticed us, and I went ahead and played along. The Mustang lurched to the left toward the interstate on ramp, and Enrique put the pedal to the floor.

At home, lunch came and went uneventfully, and soon after, I was sitting on the cool basement floor sorting my baseball card collection into separate teams. I caught a faint whiff of a sour, rotting smell as I sat alone in the unfinished section, like I had many times before, and immediately knew the source. I had never enjoyed eating vegetables, like many children. Mom had served Lima beans regularly for as long as I could remember, and the dry, tasteless texture absolutely disgusted me. All three of us kids were coerced to finish our meals and join the "clean plate club" on a nightly basis.

I had tried many methods of downing the horrid things, including mashing them all up into a ball of paste, and swallowing the mass whole with a large gulp of milk—or iced tea, if we were lucky. However, my preferred method of disposal had finally become to stuff the entire wad into my mouth, and then announce a sudden and urgent need to use the bathroom near the tail end of the meal.

Instead of visiting the restroom, I'd hightail it downstairs and deposit the load of reviled produce right into the storm drain found in the middle of the basement, carefully replacing the circular grate when I was finished. The evidence for my repeated crimes had been composting now for quite a while, and the scent was becoming increasingly difficult even for me to ignore.

Dad came thundering down the stairs in a good mood. "One more week, Dav! Just need to get this room painted and tiled, and it will be ready for you to move in." He was wearing grubby work clothes and had a gallon of light blue paint in his hand. "Leftover from the bathroom project last summer," he explained. "Mom thinks it will contrast nicely with the wood furniture." No one had thought to ask my opinion on the decor, but to be honest, I wasn't extremely concerned. It was going to be great to simply have a new and larger space of my own with a closet for the first time in memory.

I thanked him, and decided to go for a quick ride. Seeing Enrique head safely away from Rouge Park toward the interstate and hopefully out of town temporarily had triggered a thought in my mind. I needed to retrieve my backpack from Mandy's, and I was also hankering to present my grand license plate project plan to her once again without being interrupted.

I approached her house on my Huffy, and, as expected, the Mustang was not around. I walked confidently up to the front door and knocked. I waited for a minute, then knocked again, but heard no movement inside. I was about to leave when I looked in through the front window into the kitchen. My backpack sat on a table, right next to an open sketchbook and the collection of license plates I'd brought over to her during my last visit. Intrigued, I pushed up against the screen to get a better view into the dim room. All the lights inside were off, so I couldn't read any of her notes, but they looked neatly done and pretty extensive.

I walked around the back, and found the garage door was lowered. However, the back screen door was slightly ajar, and when I tried the handle, it rotated freely and the door cracked open. I wavered for a minute, but I knew that I could be in and out in mere seconds, giving me the chance to grab my backpack, and perhaps also steal a quick look at Mandy's project notes. The opportunity was simply too tempting, and I cautiously stepped inside.

The house was deathly still and smelled of pizza, burnt popcorn and a hint of ginger potpourri. I was surprised at how clean it was, seeing that Enrique was one of its primary occupants, and I couldn't imagine him taking the time to make sure the kitchen was spic and span every night before bedtime. The rooms were sparsely furnished, but the few pieces of furniture and audio equipment they did have around were of the utmost quality, and must have cost a small fortune, I thought.

I headed directly over to the kitchen table, slung my backpack over my shoulder, and then leaned over curiously to peruse Mandy's sketchbook, which was lying open to a page in about the middle. Below some random pencil sketches and doodles was what appeared to be a list of some sort, with the word *Plans* written at the top in large letters.

Ten checkboxes were in a column on the left side of the page, and a mix of notations were on the right. It seemed to be a work in progress, with new tasks added to the list as she thought of them. The first one read *PRPs*, and I immediately somehow recognized it as most likely a reference to Pack Rat Pete's. The box next to it was checked, as if that item had been completed.

In the margin, written in a different color was a phone number, hastily scrawled. *382-2228*. I recognized it immediately as Asperat's. I stopped for a moment and tried to postulate a possible connection between him and Mandy, but came up completely blank. Why would she be calling a random teacher from a school she didn't even attend?

Added below Asperat's number in a different color pen were the numbers *50-25-50*. They meant nothing to me, but I stored them away regardless and moved quickly down the page.

The next two items on her list were simple enough to understand: *More Signs*, and *Brainstorm*. They were checked off as well. The fourth one jumped off the page at me, and made me catch my breath as I realized its possible meaning: *Map w D.*

Could it really mean working on the map project with me? I asked myself excitedly. It almost seemed too good to be true. The box next to that task remained unchecked, as did the rest of the entire list below that one.

Task 5 was *Learn C.* I was stumped on what Mandy had been referring to with that one. Number 6 was *Get $.* I could only imagine that it meant she wanted to continue to raise money from her burgeoning license plate sign business.

The 7th one was *Finish Wanda,* and it was also unchecked. I assumed it had something to do with helping her with the basement organizing project. Number 8 was simply *MTRB,* and I realized it could mean almost anything.

My eyes had just darted down to read the final two items on her list when I heard a floorboard creak in the next room.

Alarmed, I looked up and froze, completely at a loss of what to do next. I heard the distinct and terrible sound of a pistol cocking, followed by a firm and loud voice from just around the corner. It was Mandy's.

"I don't know who is in there or what you are doing, but you have five seconds to leave from the way you came, or you'll be very sorry."

16
Scooters & suspicions

"It's me," I said, and my voice cracked pathetically. Even considering the shock of the moment, I chided myself for sounding so weak. Mandy appeared from around the corner, in a shooter's stance with the barrel pointed right at my head. It was bizarre, but she had never looked so amazing to me as she did in that moment.

She was wearing a navy Def Leppard t-shirt with red writing on it, and as she held the gun level, I caught a glimpse of her tan and toned midriff. Unfamiliar atomic bombs of attraction went off throughout my body, but at the same time it made my heart sink. I realized once again how completely out of my league she actually was, and always would be. How could she ever look at me as anything but just another generic kid in a neighborhood she desperately wanted to escape?

Her eyes flashed with anger, but I detected some relief in them as well. Clearly she had gone through life believing that she needed to be ready to defend herself at a moment's notice, no matter where she happened to be. It dawned on me that she had seen, and maybe had been forced to do, things I could never understand.

"What are you doing here? Are you crazy?" she asked, walking over to the table beside me. She laid the gun down with the barrel pointed away from us. "Glock 17, Norwegian Army, '85," she noted casually, then glared at me again to reinforce the fact that I shouldn't have been there. She saw me staring at it. "Just one of the weapons Enrique keeps lying around should the need ever arise," she added.

"I—I needed to get my backpack, and the door was open," I explained sheepishly. "I wasn't snooping, and I wasn't going to stay longer than a minute. I figured it wouldn't hurt anything and I knew Enrique wasn't around."

"Enrique is always around, or can be in seconds; you just don't realize it yet," she said flatly. "If he catches you in here, you'll become just another loose end he has to tie up. I can't believe I left the door unlocked. If he knew I'd forgotten..."

"I'm sorry. It was a mistake," I said sincerely, and looked straight at her. My eyes were completely level with hers, which struck me as odd, since only a few short weeks prior she had been obviously taller than me. She seemed to notice it as well, and it made her look uncomfortable for a brief moment. Her eyes darted to her sketchbook.

She reached over and closed it emphatically. "We all have our secrets, Dav. I'm pretty sure you have one as well." I looked back at her with a start, and her steely gaze was right there waiting for mine. I shifted uncomfortably under her knowing stare. I relaxed, however, when I realized she could have no idea what my terrible secret actually was.

She seemed to change gears and looked around furtively. "OK, you've got to get out of here," she said quickly.

"Wait, I just want to tell you more about my map idea," I began, but she shoved me toward the back door. "Not now," she said bluntly. "Meet me at that creepy playground in the old park Thursday afternoon at, let's say, around 3. I'm super busy with some things until then."

I knew the place of course, as it was on the direct route Tyson and I always took to get to the woods and the railroad tracks. I started to object, but the look on her face told me there would be little use. I told her that I had baseball practice starting up, but that I would show up at the appointed time, if I could. In reality, wild horses couldn't have made me forget the time and place, or kept me away from the spot she'd mentioned.

That night, I was back sitting in the same church pew at Crosstown. A missionary from Japan was giving a presentation, complete with a slideshow packed with images of smiling Japanese converts, gigantic spreads of food, and snow-capped mountains. When a map of that country appeared on the massive screen that extended down from the ceiling, it piqued my interest.

I saw the island of Okinawa, where she was serving, and noticed with interest how close it was to neighboring Taiwan. I looked around and realized that I was in the vast minority of people who found this type of information engaging, judging by the stifled yawns and glassy looks of the surrounding congregants.

The missionary turned off the slideshow and began reading from a text, and I slowly lost interest. After taking a few shots at counting bricks in the walls that framed the vast stained glass windows on both sides of the auditorium as I'd often done before, I looked toward the back of the sanctuary. There, a long row of glass windows shielded half a dozen elders from the rest of us. They sat in metal folding chairs, and some of them had headphones on. I wasn't sure, but thought it might have been part of a security detail in case of an emergency.

"Everyone who calls on the name of the Lord will be saved. How then can they call on the One they have not believed in? And how can they believe in the One of whom they have not heard? And how can they hear without someone preaching to them?" the lady at the front pleaded. "And so, I go."

I listened to her speaking and wished I understood my own destiny and purpose in life so clearly and simply as she did. I continued to stare back at the elders, sitting up straight in their handsome suits and ties, and remembered that it had been a hot Sunday night just like this one almost three years earlier that the Tigers had been playing in Game 5 of the World Series against the San Diego Padres. The hometown team had been on the precipice of ending a 16-year championship drought, and the city was absolutely buzzing with anticipation. Everywhere you went during those days, people had been talking about that dominant, historic team.

I had begged Dad to let us all stay home from church and watch the game, but he had insisted we go to the evening service instead. I had sat and pouted bitterly through the entire message, wondering as every minute ticked by if our team had already clinched and had begun celebrating.

I had almost wished they'd lose, which would mean I could watch a potential Series win the very next night, comfortably in front of our television at home for Game Six.

It was only later that I realized the elders in the back wearing those headphones had been tuning in to the radio broadcast of the game, and were hanging on every pitch as the pastor preached. Small gasps and an almost imperceptible commotion had erupted in the back when Tony Gwynn had flied out to left field into the waiting glove of Larry

Herndon for the final out. They had quickly composed themselves once again, and directed their attention back to the front, but I knew exactly what had transpired.

The pastor's deep voice brought me back to the present as he thanked the missionary for her presentation, and announced there was a church business matter to attend to before we were dismissed. He asked the head elder to come to the front. The man did so, and explained that there was a small change needed in the church's constitution, but nevertheless, adopting it would require a vote from all the members.

These proceedings struck me as simply going through the motions. Because for as long as I could remember, no matter the issue, big or small, not one solitary "nay" vote going against the recommendations of the board had ever been recorded.

"All in favor, say 'aye'" the head elder instructed. A chorus of voices replied in the affirmative.

"All opposed, say 'nay'" he said robotically. As he turned to leave the podium, a voice shockingly close to me broke the silence and shouted, "Nay!"

The source of the vehement objection was Corbin. Dad and Mom hurriedly ushered him out, nearly running up the aisle on our far side of the auditorium. A few polite and uncomfortable laughs rippled through the crowd as the culprit became identified. I could barely contain my laughter, and I smiled broadly—ecstatic that for once I was not the source of family shame.

That night after the sun had set, I announced to anyone listening that I was going to go on a scooter ride. Suzanne had been put to bed, so she could not object. This type of late-night escape was not a strange occurrence for me, and neither Mom nor Dad had any issues with it, judging by their lack of response. Both of them were reading quietly in the warmly-lit living room, and I departed without another word.

I was barefoot, as I nearly always was while scootering around town, tempting fate that I'd not run over broken glass or a rusty nail. The evening was warm but breezy, and for some reason, it gave me shivers.

I loved these rides at night, when I was basically anonymous, and could freely go where I pleased without fear of identification from the Biker Scouts. I headed north first, and before long I turned into the narrow alley that led straight behind Club Xanadu, and ended in a solid brick wall just shy of the major crossroad that marked the boundary between Rouge Park and Detroit itself.

A green glow from the neon sign in front of Xanadu cast an eerie light behind the club. As I got closer, the blank steel door to the back of it burst open, and the orange pulsating light and loud music from inside seeped out. Enrique, Ryne and Dustin emerged and the door slammed shut once again as quickly as it had sprung open. Enrique was enraged, and was yelling at Dustin. Ryne stood by pacing, and was pounding one fist into the other in frustration.

"Ryne," Enrique barked, turning his attention to the young leather-clad punk, who I shockingly realized was free to come and go as he pleased into the strip joint, even though he was several years too young to legally enter. His hair was spiked even higher than normal, and he appeared to have eye liner of some sort applied for the occasion.

"Kid feels guilty and it's eating him up alive. Something's got to be done—we don't need any extra attention drawn to ourselves right now. Don't just stand there, and I don't care how late it is. Go now!" he screamed, and Ryne jumped back and quickly disappeared into the shadows down the darkened street perpendicular to them. I dismounted from Suzanne's scooter and crept up next to a dumpster to listen more closely.

"And you," he lowered his voice menacingly, redirecting his venom at Dustin. "You said you found a place suitable?" Dustin wavered. "I think so," he quivered. "I stole this key before everything went wrong, but I'd have to check to see if they changed the locks on me or not after they let me go. It's totally the perfect place."

He held a key out, attempting to satiate the seething Enrique, but it did nothing. Enrique towered over him and grabbed him by the collar of his perennially-smudged white button-down.

"Get over there and confirm. We'd have to move on this within a couple of days. And don't be seen!" he stressed, and turned and reentered the club. Once again the electronic lights and pumping bass filtered down the alley toward me for a split second, and then disappeared. A dejected-looking Dustin walked the short distance to his car and started it up.

Headlights flooded the alley and I held completely still behind the dumpster, hoping the back wheel of the scooter was not exposed. Dustin was so distracted he probably wouldn't have noticed in any case, I realized. He sped by me without even turning his head, and I vowed to try my best to follow him from a safe distance and find out what he was up to.

Instead of turning onto the main road that divided Rouge Park from West Ridge, he weaved between side streets at a speed barely above idle in the general direction of the latter. It wasn't difficult to keep up with him; every few houses I'd silently push off with a massive thrust of my left leg and simply coast along the smooth pavement. When we got about a block from the church and school, he suddenly flipped off his headlights. He turned into an infrequently used service road between the church complex and Lightning Lanes, and sat for a minute or two, making sure the coast was clear.

At this hour, the campus was completely empty. A few tall spires with flood lights here and there dotted the property with a jaundiced glow, but there were plenty of shadows to hide within, when necessary. Dustin turned off his car and left it safely obscured in one of those pockets of darkness. He walked briskly farther down the service drive until he reached the row of storage units where we'd detonated Denny's multi-stage makeshift bomb. That day seemed eons ago, even though it had only been a few short weeks. I remembered seeing Dustin there that day as well, making his suspicious phone call from the lonely pay phone located at the end of the long, brick edifice.

Dustin walked into the circle of the only flood light found back in that area, and I saw him look around again to ensure he was alone. He seemed on edge, as usual. He finished a cigarette and tossed it down the bank toward the creek. I waited far enough down the service drive behind him to remain undetected.

He pulled a ring of keys out of the pocket of his sagging trousers and continued to walk toward an obscure brown door at the end of the brick storage structure. It nearly blended into the wall, and even though I'd grown up around the place, and prided myself on my exhaustive knowledge of the grounds and facilities, I couldn't remember ever having noticed that the door even existed.

He dropped the keys just then and swore under his breath. He leaned over and retrieved them clumsily, and then managed to get the door open with some effort in the dim light. He disappeared into the yawning blackness beyond, and immediately upon entry began to descend some stairs. The door closed again behind him with a rough metallic scraping sound.

He was gone several minutes. The noise, lights and music from the bustling Lightning Lanes just across the creek kept my attention while I waited for Dustin to emerge once more. I wondered if Pack Rat Pete was over there that particular evening, taking his best shot at adding to his prodigious bowling trophy collection. That thought led me to wonder about Mandy's lettering sign progress, and from there, my mind arrived quickly upon Mandy herself—my favorite daydreaming subject. I wondered what she was doing at that very moment. What I wouldn't have given to know what the last two items on her sketchbook list were.

Dustin finally reappeared, closed and locked the mysterious brown door, and strode back to his car with a new purpose in his step. I had to retreat and hide behind a grove of trees on the creek bank to avoid detection. My left foot found a sharp object in the grass and I barely stifled a shout. He hopped back into his wood-paneled station wagon, and he and his *PRTYBOY* plate roared off this time, turning right and from there onto the main thoroughfare through West Ridge.

I knew I had no chance of following him from that point on. I spent the rest of my quiet ride home in the darkness, favoring my injured foot, while I tried in vain to figure out what possible nefarious purposes he and Enrique could have in store for that secluded and forgotten location.

The next morning I arrived bright and early back at Crosstown for the first baseball practice of the summer. I was excited to see Denny's car pull into the parking lot, and he emerged from the vehicle smiling, his tanned face and windswept hair testifying to his three-week beach vacation that had just ended. Tyson arrived soon after, along with Trevor and Gregory, both of whom I'd barely seen over the past several weeks. Henry Hallas was decked out from head to toe in a blue and gold Crosstown uniform, complete with stirrups and cleats as if it was already game day, and chatted with Dad behind the chain-link backstop.

Grangeford and his father arrived in what appeared to be a brand new blue Corvette with the top down, both of their heads of hair tussled from the pleasant morning breeze. I'd never seen this particular car before, and surmised bitterly that it was yet another acquisition for a family that was quickly running out of creative ways to spend their money.

Grangeford hopped out of the car, and walked over toward the rest of the team looking as if he was officially sponsored by Nike, judging by his shiny cleats, matching attire and batting gloves, which looked like they still needed to be broken in. I shifted uncomfortably, keenly aware of my own worn tennis shoes and casual clothes, and tried to ignore his arrival.

Soon the air was filled with the familiar tings of aluminum bats making light contact with baseballs, as Dad and Henry hit soft grounders to the infielders. I was sent to the outfield with about half of the team, and instructed to warm up our throwing arms. A boy one year younger than me named Hosea, who clearly had little interest in being there, was paired up with me.

He was short and pudgy, with stringy light brown hair, and had arrived wearing nicely-coordinated baseball garb produced by Adidas that his parents had lovingly selected for him. But unless being directly spoken to, he much preferred to let his eyes wander off and his imagination run wild.

Hosea's claim to fame was the invention of a game played on the school blacktop called "Gorby-Chase," where students took turns pretending to be the infamous Soviet leader with the unmistakable birthmark on his forehead. Whoever had the bad luck of being selected to impersonate Mikhail Gorbachev would then chase everyone else around like a madman, attempting to tag others, who were then forced to join him as fellow Communists. The Cold War seemed to be finally coming to a head; just weeks earlier, Reagan had commanded his Russian counterpart to tear down the Berlin Wall.

"Hosea," I called, and he turned back toward me. "Here, catch."

I sent a ball his way with some zip on it, and he awkwardly stabbed at it and missed. It bounded past him farther into the outfield, nearly arriving at the home run fence. I made eye contact with Tyson a short way off, who was throwing a ball around with Trevor, and rolled my eyes at Hosea's ineptness.

Henry announced we would be taking turns batting, and my stomach sank. I could usually hold my own with a glove without embarrassing myself, despite my recent mistake playing with CJ, but batting in front of the whole group of boys was pretty much my worst nightmare. I secretly hoped I'd be selected near the end and we'd run out of time.

"Grangeford, run it on in, big guy. You can go first today," Hallas instructed, and set up on the mound with a barrel of practice balls. The athletic youth grinned, tossed his mitt toward the bench and rifled through his collection of expensive bats that stood in a bag next to his dad, who was leaning against the backstop to observe and critique. Finding one to his liking, he dug in around home plate with his cleats, and assumed a classic batting stance, his expression basically daring Hallas to release a pitch for him to abuse. His bat danced back and forth over his shoulder cockily.

I glanced at Hosea, who was still wandering in my general direction, having finally retrieved the missed ball. Begrudgingly giving in to my curiosity, I turned back to watch what Grangeford would do at the plate, pettily praying for him to whiff repeatedly. He took a pitch outside, regrouped, and then turned on the very next offering and launched an absolute bomb into left field. It carried toward Gregory as he gazed helplessly up at it and watched it travel well past him and over the fence.

I heard my name being called frantically, and looked over at Tyson. He was swinging his arms wildly and pointing, and then Hosea's plaintive voice joined in calling my name as well. I turned back toward him and caught just a glimpse of a huge white ball, which was close enough for me to see even the most intricate details of the red stitching.

Suddenly and without warning, I was back in the boy's bathroom at Crosstown once more. The hands which had been clamped around the student's neck released their iron grip in an instant, and I could hear heaving gasps join the sound of the stern, barking voice which was now commanding the pervert to retreat.

Air jubilantly returned into the victim's lungs, as he collapsed to the tile floor, which was greasy with urine from the notoriously-poor marksmanship of the male student body. A tall, dark-haired man bounded to the young man's side and knelt down beside him. The bedraggled intruder recoiled, and slunk into the shadows of the restroom and then disappeared. I reached out with my mind to identify the players in the macabre scene but it ended abruptly to my chagrin.

Milliseconds later the baseball collided with my face and then all I could see was white, cascading stars.

17
behind in the Count

The rest of that week passed by without any major incidents. I spent the remainder of Monday icing my face, and soon sported a massive shiner. My nose was incredibly sore, but not broken. CJ Crossdastreet snidely commented on how it looked on Tuesday morning as I loafed around in the front yard, and I was tempted to venture over and give him a pounding, but I resisted. On Wednesday afternoon, after mowing a few yards with Zane, I took the spoils over to Pack Rat Pete's and blew the wad on more cards. I cruised by Mandy's place hoping for a glimpse of her, but the house was vacant once again.

Every morning found me back on the familiar diamond at Crosstown, whiffing away at the plate, while making some decent plays in the field.

I guessed that I was probably a valuable enough fielder at first base to get some playing time, despite my batting woes. I had vowed to never make the mistake of warming up with Hosea again, and rushed to select a throwing partner almost before the words were out of Henry Hallas' mouth to ensure I'd snag someone who would look before they threw.

It appeared we would have a competitive team that year, and games were slated to begin that Saturday with a trip to a church across town called Evangel Apostolic. They were nicknamed the Lightning Bolts, and I'd always assumed it was a reference to their charismatic views on the power of the Holy Spirit.

Dad and Mom continued to take turns putting the finishing touches on my new room. It was coming together splendidly, and they estimated I could move in the following Monday. "Right before your birthday!" my mom had noted. I celebrated my special day one day before Uncle Sam, as they always liked to say. I secretly did enjoy the catchy nature of my actual birthday: 7/3/73. It was an easy one to remember and I had always liked the way it rolled off my tongue.

"What do you want to do for your birthday?" she asked me on that sweltering Thursday morning. "Last year was fun, going over to Windsor for some good old Canadian five-pin bowling," she said, cheerfully. "And the year before that was—what? Oh yes, Chuck E. Cheese's. I'm assuming you're a little too old for that now?"

"Yes, Mom," I groaned. I could only imagine my friends' taunts if we headed back there again. The chasm between the ages of 12 and 14 was proving to be even more vast than I'd anticipated. Life had seemed simpler back then somehow. A picture of the previous event was still hanging on the fridge in the kitchen.

Suzanne and I stood beaming at the camera, while a furry, costumed member of Chuck E.'s band posed behind us in the photo, which was already beginning to curl a bit at the edges. I had been wearing minuscule green shorts and an Incredible Hulk tank top. *No one has ever done the muscle-bound hero less justice,* I smirked sadly, as I observed my incredibly slender limbs showcased in the print. Suzanne had been decked from head to toe in My Little Pony. Both of us looked incredibly happy, tanned and healthy, without a care in the world.

"How about a trip up to the lake?" Dad chimed in. "You know—what's it called—Stony River. It has that huge bike path around the lake... sports, swimming—and then we could grill out. Invite a handful of your friends. What do you think?" They both looked at me with promising faces. "Sure," I shrugged. "Sounds like a plan."

The truth was I wasn't that excited about a party this time around for some reason. I couldn't peg exactly why. The nagging thoughts about Justus and the bloody knife discovery still weighed heavily on me in the quiet moments of most days. Plus, seeing Mandy later that day was the only thing currently on my mind.

A bit before three that afternoon, I left the house and headed toward the vacant park. I had spent most of the past few hours sorting my baseball cards and looking at the clock every couple of minutes or so. Two more plates had arrived for me in the mail that day. A green and white Idaho plate with the tagline *Famous Potatoes* from a great uncle, and a blue California plate from a distant family friend.

So far, I'd been able to get to the mailbox before Mom and Dad every time, and they still had no idea I'd even been collecting plates. I wanted to show them, but knew any conversation about it would inevitably lead to Mandy. And her very existence was still my secret.

I'd left all the license plates I'd already collected at Mandy's when she had hurried to usher me out the back door, and I hoped she would remember to bring them to our meeting. I nodded at Jason and Johnny, who were taking a break from their endless daily baseball practice in the shade of the beech tree, chugging on some Kool-Aid, judging by the red clown lips it had left around their mouths.

Freddy was in his front yard, but disappeared with a shot as I approached. I was relieved, because every interaction between us since that fateful day had been brief and awkward, and I could only guess what his crazed mother had threatened to do should she ever see us together. Getting still closer to the park, I passed by the triplets' house, and found I had just missed them, as I could see a trio of bikes transporting their familiar figures receding away from me into the distance.

Upon reaching the dead end, I looked around to ensure I hadn't been followed, and climbed through the gaping hole in the chain link fence, pushing aside the weeds like curtains. I was ecstatic to have not seen much of the Biker Scouts for the past several days, but I knew they were always not far away. I wondered what, if anything, had been keeping them so busy. I glanced down at my Radio Shack watch and saw that, like my father, I was exactly on time. 3:00 PM on the nose.

As I crossed the seemingly endless field, the dry grass blades whipped across my ankles. The aging park was roughly twenty acres of empty, windswept grassland, whose original purpose had been lost to time. In about the center of it, a rusting and abandoned jungle gym stood starkly against the horizon, like a modern version of Stonehenge.

Several previous generations of children had enjoyed its plentiful features, but not the current one. A swing-less crossbeam extended pointlessly out from the playground, and one of the slides was missing completely, a rough plywood board covered in crass graffiti now nailed in its place. Mandy could not have picked a better place to meet me, if isolation was the number one objective.

Mandy stood leaning against one of the support posts, perfectly still, facing in the opposite direction of my approach. She was watching a train chug by, puffing out black smoke under its heavy load. It was pulling an endless line of cars away from Detroit and southwest toward Chicago, which was a couple of hundred miles further on. Unlike my sweltering street where the air had been still, here a stiff breeze was free to gain momentum across the flat expanse. It blew Mandy's hair wherever it wanted, and she looked even more otherworldly than normal to me. I found the entire setting surreal, and we both seemed to be in a different dimension than the familiar world. She heard my footsteps eventually but didn't turn around.

"I'll be on that train someday," she stated wistfully. "Then I'll be rid of Enrique and all those beastly people he surrounds himself with. I'll ride it all the way till the tracks end."

"What would you do?" I asked, both curious to hear her answer, and also selfishly hoping she'd realize the complete fruitlessness of running away at her age. I recalled the brief escape Tyson and I had attempted weeks earlier, and wanted to tell her about it, but held my tongue. As I looked at her face full of resolve, I knew she had ten times better of a chance at making it out in the real world alone than I had.

"I'd open a gift shop. I'd sell my artwork, and spend the nights on the beach. I don't care if I have to live in a cardboard box. It would be all mine." She turned and I could see an ugly red blot under her cheek. It looked like someone had belted her with a fist. I wondered what the perpetrator had received back in response.

She saw what the baseball had done to my own face at the same time, but neither of us acknowledged the other's disfigurement. "For some odd reason, it's easy to talk to you," she commented, tilting her head ever so slightly. "You're not like other guys."

Her compliment made my pulse race, but I didn't know how exactly to take it, or how to respond, so I hurried to change the subject.

"OK, on a different note, let's talk about our map project!" I

207   *Davajuan*

reached into my pocket and unfolded the rudimentary drawing I'd made of all fifty states. I was pretty proud of how accurate it was for freehand. She smiled wanly and took it from my hand.

"It's very cool. I've decided to help you, but I can't promise anything, really. I've... well, I've gotten into some trouble. I have to finish up with some things around here and make as much money as I can. But," she said looking me straight in the eyes, "I won't be here for much longer, if everything goes as planned." I ignored her statement, perhaps hoping that would make it less real somehow.

We examined the new plates I'd just gotten, laying them out in columns on the gravel surrounding the jungle gym, and she was intrigued by them. "The more color, the better, I think," she said, sitting down and producing the others that I'd left on her kitchen table.

"We have a good variety going here. I'm thinking a quilt-like look will really make each state pop off the wood planks." She seemed to have almost forgotten all of her worries in an instant, and was growing more invested in our project by the minute. I desperately hoped that this collaboration would be enough to keep her around a bit longer.

Two days later, a yellow Crosstown bus carrying our entire Youth League squad rumbled into the dusty parking lot at Evangel Apostolic. It was a Saturday, but the facility was still filled with cars, the first game of the season obviously a big draw. The team piled out of the bus soon after it was parked, some boys carrying bat bags and others a large orange Gatorade cooler.

All eighteen of us made our way across to the visitor's bench and spread out, partnering to warm up as we'd been instructed by Henry just before exiting. Dad gave me a solid pat on the back without speaking and jogged off to greet the coaches of the Lightning Bolts.

The opposing team was dressed out in blindingly-white new uniforms with purple trim. *Evangel Apostolic* was embroidered across each chest in gold, and it was clear their team was stocked with big guys who could play ball. On our side, the only specimen that could hold a candle to any of them was Grangeford, and perhaps Tyson. Denny, Trevor, Gregory, Hosea, Leon and myself all looked pretty puny by comparison.

I told myself it was only the first game of the season, and that the stakes were low. *If we happen to get slaughtered so be it*, I thought. After tossing the ball around with Denny for a few minutes, Grangeford gathered us in a semi-circle for some stretches, and then Henry and Dad waved us in from off the field.

"Now listen," Hallas began, leaning over and putting his hands just above his knees. We all instinctively huddled closer. "These guys are good. We lost last year to them 10-1. Most of their big sluggers are back. Let's make them work for every run. Watch the ball go into your glove, and then throw, not in reverse. Hit your cut-off men. Talk out there. Be patient at the plate. Work their pitch counts up whenever possible. Anything to add?" Henry turned to Dad, imploring his own former coach for additional words of wisdom.

"What did we focus on this week? That's right, Denny," Dad nodded. "Check your signs. Every pitch, step out and check down the third base line. Coach Hallas or myself will be there, depending on the inning. Base runners, stay alert. If you don't catch the sign, tap your helmet and it will be repeated. For today's game, third symbol is the actual sign. Green light, take, hold the base, or steal." I knew the signs by heart; the memorization aspect of the game had always come easy to me. The rest, not so much.

Dad announced the starting lineup, and the first three boys he called ran and grabbed batting helmets and scrounged around for their favorite bats. Tyson and Denny were both in. Grangeford would pitch and bat clean-up. Trevor was always our catcher, and the rest of the starters were comprised of boys I wasn't particularly close to.

I sat down on the wooden bench between Gregory and Leon and settled in for the first inning. It was overcast, not too warm, and a nice breeze from the west pushed a steady stream of white, floating dandelion tufts out to right field. I traced my finger under my eye and the bridge of my nose massaging the sore spots. Leon handed me some of the peanuts that he'd brought for his predictably extended stint on the pine.

The first three innings went about as expected. We cobbled together a few walks, a hit or two, but stranded every runner except one. When Grangeford hit a solo shot to left on a full count, our bench erupted in celebration. The Lightning Bolts brought a runner home in each of those initial innings and we found ourselves down 3-1.

"Nice rip!" I called to Tyson as he unleashed a fly ball that nearly cleared the outfield fence, but was caught by an intrepid fielder on the run. He dejectedly pulled up between first and second and returned to the dugout.

"Come on guys! This game isn't over. Not even close. Let's take it up another notch!" Tyson cajoled us as he arrived back. His speech riled up the entire roster and I admired his assertiveness. He walked down behind the bench giving a hearty shoulder punch to every player he passed, including me. However, our next two batters went down in order, and it was time for our team to take the field again for the 4th. Dad came over quietly and tapped the bill of my hat. "You're in at first."

I hopped up instinctively, and I felt a surge of adrenaline as I grabbed my glove and ran out into the infield. Grangeford had moved from pitcher to shortstop, and I tossed him a ground ball as we routinely did between innings, and he promptly sent a laser back at me that made my leather glove snap. Being on the field felt good, and important. I looked up right at that moment to see Leon's family walking over to the bleachers, trying to find an open spot behind our bench. Violet was with them.

She looked perfectly put together in a tan jumper and green headband. I gulped internally and pretended I hadn't seen her, that I was too occupied with the challenge at hand to keep track of who all was attending. Denny took the mound in relief and loosened up his arm with a few practice throws to a crouching Trevor. His fastballs weren't overwhelming, but he had been perfecting a pretty nasty curve.

"Watch this guy, Denny," I called as the next Bolts batter got situated at the plate. "He doubled his last time up." Denny got him out on three pitches, and the growing crowd expressed their admiration. The bleachers were starting to fill up as a couple other surrounding games had finished. Two pop outs later, we trotted back to the dugout to hearty applause from both Dad and Hallas, and the audience behind them joined in as well.

I hadn't realized that my spot in the order would bat first in the fifth inning, and it all became very real as I sought out a batting helmet, and one of the 32" bats, a worn-looking Easton. I'd used it the previous season to send a dribbler down the third base line for my only hit of the season, so it was the closest thing to a positive superstition I could muster.

As I stepped into the batter's box after a couple of practice swings, I hoped no one could see me shaking. One valuable tip Shannon Worthy had once shared with me before one of my occasional trumpet solos at church was that the crowd couldn't see you tremble from any significant distance. "It's your own private torture chamber—no one else notices," he had assured me. I hoped that his truism extended to sporting events.

As a left-handed batter, I could see straight ahead of me down the third base line, and Dad signaled for me to take the first pitch. I stood like a statue and observed a fastball whiz past right down the middle. *I probably couldn't have gotten a bat around on it in time anyway*, I thought negatively. Dad instructed me to take the next one as well. Another strike.

I finally got the green light on a splitter in the dirt, and managed to check my swing at the last second. I dug in and waited again for the next pitch. A lazy curve that looked outside ended up right smack dab in the middle of the plate, and behind me I heard the umpire loudly ring me up for a called third strike. I smirked wryly as I heard Ernie Harwell's iconic voice in my head. *"He stood there like a house by the side of the road and watched that one go by."*

I turned and walked back to the bench with my chin nearly in my chest. A few people in the crowd thoughtfully shouted things like, "It's OK," and "You'll get him next time," but I knew it was more out of pity than optimism. Denny batted after me and laced a single up the middle. The next two batters walked, and we were in business with the bases loaded.

The crowd, which seemed to be rooting for an upset even though we were the visiting team, started to buzz, and then promptly moaned collectively as Trevor got jammed at the wrists with a heater and bounced into an inning-ending double play. Hallas was beyond livid at Denny for not taking off at the sound of the bat and getting caught in a force out at home plate. He threw his Crosstown hat to the ground and walked off in a huff, returning a minute later after managing to compose himself. I saw that his uniform was literally soaked in sweat.

Hosea finally got sent into right field for the fifth. Crosstown's philosophy was big on everyone getting at least a little bit of playing time, important game or not. A couple of batters into the inning, a hard-hit ball got past me at first and bounced toward him in right. Incredibly, without anyone else noticing, he had taken a seat in the grass and was playing an imaginary game, walking his fingers over his removed mitt, entirely in his own world.

The sudden action caught him by surprise, but thankfully the center fielder hurried over and held the runner to a stand-up double with a terrific throw. I looked over at Dad and Hallas, and couldn't decide if they were going to laugh or cry.

After some more dicey and close plays, Denny was finally able to retire the Bolts with no additional damage done, and we headed into the final frame still trailing just 3-1.

"Win or lose, you've all played really well today," Hallas admitted, and Dad seconded the sentiment. "Bottom of the order—now let's get some base runners!" I stole a glance back at Violet and our eyes met. She smiled and waved. I managed a thin smile back and tried to refocus on the game.

A vague feeling of dread started to come over me as I did the math and realized there was a sliver of a chance I'd have to bat yet again. *I could deal with us losing a close and well-fought game,* I bargained with myself. A nice and tidy 1-2-3 inning, and we'd find ourselves safely on the bus back to West Ridge, satisfied with our progress. I liked our chances at going down in order with Hosea leading off.

The first pitch hit Hosea squarely in the left shoulder, however, and he walked off the injury grimacing while being consoled by Hallas, before heading down to first base. Leon then took advantage of a dropped third strike and sprinted down to first safely as the catcher bobbled the ball back by the backstop.

The next batter, a jovial kid named Barry, worked the pitcher for several minutes before finally drawing a walk on a 3-2 pitch that was barely outside. The bases were loaded with no outs. I cheered wildly along with the rest of the team and crowd, but realized with horror that I would now probably have to visit the plate again, and possibly with the game on the line. Making the final out of the game was the worst case scenario, in my mind.

Grangeford strutted to the plate, a look of supreme confidence plastered on his face, then he turned with a determined stare and faced the relief pitcher, a large kid who was clearly tiring. The Bolts manager decided to leave him in. It proved to be a good decision, as he regained his control and got Grangeford to pop out on the fourth pitch.

Dad held his hands up, alerting that no runners could advance. Hallas slapped Ballanger on the back as he stormed back to the bench and sent his batting helmet skimming along the gravel. Mr. Ballanger was standing up in the bleachers with his hands on his head in frustration. Tyson was up next, and I took a deep breath to try to calm myself down as I stepped into the on-deck circle.

Three pitches later, an angry and dejected Tyson walked past me. "It's up to you, man," he said. "I don't know what happened. He's throwing all fastballs, so swing early." His voice sounded a mile away, like it was passing through thousands of gallons of water, but I nodded anyway. A low humming sound had taken over my entire head, and my body moved robotically, seemingly like it was on auto-pilot. I put one foot in the batter's box and looked down at Dad. He gave me the take sign once again.

"Two outs gentleman, we're running on anything," Hallas shouted, and again his voice sounded like something from a distant dream. I glanced back at Violet, and saw the entire crowd on its feet cheering, some of the kids jumping up and down in slow motion. The buzz got a bit louder. I turned to the pitcher, gripped my bat with all my might, and when he released the ball, I swung so hard I thought my shoulders might dislocate. The ball popped in the catcher's glove behind me predictably for strike one.

"Watch the signs!" Hallas yelled, and I looked down the line at Dad and received another take sign. His face was clouded, and when our eyes met for a brief moment, he seemed to make some sort of connection, and his frustrated expression turned to concern.

I swung again with every ounce of strength I could muster on the next pitch, and heard the ball snap into the catcher's mitt once more. Hallas screamed something about the signs again, but I pushed his voice to the back of my mind. I hardly dared look at Dad for my next instruction.

When I finally did, he was standing still, looking indecisively at me. After a moment, he began going through the signs, and on the third signal I couldn't believe what I saw. He gave me the green light to swing away. I saw him smile and mouth the words, "You can do this." By now the buzz was deafening, and I heard nothing else after that.

The feeling of an electric shock began in the palm of my hands and traveled up my arms as the Easton connected with the third pitch. As the pain of it began to slowly register, it was engulfed and taken over by an unspeakable feeling of joy. Incredulously, I watched the baseball travel away from me like it had been shot out of a cannon. It remained about a foot inside the first base line, and the fielder close to the bag never even flinched. Over at third base, I saw Dad push a confused Hosea toward home plate, and I suddenly forced my legs to begin the unfamiliar journey toward first.

I watched the ball continue to roll all the way to the outfield fence and sit there, waiting to be retrieved by the right fielder. As I rounded first, I could see Leon cross the plate and begin to celebrate with Hosea, followed soon after by Barry. I arrived at second base and came to a halt, fiddling with my batting gloves. I was dying to look up and see two reactions: Dad's and Violet's. But I didn't, deciding it was much more fun to imagine what they were doing, and soak in the moment in my own mind. The rest of the game after that was a blur.

18

picnic Table meditations

I hopped out of the church van back at home, riding high. My hands still rung pleasantly with the painful reverberations from the bat. I hoped it would last. I was worried that the realness of the entire sequence of events would soon begin to fade. I heard Corbin yell across the street to Jason, Johnny, CJ and Roach.

"He won the game for us! A three-run double!" He sounded as surprised as anyone else. After we'd stolen the lead 4-3, Denny had closed out the win with a bases-loaded fly out, and we'd all rushed the mound. I'd watched Leon join his family in the stands soon after and I'd finally grinned at Violet. She had given me a thumbs-up, and even her father had nodded at me pleasantly.

Standing with me in the front grass, Dad repeated himself again. "What a day—what a game! Can you believe it? You're the current league leader in RBIs, with three! What do you think about that?" he asked, slapping hands with me overhead. It was as if the fact that I'd ignored his signs to take those pitches had never occurred.

Hallas hadn't mentioned my insubordination at the post-game pep talk either. Even Hosea's bewildering decision to sit cross-legged and play make-believe in the outfield was glossed over. I realized that in some areas of life, positive results trump almost anything, and can cover over a multitude of sins. I was happy and proud, of course. But I tried to remember for sure if I'd actually even seen the pitch I'd smacked deep into right field—or if incredibly, my eyes had been closed.

The neighbor boys were drawn into the front yard by our celebration. Jason and Johnny asked Dad to come over and play with them, but he kindly brushed off their request and headed into the house with his arm around me. Corbin ran inside in front of us and shared the blaring headlines with Mom and Suzanne.

CJ and Roach paced up and down the sidewalk opposite our yard and attempted to get my attention, most likely so CJ could issue a new, fresh taunt. I was in too good of a mood to even care. Mom boldly suggested we go get pizza at Peppino's, a popular neighborhood joint. My siblings and I stared at each in awe; going out to eat at a sit down restaurant was a semi-annual occurrence, at best.

As we pulled into Peppino's a few blocks away soon after, I spied Mandy walking with Roxy along the sidewalk in the direction of Pack Rat Pete's. I started to roll down the window and wave to her, but suddenly thought better of it. She spotted me in the van as we passed, and stopped and stared at the church name emblazoned on the side. As we moved past, I could see Roxy continuing to elaborate on some story passionately without noticing us, but Mandy watched us closely as we slowed down and turned in to the pizza place's parking lot.

I was alarmed as I saw her try to walk faster and catch up to us as we entered the white stucco building, but to my relief she just missed us, and did not follow us inside. I didn't know what she'd had in mind. *Does she want to meet my family for some reason? Or tell me something important?* Either way, I didn't want to risk an awkward introduction in front of my parents and Suzanne. Corbin would definitely remember her name, and that would bring too many questions.

The last few days of June were pleasant and lazy ones, punctuated only with random sightings of Freddy or Nicolette down in the dead end. Whenever those occurred, I would quickly find something else around the house or yard to preoccupy myself with, and push the feelings of guilt and dread even further out of my mind. Mom arranged for Denny to come over one afternoon, and when his dad dropped him off, he rolled down his own window just long enough to congratulate me.

"There he is! Crosstown's own Darrell Evans. Some hit you had last Saturday! They might be moving you into the starting lineup before long," he called, and waved at my dad in the doorway. I thanked him for the compliment, then he pulled out and left.

Denny and I sipped on some lemonade Mom had made, and brainstormed things to do. We ended up just wasting hours sitting on top of the old picnic table, the same one that had always served as our soccer obstacle, in the bright sunshine of the backyard.

"What do you think next year will be like?" he asked, gazing up at a few stray wispy clouds floating motionlessly miles above us.

"Eighth grade? Probably more of the same," I said, knowing full well it would be completely different. I had measured my height the night before, and had been pleased to find I'd grown an inch in just a month. *Now I only have three or four inches and a thousand body hairs to go to catch up to the likes of Grangeford,* I told myself sarcastically.

"Which girls are the cutest in our grade do you think?" Denny asked casually. "Laura, Becky... oh, Jillian is hot! Those eyes, those lips," he offered, giggling. He started singing, slightly off-tune:

She was more like a beauty queen from a movie scene
I said don't mind, but what do you mean, I am the one

He stopped, implying he wanted me to take it from there. The words sounded vaguely familiar, but I couldn't take his lead and continue singing any further. I held my tongue regarding my thoughts on Violet. I wondered what Denny would think about my attraction to her. She never even entered his mind as far as a potential crush. Did that say something strange about him—or me? Regardless, I agreed with his assessment of the other girls, and threw out an observation of my own to keep the conversation moving along.

"Why does Tyson work so much? He hasn't had any time at all to hang out all summer," I complained. "Probably has a lot to do with his dad getting laid off," Denny replied seriously. "I overheard my parents talking about it. He really took it rough, I guess. There's not a ton of great jobs around here these days either, they said. Must be stressing them both out, wondering how they're going to scrape together enough cash for another year at CCCP. It's just the two of them, and that tuition is super steep."

I sat there in silence, realizing for the first time I'd never even considered the hefty cost of Crosstown, since faculty kids attended there free of charge. I felt bad for Tyson, and also admired him, having to pitch in and make his own way through life. I thought about the rest of the surrounding Rouge Park neighborhood, filled with blue-collar people—some divorced, some widowed. Some struggling with drug addiction and alcohol abuse—all of them getting up every day and carving out their own hardscrabble existences in a pitiless world, and inside I repented of my occasional disdain.

They had much more to be proud of than I did. What had I ever suffered through? How had I ever contributed to the modest excess my family enjoyed while plunked down right here in the middle of folks with a bit less?

I asked myself what exactly made the bankers, lawyers and dentists living over in West Ridge in their fine brick colonials—complete with lawns watered twice daily by timed sprinkler systems—think they were any better than the plumbers, cashiers, and mechanics over here in Rouge Park less than a mile away?

I looked over at Denny. He was a member of the former group, always wearing the coolest brand of shoes and jetting off on sporadic vacations, but it hadn't affected him in the same way it had some others in West Ridge. He never teased me one bit for the more spartan life we lived, content to chase after adventure and a good laugh whenever he was over in my neck of the woods.

I thought about Violet, from a stalwart family of the West Side club, just like Denny. I'd never seen her house, but I'd heard about it from other kids in my grade who had been invited with their families over for dinner. The song from Freddy's backyard that day several weeks ago filtered into my mind again:

In a West End town
A dead-end world
The East End boys
And West End girls.

I was a card-carrying member of the East End, and probably had no business setting my sights on a relationship with a girl from the

West End, I realized. Someone more familiar with life on this side of town, closer to my own station— Mandy, I thought. Then again, she seemed completely out of reach for so many different reasons.

The longer I thought about it, it seemed to me that Mandy actually belonged over on the West Side, but that Enrique's choices had doomed her to the East. She was a fish out of water; she was destined for higher places in life, and she knew it. A lot of the folks up and down my street were going to be clerks, gardeners, and barbers for the rest of their lives. They were aware of it, and had accepted it gracefully. Not always cheerfully, but they had learned from experience that making the jump from one side to the other was never an easy proposition.

In Rouge Park, I was a rarity: a kid from a poorer family going to CCCP. My education was going to be my ticket out of there. Mandy's drive and creativity were hers. Maybe we were more alike than I'd initially realized. I'd been given a big head start in life over most kids around here, and I knew I needed to make the most of it.

I hoped against hope that Ryne and Enrique's plans for Mandy's future were going to be stymied. Roxy might end up having a sordid, albeit short, career as a performer at Xanadu—but not Mandy, I vowed. I was willing to do anything I could to help her, I swore. I'd heard Shannon Worthy say before that true love is caring about the other person's well-being as much as or even more than your own. Was I falling in love with Mandy?

It was a lot to work out in one sitting. Before I knew it, it was time for Denny to leave, and I waved to him from the backyard as he left the same way he'd arrived. I sat staring up at the sky again, which was clouding over now. I felt bad for being ignorant of Tyson's situation, and an ambitious plot began to form in my brain.

I resolved to ride my bike the next day all the way down to see him at work at Revere Enterprises and take him lunch. I'd just seen a new

Taco Bell commercial that very morning touting their new 59 cent menu. I ran to the basement and pulled open the top drawer of my armoire and retrieved the envelope I'd been using to store extra cash in, whenever I actually had any. There were a half dozen crumpled-up one dollar bills inside, which would allow me to buy about 10 tacos for us to split between us, I calculated. Spare change that I kept in a mug beside my bed would supply the rest of the funds needed to purchase soft drinks.

Upstairs in my parent's sweltering bedroom, I pulled my dad's worn road atlas out from underneath the bed, where he kept it stored for safekeeping between family vacations. An entire page about halfway through it was devoted to Metro Detroit, and squinting, I ran my finger down to the crossroads that Tyson had mentioned when telling me about the place earlier in the summer.

It was a straight shot south from my house along the major road that divided Rouge Park from West Ridge, located down in a more rural suburb called Lakeview. Using the map key, I estimated it was about a ten-mile journey in each direction. I'd never been that far from home on my bike alone, I realized, and the prospect of such an adventure gave me nervous butterflies. It was a pleasant feeling, different than the ones before my trumpet solos in church, or a major class presentation. It was my own personal escapade, and I was eager to see Tyson's surprised face as I pulled up to the factory the next day with lunch in tow.

That night, I spent a good while playing Breakout on the Atari against Corbin. Since he was only five, I was able to beat him with relative ease, and after every round he'd make up some excuse, my favorite one being, "I pushed A! I pushed A!" Since there was only one large orange button on the joystick, I realized he must have heard this popular exclamation being made by a school friend who possessed a

Nintendo, complete with both A and B options.

I teased him mercilessly, until Mom finally announced it was time for him to head to bed. Watching the bouncing, pixelated ball slowly chip away at the eight layers of colorful bricks on the flickering screen made me think again about Mandy, and what she'd shared with me in the abandoned park about leaving. I selfishly hoped the multiple layers of her life in Rouge Park would hold her in as long as possible.

Mid-morning on the following day, which was a Thursday, I stopped by the kitchen where Mom was preparing stuffed peppers for the evening's meal, and I told her I'd be gone for most of the day.

"Where will you be at?" she asked without looking up from the stove.

"Oh, all over. Maybe Denny's, then Zane's, the park, who knows," I waffled. I stood there staring at her for a second watching her work, looking for the most imperceptible sign that she was even slightly suspicious. Observing nothing, I quickly said goodbye and pulled the Huffy from the shed outside. My only pre-trip check was to ensure the tires felt relatively inflated. Satisfied that they did, I patted my rear pocket to confirm I had not forgotten my wallet, and then I was off like a shot. It was going to be a hot day in early July for a long bike ride, but I felt energized and happy to be setting off on my expedition.

A few blocks into my ride I saw the triplets a bit ahead of me. It looked like they had a full load of the notorious brown paper bags again. I decided to take a slight detour and follow them as they turned into a side street. Dai came to a stop halfway down the block and ran up to a sad-looking pink bungalow with broken front windows. He handed a bag inside the window and sprinted back to his bike in a flash.

The other two triplets performed similar deliveries on the other side of the street as I followed from a safe distance. Just then, Duong lost control of his bike and it went skidding along the sidewalk, its handlebars scraping against the cement, dislodging his remaining brown bags. One of them tore open and scattered its glittering contents into the edge of the grass. He rushed to gather up several sandwich baggies with a small collection of white gleaming rocks in each.

I pulled up next to him and said nothing. He looked up at me with terror in his eyes as he frantically reassembled the recovered bags. "You can't say anything, Dav. Ryne will beat me to within an inch of my life again. Same for them, too!" He motioned for his brothers to go on ahead without him, trying to assure them nothing was wrong. They noticed me and hesitated, but then continued on their way down the street.

As I later learned to a fuller extent, the "crack" version of cocaine was a newer, cheaper, and even more addictive form of the infamous drug that had gained popularity in the largest, more impoverished cities all around the United States in the mid-eighties, in places like New York, Chicago, Los Angeles and Philadelphia. Starting the summer before this one, the trade had begun to spill over into the suburbs due to its inexpensive price point and ease of delivery. Now it had apparently arrived here.

It dawned on me in that moment that Enrique had most likely used his past connections in Chicago to create a pipeline to inject the new drug directly into Rouge Park, and had enlisted a horde of juvenile delinquents to deliver the goods by bicycle. The Biker Scouts were nothing more than a glorified drug distribution gang, staying under the cops' noses for the time being by appearing to be simply riding their bikes around and having fun, like kids had done on those same streets for nearly half a century.

"What have you guys gotten yourselves into?" I asked him, both surprised and disappointed. "So this is how you've had more money than you knew what to do with? Do your parents know what you're up to?"

"Of course not. No adults can know! That's the deal. And you can take that holier-than-thou attitude and stuff it—for real," he spat. "We don't have jack in my house. We're finally into some big money now, and that money is going to change everything for us. It's easy to judge if you have everything you need just handed to you," he accused bitterly. His comment hit pay dirt, and I considered backing off. But he looked scared, and I continued to plead with him to change course.

"I'm worried for you guys. Do you think this charade can last forever?" I warned. "The Biker Scouts aren't even really hiding what they're doing. You have to stop this. Who do you think is going to get in trouble if the police get wise to what you're delivering in these? You'd better believe Enrique will leave you and your brothers holding that bag," I warned, pointing at his next set of deliveries.

"It's too late. We're already in," he said despondently. "And I think you already saw what happens if you try to get out. Ryne and Chet said they'll burn my house to the ground with my parents inside if we tell anyone." He looked around suspiciously all of the sudden.

"Now, get out of here before one of them comes by here. They're always close. And, don't tell anyone—please!" He delivered his final plea in such a pathetic way that I was at a total loss for how to help them any further. I agreed for the time being and said goodbye, and turned my bike back toward my original route.

road Trip

Southeastern Michigan has some gently rolling hills but flattens out the closer you get to the Detroit River. I lived only a couple of miles from the iconic waterway, which in the 1980s was mostly known for being so dirty it was unsafe for swimming, and fishing in it was nearly pointless. Being close to the water had one benefit though: the land there was completely flat, which made riding a bike for long distances pretty ideal.

For miles, I passed by side street after side street as I traversed Rouge Park all the way to its southern border, and then entered into Northgate, a quiet suburb of brick bungalows where the houses and streets began to have a little greater distance between them. Twenty minutes after that I passed the sign announcing I had crossed into Brownsville. Larger homes on sizable tracts of land began to appear, and there were often several minutes between cross streets. The sun was getting higher in the sky when I saw a Taco Bell gleaming like an oasis ahead in the distance. I was parched, and I knew lunchtime was approaching when I pulled my bike into a rack and locked it up.

Ten bucks and ten minutes later, I continued on my way, and was relieved to see the sign announcing the Lakeview city limits before too much longer. I could ride for miles no-handed, a skill I'd worked tirelessly on for a couple summers previously, so carrying the bag of hot food wasn't an issue. In fact, I kind of relished the few looks I got as I passed folks on the sidewalk. I hoped that the ice in Tyson's large Mr. Pibb wouldn't melt too quickly. By the time I parked my bike outside two huge garage doors under the Revere Enterprises logo, my lower half was pretty sore and I was happy to have finally arrived.

The building was long, and three stories tall, covered entirely in tan sheet metal. There was a large version of the familiar logo mounted high above me, glowing light blue against the clear sky. The noise of machinery punctuated by men's voices calling out every so often wafted out through open windows as I walked toward a pair of glass doors announcing the way inside. I greeted the receptionist, and told her I needed to see Tyson Largo. She made a quick call and then went back to her typing. Her phone rang soon after.

"Revere Enterprises, Melanie speaking, how may I help you?" she said in a sing-song voice. There was a pause. "No officer, unfortunately we have still not seen Justus or Sigmund since late May, sir. Yes— Mr. Dawson has your number and I will have him reach out to you immediately if that should change."

She paused and listened for a minute longer. "Thank you for the update, sir. We are hoping for the same thing here at Revere Enterprises. Have an excellent day." With that, she hung up the phone, shook her head sadly, and went on with her work.

The steel door separating the lobby from the general plant opened, and with it a rush of warm air filtered into the chilly air-conditioned and carpeted welcome area. Tyson breezed in, completely surprised and happy to see me.

"Wow, don't tell me you rode all the way down here?" he asked incredulously. I appreciated his admiration, and then showed him the bag full of tacos and the icy beverage I had in tow. "Are you on lunch break yet?" I asked him.

"I can take it now, sure. Can you tell the foreman please, Miss Melanie?" he asked politely, and when she agreed to do so, the two of us headed outside and sat on a curb in front of the factory and ate our meal. As we talked I couldn't stop thinking about what I'd overhead Melanie say.

"Remember when you told me awhile back that two workers had been missing from the factory?" I asked Tyson. He did, and he wondered why I was interested. "I think I might know who one of them is," I shared, but chose my words carefully.

"Yeah, the guys around here talk about Justus and Sigmund all the time. Some of them were pretty good friends with them both. They sound like kind of rough characters, though," Tyson added. "Some of the stories I've heard would melt your ears. The 'lifers,' as they call the ones who do this job full-time and not just as student or summer work, live for the weekend and party pretty hard. They say it's to try to forget what a hard job this is during the other five days."

"Hey, thanks for the lunch," he continued. "That was awesome. You want to go inside and take a look around real quick?" he offered.

I definitely wanted to, not only to see the place for myself, but also to attempt to get even more information about Justus and this character named Sigmund. I agreed and we walked back through the lobby and into the stifling factory itself.

It was abuzz with the grinding sounds of metal being cut, and presses coming down with several tons of force, cutting shapes out of the aluminum sheets, which were then bent into different creative shapes to be used as gutter parts and accessories. As we walked around, I understood why every person I saw wore orange ear plugs and tank tops. It was dirty, noisy, and sweltering work.

No wonder they pay Tyson so much money to be in here, I marveled. A few grimy workers walked past us and looked at me sideways, and a few nodded silently. One man punched Tyson playfully in the shoulder, and we turned around to follow him back to his station so Tyson could introduce me.

"This is Travis Keane," Tyson said, and introduced me as well. Travis was tall, slender, with a wisp of a goatee, sharp blue eyes and veiny, muscular arms and hands. "He's been here at Revere for twelve years," Tyson bragged, but Travis shrugged it off. He was working hard in front of a massive press, equipped with two yellow buttons shoulder-width apart, to ensure both hands were safely engaged and not pulverized by accident as downspouts were formed between the slabs of descending steel.

"We were just talking about Justus and Sigmund. Justus lives in his neighborhood," Tyson shared, raising his voice above the surrounding noise. Travis nodded. "Yeah, I miss those guys. No idea what happened. They always used to work on that riveting machine right over there," he said, pointing to an empty station in the corner.

"They got so fast at it they'd meet quota by lunchtime, and would spend the rest of the day jawing with the other guys around here, including me. I heard a lot of stories, believe me," he said, looking melancholy. "No word of those two rascally brothers in your neck of the woods?" he asked me.

"Brothers—as in actual brothers?" I asked Travis, surprised by the news. He nodded again. "Yeah, they're pretty close. Justus tries to keep 'Ciggy' in line, but it isn't always easy," he said, raising his eyebrows.

"Ciggy?" I asked Travis. "Is that Sigmund's nickname?"

"Yeah," he answered, "That guy was always puffing on Marlboros around the plant. Couple packs a day kind of guy. 'Ciggy' is just shorthand for cigarettes, you know? Justus would give Sigmund a terrible time about stuff, claiming Kents were the best. Between the two of them, they could have kept an entire tobacco farm in business, to tell you the truth." He chuckled to himself.

"It's funny, they both have their favorites in everything," Keane continued. "Justus loves to drink Heineken, while Ciggy despises it. See that tower of bottles over there? Justus adds to it every time he finishes one. Says he's 'building a pyramid to rival Giza,' whatever the heck that means. For twins, they can be polar opposites sometimes. Justus is the cynical one, and Ciggy can find the positive in anything, it seems."

We then moved on to chatting about other things, but I tucked the brand new information about Justus and his missing twin Ciggy away for further analysis. Tyson let me know his lunch break was over, and that he needed to get back to sweeping up greasy sawdust on the other side of the plant. He thanked me again with a big pat on the back, and said he'd stop by in a few days if possible.

"Keep up the good work!" I called after him, intentionally trying to be supportive after the previous day's eye-opening conversation with Denny. I hoped it hadn't sounded too sappy.

I waved goodbye to Travis as well, and he motioned for me to come back over. "If you ever see either of those two characters around, give them my regards." I agreed to do so.

"Does Ciggy live in Rouge Park as well?" I asked him. "Not sure," Travis replied. "Just know he lives alone and doesn't even have a connected telephone. He went through a rough patch a couple years ago and ended up serving some time. When he got out recently, he resolved to make some big changes in his life. Started volunteering and everything. They even gave him his job back here at Revere. That's why it was so surprising when he stopped showing up out of nowhere. Seemed like he was finally getting some momentum."

He turned back toward the hulking machine he had been working at. "Safety first," he grinned as he put his protective glasses back on. "Don't want to lose a digit or something like that crazy fool Ciggy."

On the way out, I walked past the brothers' riveting station in the corner of the warehouse. Curious, I glanced around, and seeing no one paying any attention to me, I went closer and had a look. Two metal folding chairs, stacks of cardboard boxes, brown sheets of packing paper, and the riveting machine itself made up the work area.

Besides the mountain of empty Heineken bottles and some stray bags of chips, a pile of receipts and random pieces of paper littered the work table. A half-riveted piece of gutter still hung unfinished from the riveter, saved for a subsequent shift. Everything I saw pointed to a couple of relatively reliable workers who had planned to return to the job the very next day, but then something had apparently happened that changed their plans drastically.

The top piece of paper was folded in half, and I ventured to take a closer look. It was a letter from the West Ridge Cub Scouts organization. At the very top, I saw an elaborate eagle and fleur de lis logo. It was identical to the one that was carved into the blood-covered knife I'd found hidden inside the car at CJ and Roach's place. I inhaled quickly, and scanned the letter, glancing around nervously several times.

It was addressed to Sigmund, and it served to inform him in terse tones that, due to previous negative reports the group had received from parents of the troop, he would no longer be permitted to volunteer as an assistant leader. It had been signed and dated May 24th. I folded the letter back exactly as it had been, and continued on my way.

As I exited the factory, the bright sunshine and cooler air outside was a relief. Mounting my bike to begin the trek toward home I wondered, almost out loud: *Had someone associated with the Cub Scouts troop somehow been responsible for the murder of Justus, and also the disappearance of Ciggy?*

As is true of most journeys, the way home was much less exhilarating. There was no new scenery to admire, and the rush of succeeding in my quest began to fade. I was happy to have seen Tyson and deliver the unexpected meal, so that was no small consolation. But after a couple of miles, my legs already ached and the high and hot sun pounded down on me relentlessly.

I stopped about halfway back once I'd made it as far as Northgate, and spent the last of my traveling money on a large fountain drink from a convenience store. I found a shady spot next to the air compressor station and allowed myself a break to cool off and think.

I ran through the lineup of all the individuals I was aware of who could have had a motive to murder Justus. In the very beginning, I'd had my suspicions about Joyce Stickler, but now it seemed clear she was genuinely concerned about the well-being and fate of her brother. Dustin Crabb was obviously morally capable of the crime, and had been seen hanging out again with Justus recently, but I wondered if he had the stomach for such a heinous act.

Maybe Justus had become aware of Enrique's drug distribution scheme and threatened to reveal it to the authorities, I thought. If that was the case, perhaps he'd enlisted the ruthless Ryne to take care of his dirty work. I wondered if that had been the subject of the bits of various conversations I'd overheard between Dustin, Enrique and Ryne. Was the murder of Justus the "mess" that needed to be cleaned up?

And then there was Nicolette. I still felt that the crime was well within the limits of what she was capable of, especially after having a lot to drink. Lastly, this new tidbit about Ciggy made me consider if he was another victim, or perhaps even the actual perpetrator himself.

The threatening letter warning me to keep silent was another loose end. Who could have written it except Nicolette? She alone knew about the body buried in the backyard, and that I had stumbled upon it, as far as I knew. I needed to find someone to finally share this burden with, and perhaps see things from a different angle, or at least consider options I hadn't even thought of yet.

But who is the right person to trust? I asked myself. My parents were not an option, I acknowledged. Not that they were untrustworthy, but that they would feel compelled to escalate the situation, putting Corbin at immediate and unnecessary risk. *Plus,* I reasoned once again, *nothing can be done to help Justus at this point.* A slow, deliberate plan of action was what the situation called for.

I considered Tyson, and knew that he had been a steady, reliable friend through thick and thin. He had become somewhat involved now through the Revere Enterprises angle, and would perhaps have some good advice on what to do. Mandy crossed my mind as well; however, her proximity to Enrique, who surely had to be involved at some level, made that option simply too dangerous in my mind. I determined to find the right time soon to let Tyson in on my secret burden.

Hopping back on my bike, the sounds of the journey soon took on a familiar tone, as the streets grew closer together once more, and the clicking pattern of symmetrical pavement dividers lulled me nearly to sleep. The repeated down and up as I pedaled across each street turned it into a comforting rhythm. It was late afternoon when I zoomed past Pack Rat Pete's, and finally even D & D Market, marking my final turn. I sighed and stretched when I finally dismounted in the backyard and headed into the house.

"He's back!" Mom hollered up the stairs to my parent's room. "Well, you weren't kidding about being gone most of the day. Did you eat?" she asked. I said I had. "We called Zane's place looking for you, but they said you never arrived." She stood, hoping for further voluntary information about my whereabouts, but I offered none. Dad appeared at the bottom of the stairs, and the two of them looked at each knowingly. "Now, dear?" Mom asked. Dad nodded, and in unison they announced that my room was officially finished.

"You can move in today," Dad smiled, with his arm around Mom's shoulder. "It's been a long process, but we hurried and got it finished right in time for your birthday. When your friends come over, you can show it off to them." They both looked pleased as punch, and I thanked them profusely and hurried down to take a look.

When I walked in, I was surprised to see a new bunk bed against the wall, a small desk, a bookshelf against the outer wall underneath a bank of small windows near the ceiling, and an area rug in the center of the floor. Both bunks were made, and had matching sheets and bedspreads. Mom and Dad had been quite busy while I'd been on my adventure, and I now understood why they were so proud of themselves.

It had turned out even better than I'd hoped. I immediately began transferring things from my old room to the new one. "Thank you both, I totally love it!" I yelled up the stairs, and I could hear faint laughter as they enjoyed overhearing my excitement.

I spent some time organizing my hanging clothes in the closet opposite the bunk bed. Then, I moved my baseball card collection, comprising of several long white cardboard boxes, to beneath my desk, and then worked on arranging the smattering of memorabilia and tchotchkes that finally had an official place for display on top of the desk. I drove a finishing nail into the freshly-painted drywall above the desk and moved Mandy's license plate sign from my old room, leveling it by eye. I stood back and admired my new living quarters and smiled broadly.

"Dav, come upstairs!" Mom yelled down. "The triplets are here with Queen." I couldn't remember ever seeing the brothers taking the dog for a walk, and I came up to the side door at the top of the basement stairs. All three of the boys hurried back and met me there, dog in tow.

"Hey Dav! How's it going? Your mom says you have a new room," Duong said. "Can we come down and see it?" Dai asked. I relayed that message to Mom through the screen window in the living room.

"Not today, Dav. Someone needs to keep an eye on that dog." Mom was not a fan of canines, to say the least. "Go down and pull the curtains back so they can look in—they should be able to see everything pretty well from there."

Though the triplets were disappointed at her response, I acquiesced, and headed back down the stairs to my new room. The windows above the bookcase were located right at ground level, about six or seven feet off the ground. Mom had added a small rod that spanned across the concrete-encased recessed window, and a small cloth curtain for some privacy, when necessary. I couldn't reach it from the ground to pull it back, so I climbed onto the top bunk. I glimpsed three pairs of dingy shoes and Queen's paws waiting for the big reveal.

I stretched to reach the curtain, but my fingertips couldn't quite get there. I briefly considered regrouping and trying to use the desk chair, but resolved to reach just a little bit farther. Just as my fingertips finally grazed it, I lost my balance on the bunk and realized with horror I was going to fall.

I clutched wildly at the curtain for something to support me, but it provided no resistance and came tumbling down right along with me.

The side of my head hit the bookcase on the way, completely stunning me, and I eventually landed with a sickening crunch head first onto the unforgiving rock-hard cement floor below.

The bizarre vision returned once again in an instant. The image of the boy's body lying prostrate on the chilly bathroom floor at school swirled around in my mind and then came into focus again, this time with absolute clarity. I heard him moan as the tall, dark-haired man turned the youth's pale head up toward the sickly yellow light. I recognized his face immediately, as the scene faded once more—and the pain from the real world came rushing back in like a tidal wave.

20
fractured Fairy Tale

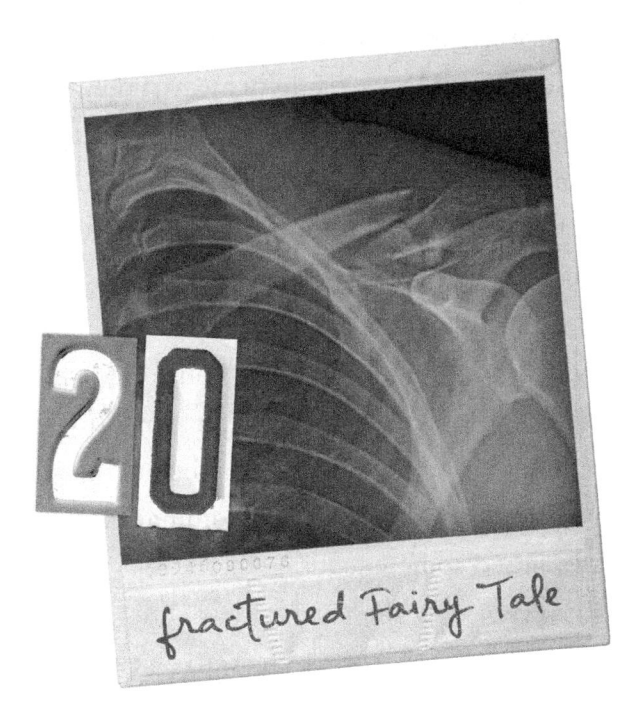

I felt blood trickling down my own face and briefly believed its source was the most concerning injury, until I tried to lift my head off the floor. Spasms of pain so intense I could hardly process them radiated outward from my shoulder, and I struggled to even make a sound. Something major was amiss, I realized frantically. I finally managed to yell for my parents, and after a few seconds I heard the triplets inquiring at the back screen door as both Mom and Dad flew past them and pounded down the stairs to investigate.

Mom was the first on the scene. She knelt down and tried to reorient me from my crumpled position wedged against the bookcase, but I screamed out and told her not to move me under any circumstances. Dad arrived a second later and stood assessing the situation, trying to put two and two together regarding the possible chain of events. He looked up at the half-opened curtain and saw the triplets, gathering again around the small window in an attempt to catch a glimpse of me. He waved them away rudely, as one would at a grisly crime scene to nosy gawkers. They eventually got the message and scampered away with wildly-barking Queen.

"Oh Dav, what happened?" Mom asked empathetically. I tried to cobble together the words to form a complete thought, but simply couldn't. "The triplets... The curtain... Top bunk... I slipped." It was enough though, and I could tell that both of my parents were struggling internally to walk the line between sympathy and lecture.

Mom brought a wet towel and gently dabbed at the blood on the side of my face, which she reported was coming from a nasty gash to my ear. Dad offered some encouragement, relaying that the cut itself wasn't too severe, that the ear had few veins or arteries to be concerned about, and that the flow seemed to be easing already.

As I lay there, still unwilling to move, I tried to explain to them that the actual crisis was the unseen structural damage to my upper chest and shoulder. I wondered if I had possibly shattered my sternum, or collarbone, or even my back, and that the agony was just registering elsewhere; or if I'd broken all of those bones simultaneously—which was feasible, judging by the amount of sheer inescapable pain.

Corbin and Suzanne had arrived to observe, and stood craning their necks around Dad to get a good look. Suzanne attempted to compare the event to when she'd crashed her bike into a tree, and I angrily denied the comparison.

"Or when I was running around the basement that one time and got my nostril caught on the armoire handle and it ripped," Corbin offered. This was a closer example I had to admit, simply due to the freak nature of that unexpected injury. His preschool class had given him a terrible time about it, as the stitches had been left in for several weeks, producing a crust of bloody snot in the repaired nostril. I was utterly confident that the pain levels of the two mishaps had nothing whatsoever in common, however.

"My shoulder," I finally gasped, "That's the real problem! I still don't want to move though, yet," I added dramatically, and with that, Mom sent Suzanne off to create a makeshift ice pack. Dad and Corbin disappeared as well, leaving me with my mom to marinate in painful silence. I nearly cried in front of her, as the implications of the event began to hit me in waves.

The baseball game on Saturday was definitely out. Pushing a lawnmower to make money with Zane? Probably impossible. My birthday party at the lake, swimming and roughhousing with friends?

I couldn't envision a way to enjoy any of it in the slightest. I stuffed the tears temporarily and gathered myself as Suzanne arrived back with some ice cubes wrapped in a dishrag.

Mom tried to apply it for me in the general area, but I rudely grabbed it from her and pushed her away. She recoiled and asked if there was anything else she could do. I could tell she was genuinely concerned and trying to help, but I was mad at everything and everybody. I sullenly refused to answer and both she and my sister eventually departed quietly.

I stayed in a heap next to the bookcase right where I had landed for what seemed like hours. I hadn't gotten a chance to plug in my digital alarm clock yet, so I judged time by the lengthening shadows that the sun cast against the far wall of my new room. I could hear footsteps above me as my family went on with their day. I couldn't decide if I wished they had stuck around longer, or if I was glad to have the privacy.

I actually just wished the entire thing hadn't happened. "Thanks a lot God," I said churlishly out loud, stifling a shake in my voice, knowing full well both my parents would have been shocked at my insolence toward the divine.

As my stomach rumbled, alerting me that the dinner hour was undoubtedly approaching, I finally tried to roll over and reach my lower bunk, not even one yard away. A shot of pure screaming pain shot through my upper body, and I returned to my initial position whimpering. Every few minutes after that, I made even bolder attempts, and eventually the promise of the comfort from a mattress and pillow trumped the agony, and I managed to arrive on the bed. Several experiments later, I successfully found a contorted position that allowed me to prop my head up and still avoid any major spasms of suffering.

Dad appeared a few minutes later, hauling two large stereo speakers from upstairs. I looked at him curiously, happy for a momentary diversion from my injuries, no matter how odd. He grinned at me as he turned sideways to fit through the door.

"Couple of things," he puffed, setting them both down. "I decided a while back it was finally time for us to get a new entertainment system for upstairs. Mom and I thought your new room would be the perfect place for this one." I was speechless, as this type of privilege was a rare occurrence.

He left again and returned shortly with the player portion of the older system, which was about ten years old. It had been a centerpiece in our living room for almost as long as I could remember. It played both records and cassettes, and in my mind, it was an absolute luxury. I thanked him as best I could in spite of how I was feeling. He nodded and continued to position it snugly against the wall next to the closet.

"And," added Mom, right on his heels, "we also thought that, under the circumstances, you could open one birthday present a couple days early." She handed me a box wrapped hastily in bright blue paper. When she saw me struggling to tear into it using my one remaining good arm, she took it back and finished the job for me.

Inside was a device in the shape of an arcade game. It was a realistic-looking version of the upright classic Ms. Pac-Man, only shrunk down to be just twelve inches high. I had seen them on television commercials before, and knew she had most likely heard me gushing to Corbin about owning one someday. I murmured a thank you to them both, and turned it on, and found the familiar beeps and theme music oddly comforting.

After promising to call up when I needed anything, including dinner, they left once more. I found it difficult to play the video game in my current state, so I eventually turned it off and contemplated their kind acts in silence. Soon I was lost in thought once more about the mysterious happenings surrounding the Mann clan. Restless sleep took hold of me without my knowledge.

In a dream-like state some time later, I glanced up and was shocked to see what seemed to be the crouching figure of Justus himself furtively passing by my bedroom window high above me. He was looking straight ahead and didn't look down at me.

I blinked several times as I lay there, wondering if I had imagined it. I had only had one significant interaction with Justus Mann in the past. I'd been waiting one day for Freddy when the lanky factory worker had come loping out into their front yard.

"I'm going to Cedar Point tomorrow. Ever been there?" he asked hopefully. I shook my head dismally. I'd been wanting to visit the roller coaster theme park on the banks of Lake Erie a hundred miles or so southeast of us for a very long time.

"I've only been there once," he had stated. "It was when I was about your age. A buddy and I took as many quarters as we could gather, and instead of standing in line for rides all day, we played endless games of skee-ball. Ever heard of skee-ball?" he had asked again, pausing until I nodded yes. I had tried my hand at the popular game that involved rolling wooden balls up a ramp into nested holes several times, and enjoyed it.

"Well, we played all day until every last quarter we had was spent. We traded our pile of prize tickets in at the front desk for a dozen plush toys. For all those, we were able to upgrade to a huge stuffed Frankenstein doll," he laughed. "Late at night, right before closing time, we got onto a roller coaster called the Mine Ride, and threw the monster right down into the big lake in the center of the twisting metal tracks. It just floated there for a bit, bobbing up and down, with the carp nipping at its ears, before sinking out of sight." He chuckled again wistfully, and stared at me waiting for a response.

"Is that what you'll do again tomorrow with Freddy?" I had asked. "Freddy? Nah. I'm not taking him. I'm going with a couple guys from work," he'd shrugged. "But, no. I'll take on all the big rides instead this time. Life is short, kid. It might be my last chance to ride the Gemini—or the Blue Streak—or that new ride they got now called the Iron Dragon."

"No more wasting time on pointless trinkets," he continued. "In the end, all the stuff we sweat and save for just ends up floating in the muck with the fish tearing into it." I had looked back at him in stunned silence. There had been something familiar in the way he had performed this last nihilistic diatribe, as I sat upright in my bed, staring up after the shadowy figure that had just passed by.

An indiscernible amount of time later, I seemed to wake again to find I was outside in the backyard alone. The moon was high in the sky and glowing with an amazing intensity, lighting up the surrounding yards while casting odd, long shadows between the chain link dividers. *How did I get out here,* I wondered? A shiver went down my spine as I gazed between the houses and saw Nicolette making her way down the street toward her house from the direction of Embers Bar, wailing as she went.

She had been beautiful once, I realized with a jolt. She had one of those faces that you could just tell, no matter what toll the years of disappointment and misery had taken. I wondered how exactly she had ended up just another vicious and angry alcoholic stuck in an unhappy marriage in this glorified hovel of a dead-end town.

In a West End town, a dead end world
The East End boys and West End girls

I heard a man's voice calling down the street after her—a familiar voice, but the owner's identity was just beyond my mind's reach. I struggled to grab onto it, because somehow I knew it was very important. He was sitting in a car that was slowly following her down the block, at barely more than an idle. His voice echoed as he recited her name, like it was coming from a time and place in the distant past. The shadow of the car crossed my driveway, and I observed that it was odd and bulbous, but it kept just out of view. My feet felt cemented in place as I struggled to crane my neck to see who it was.

Too many shadows, whispering voices
Faces on posters, too many choices

Another shadow took its place, and I realized it was that of a bounding dog. Horrified, I saw the galloping figure of Damian, the German shepherd from across the street, coming toward me with effortless speed. I slammed the gate to the backyard closed and folded down the long metal latch. My feet finally came loose and I backed away from the gate, only to see Damian leap the fence into my backyard with a casual bound.

I ran to the other side of my darkened house in a useless attempt to hide, as there were no bushes or obstacles to seek refuge in. Damian traversed the distance between us in two or three long strides, and I saw his slobbering, fanged mouth gape open and approach my shielded face. I yelled out in terror.

I awoke with a start to find Muffin licking my cheek, which, along with the rest of me, was soaked with sweat. It had been yet another bizarre series of dreams, and I was still safely in my own bed. My relief soon faded, however, as I made a quick move to prop myself up with one elbow and realized that the shooting pain in my throbbing shoulder was still all too real. The sound of my beating heart thumped like a bass drum in my ears. I judged by the dim gray light filtering through my new upper window that it was getting close to dawn.

My injured ear was tender to the touch, and I had a dull headache, but those complaints faded to the background in the presence of the ever-present shoulder pain. I struggled to get up, feeling weak from a complete lack of food and water since the freak injury. Apparently, I'd fallen asleep the previous evening and my parents had thought it best to just let me rest uninterrupted. With significant effort, I made my way up the stairs gingerly and attempted to go about my day.

"Any better this morning?" Dad asked as he folded up the sports section of the local rag, known as the Downriver Declarer. Hearing the expected answer, he tried to change the subject. "Check this out," he beamed, pointing at a small blurb on the back page. "Your game-winning double made the mid-week edition, and you're at the top of the board in RBIs in the entire Metro League, just like I predicted!"

I managed a weak smile in response, and as I returned to my

cold cereal, it hit me again that there was simply no way I could participate in the next baseball game. I didn't know whether to be happy or burst into tears.

Mom appeared with some pain pills. "I can set you up with a video or something," she offered, but I shook my head silently, and returned to the seclusion of the basement. All day long, life proceeded again above without me. I played endless rounds of Ms. Pac-Man, keeping a log of my high scores in a small notebook, crossing out each one as I eclipsed the last.

After one such record-setting session, I finally turned it off and stewed. I knew I had to see a doctor, but assumed it would be met with stiff resistance upstairs. My past history of injury embellishment was going to come back to haunt me in a major way, I feared. If I successfully convinced them to take me to the doctor, and somehow came back without a serious diagnosis, they would absolutely never believe a word out of my mouth again. I was sure of it.

"Honey, we need to talk," Mom said, appearing outside my new room. She came in and sat down at the desk. "Your birthday party is tomorrow morning after the game, remember. We can pack up the boys in the church van and head—"

"I can't!" I cried out, and the tears finally came rolling down freely. "I can't go to the game—I can't play in the game—I can't have a party! I'm hurt—bad. I know you and Dad don't believe me." I glared at her, and then my face fell.

"I know you never believe me. I probably wouldn't either, to be honest. I know I've stretched the truth in the past, but this time it's real. I promise." I stopped and tried to catch my breath with great heaves, and tried to get back control over my emotions, with some difficulty. Mom stood up and stared at me, a distant look in her eyes. Then, she studied my face for a moment, and leaned down to wipe away the tears.

"It's OK, dear. I'll be right back." She left and walked quickly up the stairs and all was silent throughout the house for a good while.

An hour or so later, Dad and I were sitting in an examination room at a nearby urgent care facility. X-rays had been taken, and we both sat silently and somewhat awkwardly in the sparsely-decorated square cell. A melancholy faded poster on which Big Bird explained the levels of pain to children was the only item of interest in the room. After what seemed like forever, the doctor returned, and I hoped my prayers for a dire diagnosis would be answered. Both my dad and I braced for the results, almost certainly for wildly different reasons.

"Well, young man. What we have here is what we like to call a greenstick fracture of the collarbone," he explained in a friendly tone, while pointing at the affected area on the developed sheet of film. The word fracture sounded quite serious, and I nearly shouted out loud in relief. As he handed my dad a stapled set of papers explaining how to nurse me back to health, I basked in the glow of having my pain officially validated in writing.

"So it's broken?" I asked, knowing that that badge of honor would earn me a huge amount of cache with my peers. "Well—technically, yes," the doctor acquiesced, "but nothing actually moved out of place, thankfully."

"Just imagine a young stick in the woods that you bend until it breaks, but it's too green inside and not dry enough to snap apart. It just bounces back and returns almost exactly to its original position." I nodded seriously at his explanation, silently savoring every word of the technical jargon.

"He'll have to wear this brace to protect his collarbone as it heals for several weeks," the doctor added. Dad took it from him and looked it over curiously. "What about sports—baseball for example?" Dad asked hopefully.

"I'm sorry, completely out of the question," the doctor apologized. So there it was: my promising season would be cut short in the prime of its young life. I made my peace with that fact internally even quicker than I would have thought.

Dad nodded, and looked somewhat disappointed. "What about," he paused for a second, "roller coasters, or other amusement park rides?" The doctor again ruled out both for the time being. I stopped and stared at my dad, confused. He looked back at me guiltily and shrugged, perhaps trying to send the message that he would have to explain more later.

"I'd like to see him again at the end of the month to check on his progress," the doctor requested, as he saw us out into the lobby, filled with other unfortunate souls. Dad agreed to schedule the appointment, and we left soon afterward.

He was still muttering about the amount of the bill as we rode home later with the windows rolled all the way down. I was taking small bites from the Whatchamacallit candy bar he'd purchased for me at a nearby gas station. It seemed like an olive branch, offered in an attempt to make peace between us for all the past misunderstandings regarding my mishaps.

I accepted the gesture both humbly and gratefully. As I savored another mouthful of the fabulous peanut-flavored crisp, I wondered what this unexpected development would mean for the rest of my summer.

home alone

21

A few days later, I watched in disbelief as the station wagon backed out of our driveway shortly after sunrise. Corbin waved to me, and Mom blew me a kiss from the front passenger seat that I usually claimed for lengthy road trips. In another minute, they were gone.

"Dav, this is going to be a difficult conversation, but we have to have it; so here goes," Dad had sighed as he walked into my room the day after my birthday. I had been passing the time by fiddling around with the new Polaroid camera my grandparents sent me in the mail as a birthday gift.

I had issued a small groan as I shifted positions on the hard tile floor. I was wearing my collarbone brace, and had also been trying to rework the wires to the speakers on the new-to-me sound system so they didn't show as obviously. His voice had been laced with regret and concern, and it commanded my full attention.

"Before, well, *this* happened," he had started reluctantly, pointing at the brace that extended over my shoulder and back and cradled the affected arm, "Mom and I had thought it would be fun to take a family trip."

"A family trip?" I had asked, my agitation growing. "Where to?" He had taken a deep breath, and lowered his eyes. "Kings Island." My eyes flashed angrily as the implications of the conversation began to dawn on me.

Other than perhaps Cedar Point, no other destination in the Midwest appealed to thrill-seeking kids like me more than Kings Island in southern Ohio. The roller-coaster extravaganza was a legendary attraction that I'd wanted to visit for years. His random questions at the doctor's office made complete sense now. To think that we all had to miss out because I'd been in too much of a hurry to show the triplets my new room seemed like more than I could bear.

"Dad, we can still go. I know the doctor said to take it easy, but I'm sure we can figure out something. Think of Corbin—and Suzanne," I had pleaded, grasping wildly for any foothold of a reason that I could come up with on the fly.

"There's more," he had continued in a melancholy voice. "The tickets we got were from that Mary lady at Farmer John's. She got a hold of them somehow for us at a discount, but they are non-refundable and only for certain dates. The dates are this week." He paused and seemed to try to build up the gumption to deal the final blow. "Mom and I talked extensively. We're still going. But you'll have to stay here."

"What?! With some kind of lame babysitter? I'm too old for that!" I had sputtered, outraged. I had stood up and paced out in the open area of the basement, waves of disappointment and resentment hitting me one after another. *I have to miss Kings Island? With the Beast roller coaster that my classmates drone on and on about at lunchtime? The Flying Dutchman, King Cobra?*

I could imagine the wind blowing back my cheeks as I whooshed down the first hill on one of the massive coasters. I'd wanted to go to an amusement park for so long. All I'd ever gone to thus far was a tiny park out in the wilderness of Kentucky with rides designed for little kids and toddlers. Dad had followed me out into the basement, and I could tell he was resisting the urge to match my intensity.

"No, no babysitter," he had said flatly. That news had stopped me in my tracks. "Mom and I discussed this as well last night. We think you're ready to stay here alone." He had smiled at my stunned reaction. "You've had a good stretch this summer, stayed out of trouble, been responsible."

The contortions of my face had softened a bit at the unexpected compliments. "We'll leave you some food, some instructions, and maybe ask a couple of adults to check in on you from time to time. I'm sorry that it has to be this way, but that seems to be the best decision for everyone involved under the circumstances."

A flurry of packing had taken place around me the rest of the evening following our conversation. Now that the elephant in the room had been addressed, and it was common knowledge that I'd have to miss the trip, the rest of my family felt free to prepare for traveling openly. My siblings handled it decently well, and managed to keep the teasing to a minimum.

I knew that secretly, they had little interest in roller coasters or thrill rides to begin with. Corbin would want to try to win a stuffed prize or two, and Suzanne would be satisfied to see some dressed-up themed characters walking around, and possibly posing for photo ops with them. *The experience of Kings Island will be totally lost on them both*, I realized with a frown. It almost seemed too cruel a fate.

Immediately after they had loaded up and backed out of the driveway the next morning—calling out from the car with last second instructions and caveats like only watching the sitcoms and cartoons highlighted in the TV guide, and being sure to brush my teeth and be in bed by 10 o'clock—the house fell completely silent.

Soon after they departed, I walked out onto the front lawn, taking in the pleasant morning sunshine, and surveying the realm I'd command for the next few days. I hadn't been outside much since the injury. CJ Crossdastreet was across the way whining about something to Roach, and when he saw me, he dropped what he was doing and came parallel to me in Jason and Johnny's yard. Roach stood planted right where she had been, working on a Blow Pop.

"Whatcha doing today? And what is that stupid contrition on your shoulder?" he began, stupidly using the wrong word. Rumor had it CJ would be repeating the same grade once again in the fall. "Your mom and dad get violent with you for refusing to do your chores? Do you have to read your Bible for an hour and write an essay on it or something?" he laughed snarkily. Once he'd figured out that we were churchgoers, it was a theme CJ often poked at to see if he could rile me up.

"Nope. I'm completely on my own for the rest of the week. I can do pretty much whatever I want. Parents left town for Ohio," I bragged loudly, wishing I hadn't immediately after it came out my mouth. A handful of Biker Scouts, none that were too high up the food chain or recognizable to me, drifted by on their BMXs right as I said it, and I hoped they hadn't understood or made a connection.

CJ looked genuinely impressed at the revelation and stopped his taunts. Jason and Johnny had been listening to our exchange through an open window and came outside to finally get a good look at my shoulder and arm brace. Roach sauntered over and gazed at it silently, cracking through the hard candy shell of her sucker noisily to access the nucleus of gum encased deep inside, like a fly suspended in amber. The brothers excitedly had me confirm the details of my fascinating injury. The triplets had breathlessly shared the report with them immediately after the accident.

"How long do you have to wear it? Does it still hurt? Was there bone sticking out of your skin? Can you ever play baseball again? Are you going to sue the bunk bed company?" The questions were simultaneously annoying and flattering. It was nice to be the center of attention again.

It dawned on me that I'd been the center of attention in my own house for several of my formative years, until Suzanne and Corbin had arrived in succession, sucking all the oxygen out of the house with their diapers, needs, cries and demands. This week would be a welcome return to some solitude and freedom to do basically whatever I wanted, just as I had brashly proclaimed to CJ.

From the corner of my eye I saw some of the same Biker Scouts returning down the block toward us, and their numbers had now grown. I excused myself from the conversation and quickly darted back inside the house. I plopped down on the couch in the living room, and experienced that frustrating feeling of indecision you sometimes have when you finally get all the time in the world, but then have trouble actually picking something to do first.

I glanced up at my 8 x 10 framed school portrait hanging in the hallway from the year before. A faint impression of pencil on my upper lip, and additional evidence of frantic erasing and smearing was obvious to me personally, but probably not to anyone else unless they were specifically looking for it. When the cellophane envelope, which contained one big glossy print and a smattering of wallet sizes, had been handed out to the class, I'd grandiosely removed mine and proceeded to illustrate a mustache as my classmates looked on in awe.

It hadn't take long for me to realize the implications of my rash stunt and switch gears to try to remove it, the efforts of which were mostly in vain. I stared at the old me for a moment, and told myself that I'd come a long way from the fallout of that past folly to where I sat now, trusted alone in my own house for the span of several days.

A knock at the door made me jump. I assumed that the Biker Scouts had become aware of my solitude and arrived to finish the job that Ryne started several weeks before. I remembered his warning to not be caught alone all too well. I peered out from behind the half-open door and was startled to see Mandy standing on the front porch. I hadn't seen her in several days, and she was a welcome sight.

She had on a pink and yellow-striped sleeveless shirt with a high, banded neck and cut-off jean shorts. Her hair was pulled back in a cute ponytail of some sort pointing nearly straight up, and her burnt orange lipstick jumped out at me like it was almost radioactive.

What is she doing here? I asked myself nervously. I gathered myself for a second in the shadow of the door, smoothed out the wrinkles from my favorite T-shirt—a bizarre mash-up of Daffy Duck and vilified Libyan dictator Gaddafi emblazoned with the corny tagline *I'm Deathpicable*—and then casually stepped out into the sunlight streaming through the entryway.

"Hurry up, let me in before any of them see," she quickly commanded, and I robotically obliged, opening the screen door. She swept past me into the living room, and took an investigatory look around the entire first floor, without bothering with any niceties or even waiting for an invitation from me.

"Cute and simple," she assessed. She smirked as she found the pencil mustache portrait. "What is this, sixth grade? Wow, you've grown." I said nothing in return, but internally, I beamed with pride.

"Before who sees us?" I asked, growing slightly concerned. She continued to peer into all the rooms on the main level, and never answered that line of questioning. "You're not armed with a weapon this time, are you?" I asked with a nervous laugh.

"So, where do we start?" she asked, ignoring me again. I saw that she was carrying an orange and brown burlap bag, and it appeared to have license plates and an assortment of tools that she'd deemed necessary for our map project. She looked at me with mild annoyance.

"What's up with that?" she asked, and I wondered if she was referring to my arm harness or the gaudy shirt. I guessed that she understood its pun, seeing that Muammar had been an extremely unpopular world figure ever since the bombing of a Berlin discotheque.

"Aren't you going to ask how it happened?" I queried, finally referring to the brace. She shrugged. "The triplets told Roxy a couple days ago. Sounds pretty painful. Are you going to be able to help on this map, or will I have to do literally everything myself?" She stood with her hands on her hips waiting for my response. Her accusation jolted me into action, ready to prove her wrong.

We set up in the open area of the basement, and a sudden epiphany struck me. I ran out to the church van, and was ecstatic to find that my Dad had indeed left the overhead projector in the back of it when VBS had ended. I called to Mandy and she helped me carry it down to where we were working. I ran the handful of steps over to my old room and rifled through some loose sheets on the floor and found the page containing the outlines of the fifty states that I'd been saving. I turned around to find Mandy right in front of me, peering past me into the dim room.

"So this is the place where the injury happened, eh?" she asked. "No, this is my old room," I said dismissively. "My new one is over here." I prayed that I'd left it relatively clean, and that I hadn't left a pair of underwear on the floor or something. We walked over to it together. She sat down on the bottom bunk and took a long look around. I reclined awkwardly with my hand on the desk, wondering where this was going.

"Wait a second, really?" she asked suddenly. She was staring at the wall above my desk now. "You bought one of my signs?" She looked at me, and I couldn't read her face well enough yet to assess if she was pleased or weirded out.

I nodded. Her perfectly symmetrical and flawless face broke into a pleasant smile. My heart ached at the sight, and her unflinching eyes seemed to pierce through me. I robotically turned and said we'd better get back to work on the map. I realized once my back was to her that for some reason I felt vulnerable and afraid. *Afraid of what exactly?* I asked myself. The truth was I was becoming deathly afraid that the girl in my basement at that moment would end up hurting me deeply in the end.

Over the next few days, Mandy and I worked on our project nearly non-stop. She would arrive mid-morning, and after the second day she would come right into the house without even knocking, and pound down the stairs to our work area in the basement. On the first afternoon, I called Tyson, and asked if he could break down a pallet from Revere and drop the wood by for us. He agreed, and showed up with a stack of perfectly weathered planks on the second morning even before Mandy had arrived.

For some reason, I decided once again to keep her existence hidden, even from him. I was somehow enjoying having this secret all to myself. I showed him what I was working on and he was pretty impressed. He said he had to leave, explaining that another hot day of toil down at the factory was in store for him. I thanked him heartily, and watched as he ran back out to his dad's car idling in the driveway.

On the second day, Mandy brought her boombox with her, and set it at the top of the basement stairs to ensure she got a good radio signal. Soon afterward, the driving rhythms of Top 40 tunes filled the basement. She seemed to know all the words to every single song.

"Oh yeah, Lisa Lisa! I love this one," she exclaimed, and then sang along with the current chart-topper while we worked.

Today started with a crazy kiss
On our way home
We were in for a surprise
Who would have known
Who would have thought that we would become lovers?

I gulped involuntarily, and wondered if she could possibly be thinking the same crazy thoughts as I was. I was pretty sure the answer would have been a resounding no. I said nothing, and continued to work on tracing the map outline onto the sheet of paper stretched out like a curtain hanging from the I-beam above our heads.

As friends we were so tight
I think I love you
From head to toe.

She stopped and looked over at me, as we lined up the pallet planks and attached them together with some wooden cleats she'd found in the alley behind Embers Bar. I held my breath, wondering what she'd say next. The light from the overhead projector behind her cast a glow around her head that was almost angelic. The lyrics of the song playing in the background were now all-consuming in my head. There was absolutely no doubt that I loved her in that moment as completely as the song described.

"You don't seem to know any of these songs. Don't you ever listen to the radio?" she asked. I reluctantly explained that my parents limited my music options, requiring that I listen to classical music and movie soundtracks instead of the era's popular hits.

"Straining at gnats and swallowing camels, eh?" she sighed. The comment took me aback. I was familiar with the passage she'd referenced from the book of Matthew, but was frankly surprised to find out that she was as well. Also, I found it slightly offensive that she felt comfortable labeling my parents with such a damning description, even if I agreed in principle with some aspects of her assessment. She returned my look and seemed to read my mind.

"You don't have to go to church every time the doors are open to know what the Bible says," she said matter-of-factly. "And, I don't mean to be harsh toward your parents. I just happen to know a lot of the things that go down over at Crosstown among some of its most illustrious members, let's just leave it at that. That freak Dustin has no filter whatsoever."

"Anyways," she continued, "I have a ton of tapes I think you'll really get into. I'll drop them off sometime and you can play them on your stereo. I'll get you cultured one way or another." She paused and looked up at me.

"Music raised me. It taught me everything I know. And it reminds me every day of what I still don't understand." She continued to rattle on about her favorite musicians and we continued to work hard together on the project well into the afternoon.

By the end of that second day we had cut out paper templates for all fifty states, and as an experiment, I attached one of them to the license plate from Minnesota with some painter's tape. I grabbed the tin snips from Mandy's bag and carefully began to slice into the soft aluminum, following the intricate lines of the template into every indentation and around every curve.

Mandy watched transfixed, her eyes following every movement of my hand and the blades. In a few moments, I completed the cut and slowly removed the paper from the surface of the car tag. I held forth the outline of the Land of 10,000 Lakes for us both to admire in the dim light of the basement. Without thinking, we slapped each other an exuberant high five, and I realized that it was the first time we'd ever actually touched.

Did I linger too long? Too awkwardly? I asked myself frantically. I searched her face for any sign of how she felt about it. She was too busy contemplating what state to do next, and scrambled to find the paper shape of Illinois. The burnt orange sun was starting to stream through the basement windows as it raced down toward the horizon when she finally excused herself for the evening.

I said goodbye at the front door and watched her walk away, and after spending a brief moment relishing our day alone together, I went straight to the kitchen to fix myself a fine dinner of corn flakes mixed into vanilla ice cream, and a chocolate pudding cup for dessert.

tragic Developments

The screen door clanged shut mid-morning again on the third day, and feet pounded through the living room above me, sounding rather loud even for Mandy.

"I'm down here, Mandy. Come on, let's get going on some more of these states," I called up. "Oh, and grab a couple of those Mello Yello cans in the freezer for us. I put them in a while ago, and they should be good and cold now. It's going to be a hot one again," I suggested loudly.

"Coming, darling!" a voice said sweetly in a falsetto from the top of the stairs, followed by laughter. I froze as Ryne, Chet and two more of their sidekicks thundered down the stairs toward me. I couldn't believe they were in my house, uninvited, and I waffled back and forth in my mind between utter fear and outrage.

"We heard you might be going it alone this week and wanted to swing by and see if you needed anything? Better be careful—as anyone can see by looking at that ridiculous thing on your arm—most accidents actually occur in the home," Ryne snickered. One of the other punks pushed me to the floor roughly while his partner trashed the table that Mandy and I had been working at, scattering random plates and tools to the ground with a resounding crash.

"Ooh, doing a little craft together are we? How adorable," Ryne continued. "Mandy never has made the best choices in friends. Speaking of friends, those pathetic triplets totally spilled the beans on you. You just can't seem to stop digging around in things that don't concern you." He glared at me now, his nostrils flaring.

"So, just to make sure you don't get any ideas in your head about involving your parents, or the police, I thought we'd come by and clear things up. Something real big is coming up, and I'm not about to let the likes of you get in the way." Chet had joined in with the other two, who had finished destroying our work table and had found their way into my new room like foraging rats.

The sound of glass, metal and plastic hitting the tile floor made me cringe. I could tell the contents of my desk and the objects displayed on it had been thrown clean off, and the sound of splintering wood followed close after. I stayed where I was on my back on the basement floor, struggling to think of what to do next. Ryne towered over me, daring me to fight back. But I was beaten, and I knew it.

I wondered what might happen if the boys turned their fury away from inanimate objects and toward me instead. *Is that what happened to Justus?* I asked myself. *Had he gotten in the way of their plans—or more specifically, Enrique's? A half dozen of these rabid dogs could have brought Justus down without too much trouble, perhaps at the craven club owner's instruction,* I realized.

A polite knocking at the front door upstairs startled everyone. Ryne lifted his hand, and the other three boys stopped their destructive plundering at once. He motioned for me to not say a word. Another series of knocks followed. I knew it wasn't Mandy, simply because she wouldn't have waited for my reply. I wondered who it was, but remained silent.

The voice of Asperat now traveled into the house, as he called my name and waited to hear something back in return. I could imagine him peering in the front screen, shielding his eyes from the bright sun to assess what I might be up to inside. No doubt my parents had arranged this visit previously to ensure I hadn't burned the place down. Awkward silence followed as all four of us remained motionless. Chet walked up to whisper something to Ryne, but was pushed away dismissively.

Without thinking, I impulsively leapt to my feet and shot up the stairs like a bolt of lightning. A shock wave of pain traveled through my collarbone as I'd used my bad arm to propel me forward, but I completely ignored it as I scrambled to safety into the kitchen, and gathered myself as best I could to answer the front door.

Asperat waved at me, and he looked relieved that I'd finally made an appearance. Farther back in the house I could hear soft steps ascending the stairs to the main floor in my wake, and a familiar creak notified me that the vicious goons were slipping out the side door and into the back yard.

"OK if I come in, Dav?" he finally asked, tilting his head slightly, and I realized I had been frozen in place staring ahead at him for an uncomfortable second or two. Not wanting to risk him seeing the tumult in the basement, I stepped outside with him, smiling broadly. "Kind of messy in there," I grinned. "Not to worry, I'll have it all back together when my parents arrive home tomorrow. Have you heard from them at all?"

He replied that he had not, and confirmed that this drop-by had indeed been commissioned by Mom and Dad. After a few pleasantries and standard questions as to my activities and well-being, he grew quiet. He looked down the block wistfully for a moment, and then turned back to me. "Are you sure everything is OK, Dav? You seem to have something heavy on your heart, just below the surface. Forgive me if that's too intrusive, but I wanted to ask just in case you need to confide in someone."

I studied his face, and for one alarming moment I considered telling him all about Nicolette, and Justus, and the bloody knife, and missing Ciggy, and the drugs and the violence and the Biker Scouts and the threat to Corbin; but I pursed my lips and shook my head.

"Everything is good," I lied instead. He nodded, and continued to gaze down the street toward the dead end for another moment. Finally, he said he'd be off, and I stood up along with him from the concrete front steps where we had been sitting and bade him farewell, thanking him for the impromptu visit. He drove away from the house seconds later, passing the triplets' house and disappearing from view.

I looked up and saw the three Ly brothers coming around the corner toward my house, and bolted inside, closing the front door quickly. They were the last ones I wanted to see at the moment. I was angry that they'd so easily thrown me under the bus to Ryne and his minions. I closed the front shades, and then with a deep breath, braced myself for the thankless task of cleaning up the lower level after the pillaging intrusion.

The sight of my new room enraged me and, being alone, I angrily swore and spat Ryne's name as I picked up the mess. The wooden chair to my desk was in pieces, the legs and back separated from the seat. I imagined Freddy's voice gleefully chanting his favorite hit again:

You think you're mad, too unstable
Kicking in chairs and knocking down tables

The sign Mandy had made was on the floor, dented and splintered, one letter hanging from a single nail. The rest of my things could be salvaged, but I knew the chair had to be fixed before my parents saw it, or the questions would never end—eventually leading straight to Mandy, the Biker Scouts, and everything else.

Down the street, I knocked on Dmitri's front door. I hoped the convenience store owner would be home, and awake. I was partially correct, as a groggy and unkempt Dmitri answered the door rubbing his eyes, dressed only in a tank top and boxers. Once he recognized me, he opened it wider and, after looking up and down the street, ushered me inside.

His house was a mess, and full of half-filled cardboard boxes. Dagmar appeared, with a load of dinner plates and saucers wrapped in off-white packing paper. She gave me a weak smile but said nothing, and continued on a beeline to the nearest box.

"Are you leaving?" I asked, the sad answer already obvious to anyone. I hadn't seen a moving sign out front. Dmitri scratched his head, and seemed to consider several ways of responding to my query.

"Lansing. I have a cousin there. This mess with the crack, the gangs, the pressure—it hasn't reached over that way yet. We can start over again there. And leave this chapter behind." He talked in a low voice, and it was clear that Dagmar wasn't pleased with the decision.

"I understand," I said gravely. I told him about the incursion and damage to my room. I asked if he had any wood glue and some clamps I could borrow, and after expressing his outrage at my own predicament, he disappeared into a back bedroom momentarily and returned with both. I promised to return them as quickly as possible, hoping for a clue as to when they would be leaving. He didn't offer any more specifics, except to warn me not to share the information with anyone. I agreed, thanked him and returned home to continue my repairs.

I was crestfallen to see that Mandy had arrived in my absence, ready to continue our work. She had begun putting our project area back together, righting the table and the overhead projector, and cleaning up the scattered license plates and dozens of wire nails. She was now standing in the middle of my new room gazing at the damage in shock. She was wearing jean shorts and a black Chicago White Sox ball cap, and even though I was not a fan, I thought the hat looked good on her.

She looked at me angrily and skipped over pleasantries or a morning greeting. "What happened down here? Who did this to your things?" I didn't answer, and she pressed me further. "Fine. Keep all your secrets from me." She looked extremely perturbed, but continued to pick up more objects from the floor. She attempted to put them all back on my desk in the right place, failing utterly.

"What do you mean? What 'secrets' exactly?" I asked, my curiosity piqued. She turned toward me once again. "I've known for some time you have a secret, Dav. The way you look around outside, the way you refuse to go into the dead-end in front of Freddy's, the random questions you ask—I wish you trusted me." She walked back out of the room, and finished cleaning up the random tools on the ground in the basement. Thankfully, that area was already nearly back to its original state. I followed her, my confidence and ire growing somewhat in conjunction.

"OK. You really want to know, do you? It was Ryne, Chet and those other employees of your dad. I mean—sorry—your step-dad." I retreated from my accusation somewhat mid-sentence, when I saw from her eyes that she was offended by my statement.

"That's a good start. Mind telling me why they decided to march right in here and raid your place? It couldn't have been because you happen to ride an off-brand bicycle. What else did you do? Or—what else do you know?" she returned. Now that I had started, more came tumbling out.

"The triplets told me everything—how the system works, what they're delivering. I told them to get out of it, but they can't. They must have tattled on me to Ryne. And it sounds like he's worried, because something really big is going down soon." Mandy grimaced at the last statement, and nodded quietly. Apparently this revelation was not news to her.

"Yes, that's true." She looked at me intently, then continued. "OK. You trusted me, so I'll trust you." She sat down next to me and huddled up closer. "He doesn't know that I know, but Enrique is expecting a massive shipment of drugs in the next few weeks. It's the biggest deal he's ever done, and it will set him up for life if it goes down without a hitch." She set her jaw and stood up to pace.

"I'm talking big money this time. I'm still hazy on some of the details, but I overheard him on the phone a few nights ago. I'm sorry you've been pulled into all this," she sighed. "I'm not sure what to do about it." She sat down in a metal folding chair and looked lost in thought.

"Let's think about something else, then," I suggested, motioning back to our project, and pulled up the second chair next to her. She handed me the tin snips, and for a while we worked silently, not having to even tell the other person verbally what to do next. We were ticking through the states one by one, and gaining steam as we became more dexterous with the metal and snips.

It was another sweltering July day, and even though we were in the basement, the air was humid and thick. I looked over at Mandy, hard at work, straining over a particularly stubborn piece of steel, her skin glistening with sweat. It dawned on me that we were both artists at our core. We were visual people, and an image or a simple glance meant more than a thousand phrases could ever hope to. Spoken words would never be able to convey the full complexity of what we felt—for others, or even for each other.

"How will we know where to attach each state?" she wondered, looking at the rectangular set of planks that we'd sanded and stained. "The overhead projector again," I replied. "Let's attach Minnesota as a test."

I flipped the switch of the projector in an attempt to cast the map image onto the upright plank canvas, but the bulb had apparently been smashed in the melee. Frustrated at the delay, I searched some nearby shelves for a replacement, but it appeared to be a special custom bulb.

"There's something else, though—isn't there?" Mandy asked abruptly. I paused where I stood, looking the other direction. Every ounce of my being strained against telling her my secret. I walked back over toward her and looked deep into her huge green eyes, as big as saucers, staring at me expectantly, and I wanted to dive right into them.

In an instant, I shook off all my inhibitions and vowed to take the plunge. In an onslaught of words, the details of that fateful day a few weeks prior gushed forth. She listened in silence for the duration of my sordid tale.

"I can't get his face out of my head, Mandy. The dead eyes, staring at nothing. The dirt caked in his mouth. The fact that Freddy won't ever see his own father again. That he's still buried in that backyard just a stone's throw away. That I haven't found the courage, or taken the opportunity, to tell anyone in the world. Am I a horrible person?" I asked her.

She looked rather pale, and it took a couple of moments for her to reply. "Well, you said you hadn't told anyone. You've told me now," she smiled weakly. "It can be our secret. No one else in the world has to know. No one else would be able to understand. Let's keep it that way forever, Dav," she urged.

That suggestion made me feel cold in a way I hadn't expected. "No, we really should tell someone else now, right?" I asked. "You'll help me do it, won't you? I just don't know if I have the strength." She looked away.

"Plus, I think there is one other person that knows and can corroborate my story," I continued. She turned back to me with a start. "Wanda said she saw someone else digging back there behind the garage before Freddy and I were. I've been dying to ask her about it, but didn't know how without explaining why."

I thought I heard a floorboard above me creak every so softly. My blood rose subconsciously, as I was sure that the Biker Scouts had returned to finish the job they'd started with me earlier. But then I heard a soft meow and determined it was most likely just Muffin performing one of her random afternoon chases after phantom shadows. It reminded me it was time to feed her, so I filled her bowl which sat just outside my room with some dry chow. She heard it and bounded down the stairs to dig in ravenously.

"There's more," I continued, carefully. "I found the knife the killer may have used on Justus." Her eyes darted back to me expectantly. "Do you have it here?" she asked slowly and dreadfully. I shook my head. "It's still hidden safely, for now," I replied cryptically, and didn't offer any more details on its whereabouts.

Mandy sat back down in the metal chair. She started to say something else, but held back. After a deep breath she started again. "The police might think you did it, Dav. It's—it's too risky. Too many variables—yes," she nodded to herself. "Better not to involve anyone else in it. No one can bring that poor man back now." I knew what she said was true; I'd consoled myself with the same fact often.

"Don't you think that some secrets should remain that way forever, if they don't hurt anyone? I don't want to see you get blamed for something you had nothing to do with," she said. It had never dawned on me that my confession might bring unwarranted suspicion in my own direction. It caught me off-guard and I paced in front of the washing machine.

She suddenly stood up, and looked conflicted. "I have to go," she announced. "Now?" I asked. "It's still pretty early," I argued. "My parents come back tomorrow, and then we'll have to stop meeting this way."

"Why?" she asked. I didn't have a good answer to give her off the cuff. The truth of the matter was that they almost certainly wouldn't have allowed me to hang out alone with a member of the opposite sex, but I avoided admitting that to her outright. "It's—well, it's complicated," I waffled.

She looked frustrated by my ambiguity, and then promptly bounded up the stairs and out the back door. "See you tomorrow!" I called after her, but I didn't hear anything from her in reply. I sat for a long while alone in the folding chair, listening to the birds chirp from the open side door screen, wondering if, and hoping that, my trust in Mandy had been well-placed.

I woke up earlier than normal the next morning to get a head start on cleaning the house from top to bottom. Mom had called from the hotel in Cincinnati the previous evening and let me know that they would be arriving home around lunchtime.

I fixed myself some more cold cereal for breakfast and sat shoveling large mouthfuls between sips of orange juice when a flashing blue light caught my eye through the kitchen bay window. I stood up, and squeezing between two dining room chairs, pushed back the lace curtains my mom had sewn and craned my neck to see what was going on.

Two police cars with their lights ablaze were parked at odd angles the next street over, right next to the triplets' house. I could see several officers walking swiftly in multiple directions, and a small crowd of onlookers gathered. One officer was trying to corral them all and get them to back away from the scene.

My heart jumped into my throat as I imagined what might have happened to one of them. I hurriedly pulled on my shoes and socks and ran outside into the cool morning air, making a beeline for the growing crowd, and caught sight of the somber face of Officer Devon Collier almost immediately. He looked at me for a split second, an inkling of recognition crossing his face, but then returned immediately to pushing back the throng. As I worked my way closer, it became obvious that the center of attention was not at the Ly house after all, but a few doors down.

An ambulance was parked in the driveway of Wanda's house, and several emergency personnel and additional officers were going in and out of her propped-open front door every few seconds. I elbowed my way even closer, and saw CJ, Roach, Jason, Johnny and Roxy standing shoulder to shoulder in the first row of observers, almost on Wanda's front lawn. Roxy had tears streaming down her face, and seemed to be carrying on in an hysterical and dramatic fashion. It was hard to hear what she was saying above the general din of the crowd.

"Back up please, everyone. This is an active crime scene! Please go back to your homes and make room for the professionals to do their jobs," Officer Collier demanded loudly. His partner, Officer Simmons, continued to firmly push everyone back, and soon I was trapped between the baseball-loving brothers from across the street.

"What's going on?" I asked them, as I struggled to stay upright. "Not sure—we got here right before you did. Ask Roach. She was here even earlier," Johnny said loudly. I pushed myself toward the rotund redhead and put my head close to her ear. "Do you know anything about what happened?"

She was chewing gum wildly, and nodded, excited to share her valuable information with someone else. "I heard that Mandy came out of the house screaming and yelling for help. She said it was an emergency and to call the police. They got here a couple minutes later and went inside. Roxy was here for some reason too—maybe trying to help Mandy." I looked over at Roxy, her thick black mascara running down her face in dark rivulets. She turned in my direction.

"I just can't believe it," she moaned. "What did Wanda ever do to anyone? And poor Mandy. To see someone like that, covered in so much blood." At the mention of Mandy's name, I started looking around frantically. Why had she been over here this early? Had she been injured as well? Was she being interviewed by the police? I couldn't see her anywhere. I desperately wanted to find her, to know that she was OK.

Seconds later, four more officers joined Collier and Simmons and urged the crowd even further away from the property. I backed away from the main group, and passed by the opening to Wanda's bungalow from a distance, squinting into the main corridor, hoping for even a fleeting glimpse of Mandy. A couple of emergency personnel and a detective were pacing around the back room, clearly visible from my vantage point.

On the ground behind them was an ominous white sheet, covering a completely still, small figure.

Wanda was dead.

23

Digging for answers

I drifted aimlessly down an empty street some time later, a cool misting rain hanging in the air, and I wondered how this could possibly have happened. *The timing is too perfect to be a coincidence—isn't it?* I asked myself. To have finally told another living soul about the body, and Wanda's possible knowledge about it, and then to have her wind up dead the next morning stretched my imagination to its breaking point. I was a fool to trust Mandy, I thought. I was livid, and I needed to talk to her. I changed course and arrived at her house, but it was dark and silent and no one answered my repeated pounding.

I continued to walk down her block away from the crime scene. Whenever I closed my eyes, I could see Wanda's face glaring at me, her dry and tanned smoker's skin wrinkling up in consternation, asking me why I hadn't told anyone my story soon enough. I stopped and leaned against the graffiti-covered cement wall in the alley I'd wandered into.

In my mind's eye, Wanda's face slowly morphed into that of my old pastor, and I watched him as he repeated his prophetic adage from the pulpit. "A truthful witness saves lives." My blood ran cold as I realized that I was as much to blame for Wanda's death as the perpetrator. I could have warned her, but I had been too afraid, too hesitant.

I'd listened intently minutes earlier from outside Wanda's place as a sobbing Roxy had recounted the sequence of events to Collier and the Rouge Park detective, a short balding man with squinty eyes. He'd taken down notes on a small notepad, while the blue flashing lights reflected off his thick-framed glasses.

Roxy had been letting her dog out to do its duty one block over earlier that morning when she'd heard a familiar-sounding voice frantically calling for help. She had darted over to Wanda's in the direction of the sound, and found Mandy on the porch, her hands covered in blood, pointing inside the open door, her face drained of all color.

"She's dead, Roxy! Someone cut her throat, someone's nearly taken her head clean off! She's dead," she'd repeated softly, almost to herself. Before the police could arrive, she'd run off toward her own house, carrying on about having to wash the blood off her hands.

Roxy had pleaded with Mandy not to leave, but the girl had continued to sprint into the distance without even turning around to look back. The detective replied that it was indeed unusual, but completely understandable due to the shock of the discovery, and that the authorities would follow-up with her in due course.

"When she calms down, she will most likely seek us out. We'll keep an officer posted here in the interim," he continued, and consoled Roxy with an arm around her shoulder. He motioned for her to continue to speak with a female officer on the front porch who provided her with a blanket and a warm smile.

Duong had stepped forward and offered that Queen hadn't been barking at all during the night or early morning, which was unusual, and that it could mean that any intruder was someone familiar to the neighborhood. "She goes insane if a stranger is lurking around any of these houses. Must have been someone she recognized," he surmised, and Collier thanked him, somewhat dismissively.

I, on the other hand, thought the piece of evidence was rather compelling. I knew from experience that Queen could keep Rouge Park awake a quarter mile in every direction if the cause was right.

Just around the corner of the cement wall I was now crouching against, I heard a bike screech to a stop. I was on the opposite side of the entrance to Embers Bar, and I heard a voice I despised speaking. "It's all set now. Tell the boss problem solved." Ryne said nothing else, nor was there any response to his news, and I could hear the metal chain of his bike engage and he took off. I peered around the corner seconds later and saw no one. Whoever he'd delivered this news to had already disappeared.

I could only assume this opaque reference had something to do with Wanda's death. Was she the problem that had needed to be taken care of? If so, was this enough evidence to take to the police? Or was I imagining things again and putting the pieces back together all wrong?

I realized with some alarm that my parents would arrive home soon. I still had a lot of putting the house back together again to do, and needed to take off the clamps from the repaired wooden desk chair, so I stood up and headed home. As I got closer to my own house I could see that most of the curious neighbors had dispersed, and only one police car was still present on the scene in front of Wanda's.

I walked along the triplets' fence, and a piece of Styrofoam and plastic that the wind had blown up against it caught my eye. I reached over the fence and grabbed it. It was from Farmer John's, the local grocery, and the label revealed it had recently contained several valuable ounces of Eye Filet. Feeling unusually conservationist, I carried it home with me to dispose in the trash properly.

Before long I was working in the kitchen when the sound of my family pulling into the driveway caught my attention. I put the last plastic cup away into the cupboard, hanging the dishcloth on the oven handle neatly. My parents would be impressed, I knew. Suzanne and Corbin sprinted into the house, gushing about their escapades at Kings Island, with my parents lingering behind to begin the arduous task of unloading the luggage. I tried hard not to be jealous and to be happy for them.

"We saw every single one of the Looney Tunes characters!" Suzanne exclaimed. "There was a huge roller coaster that went upside down," Corbin added. "Yeah, but you didn't ride it," Suzanne needled, followed by Corbin protesting that he wasn't tall enough, or he most certainly would have. Suzanne countered that she doubted it, as he'd chickened out of a smaller coaster he could have ridden, and they continued their debate as they proceeded to their rooms.

Mom said she would have the pictures developed soon, and that they'd filled several rolls of 24 exposures each. Dad was already unscrewing the car topper from its moorings, and preparing to haul it once again back down to the basement. Mom began to bring the suitcases up to the porch as a staging area. I offered to help them both.

They beamed at me, and the laudatory comments continued to pour forth as they walked through and observed that the house looked pretty much identical as to when they had left, and perhaps even better. In the basement, they both stared with interest at the work area, but I'd hidden the cut pieces inside a cardboard box, and they said little more about it, which was a relief to me.

When I realized I had both of them present, I took a deep breath. "Something terrible happened while you were gone," I started, unleashing a flurry of worried questions. I brushed their wild guesses aside, as they generally centered around what appliance or houseware I had accidentally destroyed. "It's not any of that. I wish it was, though. Wanda was killed."

They both looked straight ahead in stunned silence. The rail-thin widow had been a fixture in the neighborhood since we'd moved in. While neither of them had ever been particularly close to her, they both sat down in the chairs Mandy and I had been using, and tried to get their minds around the shocking news.

I described the morning's events in detail and answered their questions, which seemed to lead ever closer to the rest of my bizarre tale. With my pastor's booming voice echoing in my ears, and the image of Wanda's face pleading with me seared in my mind's eye, I vowed that it was finally time to reveal all that I knew to them.

"There's more," I said quietly. "I realize now I should have told you both a long time ago, and I wanted to, but—well, it's a long story. This is going to be hard to believe, the hardest thing ever perhaps; but I promise you it's the honest truth. If you've ever thought you could trust me even a little bit, please—this is the time now!" I stopped for a second and tried to calm my nerves.

I knew that the incident with my collarbone had earned me some rare cachet, and that with this move I was cashing in every single chip—I was going all in. "Remember the night that Asperat was over for dinner to help with the new room?" They both looked at each other and nodded.

They sat entranced as I told them the story. It was my second retelling in as many days, and it was becoming easier to form the awful words. With each sentence, the truth became more real, and the

279 *Davajuan*

fear lurking in the back of my mind that this had all somehow been just a figment of my imagination began to fade. The looks of shock and disgust on both their faces emboldened me to leave no details out this time. Mom stood up and embraced me, as if the thought of how difficult it had been to make a discovery of that kind—and then keep it secret for as long as I did—had dawned upon her all at once.

"I had heard that Justus had been missing for some time from Rhonda's parents down the block. But this—who could have predicted?" she said slowly, shaking her head while still processing the grisly details. She suddenly took a step back, and examined my face closely.

"Why didn't you tell us sooner, Dav?" she asked. Dad was standing now as well, pacing the basement floor, his hand covering his mouth. His mind had already fast-forwarded to the next steps of how and when to alert the authorities, I surmised. At the sound of Mom's pointed question, he stopped and looked at me as well, eyebrows raised, waiting expectantly.

I had not mentioned the threatening note. It was still safely folded and tucked up in the ceiling of my old room. A jolt of dread shot through my body as, for the first time, I allowed myself to consider the terrible question of whether the letter could have been created by Mandy herself. She, of course, had been working at Wanda's frequently. As far as I knew, she was also still the only other human who knew I had discovered the body, and that Wanda had been the lone possible witness.

Roxy's report about the blood on Mandy's hands certainly fit the horrible theory that was forming in my mind. I decided in a flash to keep the note's existence to myself until I knew more about her possible involvement. *I need to talk to her in person first*, I told myself firmly.

"I was scared," I admitted. "I tried to tell you that same night, but the words wouldn't come out. Then, other things got in the way. My injury, your trip to Ohio… I just couldn't ever find the right time." My parents both took deep breaths, and continued their pacing. Mom turned and scolded me.

"That's not a good enough excuse, Dav! The Manns are looking for answers about what happened. You *had* the answer—as terrible as it is—and you absolutely should have told someone." She gnawed at a fingernail. "Will Dav be in trouble with the police for waiting so long, dear?" she asked my dad.

"That's no longer our top concern," he said slowly. "A man is dead, and now another crime the next street over has been committed. Are they related in some way? It seems likely. I'm not sure what's going on over there in that dead end, but it has to stop. We have to go right now and do the proper thing," he said stoically, a resolved look on his face. "Get ready and we'll head over to the Rouge Park Police and have you make a statement Dav, before things get any worse."

The police station smelled old and important. A few officers loitered about the lobby with paper coffee cups, and a couple of irritated folks stood in line waiting to pay fines for minor traffic infractions. At the mention of needing to report a dead body, we were ushered immediately back into the inner workings of the station and taken directly to the detective's office.

Devon Collier hurried in to join us, and within minutes of hearing the key points of my story, we were following him and the balding detective back north through the city of Rouge Park in Collier's squad car with its lights ablaze.

I was petrified and nervously excited at the same time. I looked over at my dad behind the wheel, his lips pressed together and lines of concern around his temples. He was a young man still really, in his late thirties. He looked a lot older to me in that moment. A feeling of dread was forming deep in the pit of my stomach, and I knew it would be excruciating to watch as Freddy and his pathetic, ragamuffin sisters became aware of their father's fate.

It reminded me of a similar feeling in the pit of my stomach I'd had a few weeks previously, not long before the school year had ended. My friends and I had been sitting in Art class, run by a specials teacher, allowing Mrs. Townsend to have an hour of prep work and to catch her breath before dealing with the likes of me again. Both Denny and I possessed some raw artistic talent, and we firmly believed that gave us license to mercilessly critique the attempts of the kids around us with less innate ability.

After loudly lampooning one particularly brutal rendition of a castle on one girl's paper, the Art teacher sent us both out into the hallway to await discipline. Denny and I laughed ourselves silly sitting in the barren corridor alone on the carpet, but after five and then ten minutes had passed, we became bored and nearly despondent, our ammunition of things to mock finally depleted.

Looking out the side doors of the school building, a large expanse of grass had fallen under the shadow of the neighboring old folks' home that shared the Crosstown campus, in addition to the church and school: Sunset Acres. It was a ten-story rectangular high-rise structure, housing hundreds of senior citizens, and at the very top was a small square room with large glass windows on every side, known colloquially as the Penthouse.

The Penthouse was a source of many myths and legends among the youth of CCCP, since few had ever successfully visited the top and looked out in all directions. Those who had reported that you could see Canada in one direction, downtown Detroit in another, and almost as far as northern Ohio in yet another.

"Bet you can't get to the top of Sunset Acres and be back before the teacher comes out here," Denny said temptingly. It was common knowledge that leaving the school without permission was a canonical rule with potentially devastating consequences if broken. I considered his dare. I had looked outside, and the allure of the tower was almost too much for me to bear. I stole a glance inside the art classroom, and saw that the teacher was completely immersed in helping students with their drawings.

"I'll see that bet and raise you one," I had bragged. "I'll wave to you from outside the Penthouse in under five minutes." Denny looked at me, awestruck. I had bolted through the door to the outside and ran at top speed through the lush grass lawn between the two buildings. True to my word, I entered the retirement home, walked confidently to the bank of elevators, and pressed the warm, glowing letter 'P'. Every second that ticked by felt like an eternity.

When the doors opened once more, I wanted to take the time to stop and absorb the amazing sights visible from the small, well-furnished entertainment room, but my mission was clear, and time was my enemy. A whoosh of wind unexpectedly hit my face as I opened the door leading out onto the stone-covered roof of the building, roughly a hundred feet in the air. I walked gingerly toward the edge, the dizzying height forcing me to carefully consider every step as I approached a short wall ringing the outer rim.

I had gazed down toward where I'd been just minutes prior, and saw the tiny figure of Denny barely able to contain himself as he pressed against the glass door and pointed at me silently. I gave him an exultant and exaggerated wave, and then began to retrace my steps as quickly as I could.

The adrenaline rush on the return journey had been palpable. I could already almost hear the tale being retold, and embellished upon, as it spread throughout the student body. I would be a legend, right up there with the audacious kid that had traveled from room to room during the school day through the dropped ceiling system. It never dawned on me that, coincidentally, he was no longer enrolled at CCCP.

As I had burst through the exterior doors of Sunset Acres, and began my triumphant trot back over to the school, I had been petrified to see that Denny was no longer waiting for me alone at the side glass entrance doors. Our teacher had been several yards outside now as well, standing with her arms crossed, a look of disdain and perhaps a hint of respect at my audaciousness on her face.

"You have some nerve," she had admitted, as I drew closer. She turned and started walking, the implication to follow her directly to the principal's office abundantly clear. Denny whispered plaintively that he had not ratted me out, and I believed him. The ensuing heated conversation, suspension and near-expulsion had actually been the culminating event that prompted my original decision to run away to the woods with Tyson, which now seemed juvenile—and like it had happened eons ago.

In stark contrast to that past feeling of dread, as we pulled up in front of Freddy's house with the police I told myself that I had no need whatsoever to be nervous. I had done nothing wrong. Someone else was the perpetrator this time, and I was going to get to play the hero for once, exposing crime and putting a stop to whatever monster was taking out Rouge Park residents with a callous ferocity.

As we got out of the car, I looked around, half expecting Enrique, Rync, Dustin or even Nicolette to come running up to us, confessing to the crimes and begging for mercy. But no one did. Freddy looked up from his chalk drawings on the porch with a blank, confused expression. Inside, Nicolette was yelling at the girls for breaking a dish. I stood next to Dad on their front grass and waited. Collier and the detective explained the reason for their visit to Nicolette, who looked unkempt and angry as ever as they notified her through the front screen.

At the mention of a body, her shoulders fell, and her expression changed. Her hands went above her head and she grasped at her hair, her face crestfallen. She led the way to the backyard like a zombie, and Collier motioned for me to follow. Freddy watched the entire scene as if in a trance, and I could tell he wanted to ask me what I was doing there, but he couldn't seem to find the words.

It was the first time I'd been in the Mann backyard since the night of the discovery. Though I'd been there dozens of times in the past, it all seemed like a dream. Details I'd never noticed before were jumping out at me, overstimulating me with input. The drooping vinyl siding on one corner of the front of the garage. A rusty bike chain that had left lasting orange streaks on a section of broken cement pavement.

I'd played there so often before and never noticed a thing, I realized. That had been before the cruel reality of what some people were capable of had opened my eyes to a harsher world, a world I wanted nothing to do with. The world of Enrique, spiked hair, drugs, knives, threats and loss. *At least this will be the first step in putting a stop to it all,* I thought.

Behind the garage, the detective and Collier asked me to point to the spot. Nicolette was yelling again, nearly incoherently. "What did you do?" she asked me, outraged. "Are you responsible for this? What did you do to Justus? I'll strangle you!"

I wanted to speak up in my defense, but was afraid to say anything at all. Collier tried to calm her down, and explained that I was not a suspect, but a key witness. Nicolette shoved the arms of the detective away and tried to get closer to where Collier had begun to dig, but was restrained.

"You need to back away, ma'am," Collier instructed. "This is a potential crime scene from this moment forward," he said grimly. Nicolette's carrying on only increased in volume at that statement. The officer looked up for reassurance from me that his shovel was positioned in the right place, and I nodded gravely.

I glanced behind me and saw that a motley crew had gathered again at the mouth of Freddy's driveway, containing a lot of the same characters that had been craning their necks at Wanda's just hours prior. I felt rather important in the center of the limelight, but tried to brush off the feeling, turning back to the dig, and then setting my jaw in preparation to once again confront the decomposing face I'd seen so many times during the weeks beforehand in my haunted dreams.

With each shovel-full of dirt, the anticipation rose, until I thought for sure that each plunging stab by Collier would be the one to thud dully against poor Justus's skull. For the first time, I wavered. *Had this been the exact spot?* I was sure of it. I could still picture myself there, exactly where I had been standing that fateful night—within inches, I could have sworn. The soil was loose, and the digging was easy and swift. More dirt soon was displaced, and the hole was now plenty deep enough to have exposed what I had previously found.

I grabbed the top of the back fence that separated Freddy's yard from Wanda's and steadied myself. I looked into her backyard, and thought I could almost see the old crone staring at me from the deck, grinning. Grief-stricken relatives and friends who had gradually gathered to arrange her affairs looked oddly back at us, as if we were attractions at the circus. *It had not been my imagination. It had all happened, just the way I'd remembered it—over and over again.* Or had it?

I finally dared to look across at my dad. His eyes were transfixed on the expanding hole, now big enough to put an oversized armchair into. He did not return my gaze. Collier was soaked with sweat, and for the first time in a while he looked up at me from the hole below, expectantly.

"Well?" he asked. His face was red, and he rested for a minute, leaning on the shovel, taking in deep, irritated breaths. He somehow managed to hold his tongue any further.

Nicolette swore, and stomped off toward the front. The crowd engulfed her, as questions and theories swirled around the writhing group like a summer storm. Collier dug a couple more feet in every direction, his ire growing right in step with the stifling humidity of the mid-July afternoon.

I kept staring at the hole, praying under my breath for the hideous head to magically appear. But I knew that it was in vain. My knees almost buckled and I felt frozen in place. The body was gone.

24

bass Boost

Seven terrible days passed. They seemed to be the darkest of my life, and a cloud of depression parked itself right over me and refused to blow over. I spent most of my time alone in my room in the basement, coming out to eat meals quietly—or if I was especially bold, head outside to lay on my back on the picnic table and look up into the empty sky. I made sure to completely avoid all the neighborhood kids, especially the Biker Scouts.

I spent hours trying to figure out how it had all gone so wrong. After the initial shock had worn off, I'd tried to piece together a theory, but there were too many holes in each of them. *Who had moved the body? Where had it been taken? Had there even been a body? Of course there had,* I told myself, repeatedly pulling back from the dangerous precipice of self-doubt that I knew might cause a swift descent into madness. Justus and Wanda were dead, and someone was responsible. But who it could be, I couldn't quite figure out. *Or maybe,* I thought as my blood ran cold, *I know exactly who it has to be, but don't want to admit it to myself.*

In the middle of the second night, a thought hit me like lightning. The knife in Roach and CJ's driveway. Of course! It would be irrefutable proof that my story had been true after all. I got out of bed without a sound and crept up the back stairs. At the side door, I released the dead bolt as quietly as possible. Corbin tossed around in his bed a few feet away from me, and I stopped and stood silently by his bedroom door until I was sure he was sound asleep once again.

Outside, the night was warm and pleasant. No one was around. I stole across the street and headed for the dark outline of the rusted car just a few houses away. Damian stood staring at me from over the fence with red eyes like a sentinel. Queen barked wildly from the triplets' property, and I came to an abrupt stop, unsure if she was reacting to me, or something else entirely. Her barking eventually stopped, and I arrived at the ghostly frame of the old car and crouched down inside.

It was dark but I remembered exactly where the knife was concealed. My heart raced as I imagined the vindication in store for me when I presented the bloody evidence to Collier and the detective. It would certainly be enough to prove a crime had been committed. Perhaps they'd even be able to determine that the blood on it belonged to Justus.

My hand came to rest on a soft, weedy patch of earth where I knew the knife had been. Frantically, I felt all around the area, and I knew within seconds that I'd been stymied yet again. The perpetrator was good, staying at least one step ahead of me. They'd covered their bases incredibly well. My last scrap of hope had disappeared right along with the Cub Scout knife with the fleur de lis carving.

I returned back home dejectedly through the side door and laid awake on my bottom bunk until dawn. I came to grips with the fact that only two human beings could have known where that knife was at: the killer, and Mandy Willows. I hoped with everything in me that they weren't somehow one and the same person.

I tried listening to the Tigers on my stereo the next few evenings to pass the time, as they spanked the Seattle Mariners three games in a row to climb to fourteen games over .500. I wondered if somewhere close by, Dustin Crabb was tuning in nervously as well. They came one run short of a potential sweep, falling 5-4 in the series finale at Tiger Stadium. As Harwell signed off for the night, I switched off the radio and fell into yet another, fitful sleep.

After a week or so of this morose cycle of helpless thoughts and inaction, I finally heard a knock on the front door upstairs, and Mom hurrying to answer it.

"Oh, hello, Tyson! So nice to see you. How has your summer been? Come in, come in," she said cheerily. Tyson responded with some pleasantries of his own as he stood in the entryway, and then eventually asked if he could go downstairs to see me.

"Of course. But," she added in a lower voice, "I have to warn you. He's had a rough stretch. He has a lot going on in his head right now. I'm sure he can tell you all about it. Maybe you can help." He agreed to try, and bounded down the stairs in my direction.

My room was a mess, and I scurried to make it more presentable. He greeted me at the door, and came right in, plopping himself on my lower bunk. He had on a shiny new pair of basketball shoes, and a cool Pistons tank top. I continued to tidy up, and he leaned over and picked up a stack of my baseball cards.

"Your collection is coming along," he commented, and reached into his pocket to pull out three packs of cards. "I stopped by Pete's on the way. They had a sale on '86 Fleer basketball. Basically giving them away to clear out room for next season's cards. Thought you might be interested," he smiled. "Jordan, Bird, Magic—you never know who might be inside."

"Thanks—but Fleer cards are cheaply made, literally a dime a dozen. No one collects basketball cards. Plus, I've already got a few of those Jordans already. Baseball cards is where it's at," I said, more rudely than I initially intended. I turned away from the pile of clothes I was stuffing into the bottom of my closet and smiled weakly at Tyson.

"Look—I know you're trying to help. I heard my Mom upstairs. But, the truth is, I don't think anyone can help me now. I'm kind of at a dead end." I leaned against the far wall of my room and let my head droop between my shoulders.

"Alright—that's it. Come on, Dav. We've been in a ton of jams before—" he started to say. I cut him off. "No, you don't get it. This one is different. If I told you what's happened, you'd begin to understand," I argued without looking up.

He got up and walked over to the desk, looking at the items I had on display. "Why don't you give me a shot, then? If I can't help, I promise, I'll leave you alone and you can get back to doing nothing for the rest of the summer." He looked at me for a second. "I have an idea, come with me," he commanded, grabbing me by the arm and forcing me to stand up. I grimaced, and glared at him, pointing at the brace. He ignored my moodiness and headed up the flight of steps without me.

Once we were both outside, he instructed me to pull my bike out of the shed, and he waited on his own at the end of the driveway while I reluctantly did so. I looked around for signs of any other kids, and seeing none, I followed him at a small distance as he headed down the street. He circled back and rode next to me. I started to warm up, appreciating the extra effort he was going to. It was nice to have a friend like Tyson, and I vowed to try to stop taking him for granted.

Since the debacle behind Freddy's garage a week earlier, my dad had hardly spoken to me, other than to instruct me to perform my chores, or call me up for a family meal. Mom seemed more sympathetic, but I knew that they were both completely mortified by what had happened. In their eyes, my greatest lie to date had been exposed in front of dozens of people, and the city authorities to boot.

I wondered if they could ever believe a word out my mouth again. Their invitation to accompany them to Wanda's funeral had seemed like a formality. I had quietly declined, knowing I couldn't possibly bear to see her friends and family mourning her untimely demise. I replayed the fallout of the wild goose chase once again in my mind.

Collier and the detective had left the scene hurriedly in their squad car that day, minutes after abandoning the dig, clearly agitated and somewhat embarrassed in their own right at having fallen for the false alarm.

"This is an outrage! How dare you invade my property and go digging wherever the heck you want? I'll be talking to my lawyer!" Nicolette had called after them as they pulled away from the curb. "Stop wasting time listening to that kid's tall tales and do your jobs—find my Justus!" I'd slinked away just in the nick of time during her diatribe. A few of the gawking kids noticed me leaving the scene—but I was one step ahead of them, and I'd run the last few yards to the safety of my own house before anyone could interrogate me further. I knew I would probably never live the whole thing down.

Soon Tyson and I arrived at the surprise destination, a few blocks further than I typically ventured. He pointed proudly at a new business that had just opened up called Spadz Pizza. It was a strange and wonderful sight to behold: an abandoned car wash that had been converted into a drive-through fast food joint. We waited on our bikes behind one car, and then pedaled up to the window when it was our turn. The teenage girl at the register looked at us sideways, but allowed us to order two slices and a small drink anyway.

We sat next to our bikes on the sidewalk in front of Spadz and enjoyed our greasy snack as traffic sped by noisily, and the world seemed to lighten a bit. I asked Tyson how baseball had been going without me. I had wanted to ask Dad, but had avoided doing so ever since my season-ending injury.

"We're pretty good. Hallas is pumped. We still haven't lost. Grangeford is mopping up the competition. He already has seven home runs and leads the league in a bunch of categories," he reported. Tyson glanced at me to see my reaction but I refused to cave. "Funny thing is, you're still there at the bottom of the leaderboard for RBIs in the Downriver Declarer, even after all those games." I finally gave in, and we both had a good laugh over the improbable stat.

"How's Leon doing?" I ventured. Tyson looked at me suspiciously, and put two and two together. "He's been fine, I guess. A couple of good hits so far. Nothing spectacular. Why don't you ask me about the person you're really interested in, though?" he teased. I hadn't seen Violet for a long while, and imagined that she was having a pretty good time down at Disney World. I hoped she was thinking about me from time to time, too.

We arrived back to my place an hour or so later, and were both surprised and happy to see Denny sitting on the porch in the shade, looking bored. He had ridden his skateboard the entire way from his home in West Ridge. We headed down to my room together, and as Tyson lounged on the bed and played Ms. Pac-Man, I decided to ask Denny about the knife markings. I sketched the fleur de lis logo on a scrap of paper, and showed it to him, and he recognized it immediately.

"Yeah, I used to have one just like that," he nodded. "In fact, I still might, somewhere in the attic or something. They gave them out a couple years ago to all the boys in my Cub Scout Troop. Why do you ask?"

I brushed off his question for the time being. "Did you by chance ever have a leader at Cub Scouts called Sigmund, or Ciggy?" I ventured. I knew it was shot in the dark, but I was going to give it a shot regardless. Tyson sat upright and stared at me, wondering what the missing factory worker could have to do with my line of questioning.

Denny immediately recognized the name. "Yeah, who could forget that guy. Mr. Sigmund, the kids all called him. He was a strange one, kind of interesting to hang out with at first, but I think he got canned after I left, or so I heard. Never got a great vibe from him, if you know what I mean. One of the nastier kids called him 'Freud' behind his back. Sigmund Freud, get it?" I didn't explore the nuanced response further, because my mind was busy racing.

"Come on, Dav. You can't just throw out something like that and not fill us in on the details," Tyson coaxed. "You owe us an explanation. This has something to do with why you're down in the dumps, right?" he pushed. Denny looked at me inquisitively, unaware that I had been moping around recently.

"What's wrong?" Denny asked. "Your collarbone still giving you fits? My shoulder's killing me from pitching yesterday." He rotated his throwing arm, wincing.

I replied negatively to Denny's naïve guess, and hemmed and hawed a bit longer, stalling. *I can't bring these guys into the situation can I?* I asked myself. I looked at them both for a minute, as they waited expectantly to learn more. They'd both stuck with me through thick and thin ever since I could remember, and I had to believe they would now as well. I took a deep breath, and struck forward, knowing there was now turning back. I swore them to secrecy, and went over to my old room and pulled the threatening letter down from its hiding spot.

I came back in and handed it to Tyson. "Here's why I haven't told anyone. I couldn't take the risk." Denny took it from Tyson and looked it over. "I recognize that writing. Just don't know from where," he said. He looked at me earnestly. "Now tell us what this is all about!"

I started from the very beginning, and left no detail out. The two of them sat at rapt attention, their faces rising and falling with every new development. They recoiled when I described the discovery of Justus. Their eyes popped when I revealed the existence and then the disappearance of the tell-tale knife, and the pieces seemed to come together even more when I mentioned Wanda's gruesome death.

I carefully wove the story without mentioning Mandy, though how someone would have known to move both the body and knife without her involvement still stymied me. I wondered if I was doing so simply to prevent one of them from coming to the inevitable conclusion that the girl I had an overwhelming crush on was somehow involved in both crimes.

Tyson held the threatening note up to the light that streamed in my room from outside and suddenly pointed at something on it. "Have you seen this marking?" he asked me, curiously. I bolted over to his side and looked at the paper. A faint watermark was imprinted in it, and as I squinted I could make out that it read *Downriver Bank and Trust*. I took a moment to consider the surprising new lead. I was surprised I hadn't taken the time to examine the note more closely myself.

"Maybe someone who works at the bank wrote it!" Denny offered. "Or, anyone who does business there," Tyson added, more somberly. "That narrows it down to only a couple thousand people." He turned to me.

"Sorry, maybe it's not as good of a clue as I thought." We all sat in silence for a moment. "Try talking to your folks again and tell them everything you've told us!" Denny urged. "Your dad seems like a reasonable guy. I'm sure he'll come around." I shook my head dejectedly.

"You're talking about the man you see when he's over at Crosstown. Here, with me—after all the times I've let him down, it's a completely different deal. He'll honestly never believe a thing I say again." I paused. "But seriously, guys. Thank you for believing me. It means a lot."

Mom called down and notified me that the rest of the family was heading over to Value Village, the thrift shop located down in Northgate. I bounded halfway up the stairs and asked if she would please keep her eyes peeled for any used Hardy Boys books that I hadn't read yet, in a low voice to avoid my friends overhearing such a juvenile request. Somehow sharing my predicament with them had begun to lift my spirits even more. She smiled and nodded without responding audibly.

When I returned to my room, we discussed the situation again at length. Denny thought it sounded like Nicolette might have killed Justus in a rage, moved the body later, and then—having somehow overheard Wanda tell us about the person she'd seen digging—finished the job. I could see the flushed face of the angry housewife in my mind, and told them both that, while possible, I didn't think Nicolette possessed the acting chops to pull off such a performance as she had in front of Collier during the dig.

Tyson surmised out loud that the killer could just as easily have been Dustin Crabb, for different reasons. I knew he had no love lost for the smarmy ex-principal. He suddenly remembered something and pulled a cassette out of his pocket. "Your folks are gone now, right?" he said, a boyish smile taking over his face. I nodded. He held out a plastic case containing the newest album from Prince.

"Let's see what this baby can do, then," he grinned, and popped it into my dad's old stereo. The first song began to boom through the two tall speakers with rich and full-bodied tones, the vibrations of which nearly shook the Third Place Pinewood Derby trophy I'd earned years ago right off the edge of my desk.

"Turn it down, Tyson!" I ordered, but the truth was I was actually thoroughly enjoying the luxury of playing rock music loudly, without any fear of parental retribution. Prince's voice pumped through the entire empty house, and the three of us just sat and soaked the lyrics in:

Here we are folks
The dream we all dream of
Boy versus girl in the World Series of love.

The connection between Mandy and I had grown so much during the week we worked on the map together. But I hadn't laid eyes on her since the last time she'd rushed up the stairs and out my back door, the day before Wanda's body was discovered. I couldn't shake the feeling that somehow we were heading to an ultimate confrontation, one that would most likely drive us apart once and for all.

Tell me, have you got the look?
You walked in, I woke up
I've never seen a pretty girl
Look so tough, baby.

I remembered how Mandy had looked when she'd confronted me in her kitchen with the loaded gun. Fierce and unafraid of anyone or anything that crossed her path. She was someone who was willing to do whatever it took to protect the things in her life she valued. I found it both admirable and rather frightening, I realized in that moment.

You sho'nuf do be cookin' in my book
Your face is jammin'
Your body's heck-a-slammin'

No argument could be made on those points about Mandy in my book, either. Part of me wished the two boys could have known about her. They'd both have swooned over her. But I continued to resist revealing her existence to anyone at all. She would remain mine alone to pine after.

Soon all three of our heads were bobbing up and down to the catchy beat of the single, which Denny said had been released on the local radio only the day before, and we were all no doubt completely immersed in imagining different girls in our own minds, when a yell pierced the deafening atmosphere. We all jumped.

My dad was standing in the door frame, his face contorted angrily. I dove for the power button and the room became instantly silent once again. My friends both sat still, woodenly refusing to make any eye contact with Dad. They both seemed to want to melt quietly into the brightly-painted baseboards.

"What—is—the—meaning—of—this?" Dad stammered. "You know this type of blasphemy isn't allowed in our house!" I stood in front of him, trying to come up with a reasonable explanation, but came up utterly blank.

"It's my fault, sir," Denny suddenly said, breaking the awkward silence. "Dav showed me this new sound system down here, and we just wanted to test out the bass channel really quick." I stared at him, dumbfounded, wondering if the tall tale would be accepted as remotely plausible.

"The bass channel?" Dad repeated, cocking his head. "Yes!" Denny added. "This thing really can belt out quality music. Dav said he wants to fully experience the complete range of tones possible whenever he listens to the required amount of orchestral arrangements for music class." I wanted to cheer out loud for Denny, but managed to hold in my applause. He'd spat out that entirely reasonable explanation without missing a beat, and it had been a thing of beauty.

My dad scratched his brow, and explained that he'd simply returned to retrieve his wallet, and warned us to keep the dial on acceptable stations from that point on. As he ascended the steps once again, Denny ejected the offending cassette and safely pocketed it. "No more Prince for a good, long while when I'm over here!" he promised, and all three of us barely suppressed raucous laughter.

Late that night, the catchy song replayed through my mind over and over as I lay on my bed. As I thought again about my visit to Mandy's kitchen table, and replayed the sequence of events that had happened there, I found myself browsing her personal journal once again. Somehow, I'd almost forgotten about her cryptic to-do list, and in my mind's eye, I scanned down the ambiguous items once more. I stopped with alarm when I reached the seventh entry.

It now had a completely new meaning, I realized as I considered it with despair. It had simply read: *Finish Wanda.*

no Tips allowed

My collarbone was beginning to heal. Near the end of July, I slid my brace off several weeks early, and vowed to keep it off from that moment forward. I'd quit the Ibuprofen regimen after ten days, and the feeling now was one more of stiffness and itchiness than pain. I decided I needed to work again and begin to save some money, but after one push on the lawnmower in the backyard, I realized cutting grass was not an option quite yet. I called Zane and broke the bad news to him. He understood, and let me know he'd be asking another friend for help the rest of the summer.

I'd heard at church that both Trevor and Gregory had scored jobs working in the dining room at Sunset Acres. They both made several dollars an hour, and worked as much as they were allowed to. I walked into the kitchen one morning and saw Mom already putting the finishing touches on the evening meal and sliding it into the fridge.

"Mom, I want to work at Sunset Acres," I said flatly. She looked at me oddly, the very name of the retirement tower seeming to bring back a flood of negative feelings. "Are you sure that's really the best place for you to get a job?" she queried, and I could easily read between the lines that she had serious questions about whether it would be a good idea, in light of the events of the past school year. I forged ahead regardless.

"Trevor and Gregory are working there already. They can show me the ropes. Sounds like it wouldn't be too hard, plus I could start to save some money for college, or something like that." I slid that last rationale in right at the end, hoping it would be the deciding factor, while not intending any of the generated funds to actually go toward my future education.

She seemed to waver, and then finally agreed that I could at least investigate the option. She made me assure her that I would mention our upcoming trip to the beach upfront to whoever was in charge there. I did so, and I imagined that she was secretly happy to have me up and about again and actually doing something, instead of wasting any additional time downstairs in solitude.

A quick phone call to Sunset Acres led to an immediate job offer from the woman I spoke to, someone named Janine Lucero. It seemed they were extremely short-handed, and Janine asked if I was available to work even yet that same afternoon. Surprised, I agreed, and took the job on the spot. I started to mention that I'd need a couple of upcoming weeks off, but the other line went dead abruptly. Clearly, Janine Lucero was in quite a rush. Mom was pleasantly surprised to hear the news, and agreed to let me head on over.

As I pulled on some socks and shoes by the back door, I told myself that I couldn't keep hiding forever. If the Biker Scouts were going to find me anyway, and threaten to beat me senseless, why put off the inevitable? I was done running away. I set my jaw and marched to the backyard to get my bike. I walked it down the driveway, into the exposed and open air for anyone to see, and began to pedal toward West Ridge, my head held high and defiant.

I waffled but eventually gave in to the relentless magnetic forces pulling on me and steered past Mandy's house on the way. Everything in me told me to take a different route, but the temptation was irresistible. I couldn't fathom what she'd been up to since I'd last seen her. Was she having trouble coping with the brutal death she'd discovered—or had it all been an act? I just knew I wanted to see her. I needed to ask her about Wanda—have her explain to me that I was way off base with my growing suspicions.

I was to have no such satisfaction for the time being, however. Like so many times recently, her house appeared to be empty once again. The doors were closed, the shades drawn, and the Mustang nowhere to be seen. *Maybe it's for the best,* I sighed, partially relieved. I didn't even really know what I'd say to her first had I seen her.

My first shift at Sunset Acres was a circus. As I walked into the towering building once more and pivoted in the direction of the dining area—this time as a legitimate visitor and not an intruder—sweet sounds of violin music and the sight of fine linen tablecloths greeted me. I hastily donned the white shirt and black pants that I'd been instructed to bring along with me, and hurriedly filled out the paperwork that the flustered but attractive Ms. Lucero shoved at me in the back hallway, before she stormed off to put out some other fire.

Trevor and Gregory were both working that same afternoon time slot, and they hastily tried to explain the basics of the job to me. Dressed in the same minimalistic uniform as myself, they peppered me with random instructions as we hastily filled the salad bar with ice, and began to arrange the individual ingredients in organized rows.

"Thanks a lot for coming, Dav. A couple other guys quit yesterday and we really needed the help. Even with you, we're still terribly short-handed," Trevor huffed, as he scrambled to transfer four canisters of dressing from a massive tray to corresponding holes he'd carved into the ice. Gregory concurred.

"Listen," Gregory added, stopping for a moment. "There's a couple of people you need to know about. One is Lucy. She has been known to, well..." He looked sideways at Trevor, who raised his eyebrows and closed his eyes, signaling for Gregory to spit it out.

"She has been known to use the bathroom at, how shall we say it, inopportune times. Just keep an eye out. She usually sits over there in the corner." I stood speechless at this revelation, and Gregory continued. His ruddy face was glistening with sweat, but he was clearly an expert on what it took to properly service the place.

"The Sellers sit right here. Sweet couple, no issues at all," he said, moving briskly on to the next section. "Walter sits here, really nice old English gentleman. Super good manners. And this," he paused for effect. "This is where the Four Horse Ladies of the Apocalypse sit, every single night, without fail."

"To say they're tough customers would be the understatement of the year. You'll see what I mean," Gregory cautioned, and then excused himself to run to the back for more napkins. He returned and the three of us began to fold them neatly. I watched them and tried to mimic what they were doing, clumsily at first.

The first floor dining room was clearly the center of social life at the retirement home. Dozens of senior citizens and their walkers began to congregate in the lobby outside the double swinging doors a few minutes before 4 pm, clamoring to be fed. Lucero click-clacked out into the dining room, her eyes ablaze.

"Come on, you sluggards! Hurry up! Dinner has to be served in just a few minutes!" Trevor rolled his eyes at me, and grabbed my arm. He dragged me with him to the back room behind the salad bar, where a staged sea of pre-wrapped dinner plates awaited us, with several round brown serving platters stacked on a nearby table. He took one, and handed another to me, and removed the wrap from each plate carefully.

"Watch what I do," Trevor instructed, loading seven or eight of the heaping plates onto his serving platter, then launching it up above his shoulder, eventually balancing it with one open palm. My eyes bulged. I didn't think I'd be able to do it, especially using my left arm. I'd have to do it right-handed, I realized, and it made me nervous.

There was no time to argue, however, as the residents had all been streaming in to take their seats, chattering all the way. "Oh, look, there's a new boy today," one woman called out to her table mates as I staggered toward them with the platter. "Let's see how the young whippersnapper does!"

I managed to serve each of the four old crones their food without any major mishaps. I returned and poured them each a piping hot cup of coffee, as they'd demanded. After taking a quick sip, the apparent leader of the group sputtered, "This stuff isn't hot enough. Put it in the microwave for 30 more seconds!" I did so, and was shocked to watch her down the scalding beverage as if every nerve in her mouth and throat had withered away while Carter was still President.

Gregory came rushing over to me. "Lucy served herself salad, right into the folds of her dress instead of a plate. When you get a free second, can you help me clean up the mess?" I agreed to do so, and after checking on Walter and the Sellers, hurried to the back to retrieve a mop and bucket.

I looked through the kitchen and into the back manager's office, and was surprised and disgusted to see Ms. Lucero planting a wet, gaudy kiss on none other than Dustin Crabb. *You've got to be kidding me,*

I shook my head to myself. *She's dating that character? Then there's hope for absolutely anyone.* I wondered how Crabb had ever convinced anyone over at Crosstown that he was hiring material in the first place. I moved closer to them as I looked around for the needed cleaning supplies.

"Are you sure, baby? That sounds expensive!" laughed Janine in a playful way. "I thought cash was tight right now while you're between jobs. I know Great-uncle Garland is trying to use his connections to find you a cushy gig at another area school, but in the meantime don't you still need money to pay back that ruffian Enrique?" Dustin waved his hand at her comment dismissively.

"I've got other irons in the fire, babe. Forget old Garland Shay. My luck is about to change. Enrique agreed to a huge parlay bet on the Tigers. What Willows doesn't know is that I've got major inside info. It's a can't-miss deal." He leaned closer.

"Get this—I have a friend who knows Morris Madden—you know, the relief pitcher?" Janine's pretty face appeared completely blank. "Anyway, he was over at Morris' pad and he says team morale is just terrible. Apparently Sparky is unhinged. They're going downhill fast." He sat down in Janine's office chair triumphantly, and spun around in it.

"It was a fool's bet for that overconfident lout to make, and I'll be happy to take his money when the Tigers miss the playoffs," he bragged. "Not that he needs it all anyway. Enrique's got a shipment worth a cool half million coming in. It'll generate more than enough to pay me—and still live like a king." Janine whistled at the amount. "Where's he going to keep that type of coin? Not at Downriver Bank, for sure!" she guessed.

I scurried off to help Gregory clean up the salad debacle, and then attended to Walter and the Sellers in between fulfilling audacious requests from the Four Horse Ladies. The Sellers were a warm and friendly couple who thanked me profusely every time I stopped by their table. They ate their meals in a timely fashion and soon excused themselves. I watched them slowly make their way together over to the elevator bank in the lobby and disappear.

Walter, a heavyset and polite gentleman in his mid-eighties who possessed a pleasant British accent, asked me to sit down with him in the extra chair. After glancing around and seeing no other immediate fires to extinguish, I complied.

"And what, may I ask, brings you to us, young man?" he asked. After considering his question for a second, I explained that I needed money, and that the staff was short-handed. "I go to school and church right across the way," I added.

"Ah, yes. Crosstown Christian. Fine establishment. Do you happen to know my daughter, Darcy Townsend?"

I remembered that I'd heard Mrs. Townsend's full name a handful of times before, and I nodded. "She was my homeroom teacher this year," I smiled. He beamed, and we discussed her at length. It was clear that he was proud of her, and that they had a positive relationship. I asked the kind man if he had any other children, and his face clouded.

"Yes. I have another daughter. She almost never comes to visit these days. You see, I was already middle-aged when she came along, rather unexpectedly. I'm afraid we've grown far apart since she ran off with a bad egg." He grunted as he reached down to his back pocket, and pulled his wallet out. He opened it to a faded, color photograph of a vivacious and smiling young woman. "Her name is Nicolette."

I sat in stunned silence. It was hard to believe that the Nicolette I knew now was the same person in the photo. I resisted the urge to share with Walter that I already knew exactly who she was.

"She also attended Crosstown. Her future seemed so bright. She was dating a nice young man there at the school, and then," he paused. "Well, I suppose I let my guard down. Her older sister was going through her own tough stretch at the same time, and I took my eyes off the ball, so to speak. Thankfully Darcy met a fine young man who helped her turn her life around—and now he's her husband." He looked out the window across to the church. "The struggles I've had with Nicolette have been the hardest thing I've ever dealt with. I feel responsible for how things have turned out."

I told him that he should not. "I heard a wise person once said that our own choices define us, and are solely what determines the trajectory of our future—for good or evil."

He smiled sadly. "And who came up with those insightful words?" he asked, as I stood back up to begin cleaning the dining room with my friends. I clearly remembered that day in class when Ms. Stickler had shared the quote with our entire class after being introduced to us by Mrs. Townsend.

"I was told it was your daughter."

Once all the dishes were cleared and the salad bar deconstructed, Gregory and Trevor invited me to sit down with them at a table in the back. They explained that at this time every evening—after Janine would leave early with instructions on what still had to be done and a terse reminder to lock the place up—the extra, uneaten food became free reign. Trevor took a loud bite out of a whole red onion and I grimaced. Gregory wheeled out a cart full of extra servings of tapioca pudding and we greedily dug in.

"You did well for your first meal," Trevor complimented me, with a mouthful of tapioca. "Let's hope you last longer than the last two guys." I asked what had happened to them.

"They got into a huge ketchup fight here in the back after a meal. Looked like a murder scene. They were fired on the spot." Gregory replied wryly. For some reason the innocuous comment made my blood run cold and I felt faint. I hadn't come to grips with Wanda's death yet, and the weight of my role in it actually seemed to be growing every day.

Why hadn't I done something? I interrogated myself for the thousandth time. The guys noticed that I'd become despondent, and sought to bring me back to the conversation with more hilarious tales that had transpired there at Sunset Acres, but it didn't help. I wondered if I'd ever be able to get the crushing burden off my back.

The rest of that week continued to fly by. On the second day at Sunset Acres, Janine asked if I was available seven days a week, and—drunk with the prospect of a bulging wallet—I immediately agreed. It was tiring work, but Trevor and Gregory made it much more tolerable. I was enjoying getting to know Walter, and usually sat down with him for a short stretch after every meal. Even the Horse Ladies and I had found a sort of symbiosis, as I attempted to meet their every whim and match their pointed barbs with my own witty retorts.

On Friday after dinner, Walter pulled me aside, and handed me a folded up $20 bill. "The powers that be don't like it around here when we tip, but I don't care a whit. This is for you." He shook both of my hands warmly as he gave it to me, and I thanked him profusely.

That evening Dad arrived home from coaching Crosstown, and dropped his duffel bag in a heap at the door. "How'd it go, hon?" Mom asked from the back of the house, where she was folding Corbin's clothes and putting them neatly into drawers. "We got shellacked by the Trojans," he said glumly. "Grangeford hit a couple dingers, but the final score was 12-6. Poor Hallas got ejected." Mom came out and gave him a conciliatory hug. He looked over at me, and nodded. We still hadn't spoken properly since the missing body debacle.

"Just a reminder, Dav, we're leaving for the ocean trip on Monday. Mom says you've been working pretty hard at that Sunset Acres job." I nodded. There was an awkward pause. "You did tell them about needing that time off when you applied, correct? We'll be gone until the following Friday." I reiterated that I had, knowing full well I'd never actually gotten the chance to apprise Janine Lucero of the situation. A feeling of dread began to build as I anticipated her reaction to the news. I told Dad that I would remind her of it again the following day, and that it shouldn't be an issue. He announced he was hitting the shower, and I retreated to my bedroom.

I got out my collection of baseball cards, and rifled through every Tiger card I had. My Topps set was nearly complete, stacked into columns by team, and I'd recorded every card number in order in a spiral notebook. There was no Tiger player named Morris Madden to be found. On a whim, I went back upstairs and found the latest edition of the Downriver Declarer, and scanning the sports section, found the box score from a recent game against the Oakland Athletics. There, in the pitching column as a reliever, was Madden's last name. *So,* I nodded to myself, *Maybe Dustin really does have an inside source on the roster.* I wasn't sure what to make of it.

The next day was a Saturday, and it also happened to be the first day of August. I was up earlier than normal, and as I crunched my cereal and tossed back my customary cup of juice, I marveled that so much of the summer had already gone by so quickly. Corbin sat at the other end of the kitchen table, working a Flintstones chewable vitamin around in his mouth. He asked if I was excited to go to the ocean and play on the beach with our cousins from my mom's side of the family. I smiled at the thought. It was indeed a highlight of every summer, and the prospect of the impending adventure prompted me to jump up, and get ready for yet another shift at Sunset Acres.

I arrived well before my shift began. I walked into the facility and made my way back to Janine's office. I was surprised at how quiet it was in the dining room and hallway. The lights were all off but the sunlight streaming in the windows gave the whole space an eerie blue glow. She sat at her desk, examining an invoice, wearing glasses, quite put together and attractive as always.

She saw me through the office window and motioned me in. Being alone with her was a bit unsettling, and as I entered she put down the invoice and looked deep into my eyes. Her eyebrows were immaculately manicured, and her makeup flawless. I gulped and prepared to speak. She beat me to the punch.

"I heard Walter gave you a $20 tip. Those are, unfortunately, not permitted here at Sunset Acres. You will have to return it to me at once, and agree to never accept a gift from one of our vulnerable seniors again." I stared at her, trying to compose a response.

"Why? He just wanted to thank me. I don't see—" I began to retort. She cut me off. "There's really no discussion to be had. It's been a policy here for a very long time that we do not allow our residents to be bilked by clever teenagers." Her lip curled snidely. "Do you think you're the first kid to think of this? It starts with a small amount, and eventually people get themselves added to wills and trusts." I looked at her incredulously. I reached for my wallet to return the bill, but she continued on.

"If you won't return it, the solution is simple. It will be docked from your next check." She picked up the invoice again, and began to compare its contents with a spreadsheet on her desk. "Will there be anything else?" she asked without looking up.

"Yes, there is," I stammered. I tried to regain my composure. "I—well—I need to have the next couple of weeks off. I know I should have mentioned it earlier, but there really wasn't ever even an interview, was there?" I attempted to explain. "I am going on a family vacation—" She held up her hand, and cut me off again mid-sentence.

"Absolutely out of the question. Ridiculous," she said curtly. "You've just started working here, and you've seen how short-handed we are. Sometimes I marvel at the level of pathetic, pubescent fools this place forces me to work with," she fumed. "For you to think even for a second—" This time it was Janine who was cut off abruptly.

"With all due respect, I have to step in here. Who exactly are you calling a pubescent fool? My son?" I heard a stern voice ask. I wheeled around, shocked to see my own father enter the office. His face was flushed, and his eyes flashed at the manager as he spoke.

She looked stunned ever so briefly, but quickly recomposed herself. "I know exactly who you are. You started teaching over there right after my time, however, and have no sway over me in the slightest. You can remove yourself from my office this moment," she seethed.

"I'm also his father. And I'll advise you that even though I am far from the most important person over at Crosstown, I am very close friends with some of the ones who are. They'll be hearing from me in no uncertain terms regarding your horrific managerial style—and general lack of manners." She looked greatly put out.

"As it just so happens, my boyfriend has the ear of someone quite important across the way as well," she snapped coldly. "None other than the head honcho himself." Her eyes flashed.

"I gather Dav did not tell you about this upcoming trip?" Dad queried as he glanced at me, then refocused his attention on Janine. "No, he most certainly did not," she spat back. "I'll expect him to fulfill his commitments and be here on Monday, all the same," she nearly hissed. "Anything less will result in a dark mark on his employment records, and obviously no reference would be given."

My heart fell, wondering how in the world I'd be able to meet her requirements, while the rest of my family frolicked down south at the ocean. I'd let my dad down yet again, in a new and creative way—and caused him extra work and hassle to boot, I realized sadly.

"He won't be here on Monday, Ms. Lucero," he said, glancing

down at her shiny name plate. "I've heard a lot about you from one of my former students, as it so happens." I raised my head with a start. "And he won't be working here even this afternoon. Responsibility is important, but family comes first. Come on, Dav. Let's get out of here." He turned and walked out of the small office, and the only person more shocked than me was perhaps Janine herself, who stood up from her chair, speechless.

Dad continued talking as we crossed the threshold. "And—Ms. Lucero," he called back as I caught up to him. "He'll be keeping the tip." We walked triumphantly down the short hallway side by side, through the dining room, and out the door of Sunset Acres.

26

method acting

Dad's gesture had meant a lot to me. We rode home in the church van silently. I never did ask how he happened to be there to overhear Janine's rant. I was simply happy that he had been. Things seemed to begin to thaw between us.

That afternoon, I called Denny. I had asked him to dig up a list for me, and wanted to know if he'd acquired it yet. He said that he had, but that he was heading off any minute for a shift at Farmer John's. He asked if I could swing by there and get it from him, and I agreed.

I walked into the air-conditioned grocery not long after that, and finally found the register that Denny was bagging at, located two-thirds of the way down the row of more than a dozen checkout lines. Light instrumental music played, and a sea of shoppers marched around, their orange carts filled to the brim.

He was assisting a cashier named Mary, a friendly chatterbox of a woman who seemed to know everything and everybody. I'd met her several times before, as my mom enjoyed shopping there every couple of weeks. Mary was pretty much a savant when it came to names, birthdays, and other bizarre tidbits.

I saw a small folded pile of the same orange and brown embroidered bags that Mandy had been carrying plates around in. Each had a smiling face of Farmer John himself hand-stitched into the front. Apparently they were distributed as necessary to crabby eco-conscious customers that eschewed both paper and plastic, for a small fee that supposedly went to save trees in the Amazon.

Denny was hard at work trying to keep up with a huge order as it slid toward him on the conveyor belt, and when he was finally done, he turned to me and pulled a note from his back pocket.

"Here you go, Dav. That's every single one of them. Care to tell me why you wanted to see it?" he pried. Mary turned and squinted at me with her coke bottle glasses. She pushed her wild, straggly hair away from around her eyes and greeted me.

"Well hello, Dav! Good birthday last month? I was so glad your dad accepted those tickets. How was Kings Island?" she asked as she began running up another load of groceries. I didn't want to go down that road, so I politely replied that it had been terrific. "Fourteen now?" I nodded, impressed that she had retained the knowledge, but I was not surprised. A random thought crossed my mind.

"Mary? Can I ask you something? Who around here buys a lot of Eye Filet?" She stopped in the middle of counting soup cans and stared at me.

"What kind of a question is that?" she laughed. "Now hold on, I didn't say I couldn't answer that for you," she cajoled indignantly when she saw my expression fall. I looked back up at her expectantly.

She resumed scanning items from the conveyor belt, clearly deep in thought. Minutes passed, and I chatted casually with Denny in the meantime, and even stepped in to lighten his bagging load when he fell excessively behind on another large order.

"It's fine, Mary," I finally said. "Just a hunch I had about something. You can tell me next time I'm in here, if you remember." I said goodbye to Denny, thanked him for the list, and headed back toward the exit. Mary, clearly flustered, called after me, saying that she would do just that.

"I don't ever forget anything, Dav! It will come to me, mark my words!" she hollered. I waved to her in thanks, and left through the automatic doors.

Right around the corner from Farmer John's was a massive strip mall, with a gigantic Sears location as its anchor. I'd been there numerous times before. If I ever had even a few extra dollars, I could often be found inside, splurging on a sundae from Sanders, which was embedded into the sprawling retailer. During the 1960s, it had been the highest grossing Sears in the entire world. I'd even heard that an elephant had walked right down the major thoroughfare out front when the store had opened after World War Two as part of a huge extravaganza.

I walked down along the seemingly endless facade of Sears, and gazed up at the huge blue block letters spelling out the iconic name, standing out sharply against the brightly painted white brick. The popularity of the mall had fallen somewhat throughout the 80s, but that day it was still bustling and as busy as I'd ever seen it.

Families walked down the broad sidewalks, enjoying ice cream cones, and carrying numerous bags from the day's haul. I stopped and looked inside a couple of stores along the way. A popular shoe outlet had endless new models already on display in the front window in anticipation of the impending school year. I gazed wistfully at a couple of pairs, knowing full well even without seeing the price tags that they were completely out of my reach.

The previous summer, Mom had taken me back-to-school shopping, and after buying a few new pairs of khakis, socks, and underwear at Sears, we had stopped in at this very shoe store. It had been on a whim, after I'd nagged her extensively, since we both knew the prices there were usually exorbitant. After some browsing, I had been ecstatic to find a pair of black Reeboks hidden on a shelf near the back, on clearance. They had been called Reebok Rads, and they were designed for skateboarding.

Originally quite expensive, they had been marked down 75 percent, due to being several seasons old. None of that bothered me in the slightest, and I ran up to my mom with them.

"Look at these. Reeboks! I've never had a pair of shoes this nice. Aren't they awesome? And they're in my size, or close enough to it. Can we please get them?" I had asked her plaintively. I was bordering on making a scene and she attempted to calm me down with a few pointed questions. Were these shoes really something I would use? I admitted that I had little experience skateboarding, or much intention on doing much more of it in the future.

My only real stint of skateboarding had ended badly in the basement on my right hip a couple years previously. From that point on, the skateboard had served little purpose other than to propel a harried Muffin across the basement floor when I was particularly bored.

The name brand was the thing that excited me most. I'd spent my entire life up until that point wearing off-brand shoes that, while they did the basic job, were a far cry from the Nike, Adidas, and Lotto brand shoes that most of my peers regularly sported. I found the rich, leathery smell of them intoxicating. Mom had looked them over skeptically for a few minutes, examined the bargain basement price, and looked back at me again. Then she had grabbed my arm jovially and we had headed to the register together.

As I stood gazing again at the shoe display and reminiscing, I noticed a figure standing behind me, motionless, in the reflection. I whirled around to see Mandy standing there on the sidewalk. She looked tired, her face careworn, but still gorgeous in her own unique way. I stammered for a minute, and then asked how she had been doing.

"I can't really talk here," she replied. "I'm going to see a movie. Come with me." She motioned toward the other end of the strip mall, where the Rouge Park Eight Theater anchored the place, opposite Sears. I hesitated, not knowing how to explain to her that, along with a sundry other prominent features of worldly culture, movie theaters were also completely taboo for Crosstown Church members.

"Please. It will help take my mind off other things." She looked at me and managed a sad smile and my heart swelled. "It might help you, too. Plus, it's air-conditioned and they've got popcorn. My treat." Instinctively, I looked around, wondering if anyone from Crosstown would see me. I was shocked to realize I was actually considering her offer. I recognized no one, and I had absolutely nothing else to do for the rest of the afternoon, so I gave in. We slowly walked together down the pavement toward the theater.

"What have you been up to lately?" I asked casually, but we both knew it was a serious question. "You seem to have a lot of things on your plate," I said pointedly, recalling her to-do list and its chilling entry about Wanda with a shudder. "Are things going the way you had planned?" I looked her directly in the eyes. She stopped walking.

A sudden random and terrible thought crossed my mind as I waited for her reply. Number 7 on her list had been to *Finish Wanda*. Now, Number 8's cryptic acronym shook me to the core: *MTRB*. What if, somehow, it had stood for *Move The Rotting Body?*

"I hope you know that I had nothing to do with what happened to poor Wanda," she said, eyes flashing. I desperately wanted to believe her. "When I arrived that morning, it was already too late. I should have been there for her. Maybe if I had been I could have stopped it." Her eyes welled up, and I couldn't recall ever seeing her this close to shedding a tear.

"It's not your fault, Mandy," I consoled her, my relief growing as I became slightly more convinced of her innocence. "But do you have any idea who did it?" I asked. She nodded up toward the marquee, and I gathered that we would continue the discussion once we had tickets and were safely inside. *And without a doubt,* I thought, *only when she is good and ready.*

We both examined the choices for features and show times. The latest Superman sequel, Harry and the Hendersons, and Adventures in Babysitting were our finalists. Mandy really wanted to see the babysitting movie, but it was rated PG-13 and I knew I'd be in even deeper trouble if I were somehow caught viewing that title. We eventually settled on watching the final installment of Christopher Reeve in tight red pants battling the outstanding Gene Hackman as Lex Luthor. Mandy bought us a towering barrel of popcorn soaked in butter, and we proceeded to our seats.

I found the theater amazing, having never darkened the door of one previously. A few dozen other patrons had bought tickets to our showing, and the soft hum of voices and ambient music that played as we waited in the half-light was exhilarating to me for some reason. It was all brand new to me. Mandy put her head next to my ear as the lights darkened even further.

"When I got to Wanda's it was still barely light outside. I knocked, but the door was slightly open. I found it odd, so I went inside and I found her lying on the floor, blood everywhere. She was already almost gone. But she tried to tell me something. All she could get out, two or three times, was the word 'chess.' I tried to get her to say more, to finish what she was trying to say, but she was choking on every syllable. A minute later she was gone," she said, her voice cracking at the end. I looked over at her in the dimness sympathetically.

A trailer came on for an upcoming movie called The Princess Bride. It looked pretty entertaining, and I filed it away for future reference, but what Mandy had just said was more interesting to me in the moment. "Chess? What could that mean?" I asked her.

She explained that Wanda did enjoy playing the game of strategy, and had taught her some of the basic strategies. But Mandy couldn't guess what Wanda had meant with her dying words. "I've been wanting to get better, and I even thought about getting a tutor, but," she said with a somber voice, "obviously other things have come up." I wondered what things she was referring to. *Maybe she's successfully made her way down to the final couple of items on her list,* I thought, alarmed. I hadn't ever gotten the chance to read what the last two were. All I knew was that I hoped they somehow included me.

The movie began, and I felt her hand silently grab mine between the plush seats. Electric waves shot up my arm and from there, throughout my entire body. I kept my hand rigid, not knowing what else to do, or perhaps I was just scared to see what might happen next. I hadn't held hands with a girl since Violet and I had shared our secret grasp many years before.

As the screen came to life and the audience was warned of the many dangers of nuclear proliferation, what Wanda had uttered with her final breath started to make sense to me in a new, surprising way.

Combined with Denny's list, a flicker of a theory was beginning to form in my mind.

In the middle of an epic fight scene between the Man of Steel and a glowing, nuclear-powered sort of WWF wrestler, Mandy looked down at her watch, which was emitting a faint green glow. She leaned over to me again as she stood up. "I have to go. I'm sorry," she whispered.

"Now? The movie's almost over," I replied hoarsely. She insisted, and pulled away. "Call me," she instructed, but she jogged up the dark aisle before I could remind her that I still didn't actually have her phone number. I looked back at the massive screen for a second, and then jumped up myself, intent on finding out where she had to be so urgently.

Out in the crimson-colored carpeted hallway, there was no one to be seen. *She must have nearly sprinted out of here*, I thought, rather irritated. At the front glass doors I looked out and scanned the mass of people outside the theater, and quickly realized it was hopeless. She was gone.

There were two phone booths in the lobby, and I was disgusted to find one of them was occupied by Ryne. He was looking the other way, and I ducked out of sight to avoid being seen. I crept closer to the back of the booth he was occupying and leaned up against a rope stanchion, attempting to look as casual as possible.

"Stop being so nervous. I told you, the kid heads out to camp in a couple weeks. The problem will be solved by then," he sneered. He paused briefly and listened. "He won't talk. I've made it clear as day what happens if he does." My blood ran cold. Was Ryne talking about me, or someone else?

"Everything is all set. This thing is happening. In ten days, it will all be over, and we'll be rolling in it," he said soothingly. He looked down at his own watch. "Shoot, I have to go. I'm meeting my girlfriend for a bite to eat at Big Boy." He hung up the phone and darted out the door, never even glancing in my direction.

I seethed at him inside, but even more so at Mandy. *Still going out with Ryne?* After all that he had done, after all she'd done with me? *That's it,* I swore to myself. I was done with Mandy and her bizarre mind games once and for all.

The next night I was back at Crosstown for the Sunday evening church services. During the summer months, Mr. Townsend ran the youth program, and it was known as Great Stories, Bible Stories. He was a logical, matter-of-fact sort of man, but patient and relatively good-natured as well, gifted with a dry sense of humor that I rather looked forward to.

At the beginning of each session, he would start up an old 8 mm film projector, and a familiar theme song would play, featuring a chorus of male voices singing robustly in unison:

Great stories Bible stories
Stories that are true
They tell of God
And his love for us
And his power too.

After we'd all filed into the small chapel near the back of the church and been seated, Mr. Townsend quieted the couple dozen of us down and cranked up the projector as always. He asked Gregory to lower the lights, and we proceeded to watch a short animated film about David and Goliath. As it played, I scanned the attendees, and was a bit surprised and chagrined to see Violet sitting right next to Grangeford.

Typically on these hot Sunday nights, the two seating sections were split pretty much down the middle by gender; not by dictate, but voluntarily. Denny and I were at the end of a row of a half dozen boys, but several couples had paired off near the front this week, in what I considered an egregious breach of protocol.

In the middle of the film, Violet and Grangeford broke into a fit of shared laughter over something. I clenched my jaw and hated them both in the moment. *Grangeford has moved in and stolen the limelight from me on everything else... Why shouldn't he do the same with Violet?* I thought bitterly.

The film eventually ground to a halt, and Gregory dutifully raised the room lights once more. Townsend announced it was time for a sword drill, and the room buzzed. These contests of Scriptural agility were a mainstay of youth activities at Crosstown. Speed, grace under pressure, and an encyclopedic knowledge of the Bible were the keys to success.

Denny, Gregory, Violet, and myself all possessed certain of those skills, but none of us had them all. Grangeford was considered a rare three-tool player, with a bonus fourth attribute—utter and inexhaustible confidence—thrown in for good measure.

He had smoked the field nearly every previous Sunday night since summer had begun. I resolved to give him the run of his life. I flipped through the pages of my Bible, and stretched the leather cover, like a professional card player shuffling through a deck before a big hand. Mr. Townsend raised his arm, and in unison the entire room of kids lifted their Bibles over their right shoulders, locked and loaded. He announced the first Scripture passage, and immediately the high-pitched sound of thin, membrane-like pages being rifled through frantically filled the room.

I stood up and shouted. "James 3:16: For where envying and strife is, there is confusion and every evil work!" I somehow resisted the urge to look over at Grangeford and Violet, and stood for effect a second longer than necessary, the irony of the passage in question completely lost on me.

"Good job, Dav. One for you," Townsend announced, and wrote a dash on the chalkboard next to my name. I got two of the next three as well, and seemed to be on the fast track to victory.

Gregory and Denny scored a couple wins as well, and I continued to rack up points and extend my lead. I finally glanced over at Grangeford and Violet, anticipating their crestfallen looks at being so soundly beaten. I was outraged to find that they had disengaged from the contest completely. He was doodling something inside the front cover of her Bible, while she was laughing and playfully punching his arm after every flourish of the pencil.

That sly dog, I thought to myself. I was angry at him, but found myself still admiring his tactics. Once he'd seen I was on fire that night, he had found a way to score points in pursuit of an even bigger prize. *Who cares about winning a stupid sword drill?* I asked myself. I began to pout inside, and for the most part, I quit trying for the rest of the evening, allowing Gregory to squirt past me in total finds to snatch the evening's victory.

Mr. Townsend released us a little earlier than the adults, and we all spilled out onto the blacktop behind the church and milled around, catching up with one another. Discussions surrounded the upcoming church sleepover that was always a highlight of every summer. Again standing in the long shadow cast by Sunset Acres, Denny laughingly recalled my ill-fated trip to the top of the behemoth building. Some other kids around me who attended other area schools were not as familiar with the story, and they turned to listen.

"And I'd do it again in a heartbeat. I'd take that basketball over there with me and throw it right into the creek," I bragged loudly, hoping to get Violet's attention with my reckless bravado. It drew some whistles and laughter from the throng. Violet simply rolled her eyes and looked disappointed. Grangeford's ears perked up and he walked over to me.

"Oh yeah, tough guy? Why don't you do it right now? Sounds like something I'd really like to see," he challenged me coolly, prompting some nervous giggles and chatter. I couldn't believe it—I was trapped again. *How is this jerk always staying one step ahead of me with such ease?* It was like playing against a master chess player. I scolded myself. I knew there was no backing down, not with this many—and especially Violet's—eyes on me, waiting to see if I would walk the walk, or if I was simply full of hot air.

"Don't do it, Dav. You've got nothing to prove. Our parents will be out here in a minute," Violet advised earnestly. She sounded slightly condescending to me in that moment, and I blew off her suggestion like I hadn't even heard it. I grabbed the worn basketball from against the church wall and headed off. I didn't care what happened to me this time—somehow the adrenaline made me feel invincible.

I made my way once more carefully out onto the roof beyond the Penthouse. The sky was a deep amethyst, and the sun burned hot and red in the west directly in front of me. A cool wind blew into my face, and a plane with Northwest Airlines markings moved slowly overhead, making its final descent into nearby Metro Airport. Weeks later I would recall the mundane sight when a similar passenger jet famously crashed across town shortly after take-off, killing all but one. I moved closer to the edge of the roofline, and was ecstatic to see a small group of observers gathered around Grangeford and Violet.

Instead of throwing the ball behind me down to the creek below, a sudden epiphany hit me. I turned back toward the west.

"Here, Grangeford! Catch this if you can!" I called, and heaved the ball up into the gusting wind with all my might. It traveled another twenty feet higher into the air before gradually, gravity took its relentless toll and sent it hurtling down toward the group of kids with amazing acceleration.

Gregory made a brave attempt to catch the ball, but thankfully he was a bit late to get over to it. The basketball hit the packed grass with a boom, and proceeded to bounce over a thirty-foot maple on the church grounds effortlessly. The ball continued to travel all the way back to the main parking lot, and I watched with satisfaction as the group chased it down en masse, like kindergartners playing in a soccer game for the first time.

I was not in a hurry to leave. I felt alone and powerful at such a height. I had shown them all that I was a man of my word. I marveled at the 360-degree view once again, savoring every morsel of it this time before I'd have to return back to mundane earth. The sky seemed to turn a deeper blue with every passing second.

I looked past the high school and could make out the figure of Henry Hallas alone over on the baseball diamond. He was tossing baseballs to himself from a bucket, and doing his best to launch home runs to left field. He tried again and again, but never could quite clear the fence, reaching the warning track with more than a handful. Dad had told me before that Hallas had missed the pros by a hair. *It can be hard to let go of the past and admit that the dream is over,* I thought sadly. My dreams about Mandy seemed to be drawing to a close as well.

Grangeford had given up chasing the basketball and joined Hallas on the field. After a short chat, he continued on toward the back of school property alone. I watched him with curiosity until I lost sight of him as the high school building obscured what he was up to.

My eyes scanned over toward the row of storage garages. I laughed to myself as I remembered Denny's nascent bomb-making debacle, and recalled seeing Dustin entering the unfinished portion located at the very end late at night, next to the same pay phone I'd also seen him suspiciously using soon after getting fired from Crosstown.

I was surprised to see another person that appeared to be Mr. Asperat doing something with the bricks outside the garage in question. I studied him from afar curiously. He was alone, and being behind the high school as well, completely out of sight from the rest of the campus. He seemed to be stacking the bricks in rows, and he kept examining his work, and then adjusting them once more.

After a while of doing so, he disappeared from view momentarily, due to the slant of the garage roof. Right when I thought I could stay no longer, he appeared again and, looking hard at the bricks for one last moment, trotted down to his red VW that was parked next to the creek, and took off.

27

Surf & sardines

I awoke mid-morning the following day, and it took a second for me to groggily recall where I was at. We were speeding down an interstate in rural Ohio, and I was sitting awkwardly positioned in the front seat of our station wagon where I'd fallen back asleep. In the mirror behind me, I could see my mom reading a magazine and Corbin playing with an Etch A Sketch. All that was visible of Suzanne was a tangle of blonde locks peaking above a pile of blankets. She enjoyed sleeping through the majority of most of our family road trips.

I yawned and rubbed my eyes. Dad was locked in, like he always was on these epic journeys, content to entertain himself with his own thoughts. Unlike most other families I knew, these trips were mostly peaceful, as everyone in the car was quite content to be left to their own devices. I pulled out my spiral notebook and began to prepare to tally the license plates I saw along the way. We were bound to see some more unusual ones on that particular route, I knew.

For some reason though, the counting activity had lost some of its excitement this time around for me, I realized a few minutes in. The sight of the license plates themselves on the back of cars streaming past us were leaving a bad taste in my mouth, and I knew exactly why. I had stayed up late the night before, packing up all the pieces, parts and tools from the map project. After I knew my parents had gone to bed for the night and the house had become completely still, I had slipped over to Mandy's house through the darkness, left the large box and the stack of distressed wood planks I'd deconstructed next to her garage, and departed like a ghost.

As the green mile markers passed by in a blur, I sat quietly and contemplated the events of the summer up until that point. I was shocked at how commonplace the idea of Justus' and Wanda's violent deaths had become within my own mind. Upon further reflection, I was horrified to come to grips with the fact that Freddy and his sisters were still living under a cloud of doubt about their own father's whereabouts. I glanced over at my own dad again, and couldn't imagine the vast range of emotions they must have been experiencing.

My mind drifted to the impending massive drug deal, Enrique's callous calculations that would enrich himself and further doom the citizens of Rouge Park, and how it was driving good people like Dmitri and Dagmar away for good. I wondered how Ryne, Chet and the rest of the neighborhood teens had gotten to the point that they were willing to sell their own souls for a few stacks of bills. I thought of the washed-out future for girls like Roxy, Roach, and maybe even Mandy—with few options besides aspiring to be a dancer, ogled nightly on Club Xanadu's seedy stage.

We had passed into Pennsylvania and I was still milling over the things I'd heard about Ciggy, the conversation with Travis Keane, and the endless tidbits I'd gleaned from people along the way. I marveled at how different reality was for so many people, when compared to what was evident on the surface to a casual observer. The deeper one burrowed down into other people's truths, the scarier things seemed to become I'd found.

I pictured the hobo once more, and pored over the details I'd observed that day. He'd looked familiar to me, like an image of someone else reflected in a rippled pool. It suddenly came to me all at once who the hobo was, and it seemed hilariously obvious as soon as the thought had metastasized: the hobo was Ciggy, of course. The Revere logo on his hat, hiding within reach of Justus' house, yelling Nicolette's name in the drain system. It all fit. *Was Ciggy the actual perpetrator of the crimes?* I wondered. I swore that I would figure out a way to find out for sure.

Late that same night, our station wagon wearily turned into a gravel driveway and Dad put it into park. My siblings and I scurried out, climbing over whatever obstacles were in our way, and the salty sea air greeted us warmly. The 8-bedroom beach house, a sprawling cube of wood high up on stilts, stood out like a hulking mass against the backdrop of the ocean itself, and it was my idea of absolute heaven.

My mom's side of the family had gathered there on the Outer Banks of North Carolina every summer for as long as I could remember. My grandfather and grandmother graciously footed the bill for everyone, making it an ideal vacation for a family like ours with not a lot of cash to spare. These trips, like all other aspects of life on my mom's side, was a strictly-managed, but still rather fun, series of days that were chock-full of activities on a rock-solid itinerary.

The house was a maze of pine-paneled bedrooms, designed to accommodate at least twenty guests. As we entered, our entire family was greeted with hugs from adults and with wild whoops of excitement from my cousins, who numbered over a dozen. We ran off toward the cluster of bedrooms that housed the younger generation. The rest of the night was occupied with catching up, unpacking, and eventually collapsing into bed and gradually nodding off. The tropical air coming in off the ocean, combined with the loud whir of numerous box fans, was a perfect recipe for sleep.

In the morning, everyone in the house gathered bright and early in the common area for a group breakfast of pancakes and bacon, after which the dishes were done assembly-line style. Grandpa had run the griddle, and now, glistening with sweat from the humidity, instructed everyone to be seated, and we all acquiesced.

The kids found spots on the hard wooden floors, surrounding the few choice seats that were available only to the adults. My grandfather was a thin and tall man, who commanded respect with his quiet but confident Jersey accent. He'd done his part for his country out in the Atlantic with the Navy forty years prior, and the strict training he'd received in those formative years had followed him throughout the rest of his life.

He opened his worn Bible and read from John 8. "If ye continue in my word, then are ye my disciples indeed; And ye shall know the truth, and the truth shall make you free."

As he always did for the cousins, he issued a challenge. "That's the memory verse for this week. Seek the truth. It will guide you throughout your life as it has mine. Any of you children who can recite it by the end of the week will get a prize," he said as his eyes danced.

I shuddered. I desperately wanted to know the truth. I yearned to know what had happened to those innocent people back in Rouge Park. I knew I bore a small part of the blame for Wanda's fate. It felt like a chain wrapped around my neck, dragging me down slowly. I wanted to be set free from it, once and for all, and I knew that learning the full story was the only way that was going to happen.

I spent the week having the time of my life. Rouge Park seemed to be a figment of my imagination. In between building endless sand castles and imaginary cities along the shore, I would wade out with a raft and float on my back in waist-deep water just past the massive breakers. I rose and fell with the waves, looking up into the cloudless sky.

In the evenings, I ate heaping piles of hot food lovingly prepared by my mom and three aunts, and at night, I slept more soundly than I had in all the weeks since discovering Justus. His ghoulish face no longer visited me nightly, and the stresses of life in the city, the Biker Scouts, and Wanda's demise began to fade away, like sand being eroded slowly by the relentless tide.

One morning, I walked out to the beach early by myself. I stood looking up and down the coastline, and lost myself in the endless, mesmerizing waves. There was a long pier to the south of us, extending out into the water to what must have been a staggering depth. A little light on the end of it blinked at me every few seconds. I stood learning its pattern when I was startled to feel an arm around my shoulder. My dad had joined me.

"It's been quite a summer, hasn't it, Dav?" he asked, and I knew the statement was laden with more meaning than met the eye. I agreed, continuing to gaze out into the dark water, which was nearly indigo. "I'm glad we're here together," he said.

"Thanks, Dad," I replied. "For what, Dav?" he asked.

"For bringing us here to this place. I really needed a chance to clear my head. And get a few things sorted out in my mind, about what's happened. Everything's going to be alright, I think. Do you?" I asked, turning toward him.

"I do," he smiled. We continued to stand side-by-side on the sand for quite a while that morning, until hunger drove both of us back over the dunes to the beach house for another scrumptious breakfast.

My skin darkened substantially in the brutal sun until, on the morning of the final day when I looked at myself naked in the bathroom mirror, the dividing lines on my torso were as stark as night and day. I thought I resembled a shipwrecked sailor wearing bright white shorts. I walked closer to my reflection and did a double-take. Minuscule sprigs of dark hair were appearing under my arms, and a solitary thick hair now sprouted bizarrely from my chin. Mom had been right after all, I thought as I stood up as straight as a statue, my head nearly passing out of the mirror's reach. It had indeed been what she had oddly entitled 'a growing-up summer.'

I awoke with a start before the sun rose on the morning of our departure. It was still almost dark, and the red glow from my cousin's alarm clock read 4:45 am. The low noise of snores from the handful of boys scattered around me on neighboring cots reminded me of where I was. I didn't want to leave. The week had flown by, and I knew what awaited me back in the Great Lake State. The stray pieces and parts from my dreams had come together to form a theory—an answer to all that had been going on back home. I knew what I had to do. I just didn't know if I'd have the nerve to actually do it.

"And the truth shall set you free," I'd recited, winning a smile of approval from my grandpa the evening before. He had handed me my personalized prize for the feat: an oversized vintage-looking metal key. I'd thanked him, and wandered off examining it closely. It had an antique look, and the word *TRUTH* was carved into it, and it must have weighed several pounds. My grandpa had followed me out onto the porch.

"Is everything OK, Dav?" he had asked. We both stood along the railing watching a lizard dart among the long beach grasses on the dunes beyond us.

"I'm not sure," I had admitted. "Have you ever known you had to do something, but didn't want to? Wished it could just all go away, and hoped that if you would just put your head under the bedspread, someone else would magically fill in the gap?" He nodded somberly, but said nothing more. He put his arm around me, and we silently reflected on tough situations in our own past and present.

The drive home was a monotonous slog. Washington, D.C. was a nightmare, all five lanes of northbound traffic clogged with a million other travelers leaving the eastern seaboard. It was nearly 100 degrees as we neared the Potomac at a crawl. Dad went into his familiar rant where he said every possible word in the dictionary without actually swearing, repeatedly vowing to never again fall for the temptations of ease that Interstate 95 appeared to offer on paper.

Corbin moaned, and it was too hot for even Suzanne to sleep. We pulled off on an exit with what seemed like the rest of Virginia and attempted to get some food. Mom tried to change the subject from the sweltering air in the car as we languished in a horrendously long drive-through line.

"You have that church sleepover tonight—if we can get you home in time," she offered. In the excitement of the beach week I'd forgotten about it completely. It seemed to be a long shot that we could possibly make it back at our current pace. "Did you invite any of your neighborhood friends like Mr. Worthy asked you to?" she queried.

I'd mentioned it to the triplets in passing the week before, but crudely hoped they wouldn't come. Crosstown was big on spreading the word about activities to our heathen friends. I didn't really pull my weight on their requests most of the time. Shannon Worthy had met the triplets once at a church carnival, and they had been on his radar ever since. I was, in truth, coldly indifferent to the state of their souls. The realization of that stark fact brought on a pang of conviction, and I resolved in my mind to change my attitude when I saw them next and encourage them to attend again.

Hours later, I walked briskly down the halls of Crosstown Church, sleeping bag and backpack slung over both shoulders. We'd arrived back home after our epic trek at almost nightfall, and even though my parents had offered me the opportunity to skip the activity—a rare choice—I had insisted on attending. The prospect of free pizza, late-night movies, and capture the flag in the dark was too exciting to pass up, no matter how exhausted I was from our road trip. I entered the chapel, and scanning the crowd, saw Tyson and Denny and some other guys and hurried over to join them.

"Hey, we were beginning to think you wouldn't make it. Pizza's already cold," Tyson said, and he and the other guys proceeded to pepper me with questions about my vacation. I grabbed three lukewarm slices and wolfed them down as the boys talked about other things, and my eyes traveled over the assorted kids that had broken off into scattered groups around the crammed chapel.

I spotted Grangeford and Violet, chatting casually with a handful of other guys and girls. *Apparently, something serious is brewing between the two of them*, I realized, fighting off raw feelings of jealousy. *Fine—no skin off my teeth*, I resolved icily. *She can find out what a tool he is the hard way.*

"Let's talk Worthy into doing sardines this time instead. Capture the flag is cool but we've done it the last two years in a row," Denny urged. Zane, Trevor, Leon and some of the other guys agreed, but I was non-committal. I actually preferred the war-like conditions and excitement of the latter activity, but didn't want to push against the tide too hard. We continued to debate the pros and cons of both games until our gregarious youth leader appeared right at my side.

"Oh good, you're finally here, Dav. Your guest was beginning to wonder where you were. So excited you decided to invite Mandy to our church sleepover! We simply love hosting visitors here at Crosstown," he beamed, nodding back to the girl I could sense dutifully standing just behind him. I froze, and stood staring straight ahead at the other boys. They looked from her, to Shannon Worthy, then to me, and back to Mandy again. They seemed as surprised and speechless as I was.

I knew from the boys' facial expressions that Mandy was looking as put-together and gorgeous as ever. I finally forced myself to turn toward her and immediately confirmed my suspicions. She had on cut-off jean shorts, a seafoam green Miami Vice T-shirt, and a pink headband. Her KangaRoo shoes were also pink, with green laces, and completed the ensemble perfectly. She waved hello, and smirked at my shocked response.

"Thank you, Mr. Worthy. I'm really happy to be here tonight," she replied sweetly, and Shannon moved on to the next group of kids. "Hello, guys," she said to my friends, and I thought several of them might faint. I excused myself, and grabbed her by the arm and marched off to the far side of chapel with her in tow. She jerked away and said she could walk all by herself.

"I'm sorry. I'm just kind of—surprised to see you here," I stammered apologetically. "Why exactly—are you here?" I finally managed.

"What do you mean? Isn't anyone allowed to come to these church things?" she asked. I sighed. "Of course," I allowed, still trying to ascertain how this had all come to happen. "How did you know about this event, though?" I stood waiting expectantly for an explanation, still incredulous to see her. I wasn't exactly sure how I felt about sharing this setting with her. And, I was also still livid that she'd ditched the movie with me to go out with that idiot Ryne instead.

"I came looking for you several times last week, but no one was home. The triplets finally told me where you had gone. And they said you'd most likely be here tonight. So I caught a ride and came here," she smiled. "I thought you'd be happy to see me."

"I am—I am. Don't get me wrong," I said shiftily. "But I thought all your free time would be spent with that crooked boyfriend of yours. Don't you have to get over to Big Boy again soon?" I asked accusatorily. Just then, Worthy announced it was time to gather and discuss the night's activities. As we formed a thick circle around the leaders, Violet caught my eyes from the other side. She looked genuinely curious about who Mandy could possibly be, and maybe even a little flustered. It made me feel happy.

Worthy explained that we would be playing sardines, and what the rules would be. A mix of cheers and moans erupted from the crowd. The lights would all be completely turned off throughout the expansive church complex. Three names would be drawn from a hat, and those kids would have five minutes to hide. Then, the rest of the throng would seek them out and hide along with them until everyone had found one of the resulting groups.

The smallest group, and thus the most well-hidden and hard to find, at the end of the game would win. A buzz of excitement and chatter broke out among all of us, and everyone threw a scrap of paper into the hat to see if they'd be one of the lucky three. Trevor and a girl in the grade below mine had their names drawn.

I was surprised to hear my name called third, and mere seconds later, Shannon Worthy declared that the countdown had started. The lights began to go out in sections, starting with the chapel, and moved north and south throughout the campus until—within a minute—

complete darkness reigned. I ran like a gazelle out of the chapel, and then felt Mandy unexpectedly grab my hand. She had slipped out along with me, unnoticed.

I knew exactly where I wanted to hide. Over in the old elementary gym, there was a long-forgotten locker room, a remnant from when the high school had played their athletic competitions in that building, instead of across the street. It had been converted into a storage closet of sorts a decade or two prior, and had now degraded into a maze of boxes and other discarded things that didn't have a home anywhere else in the church complex. It was little known to most of the kids, and the nondescript white, windowless door was often locked. It was open by chance that night, however, and we both crept inside.

Mandy and I climbed over whatever we found in our paths as we attempted to get to the very back of the chamber, in what had once been a ceramic-tiled bank of showers. Over the years, it had become stuffed right up to the ceiling with all kinds of paraphernalia. At the top of the pile I felt around and discovered a stack of old mattresses. I grabbed Mandy's hand and pulled her up with me to the pinnacle, and we grew completely still, laying side by side in the utter blackness. Just then I heard the youth pastor's whistle, faintly alerting us from a distance that the search had officially begun.

Wild whoops and hollers filtered all the way into our hiding place, but soon died out again as the seekers headed in other directions. It was silent once again. I could hear my own heart beating like a snare drum. Every breath seemed to be a hundred decibels. Mandy lay motionless and speechless next to me for a long while.

"I'm glad I got to see you," she finally said in a whisper. "I would have really regretted it if I hadn't come tonight. I may not see you again for a while. And I don't know what the heck you meant about meeting someone at Big Boy. That place is gross," she added.

I explained overhearing the conversation about the impending lunch date with Ryne at the movie theater. She insisted it had not been her that he was meeting.

"He's been going out with Roxy for a good while now," she said softly. "And—I can't believe it—but he's converted her into a paying customer as well. Yup, she's taking those damned drugs. I told her to stop, but she says I'm just jealous. I feel responsible for introducing her to him. This summer is full of regrets, it seems," Mandy lamented.

I lay still and considered what she might mean. I was afraid to ask. "Do you have any other regrets?" I whispered back instead. "Not about those things, per se. But about life in general," I clarified. "What would you do differently if you could do it all again?"

She thought for a moment. "I regret all the time I spent admiring Ryne, trying to impress him. I see him for what he is, finally. I regret putting up with Enrique's choices for as long as I have. The last one—well, I've never really told anyone else about it. But, I think I want to tell you now." I tensed in the darkness, not knowing what to expect.

With considerable relief, I'd finally come around to feeling rather confident that she wasn't personally involved in the crimes, but the way she'd said her last statement made me waver slightly. I desperately hoped that I wasn't about to hear a confession. She began again.

"When my Mom was dying, it was hard for me to watch. The last few months, I rarely even visited," she remembered wistfully. "On my very last visit, she was delirious, over the moon on morphine, to help manage the pain. She had to be strapped to the bed, a painkiller drip attached to her arm." Her voice quivered slightly with emotion. "She pleaded with me to set her free, said they were trying to kill her. I tried to reason with her, to tell her it was for her own good. But she wouldn't listen, she couldn't understand. It was too much for me to handle in the end."

"I escaped, running out of the room down the glossy hallways, which smelled overwhelmingly of antiseptic and death. Have you ever noticed how perfect hospitals look on the surface?" she asked, bitterly. "But it's all just a facade, hiding the horrible truth underneath."

"I just kept running farther away, in tears, unable to stand it any longer. I didn't know it, but it would be the last time I saw her alive. If I could do it all over, I'd turn right around and go back, stay close to her. I'd stay with her that entire day, no matter how difficult it was. But—I can't," she said flatly. "I can't go back to her. And so, I have to live with that fact. And try to remember that whenever there is someone else important in my life, I should make sure to let them know it, beyond a shadow of a doubt."

With that, her lips met mine, and simultaneously in my own head, an explosion of vibrant fireworks in every color filled the inky darkness of the abandoned locker room all at once, putting even Denny's most impressive homemade bombs to shame. Almost immediately though, we heard someone else entering the cluttered locker room, and I knew immediately from the sound of their voices that it was Grangeford and Violet. Mandy pulled away from me abruptly, and we resumed hiding in the darkness, trying not to move a muscle.

But one thing that Mandy had just said stuck in my mind, ruminating there: Staying close by to the ones we love, no matter what terrible things have happened. Her insightful phrase cemented something I'd been working over in my mind for a while, and now I knew exactly what I had to do next.

28

piercing the Fog

The next night I sat up with a start. I had heard a series of gunshots, or so I thought. *Was it just another of my crazy dreams?* I asked myself. Muffin jumped off me down to the chilly floor, clearly annoyed. Then I heard another report, faint but clear, even from my basement bedroom, and knew what I'd heard was completely real.

I hurriedly pulled on some clothes, and stuffed my feet into some shoes that I knew my parents wouldn't freak out about should they become caked with mud, and sneaked out the side door.

Now's as good a time as any, I said to myself as I walked down the driveway. *Time to get to the bottom of everything.* The first light of morning was appearing behind me to the east. The air was thick with a heavy fog.

Somehow I knew what direction the shots had come from. I began to jog slowly in the direction of Embers Bar, and cut through the alley behind it toward Mandy's street. From behind a fence one block over from hers, I could just make out the front of her house. Two windows had been shot out, along with the large pane of glass inside the front door. Two adult male figures were milling about just inside, and the Mustang was awkwardly parked sideways in the middle of the yard, as if Enrique had just arrived in a terrible rush.

I wondered if rival drug peddlers from Detroit had gotten wind of what Enrique and the Biker Scouts were up to, and that they were none too pleased. Someone had sent a message, clear and unambiguous, that this intrusion wasn't going to be taken lying down. I strained my eyes to see if anyone had gotten hurt, but the fog was too thick. I lingered for a moment to try to catch a glimpse of Mandy, but I never saw her. I eventually headed down the street backing up to hers, toward the infamous park.

The rest of the church sleepover had been a blur. Grangeford and Violet had been the first to stumble upon our hiding place, and eventually, a swarm of kids had crammed noisily into the small space with us, revealing where we were at in a gradually more obvious fashion. When it was over, I was somewhat glad, because I was growing tired of witnessing Grangeford and Violet's annoying flirting.

Mandy and I had hung out off and on the rest of the night, ignoring the stares and whispers from my friends and the rest of the youth group. After a game of dodgeball, more food, and a sappy movie, some of the kids had rolled out their sleeping bags and the chapel had slowly grown quieter. Mandy had gotten up from where we were sitting to use the bathroom.

I must have dozed off, because when I had opened my eyes again, it was morning and kids nearby me were packing up and staggering out to their parents' waiting vehicles in broad daylight. I looked around for Mandy, but didn't see her. Tyson and Denny were gone too. Shannon

Worthy walked over to the padded seat where I'd apparently slept away the last hours of the sleepover, a big grin on his face.

"Well, that was fun, wasn't it?" he had mused pleasantly. I had nodded back groggily. "You know, right before I went off to college, your dad ran some of these church activities. He was one of my favorite young teachers back in the day." His cheeks were flushed from the night's strenuous activities, and his kind blue eyes had studied me intently. "Now, Dav—don't take this the wrong way," he had said, as he sat down next to me and stretched, lowering his voice.

"All kids are invited to come to Jesus—you know I believe that with all my heart. He's created each one for a special purpose. But I want you to be careful. Make sure you're thinking through who you're associating with. That girl Mandy seems like trouble to me."

I had followed his eyes as he was staring out the door of the church. Janine was outside, climbing into Dustin's car in the driveway between the church and Sunset Acres, and the two of them had screeched away noisily. Shannon Worthy watched them go, his jaw set. I had glanced back and I realized he was trying hard to hide his consternation. I wondered if somehow his warning about dangerous women who weren't to be fiddled around with had been rooted in a past relationship with Janine herself.

"She is trouble," I replied flatly, not looking at him. "But I don't care." I had gotten up and walked straight out of the chapel without another word to him.

I hadn't seen Mandy since she left the overnighter unannounced, and as I climbed through the jagged hole in the dead-end fence that opened up into the park, I desperately hoped that she hadn't been hurt in the drive-by shooting. However, my current mission did not involve her directly. Finding out her condition would have to wait. The old playground stood out starkly like a sentinel against the fog that covered the ground. I continued past it toward the railroad tracks, and crossed them carefully into the woods beyond them.

I'd not been back to this place since the fire escapade with Tyson several months prior. The trees looked haunted and different in the heavy morning mist. I climbed down to the drain opening where I had last seen the hobo, looking around every few seconds for a glimpse of him, or a sign he had been there recently. Seeing nothing, I lowered my head into the drain and called out.

"Ciggy? Hello?" I was sure he'd be surprised to find out his identity had been discovered. I hoped it would be enough to get him to show himself and provide me some much-needed answers. I called again, but the sound of my own voice just echoed through the seemingly endless misty tunnels.

A voice startled me and I whipped around quickly, nearly slipping in the muddy ravine.

"Henry Ford once walked these same woods, did you know that?" the hobo said. He was about thirty feet behind me, and dressed exactly as he had been that fateful day back in May when I'd last laid eyes on him.

"See those arches placed over the railroad tracks going as far as the eye can see?" he pointed. "Made of concrete, from when Ford tried to electrify trains. Called catenary arches, I think. Turns out it took a whole crew an entire week to remove just one of them. Looks like they're staying right where they are till the end of time."

I heard Freddy's voice again, singing from the top of the garage:

We've got no future, we've got no past
Here today, built to last

"Henry was exploring possible places to build his next big automotive complex," he continued with a raspy voice. "This tract of land was unfortunately just a tad too marshy," he said, pulling out a knife and examining it thoughtfully. "It was perfect in every other way," he mused, walking a few steps closer to me. I looked around warily, and realized he was slowly cornering me.

"Close to the tracks, close to the River, right smack dab on the route between Detroit and Chicago. Just that one small thing changed everything, my grandpa used to say," the hobo continued. "Ford built in Dearborn instead. So instead of Rouge Park becoming a bustling metropolis, it's the dying husk you see now," he said, motioning around him. "Not much of a future. For this place," he added, "or for you and me."

He stepped closer, and the look on his scraggly face frightened me. "So, you know who I am, do you?" he asked. "You might think you know about me, but I have my doubts," he chuckled sarcastically.

"Sigmund Mann. That's right," he nodded as he continued. "But what exactly is that to you? I've never seen you in my life, kid." He was now only a couple of yards away from me. The knife gleamed menacingly in the growing daylight. I looked behind me and saw the steep stone incline up to the railroad tracks was quickly becoming my only viable escape route.

"But you're not Ciggy—are you?" I stated. He stopped suddenly in his tracks, and for the first time looked frightened and unsure himself.

I locked eyes with him. "You're Justus Mann. I should have figured it out a long time before this. The signs were all there the first time I saw you. I'm surprised I didn't recognize you right away. But the fake beard and bushy eyebrows you bought at Lynch's were a nice touch," I added, and continued to press him.

"The bag I found from Lynch's was a valuable clue. That's a costume store, isn't it?" He stood expressionless. "You just want to pretend you're Ciggy in case anyone like me happens to stumble on you out here—right?" I asked pointedly. He seemed flustered, and stammered as he tried to form a response.

"Justus is dead!" the hobo finally yelled. "Now that crazy Enrique can't get his hands on him. No more traps and deceptions, no more deliveries of his poisons, no more crushing debts. The mess is over. He's escaped them for good," he nodded, looking more sure of himself as he spoke the words.

"Ciggy hates Kents," I countered. "But I found Kent butts outside the drain opening where you'd been hiding. And Justus loves Heineken. You were holding a bottle of it that day I saw you back in May." It was clear my mounting evidence was beginning to weaken his resolve.

"You can protest all you want, but I know it's you, Justus. The wedding ring I saw that first day should have been obvious as well. Even though you were trying to pretend to be Ciggy, who is single, you just couldn't take it off, could you?" He lowered the knife and his head bowed.

"She's important to you, isn't she. Even though you probably think that Nicolette is the one who killed Ciggy? That's why you needed to find a place to hide close by; to keep watch over your wife and kids—right?" His eyes were welling up with tears as he lifted them again toward me.

"She's innocent?" he asked, breathlessly. I nodded. "I'm pretty sure I know who killed him, and why —and it wasn't Nicolette," I stated firmly. "And the very same person killed Wanda Kogan to cover their tracks." He sat down on a large outcropping of rock near the opening to the storm drain, and looked lost in thought.

"What I don't understand, though, is why you buried your brother in the backyard behind the garage?" I asked him. He looked at me angrily.

"I didn't do that!" he insisted. "I came home one night, drunk and frantic to get out of Enrique and Dustin's clutches once and for all. I was going to make things right with Nicolette, clean up my life—start things fresh again," he remembered wistfully.

"But, I found Ciggy lying dead right in the center of the living room on the afghan rug. I thought Nicolette had done it, in one of her drunken rages. No one else was around. I realized I'd be framed if I got caught there—I didn't have time to do anything else except grab some clothes and a few bucks and run." He looked at me again with haunted eyes. "Do you think someone killed Ciggy by mistake?"

"I do," I nodded, though I was surprised to learn that Justus had not discarded the body himself. *Who else would have had the time and opportunity to do so?* I thought. He kept talking.

"I barely escaped that night. Just as I climbed through the fence into the park, I saw Enrique, Dustin, and a couple of the Biker Scouts barge into my house. They had flashlights, and I could hear them joking and laughing it up. They must have been coming for me. When they saw Ciggy on the floor, they probably thought it was me, and believed someone had beaten them to the punch," he surmised.

"Or they were coming back to clean up a mess one of them had made previously," I countered, recalling the conversation I'd overheard to the same effect. I asked Justus to describe which Biker Scouts he had seen entering the house that night. When he had done so, I sat down on a rock across from him, separated only by the water cascading out of the culvert, and we stared at one another momentarily, both our minds racing.

"You don't know how many times I almost jumped onto the back of one of these train cars and headed to Chicago," he said as he shook his head, just as a graffiti-adorned trail of boxcars rattled and thundered past overhead. "But, I just couldn't. I can't give up on

Nicolette. I've let her down, kid. And just when I resolved to turn things around for both her and me, this craziness all goes down." He got up restlessly and walked up the embankment, heading away from the tracks and into the woods. I instinctively got up as well and followed him.

"Why did Ciggy get kicked out of leadership in the Cub Scouts?" I blurted out from behind him. He stopped walking and turned to look at me again. His face had grown gaunt during the past months, and his blue eyes gleamed with an unhealthy vividness.

"Some kid reported him. Said he was doing weird stuff to him at the meetings. He'd had trouble like that at other jobs in the past, I hate to say. I never wanted to believe it, but the head honchos at the Cub Scouts were convinced." He paused. "Ciggy went through some tough stretches like all of us did, man. I'd hate to say the drugs were completely to blame, but after he first went down that path, he was never really the same. Old demons became his permanent masters," he admitted reluctantly.

"What I don't understand is why you didn't go to the police?" I asked next. Even as the words came out of my mouth, they had a strange taste, as I realized that, of course, I'd been guilty of the same mistake.

"You don't get it, kid. I had to disappear from the face of the earth. Enrique and the Xanadu crew were going to silence me, one way or the other. They got Ciggy instead. Since I couldn't do anything for him, I figured it was best to try to turn lemons into lemonade and stay dead."

"Plus, with me out of the picture, those maniacs have finally been leaving Nicolette and Freddy and the girls alone. I couldn't risk that changing should I miraculously reappear. I'd love to see the looks on their faces, though, if I did," he chuckled. He leaned against the tree

I'd seen before with the R + N carving etched into its crumbling bark.

From here we could see through the remaining trees of the small forest out into the empty windswept park. The fog was beginning to disperse, and the playground came into view. Justus stared at it nostalgically.

"Oh, man. That old set has seen some things in its day," he admired. "We played on that when I was about your age. The four of us had some great times there. Of course, it wasn't falling apart and decrepit like it is now. It was freshly painted in bright colors, with rubber swing seats that smelled like a brand new car. They'd play baseball games on that field, sell hot dogs and popcorn... Those were the days," he smiled sadly.

The rusted-out backstop was leaning heavily to one side now. The diamond was completely overgrown, and besides the playground set isolated in the middle of the field, the park was uninhabited and had fallen out of use completely.

"I fell in love with Nicolette right there," he pointed. "That very spot. We'd swing to our heart's content until it was pitch dark and my folks called me and Joyce home." It was difficult to imagine my prickly principal as a carefree girl. "Of course, that didn't make all my friends happy. She had been with someone else before me, another kid on the block. I'm not sure he ever got over it, to be honest, poor guy," he added.

Just then another train burst into view, obscuring the park in a noisy rush of grinding metal. After it passed, he looked at me again expectantly.

"I have another question," I continued. "I believe that the weapon used on Ciggy was a unique knife, a kind they gave out at the Cub Scout troop he was leading." I described the knife, and its engraving in detail, and Justus nodded excitedly.

"Yeah, Ciggy had one of those. In fact, he left it over at my place a while ago, and I'd put it on a small shelf by the front door hoping he'd remember to take it home with him the next time he came over." His face clouded. "I never would have guessed it would have been used to take him out." His face contorted.

"I just can't believe I'll never see him again," he mused. I could see his anger growing as he thought about his predicament and the chain of events leading us both to this isolated place.

"I know that Ciggy was far from perfect, but they can't get away with it," he fumed, stomping around back and forth on the soft earth. "I want to be vindicated. I want the culprits to pay. I want that demon Enrique and his cretin Dustin behind bars. And, above all, I want to return home." He stopped and tried to catch his breath.

"I'd love to see you reunited with your family, Justus. Maybe you can still put the pieces back together with them and get a new start," I offered. "I also have a person I'd like to see cleared as well," I added. I felt bad that I'd suspected Mandy's involvement for as long as I had.

"Not to mention poor Wanda," Justus contributed. "When I saw the commotion and the lights, I just had to know what was going on. It took me a day or so but I finally crept over long enough to figure out that she'd met some sort of untimely end too. I'd wondered if the two crimes were connected for my entire time out here. Something told me they had to be." He stumbled, and reached around for a soft place to land.

"You're hungry. And exhausted from exposure," I chided. I promised to return that afternoon with food, water, and additional blankets. He thanked me, then gazed at me directly, his eyes boring holes into me with their intensity.

"What do you think? Can you help me?" he asked, desperately.

"Yes, I think I can now," I replied.

When I got home, Mom greeted me at the door. "There was a phone call for you," she said, looking at me oddly. My heart raced, hoping to hear that it had somehow been Mandy. I wanted to hear from her so badly that I no longer cared if my parents knew about her existence or not. I braced myself for the news.

"It was Mary from Farmer John's. You remember her, right? Funny woman, remembers almost everything it seems. Strangest thing," she continued, looking down at her note. "She said, 'I remembered who had been buying a lot of Eye Filet lately.' Does that make any sense to you at all?" Mom asked confusedly. I nodded, and she shared the name with me.

"One more thing!" she called after me as I headed down the hallway. I ran back to the kitchen entryway where she stood holding a small package that looked like a folded-up manila envelope.

"This arrived for you in the mail just now," she said pointedly. "It doesn't have a name in the spot for the return address. Any idea what it could be?" She looked at me quizzically. I shrugged and took it from her open hand and examined it. It had a postmark near the top from a day earlier, in Ann Arbor, which was located about half an hour west of Rouge Park by car. I told her honestly that I had no idea what it could be, or who it could be from.

I thanked her for relaying the message from Mary and continued downstairs to my room. I looked up at the key my grandpa had given me, where I'd hung it on the wall below Mandy's sign. The word *TRUTH* glowed eerily as the light caught it just right, and I hoped the verse he'd had us all memorize would come to pass. I closed the door, took a deep breath, and got to work.

29

Sticks & Stones

Two days later, I was bouncing along Interstate 75 heading into the wilderness. I was squirming in a vinyl seat on a school bus, trying to get comfortable next to Tyson. He was busy with a handheld baseball game, and every so often he would yell out something to the effect of, "No way, that was a home run!" or "Had him at second by a mile!" I asked him if I could have a turn and, surprisingly, he handed it over to me.

I was happy for the diversion. We had pulled out of the CCCP parking lot a couple of hours previously, headed due north, to a place called Camp WeSaLi. The small religious camp was forged out of the endless forests surrounding Houghton Lake. I'd been attending camp for a week there every summer in late August since I had been old enough to enroll.

"Why's it called Camp WeSaLi?" a newer kid a few rows ahead of us asked out loud. Denny pounced. "It stands for We Say Lies," he reported with a straight face. "You're actually not allowed to tell the truth there. Try it with your counselor, you'll see," he grinned, eliciting guffaws from the veteran teens on the bus.

In reality, the acronym stood for We Save Lives, and the unambiguous goal of the establishment was indeed aimed at doing so—on the spiritual plane, that is to say. Every day was a carefully-orchestrated schedule of personal devotions, chapel services, games, and free time. We were rustled from bed at 5:30 am and often didn't get back into our bunks until nearly midnight. It was always a tiring but exhilarating week that I both looked forward to, and also approached with a fair amount of dread due to the sheer amount of activities.

"Check this out," Denny said, popping up from behind the seat in front of me. He held a can of gold spray paint, which he withdrew quickly and deposited back into his gym bag. "Make sure you're on my team for the week, Dav. You'll understand soon enough. My sister went to camp last week and I've got inside information."

It reminded me of Dustin's wager, and his supposed rat in the dugout, Morris Madden. I'd checked the Tigers standings earlier that morning while at the breakfast table. They'd won 5 of their last 6, and were now just a half game behind the Blue Jays for first place in the division. I imagined Dustin had to be chewing his fingernails down to the quick.

Dad had taken me to Crosstown bright and early that morning. As we'd driven silently through the bright Saturday morning sun, I'd craned my neck to get a good view of Mandy's house as we'd passed. The house was still dark, and I had seen no one about, or in the yard. The Mustang was parked there, but we passed by too quickly for me to see whether or not the shattered windows had been attended to yet.

I noted sorrowfully to myself that it would now be another whole week before I'd have the chance to see her again. I really just wanted to ensure that she was OK. There was so much I wanted to fill her in on about Justus as well, and the stunning conversation we'd had. I had tried to swing by her house later the previous day to try and find her, but too many Biker Scouts had been milling about the place. Apparently the entire organization was on high alert as the big day of their anticipated deal approached.

Further up toward the front of the bus, I could see the backs of Grangeford and Violet's heads tilting toward one another, in a row to themselves. She had her hair braided and tied off in bright purple bandies, and he had clearly just gotten a fresh buzz cut. The front tips of his hair were spiked using some sort of cementing gel.

A row or two behind them I spied the flaming red hair of Chet Wiggins. I was rather surprised he'd agreed to be sent away for an entire week to Camp WeSaLi. *Perhaps he'd had little actual choice in the matter,* I reasoned. I recalled overhearing Ryne mention that someone would be out of the picture at camp soon enough. Could he have been referring to Chet?

He wouldn't sit down, even though Worthy admonished him to from the front every few minutes. He insisted on propping himself up against the wall of the bus, bragging to anyone who would listen about how much cold hard cash he'd brought with him to waste at the popular snack cantina. I hoped he'd get assigned to a different cabin than me. He saw me and made an ugly face.

Soon, we began to fly past endless pine trees as we wound our way ever further north into the Michigan wilderness. Cities and freeway exits became farther between one another, and finally we could see the glimmering surface of Houghton Lake itself on the horizon. It was a massive body of fresh water, smack dab in the middle of the lower peninsula.

The bus rumbled over a gravel trail for a few hundred yards and came to rest in a clearing, skirted on three sides by a chapel, a dining hall, and a gymnasium. A dozen cabins dotted the woods just outside that inner ring. Counselors spilled out of the chapel and surrounded the bus, greeted by screaming kids. I was ecstatic to learn that Denny, Tyson and I were all grouped together, and dragging our sleeping bags and suitcases, we made our way to Cabin Five.

Out of the corner of my eye, I was irritated to notice Grangeford following close behind us to the same cabin, but I was relieved to see Chet veer away toward Cabin Six. His demeanor had suddenly changed for some reason, and he looked like he might be sick. At least I'd be free of any Biker Scout antics while in the safety of my own lodgings.

That afternoon, we made our way down a trail to the bathhouse to change for lake activities. Like the locker rooms at the Community Center, the bathhouse was one of my least favorite places on earth. The boys found it intriguing that the only thing separating us from naked girls was a cinder block wall that extended only down to about knee level.

"Keep on your side ladies, or there might be an unintentional snake sighting!" Denny called out from a wooden bench in the general direction of the girl's changing quarters. Tyson and Trevor laughed loudly at the audacious statement.

"In my case, pythons," Grangeford boasted loudly, while he flexed both biceps, and through the open air above all of our heads, one could hear both the shocked giggles of the girls from over the wall and stunned laughter from the boys intermingling. As he brazenly stripped down in the center of the large room without a hint of modesty, there was no longer any reason to imagine that he had embellished his claim.

He was a grown man for all intents and purposes, and I was not. *No wonder Violet prefers his company to mine,* I fumed to myself. If there had been any way for me to despise him any more before this exhibition, that possibility withered once and for all. As I shielded myself and changed hurriedly alone in the corner, I literally saw red.

Out at the lakefront, I tried hard to think about something else. I got in line to ride the jet skis, which I'd always wanted to try. I was finally old enough to ride them, and was happy that changing into my trunks quickly had paid off in at least one unanticipated way. I was the very first in line, and soon mounted a Kawasaki model in waist-deep water, and brought the watercraft to life. After a quick primer from the lifeguard, I tentatively eased out onto the lake.

Minutes later I was skipping along the surface at forty miles an hour. It was smooth as glass, and the sun reflected off the water so intensely I thought it might blind me. For some reason, it didn't bother me. It was a surreal experience. The rest of the world—with all of its pressures, problems and heartaches—disappeared behind me along with the rest of civilization. Soon it was just me, the jet ski, and the lake itself. Nothing else seemed to exist. It wasn't a lonely feeling; it was euphoric.

I vaguely recalled the lifeguard's instructions to only go out as far as the first buoy, and to bring the jet ski back to shore within just a few minutes so the next camper could have a turn. But I didn't want to do that. Every part of me wanted to simply keep going—to see if there was a point at which it was too far to ever return. The butterflies in my stomach began to build as I ventured farther and farther out into the deep blue water. The desire to escape was becoming all-consuming. I understood more clearly than ever before what Mandy had described back on the playground earlier in the summer.

Mandy's escape. Was that what she had been referring to at the church sleepover? The allusion that she might not see me again for a long while echoed in my ears. I gulped, and realized that perhaps she had been timing her schemes to the same week of the massive drug deal. *Could the two be intertwined in some way?* I wondered.

I had slaved over a lengthy letter down in my room over the two days leading up to camp. Every word had been fastidiously reasoned out and finessed. I had needed to be sure of everything I'd laid out in my missive.

"We Save Lives," or WeSaLi. "Rhymes with Denali," Denny had laughed on the bus earlier that day. *Would my letter be able to save a life?* I asked myself. I hoped that if it was able to, it would finally bring me the peace I'd been seeking ever since the morning Wanda's body had been discovered.

When the letter had been complete, and I simply couldn't look at it one more time, I had sealed it in an envelope, and walked down the street toward Embers and D & D Market to the blue mailbox standing guard on the corner. I'd pulled down the creaking door of the receptacle several times, and then tentatively withdrawn, knowing that once the letter left my hand, a sequence of unstoppable events would begin.

Was I correct? My theory seemed sound. Was I making the right decision? I wished I could have consulted Mandy, but she wasn't around. I'd have to go it alone on this one.

By that time I was out in the middle of Houghton Lake, more than a mile from anyone or anything else. I turned off the idling engine, and came to rest on a series of gentle swells. The complete silence and solitude was startling. Only the sound of the water kept me company as I recalled every syllable of the letter I'd written. I imagined it being read at that very moment a couple hundred miles away, and hoped with everything in my being that finally, out there surrounded by a billion gallons of water, the truth would set me free.

But I knew I couldn't stay out there on the lake alone forever. I eventually reluctantly turned the jet ski back toward the dock, which was just a dot on the horizon, and upon my return was greeted with stern lectures and disapproving looks from both the staff and the kids waiting impatiently in line for their turn. It had been worth the reprimands.

The next few days at camp were consumed with activity, and my loathing of Grangeford gradually faded. Whenever I did see him, I would simply look the other way and laugh about something else with one of my friends. We were having too much fun for me to dwell on negativity, and the fresh crisp air and bright sunny weather lifted my spirits greatly.

The theme of the week was from the classic book Treasure Island. The guest speaker for the nightly services was a pastor from another area church who dressed up as Long John Silver, and shared passages of Scripture, which he described as our maps in life.

During the day, rocks painted gold and silver were scattered throughout the sprawling camp by the staff. Whichever cabin found the most treasure daily won the significant privilege of not cleaning up after themselves in the mess hall at night. Denny's shrewd thinking and surreptitious spray paint can guaranteed that we never lifted a finger after a single evening meal during the entire week. Not long after every breakfast, we had miraculously already "found" more manufactured precious stones than the wheelbarrow that each cabin was given could handle.

One night during the service, my eyes met Violet's. She smiled at me sadly, then darted on. It suddenly dawned on me that maybe I had gotten things completely backwards. I'd once wondered if my family would believe that Violet was 'good enough' for me to be romantically interested in. Almost as if she was a tier below myself, simply due to being black.

I was ashamed to admit it, and was stunned to realize that perhaps the opposite was true—that I would be a step down for her. It was a stark reality to confront. *East End boys and West End girls.* It seemed to me to be the recurring theme of my life. All that the West promised seemed to be tantalizingly just out of reach for people of the East like me.

A sudden burst of laughter from the crowd demanded my attention. The speaker had appeared again from behind the podium, this time wearing a horrific mask. The demonic face had glowing red eyes, and as he crept down the center aisle, it unexpectedly unfurled a pink paper tongue from its mouth. It rolled down to the floor, and continued on right toward where I was sitting. I kept thinking it would stop, but the paper seemed to have no end.

I had that strange feeling again, like I had felt when I had discovered Ciggy's buried head, or when I had visions of the mysterious scene in the boy's bathroom at Crosstown. Was this real? I pinched myself to confirm. But, was I just pinching myself in my sleep? There seemed to be no way to know for sure. The room spun ever so slightly, throwing me off balance where I sat.

The demon and his otherworldly tongue came even closer to me. I wondered how the pastor had made the red, lifeless eyes look so realistic. He began to speak in a hissing voice.

"Lies, lies, all I say are lies," he droned. He had come to a stop right in front of me. "Come on, kid," he urged. "Come and cut off my tongue and end the lies forever." I felt sick to my stomach and the room reeled a bit more. He produced a pair of wickedly sharp scissors from under his ragged robe.

I tried to wake up, but could not. I looked around and saw the eyes of my friends, and of nearly every camper there for the week, staring at me. Some were laughing, some looked spooked, some looked bored—like they'd seen the act before. The demon's caressing voice brought me back to the present.

"Kid, it's the only way to put a stop to it all. Cut off my tongue and end the lies!" His voice had risen to a scream, and I robotically grabbed the scissors out of his gnarled hands. I closed my eyes and cut the ruffling tongue off near its base and nearly fell back into my seat, strangely exhausted from the effort, the cheers and jeers of a hundred voices around me forming a surreal backdrop.

I wanted to open my eyes and see that the entire summer had been just a bad dream, a grand lie in and of itself. That Ciggy and Wanda would still be alive, that I had been able to finish the baseball season and make my dad proud, that I'd never even met the likes of Ryne and Janine. There was so much I wanted to change, to undo. *Why hadn't I just listened to the Psalmist and told the truth in time? Why hadn't I trusted my parents to do the right thing with the information I'd gathered?* I nearly opened my eyes to see if my wish had somehow come true, and I would be back in the safety of Mrs. Townsend's sterile classroom.

Then, I remembered Mandy. If the entire summer were to disappear in a puff of smoke, so would she right along with it. Her existence was hopelessly intertwined in it all. She'd been there every step of the way; the rises and falls of our unusual and unexpected relationship, that no one else on earth would ever hope to understand, defined the last three months of my life as much as any of the other things I wanted to obliterate. So, I just kept my eyes closed, and prayed instead that every moment of it had been real after all.

I found myself later sitting with a smattering of other boys around a massive bonfire, the spires of which reached far up into the flawless starry sky. Away from the fire, it was utterly dark. We were far from civilization, and the only other time I remembered seeing inky blackness like it had been in the drain pipe under the tracks. The fire was incredibly hot, and each of us sat holding a long stick that Worthy had reverently distributed.

"Boys," he continued, "This week we've learned much together. You are each God's wondrous treasures, not created for destruction. He made you to be reconciled to Himself. Every one of you is redeemable. It doesn't matter what you've done in your life up until this moment." He stopped and the only sound for what seemed like miles was the crackling of the red-hot embers.

"If you've made a decision in your life for Christ this week, to follow him and the map the pastor laid out in the Holy Scriptures, I want you to throw your stick into the fire," he urged. I had always felt uncomfortable at these type of demonstrative spectacles. I lowered my head and tried to avoid Worthy's plaintive gaze.

A couple boys on the other side of the fire solemnly tossed theirs in, and the sticks were utterly consumed before even hitting the ground by the unfathomable heat. I glanced at Denny, who held his firmly next me, and was surprised to see Tyson release his to be burned.

Grangeford joined Tyson in the gesture, and a few others also followed suit. After another minute, I heard a small cry and looked over to see the anguished face of Chet Wiggins. With a quivering hand and tear-stained face, he tossed his stick into the center of the fire as if it was a cursed talisman. Worthy darted to his side and sat down with him.

As the meeting began to break up, and my friends and I rose to reluctantly head back to our cabin for the final night, the two of them remained huddled next to the fire. I glanced back as I crossed the pine threshold, and saw that Worthy and Wiggins were still lingering there. I wondered what they were discussing. I didn't know what to think about Chester Wiggins and his repentant heart. Was there redemption available even for him? I wasn't sure if I even wanted there to be. The thought frightened me and I pushed it away.

Two unexpected things happened when our bus wearily pulled back into the asphalt lots of Crosstown Christian the next day.

First, as we sleepily dragged our belongings down the steep stairs to the concrete surface, Worthy took Grangeford aside and spoke to him privately. Despite Shannon's best intentions, the devastating news somehow rippled through the densely packed crowd of teens and parents.

Mr. Ballanger had left his family and run off to Aruba with his secretary from the bank. It was the first time I'd ever seen Grangeford cry, and it was also the last. I found out later that he and his mother had packed their glut of shiny things up within days and headed off to St. Louis to live with a distant relative.

Second, a squad car was parked a short distance away from the bus. The interior was too dark for me to immediately notice who was inside. As Chet stepped off the bus, Collier and Simmons quietly exited the vehicle and met him in an open area of the school lot. After a brief discussion, I watched as the two policemen escorted him to the back of the patrol car. Chet's sins had found him out.

I stood watching after them for a good while, still hoping that I'd done the right thing. My summer had been filled with the wrong choices, and I wondered if perhaps this one was just the next in the recurring series. It was clear this time, however, that the letter I'd written outlining an ironclad case against Chet had not fallen on deaf ears over at the Rouge Park Police Station.

Mary's message about the Eye Filet, and the local family that bought the steaks most often, had been a valuable clue pointing to Wiggins. Once I'd reasoned out that someone had wanted to keep

Queen quiet the night Wanda was murdered, the pieces had begun to fall into place. Wanda's dying gasp about chess had not been in reference to the board game at all; it had been a feeble attempt to expose the perpetrator by name.

The list Denny had provided me had yielded even more information than I had hoped. Not only had Chet been a member of Ciggy's Cub Scout troop, but his own father had been the replacement leader after Ciggy had been ousted. Clearly, Mr. Wiggins had believed a steady hand was needed to restore some semblance of order to whatever mess Ciggy had made of the troop.

I'd also finally remembered where I'd seen the crude scrawling on the letter threatening Corbin—on the napkin Chet had flashed across the lunchroom at me calling me a reject.

I shuddered to imagine what exactly Ciggy had done to Chet. Apparently one of Ciggy's short-lived jobs after getting out of the clink had been as a janitor at CCCP. I had realized with horror that somehow, I had been channeling a vision of one of the many times Ciggy had attempted to assault Chet in the boy's bathroom at Crosstown. The tanned, veined hands—one missing a pinky finger just like Travis Keane had described. I could never know exactly how it had occurred, or how often—and if Chet had been able to escape Ciggy on other occasions like he had in my vision—but clearly the encounters had been enough to drive him to eventually commit murder.

Once Chet had observed me digging in Freddy's back yard, he must have determined Ciggy's body had to be moved, I reasoned. Who, if anyone, had him helped in that grisly task I did not know and could never prove. Apparently, at some point Chet had gleaned from my conversations with Mandy that Wanda needed to be silenced as well. I thought back to the day he and Ryne had trashed the basement, and wondered if Chet had overheard us then.

The Cub Scout knife Chet had used to dispatch Ciggy had been hastily discarded in the rusted car. He must have returned soon after to dispose of the telltale blade. Additional conversations I'd heard over the summer about messy situations that needed to be cleaned up now made much more sense in light of Chet's guilt. The Biker Scouts, Dustin and Enrique had to have known about the murders, and been alarmed that they might scuttle their plans—but proving any connection to them would be nearly impossible, I realized dejectedly.

I imagined that the police were tearing apart Chet's room at that very moment looking for more incriminating evidence. I thought back to Chet's tearful confessional the previous night at the bonfire. I could only imagine what he'd said to Worthy. That he feared he was in too deep, that it was too late to go back. Can God forgive anyone, he must have asked? It was a question we would both have to mull over for a long time.

30
Breakout

On Sunday morning, I staggered upstairs after a night of zombie-like sleep recovering from the rigors of camp life. I looked outside briefly, and the streets seemed strangely quiet. I assumed my typical position at the kitchen table, knee up by my chin, shoveling down spoonfuls of Trix cereal while examining the back of the box, trying to solve a crossword puzzle about rabbits.

Then I noticed Duong ascending my front steps urgently. I jogged over and swung the door open. He said nothing, but handed me a fresh, crisp copy of the weekend edition of the Downriver Declarer. It still felt warm off the presses. I stared at the front page headline, and pursed my lips. I looked at him, and could see the gratitude in his eyes. *At least I gave someone good advice during this whole debacle*, I thought. I began to read the article, and it hardly seemed real.

LOCAL YOUTH DETAINED, QUESTIONED IN CONNECTION WITH CRIMES

Drug Ring Exposed, Multiple Arrests Made

ROUGE PARK, MI August 23rd – A fifteen-year-old local boy has been detained for questioning by Rouge Park Police in connection with two unsolved crimes: a missing person case, and a homicide.

Chester Wiggins, of West Ridge, was arrested by authorities in the parking lot of Crosstown Christian Church on Saturday afternoon without incident. Sources say he is currently enrolled as a student at the adjoining school.

Police spokesman Geoff Kuiper told the Downriver Declarer that Wiggins is being questioned regarding the disappearance of factory worker Sigmund Mann of Rouge Park, and the July 10th homicide of 78-year-old Wanda Kogan in her Rouge Park residence. Kuiper declined to say whether a motive had been established, or if a weapon has been recovered thus far in the case.

In an apparent connection to information gleaned from Wiggins while under interrogation, Declarer reporters have learned that additional arrests were made throughout Rouge Park on Saturday afternoon and well into the evening.

Sixteen-year-old Rouge Park native Ryne Daulton was arrested on charges of drug possession, intent to distribute a controlled substance, and third-degree assault. He is awaiting arraignment, which will occur possibly as early as Monday morning, in Wayne County Juvenile Detention Center.

Also brought in for questioning were sixteen-year-olds Tyler Salter, Wade Bonner, Andy Provenzano, and fifteen-year-olds

Patrick Venoy and Drake Stevens, all residents of Rouge Park as well. They are also being held in the Wayne County Juvenile Detention Center awaiting possible related charges.

Thirty-eight-year-old Dustin Crabb, of West Ridge, was also questioned about his possible involvement in the local drug trade and subsequently released.

Police are actively searching the surrounding area for Rouge Park resident and Club Xanadu owner Enrique Willows. He is wanted in connection with a litany of alleged crimes committed in Rouge Park and the surrounding area over the past several months. The Declarer has learned Willows may have fled the area sometime Saturday evening. He may be driving a 1986 green Ford Mustang with the license plate XANADU. Anyone with information possibly leading to the apprehension of Willows is urged to contact local authorities immediately. Police warn that Willows may be armed and dangerous.

Police investigators suspect that Willows was in the process of establishing a drug channel from Chicago to Detroit and the surrounding suburbs. A large cache of drugs and cash is still unaccounted for, according to sources closely involved in the process. Sources tell the Declarer that a search of Willow's residence yielded valuable clues, as well as a slew of unregistered weapons, but no tangible evidence of either the missing drugs or the money. Once again, anyone with information regarding this investigation is urged to call Rouge Park Police as soon as possible.

Kuiper also relayed concerns about the whereabouts and well-being of Willow's stepdaughter, Mandy, aged 15. She has not been seen since earlier in the week, according to friends. Officer Devon Collier has been instrumental in the case, as well as the ensuing investigation, arrests and search for outstanding suspects. He expressed a desire to thank an anonymous source in the neighborhood for their contributions.

"The Rouge Park Police received a letter earlier this week that proved invaluable to our case. I wanted to say thank you to this person, while also allowing them to maintain their anonymity," Collier said. He would not reveal any additional details about the person or the letter when pressed by reporters.

Late Saturday evening, The Declarer caught up with Justus Mann, Sigmund Mann's brother, who had also been missing for several months. Police have cleared him of any wrongdoing in both his brother's disappearance and the subsequent murder of Wanda Kogan.

"I just want to say I'm glad to be back at home. I plan on making up for some of the bad associations and choices I've made recently," he said, as he stood by his wife Nicolette and their three children on the front lawn of his modest Rouge Park residence. "It's been a rough summer." Mann alluded to being forced to hide out in a nearby wooded area, in fear for his life from what he alleged to be a ruthless and violent drug gang, run by Willows and Crabb, with enforcement and intimidation headed by teenager Ryne Daulton.

Though police have declined to charge Crabb thus far due to lack of evidence, Mann was unabashed in his own accusations, which the Declarer reports upon here without editorial comment.

"Yeah, Crabb is involved. He's been right there with Ryne and Enrique from the start. And what a sick plan it all was—pressuring all these kids to join up, offering them huge amounts of money, and threatening them later if they ever wanted to get out. They were stripping what was once a fine neighborhood right down to the bones," he continued. At that point, an unidentified family attorney stepped in and said Mr. Mann would not be adding any further comment to the public record unless called upon to do so by the authorities.

When asked by reporters, Kuiper reiterated that the police currently suspect Willows of being instrumental in introducing the Detroit suburban area to crack cocaine. The cheaper, highly addictive substance has been taking a stronger hold in neighborhoods throughout the Midwest, and according to information gathered from other sources, this was an important new market Willows was nurturing.

"This bust is a huge win in the ongoing war against crack cocaine. But this was only one battle. As Nancy Reagan has been telling anyone who will listen: Just Say No," Kuiper stressed. "I really like how she puts it: Understanding what drugs can do to your children, understanding peer pressure and understanding why they turn to drugs is the first step in solving the problem. I think all of us can see from this situation how wise her words are," Kuiper added.

Contributing reporters: Robert Reamer, Moe Smith

I put down the newspaper and finally exhaled. It felt like a huge weight had fallen from my shoulders. It was over. Enrique had been sent scrambling. The Biker Scouts had been scuttled for good. Justus had returned to his family, and Wanda and Ciggy's deaths would be atoned for by the murderous Chester Wiggins. The triplets were safely out of the drug trade. Joyce had her brother back. All the pieces had come together like a satisfying jigsaw puzzle. But the puzzle was still missing one integral piece, I thought dejectedly: Mandy.

I imagined that she was far from Rouge Park by now. But where exactly she was, I hadn't a clue. I pushed her out of my mind for the moment, and switched gears to get ready for Sunday morning church. I left the folded paper on the kitchen table, and wondered what, if anything, my parents would think about it all.

At church, my steps felt as light as air. Life seemed to be completely back to normal. I had miraculously regained the confidence that had been sapped from me over the past few months. The absence of Grangeford and his family from their standard pew felt surreal. Violet sat dutifully with her family in her customary place, but she didn't look over at me once during the entire service.

The message that morning was completely lost on me. I spent the entire time replaying the tumultuous summer in my mind, sifting through the sequence of events and all the major players. Soon, the closing hymn was announced and I stood, a bit stunned, along with the rest of the stretching congregation.

Minutes later, the place was abuzz with polite, post-service conversations. "Do you think Jerry Falwell will really do the waterslide?" someone gushed. "PTL Network said he will in September, to eliminate millions of dollars in debt," someone else confirmed. Debt—like what Dustin, and now Enrique as well, were on the hook for. I slipped out into the hallway to avoid any more of the discussion.

Joyce Stickler stood talking to the Townsends. She noticed me, and motioned me over to the small group. Instead of the warm reception that I was expecting, she greeted me sadly, and stiffly thanked me for my part in finding her brother. In a flash, it dawned on me that while I had found one of her brothers, she had lost another in the same moment. I'd never heard her discuss Sigmund; I had no idea if they had been close to one another or not. I reminded myself too that his body was still unaccounted for.

"I hope that this means we can all get back to normal now," Mrs.

Townsend sighed. Mr. Townsend agreed. He seemed ready to ask me a question when Joyce interrupted him.

"I'm not sure I agree, Alan. How can things return to the way they were when Rene is still missing?" The two Townsends nodded solemnly and agreed.

"Mr. Asperat is missing?" I asked, taken aback. "Since when?"

"Why yes, Dav," Mrs. Townsend replied. "He hasn't been seen for over a week. Were you not listening in church? It was announced here on Wednesday night as a prayer request, too." Mr. Townsend gently reminded her that I had been up at camp all week, and she looked more understanding of my ignorance.

Joyce Stickler shook her head and looked sick with worry. "It's just not like him. He's always been such a steady rock. I'm very concerned that something terrible has happened. Something possibly related to the other unpleasantness." She looked at me inquisitively.

I said that I didn't believe so. "I'm sure everything will be fine, Ms. Stickler," I added. I turned to leave. I heard her say something odd to the Townsends.

"What was that?" I asked sharply. All three of them looked at me again in surprise.

"Ms. Stickler was just recalling an odd comment Mr. Asperat made to her a couple of days before he disappeared," Mrs. Townsend replied. "I should have mentioned it a moment ago. It was something to the effect of, 'If I ever go missing, just come break me out. Tell Dav—he'll get it.' Did I get that right, Joyce?"

"Yes," the worried principal agreed. "I'm sure it's nothing. I'd actually forgotten all about it. It was all quite strange. Does that mean anything at all to you?"

"I'm not sure," I admitted. I promised to let them know if anything came to mind.

Davajuan

That afternoon, Mom and Dad went out to shop for a new metal shed. The old one had rusted out completely, and our bikes and lawn equipment were getting rained on regularly. They reviewed the normal routine with me, instructing me as to what Corbin and Suzanne were allowed to do, and what they were not. I listened half-heartedly, wishing I could head over to Tyson or Denny's instead. This would be one of my last Sundays of freedom before the new school year commenced in just a couple of weeks.

Once they had left, Suzanne sat at the piano, working through one of her newest practice pieces. She was quite talented, and enjoyed it immensely, in sharp contrast to my feelings about playing the trumpet. I smirked to myself as I recalled the time I'd tape-recorded myself practicing, and then replayed the tape at top volume from the basement in an attempt to skip subsequent sessions. It had worked flawlessly until Corbin had spilled the beans.

My tattle-prone brother was on the floor playing the Atari. He removed the Pong cartridge and inserted Breakout. "Not this game, again," I moaned moodily. "We've played this thing to death." He mimicked my voice in a manner accurately enough to make me annoyed. I got up and went out onto the porch. It was cloudy, windless, and oppressively hot.

"We're watching Indiana Jones and the Temple of Doom in fifteen minutes," I commanded through the front screen. "Don't worry, Mom made me promise to fast forward through the part where the guy's heart gets pulled out through his rib cage." I smiled as I heard Corbin make a gagging sound, and pretended to keel over.

Suzanne stopped playing the piano. After a few seconds she called out to me. "Dav, I think there's something wrong in the basement. I'm hearing weird sounds."

I bounded inside and down the stairs. There, to my horror, I found a lake of water that had risen past my ankles. I sloshed around frantically, immobilized—pulled in too many different directions at once. Out of the corner of my eye, I saw random objects floating inside my room, like little model boats out at sea tossed by heartless waves. The water seemed to be gushing from the washing machine.

"Not this again!" I screamed, and I ran over to the faulty appliance to try to reattach the hose. This time it had broken off at the base. Fixing it quickly would be impossible. I turned to the front console and tried pressing buttons. Nothing stopped the relentless flow of water. It seemed to have malfunctioned. I remembered the basement storm drains, and my heart sank as I realized that my dreadful habit of depositing my half-eaten vegetables from the dinner table had made a bad problem infinitely worse.

The water level seemed to still be rising. I ran back up the stairs and out the front door. I began to yell for help, not knowing who, if anyone, actually could.

Down the street, a husky figure appeared, and I could tell from the bright tracksuit that it was Dmitri. He put down his gardening tool and attempted to jog down the street toward me, arriving soon after, breathing heavily. I motioned him inside, and we descended to the maelstrom.

He looked around quickly, assessing the situation. He walked briskly to the corner of the basement, and felt around with his hairy hands in the murky water, which was now up to his elbow. "Cement relief cap is right here," he stated. "You have a sledgehammer?"

I shook my head pitifully. He disappeared up the stairs and out the back door. I glanced around at the mayhem. Several waterlogged wood-grain wafers floated by, and I realized that the heartless deluge had not spared my precious baseball card collection. I moved to try to gather up the flotilla with the intention of drying them off, but stopped in my tracks. The fact was the cards were a completely lost cause.

Dmitri returned with a sledgehammer and strode urgently to the spot he'd been kneeling over before. With a couple of mighty swings, he shattered the cement cap, and the water immediately began to rush into the gaping hole he'd created. He stood back looking at his handiwork, and I wondered for a terrible moment if what he'd done would be acceptable to my parents.

Beggars can't be choosers, I told myself, and with a feeling of relief I watched the waters recede. He eventually found the water shut-off valve and rotated it. Soon, a wet mess of clothing, sports cards, and other assorted items were the only evidence that the crisis had ever occurred. A bloated Wade Boggs swirled around the drain hole before finally settling on the cusp of it. The Red Sox slugger looked up forlornly at me, symbolically announcing the fate of my most prized collection. It reminded me for a split second of the state of Dustin's sordid world, which I imagined was approaching its final lap as well.

"Dmitri," I said. "Thank you so much." He nodded sweatily. "But, I thought you and Dagmar had decided to leave Rouge Park and go to Lansing," I said, somewhat confused. He nodded again, trying to catch his breath.

"Yes, that was the plan. I had listed the house, and the corner store, for sale. But, nobody had put an offer in on either one yet. This morning, Dagmar saw the article in the paper, and we heard about Enrique, and the Biker Scouts. It was like a miracle. It was a sign from heaven, Dagmar said. And it seems I might owe you some thanks as well." He looked at me happily. "We are going to stay."

I told him how happy I was to hear the news. He offered to help me begin to dry things off, and I gratefully accepted. We soaked a dozen towels from upstairs, sopping up the remnants of water, and I began to salvage what I could of my inundated possessions strewn all over the concrete floor. I reluctantly rounded up the hundreds of ruined baseball cards and deposited them directly into the garbage can. Half an hour later, I said goodbye to Dmitri, and thanked him once again for his quick and efficient assistance.

That evening, I was relieved to leave for Great Stories Bible Stories. My parents' moods had swung all over the place upon their arrival home, from rage at the washing machine itself, to relief that it hadn't been even worse, to frustration that Dmitri had shattered the cement cap. I had made an impassioned case to them that it had seemed like the right choice in the heat of the moment, and they eventually agreed.

The Sunday youth service followed the normal routine, and during a trivia game, I quietly began to relay the story of the flood to Tyson and Denny. Only a few sentences in, as I was setting the scene, I stopped short when I mentioned that Corbin had been playing the Atari. Breakout, I repeated to myself.

Tell Dav, he'll get it, Asperat had said, I remembered. *If I ever go missing, break me out.* I heard him recite the cryptic phrase in his own voice in my mind. Then I recalled the strange scene I'd witnessed from atop Sunset Acres, when he was stacking the bricks that evening out by the storage garages. Something inside magnetically urged me to investigate.

I asked Mr. Townsend if I could use the bathroom, and he agreed after a second of consideration. I slipped out the chapel door into the empty church hallway. My footsteps echoed eerily in the dimly lit passageway. I skipped right by the men's bathroom and out the back door of the church, and made a beeline to the garages behind the high school building.

As I walked down the long line of doors, I noticed the alley was empty and still. I wondered if somehow this was the place Asperat had disappeared to. Had Enrique's gang been responsible? I thought again about when Dustin had scoped out the unfinished garage at the end of the row for some unknown purpose earlier in the summer. Had the kind teacher somehow gotten caught up in their mess and been detained? *Or perhaps his fate had been similar to Justus and Wanda's,* I shuddered to myself.

When I arrived at the last door, and examined the pile of bricks, my final reservations about my theory melted away. The bricks had been neatly stacked in a long line, exactly 8 rows high, perfectly mimicking the iconic Atari game that Corbin had been playing at my house just hours earlier.

"It's my favorite game," I remembered Asperat saying. There was no doubt that he had left this clue for someone, most likely myself. I didn't understand why, but I knew it was there for a reason, standing as a beacon outside of what very well might be his holding cell, or even his grave.

I gingerly stepped around the bricks and approached the same brown door that I had seen Dustin unlock many weeks before. I tried the handle, expecting it to be locked once again, but surprisingly, it was not. It creaked open, revealing complete darkness inside. I realized it was incredibly risky to proceed without a flashlight, but knew I had to continue ahead regardless. I stepped out of the early evening light and headed down the stairs.

Nearing the bottom, I saw a small light coming from one corner of the dank, dusty subterranean room. My eyes adjusted quickly. There was a lantern, which was the only source of light, a shovel and rope in one corner, several empty cardboard boxes in another, and a single chair in the center of the dirt-floored chamber. On it sat a smiling Mr. Asperat.

31

Pay Dirt

"Mr. Asperat!" I exclaimed. "Are you OK? Are you being held here?" I asked, growing even more confused. I looked him over and there was no sign of restraints, or anyone standing guard. That combined with the unlocked door at the top of the stairs was baffling to me.

"I'm fine! Thank you, Dav. And I'm even better now that you're here. I was wondering how long I'd have to wait. But I knew you'd figure it out before long!" he said with a gaudy smile. "I've known you were a smart cookie for a long time. And," he said with a slightly sardonic tone, "I knew all along you'd be the one I'd have to keep the closest eye on."

He got up from the chair and walked over to the stairs, turning back toward me. "Oh yes, do you recognize this?" he asked as he gestured at the gleaming knife in his hand. It was a carbon copy of the one I'd seen in the rusted car, the one I thought would be recovered at Chet's.

"Yes, that's right. It's the very knife that I tried to slit Justus' throat with. Too bad for all of us that his fool brother was there instead of him. And, it's the one I had to dispatch poor unfortunate Wanda with as well," he said with a tinge of regret, as he turned the blade over, gazing down at it. I made a bolt for the stairs.

"Oh, no you don't, Dav. You're going to stay right down here with me," he laughed. "In fact, have a seat over there in that chair, and we'll arrange for you to stay a good, long while," he instructed. When I hesitated, he brandished the knife threateningly and I eventually complied.

My mind was racing. *What is going on?* I asked myself frantically. *Is it possible that I've been wrong yet one more time—that Chet Wiggins was not the perpetrator of the crimes? Is Asperat the actual killer?* The dizzying onslaught of questions threatened to overwhelm me. He must have seen the dumbfounded look on my face, and he began to explain as he tossed me the rope.

"You look quite confused! Tie yourself up with that. When you've done your best, I'll come and finish the job. No—I'm not going to kill you. Not yet," he added with an evil grin. He looked down at the knife again.

"Wondering where I got it? Thought it was Chet's, didn't you?" he said as he pointed at me. "Strangest thing—it was just sitting there on the mantle that night when I confronted Justus. At least, I thought it was Justus."

"Why are you doing this?" I finally managed to stammer.

"Doing this, here—now?" he asked, genuinely. "Or, why did I finally snap and try to kill Justus after all these years?" I shrugged, bewildered.

"Fine, I'll start with the simplest one," he said as he sat down on the dusty stairs. "Try to imagine that you love someone so completely—

have you ever even been in love, Dav? I know you have a thing for that street urchin Mandy, Enrique's daughter. I don't mean that kind of love. I mean a love that lasts for years, decades—and then you're forced to watch the other person be dragged down to depths you didn't even know existed," he sputtered angrily.

"No, you can't imagine it," he answered for me. "But that's exactly what I've had to endure with Nicolette," he continued, eyebrows raised. "I thought I could withstand it, I thought God would help me move on; but it just ate away at me day after day, year after year, until I heard from Joyce that Justus had slinked back into the drug trade once more," he snarled, his head wagging back and forth. I had never seen this new side of Asperat. His usual demeanor around the Crosstown complex had always been one of pleasant, complete control.

"It made me snap. It wasn't ever supposed to have been Justus and Nicolette together, anyway. It was supposed to be Rene and Nicolette," he seethed as he pointed at himself, and I immediately remembered the R + N inscription I'd seen back in the woods. "We grew up here at Crosstown together. We were childhood sweethearts. Everything was going so well, so right. That is—until Justus, Sigmund and Joyce moved in next door to her."

I remembered my dream, the one where I'd seen Nicolette staggering down the street, followed closely by a creeping car. I realized now that the bulbous shape in the shadows had been Asperat's red VW, the identity of it shrouded in my subconscious somehow but frustratingly just out of reach.

"She never truly noticed me again," he said mournfully. "I was no match for that public school punk with long hair, no rules and a hot rod pumping out rock music. Have you ever lost something, Dav? Something so important to you, so deeply entrenched in your soul that you thought you might die from the loss?" he asked passionately.

I thought back to the 100-yard dash, and the anger I'd felt toward Grangeford. It all seemed rather trite now, and Justus' pessimistic words about the meaninglessness of most things rang again in my head, truer now than ever.

"I tried to forget her," he continued. "God knows I tried. I even moved away and taught at a school up north for a while. But it was no use. Her draw on me was like a magnet; it was useless to resist our intertwined fate," he protested.

"You used to play out in those woods, didn't you?" I asked him. "Where I saw the carved names. And where Justus was hiding, right?" I asked. He smiled nostalgically.

"Yes, that very same park as well. Fitting that Justus returned there when he was desperate. I followed you out that foggy morning from a distance. I wanted to see the place again. It had been a long time. Everything was in the same spot, but completely different somehow, smaller. That playground used to be our entire world. We'd play tag on it for hours, going home sweaty, happy and exhausted when our parents would finally force us to leave. I thought things would stay the same forever, just like when we carved our names in that old tree. But I was wrong."

"You stayed close friends with Joyce all these years, just to keep an eye on them?" I guessed. He smiled. "For several reasons, but yes, that's the gist of it. It seemed for a while that Joyce had made all the right choices in life. But somehow it still didn't really make her very happy. For a long while I thought I could figure out a way to win Nicolette back, if I could just keep her in my sights. But from the start Justus had an inexplicable spell over her," he said venomously.

"And, you volunteered to come help build my new room, so you could keep an eye on the place, after the murder?" He nodded coolly.

"But it was more than that, Dav. That night when I came over to your house, I realized with some alarm that against all odds you were digging in the only place I could think of to hide Ciggy's body quickly. I had become frantic and erratic once I realized what I'd done that night. What a mistake to hide him there," he said regretfully. "I had to keep inventing reasons to explain why I was always lingering in the area."

"Thankfully, I followed you out the back door while your parents thought I was using the bathroom, and that's when I realized that you would actually be my biggest obstacle," he said admirably. "Not Justus, not Wanda, not Enrique—you. Framing Chet for the crimes on the other hand was child's play. The knife, the threatening note written on bank letterhead, the coincidental connection between Chet and Ciggy at Cub Scouts, it all just fell into place," he beamed proudly.

"But the note from Chet. It looked just like his handwriting," I protested. He grinned. "It wasn't too hard to find a sample of his chicken scratch in the school records. It was quite easy to mimic. Having special access to things can come in quite handy sometimes," he added sardonically.

"And after that... you did the rest, just as I hoped you would," he said, utterly pleased with himself.

"But what about Wanda?" I asked angrily. "Why did she have to die? And how could you have known that she had seen you digging?"

He grimaced. "I'd always wondered if she had seen me after calling out to me that fateful night. Then, when I came over to your house to check in on you, my fears were confirmed. You were working hard in the basement on some chintzy project with Mandy. I listened at the top of the stairs, and I knew at that exact moment Wanda would unfortunately have to be sacrificed, as well." His countenance fell somewhat.

"I can't pretend that was an easy or pleasant task. I'm not an evil person, Dav," he lectured. "Just someone who knows what has to be done, and then has the gumption to actually follow through on it. I'm different from those fiends spreading their filthy drugs all over the neighborhood. They relish in others' destruction."

"For me, the violence was an unfortunate byproduct. I rather enjoyed my time spent with Wanda. She and I had begun to play chess together in her living room from time to time. It was just another excuse for me to frequent the neighborhood, to keep an eye on everyone involved," he continued. "But then I heard about what Wanda knew. That same night, after quieting that idiotic dog with a juicy steak, I crept inside and finished her off as quickly, and mercifully, as possible."

"But Mary, the cashier at Farmer John's said—" I began to protest. He waved at me dismissively.

"That was almost my big mistake," he admitted. "You really were brilliant on that one. I was back in the supermarket many days later, and that insane lady Mary pointed out the significance of my purchase as she rang me up. I had to redirect her several times, and convince her that she somehow had me confused with the Wiggins. I made up an elaborate story about it. I was so adamant, I eventually changed her mind about it. Strange cookie, that one. Almost as strange as the power of suggestion."

He slowly walked toward the chair that he'd tied me to. I tried to match his gaze, but his demeanor had taken on a more menacing appearance, and I quickly looked away.

"You don't know how happy I am that you figured out my Breakout clue, Dav," he said, almost robotically. "I love that you noticed the bricks—the 8 rows—that you were so observant to discover this obscure little spot, and that you remembered it was my favorite game! I'm literally tickled pink about it. I am quite disappointed that the road has to end here." I shuddered, and strained even harder at the ropes digging into my arms and chest.

"How poetic that you'll be buried alongside Ciggy here," he said, gesturing at the corner. I noticed a small pile of disturbed dirt for the first time with alarm. "Yes, this is of course where I moved his body! It's so perfect—and do you know why?" He didn't wait for my reply.

"Because this is where that fool Crabb hid Enrique's drug stash until a few days ago. That moron kept coming here for several weeks—wasn't even trying to be careful the last few times. I was fortunate enough to follow him once and realize this place would serve my own purposes as well. And when the bumbling authorities eventually find their way here—and they will—there will be two more crimes queued up to add to their lengthy rap sheets. I'll get away Scot-free, and those slime balls will rot in prison for the rest of their lives where they belong!" He laughed and drew even closer to me, and the knife flashed in the dim light.

I heard Freddy singing again, as he swung himself down from the garage roof.

Call the police, there's a mad man around
Running down underground

The police. What I wouldn't have done to see them now. "What about Mandy? Did you get rid of her too?" I cried desperately, trying to stall. He stopped in his tracks.

"No. The little romance you two had was cute in its own way, but doomed to fail from the start. She was using you," he insisted, as I shook my head vehemently. "Oh no?" he asked. "Then why did she run off without you, with a half million in cash?"

I was dumbfounded. *Well, one thing is clear. Mandy can definitely check item Number 6 off her list,* I thought. "Yes, the dirty little secret comes out," Asperat laughed. "She stole the entire load of loot for the drug deal right from under Enrique's arrogant nose. That vixen! I would have given a lot of money to see Enrique's face as he found the safe completely empty when it was time to pay up." He paused thoughtfully.

"The funny thing is, she was actually close to the truth about me, even called me on the phone once. I thought she was suspicious of my intentions, but she simply wanted me to give her chess lessons so she could play along with Wanda. Smart girl. A lot of potential. More than I can say for most of the residents of Rouge Park," he added snidely.

I finally had an answer as to why Mandy had jotted Asperat's phone number down on her to-do list. I recalled Number 5 on her list: *Learn C*. She had wanted to learn the game of strategy to connect with Wanda. The knowledge was a small consolation.

Try as I might though, I had to admit that Asperat was right; Mandy had left me in the dust, and started a new life on her own. But who was I kidding? There was no way I could have gone with her; no way I would have been brave enough to leave with her even if she'd asked me to. She had made the right choice to go alone. In my imagination, I could clearly see her getting a running start and then leaping onto the very last car of a train headed west to Chicago in the dead of night, stacks of cash crammed into an orange and brown Farmer John's tote bag.

"What happens after this?" I stalled again, and he stopped. I knew it was pointless, since no one could possibly know where I'd disappeared to. But I wanted to stretch out my last few moments as long as I could. Even the damp earth had a rich, amazing smell to it. When you know your life is drawing to a close, every detail begins to scream out at you with unimaginable significance.

"After this? Well, the final chapter of this sordid tale begins, Dav. I will be free once again to finish off Justus at my own pace, in my own way. I have you to thank, again, for flushing him out of hiding. I knew that coward hadn't gone far," he spat disgustedly. "It won't be much of a challenge."

"I'll simply stage a drug overdose of some sort, and everyone will believe it. After a short period of mourning, I will renew my relationship with Nicolette." He saw that I looked dubious.

"Yes, it is sometimes hard to spot the diamond in the rough. To the naked eye, she seems like a lost cause to some." His voice rose. "But, I can still see the real Nicolette from years ago—free and fun, gorgeous and exciting!" His eyes appeared to mist again. "Her choices led her to temporary ruin. But, there's still time to change them!" He raised his fist defiantly.

"The original Nicolette can be restored, and this time, she will be right by my side. The happy years we still have left will make these horrors fade from memory. You'll become a faded memory too, Dav. Just another pawn caught up in a scheme that was much bigger than anyone else knew."

He walked the last few steps to my chair and grabbed my hair firmly, tilting my head upward to expose my neck. I was shaking with revulsion and fear. He looked at me with pity and a tinge of regret.

I wondered if hidden pain and devastating loss like Asperat had experienced was the reason so many of the people of Rouge Park had succumbed to the temptations of Enrique's imported poisons.

"You got a heart of glass or a heart of stone," I heard Freddy's voice crack, singing once again.

"It will be quick. I am sorry that it was to be this way, but once I started down this road, I knew some unanticipated sacrifices would have to be made. The good news is that down here, no one will hear you scream." He reached back with the knife and prepared to slash at my throat.

At that moment, the brown door at the top of the stairs burst open. The silhouette of Alan Townsend appeared against the evening sky, and Tyson and Denny were right on his heels. They sprinted down the stairs toward us, and I observed the distressed but determined look on Mr. Townsend's face with relief. His expression seemed vaguely familiar.

"Drop the knife, Rene," he commanded in a steady voice. "I can't fathom what you're doing, but it stops right here and right now. I won't let you hurt the boy. Put down the knife." Tyson and Denny stood frozen in place next to him on the dirt floor. The flickering light of the lantern reflected off the barrel of Townsend's drawn weapon. I was relieved to learn that the rumors about him were true after all.

"Back away, Alan," warned Asperat. "You'll never understand what I'm capable of. I've come too far to fall short at the last second." He held the knife in front of him now, shielding me from my would-be rescuers.

I imagined that after a few moments, Townsend had left the chapel to look for me. When I hadn't been in the bathroom as I'd said, I surmised that Tyson and Denny had recounted my theory about the isolated storage garage to him. How they'd convinced him to head over here and had actually found their way down to me in time, I couldn't comprehend.

"I'm not going to say it again, Rene," Townsend said in an even tone. "Move away from Dav and put down the knife."

Asperat turned back to me. I could see him contemplating the situation frantically, the sweat beads on his forehead multiplying. I realized with horror that he still had the ability to silence me, and the truth of all that he'd done would go to the grave along with me.

"You shouldn't have gotten involved, Alan!" Asperat shouted.

"None of you will ever understand what Nicolette means to me. You have Darcy's heart. You won the grand prize in your carnival game of chance. The big stuffed animal—so bulky you can hardly carry it through the amusement park. I wasn't so lucky with her sister. And I just can't accept that twist of fate. I'll pull her out of the depths and rescue her from her choices just like you did for Darcy!" he fumed, as he pulled his hand back to slash my neck open with the knife.

The gunshot was deafening.

safe & found

32

It was the first cold day in October. I sat hunched in front of the heating grate in our bathroom, and adjusted again in an attempt to create an airtight chamber of warmth for the front half of my body. Suzanne pounded at the door impatiently to enter so that she could brush her teeth for school. I sat completely still, hoping she'd leave, thinking that it had been accidentally locked from the inside.

I felt closer to God in front of the warm register. It seemed like I could turn my face back to Him without shame after the agonizing minutes of penance I'd performed while tied up in Asperat's chair.

I thought to myself that it had been a "greenstick fracture" of a summer. I had been bent—nearly broken—but things were starting to heal right back into place. I couldn't say the same for everyone else involved, though.

I knew another bleak day at Crosstown awaited me. I smiled as I thought of Violet. We had finally broken the ice a month before, and begun to speak again. Both of us were happy to pretend that Grangeford Ballanger had never existed.

The school seemed different to me. Chet Wiggins, while vindicated of murder, had eventually been swept up in the tide that inundated Rouge Park, sweeping away dozens of young and old participants in the nascent drug trade. The last I'd heard, he had been released from a low-grade detention facility and his family had enrolled him at yet another area private school that was willing to cash the tuition checks. I hadn't seen him since the day we'd arrived back from Camp WeSaLi.

Whispers around the school said that Chet's campground confession to Worthy had been about Zane's brother Zack. It seemed that one fateful night the summer prior, Chet had convinced Zack to go out swimming in the lake in the dead of night. When he'd gone under and not resurfaced, Chet had panicked, and high-tailed it back to his cabin alone and pretended to be none the wiser. After initially being livid at the shocking revelation, I suddenly realized that I could relate to him in an unexpected way, in that I had kept a tragedy secret much longer than I should have.

On a drizzly Sunday afternoon, I had stood gazing at the long series of class photos lining the empty hallways of Crosstown. Younger versions of the faces of Dustin Crabb, Shannon Worthy, Janine Lucero, Nicolette and Darcy, and Rene Asperat all stared back at me smiling—their secret inner battles and failures hidden and unknown to nearly everyone else. I sensed a person approaching behind me, and turned to see Mr. Townsend.

I had abruptly asked him how he had known to come looking for me that day back in August. He smiled weakly, and asked gingerly if I remembered when he had also saved me from an attacker in the boy's bathroom years earlier. I nodded slowly. I had known it all along, somehow—and my lying days were over. The tall, dark-haired savior from my visions had been Townsend as well.

I realized for the first time that I had been watching my own harrowing and repressed encounter with Ciggy, not Chet's. It had been my own face I'd seen against the damp floor in my visions, and I'd hidden it from myself the entire time. Townsend explained that when I hadn't returned from the bathroom yet again on the evening in question, he'd become alarmed, and for good reason.

Mr. Asperat was gone. Very few people knew what had actually happened that fateful evening, below ground near the very edge of Crosstown property. The garage had been sealed off, and now lay unfinished once more, the pile of bricks still arranged the exact same way Asperat had purposely left it. If I ever needed to know that what had happened had been real, a simple trip back that way for a quick glimpse was sufficient.

The neighborhood was different too. A couple of weeks after school started, I had looked outside toward the dead end to see a large moving truck backed into Freddy's driveway. Hours later, the Mann household pulled out and hit the road for good. Justus and Nicolette were going to make an attempt, no matter how fragile, at life together one last time. I saw Freddy wave at me from the passenger seat window for an instant, and then they were gone.

Within days of the arrests, Club Xanadu had been shuttered. But only a week later, it had reopened under a new name, the black and green walls and awnings replaced by gaudy red and white ones. A new owner had stepped in without missing much of a beat. It was clear some things in the East would never change.

One dim evening, I caught a glimpse of Roxy hurriedly rushing up her uneven front walk. She looked pale, thinner and nervous. I hoped she'd be able to stay out of the clutches of whomever would inevitably take over from Enrique and Ryne.

Tragedy struck close to home. One morning a few weeks after that, I awoke to find Jason and Johnny's place had been reduced to a smoldering husk. A slew of firetrucks and ambulances clogged the street from one end to the other. The top half of their frame bungalow was gone. I could see inside the second floor like I was looking at an exposed dollhouse. Roach and CJ excitedly reported that the two brothers had been playing with cigarettes and a lighter the evening before. Damian had not survived the blaze. I never saw the two boys at the house again. I hoped dearly that I'd be able to take over as Dad's go-to throwing partner from that moment on.

The night before, the Tigers had played the Toronto Blue Jays in the final game of the season. The winner would claim the American League East pennant. I listened to the entire ballgame on the radio from start to finish, knowing without a shadow of a doubt that Dustin's entire life was on the line. His debt had been bought up by a rival gang on Detroit's west side, I'd heard from Dmitri.

The Tigers won 1-0. Around midnight, Dustin's mangled body was found on the railroad tracks, the same ones Mandy had hitched a ride to Chicago on just a couple of months earlier. He'd lost his final reckless bet. The self-styled *PRTYBOY* was dead. No one knew for sure if he'd been thrown there by the gang when he couldn't pay up, or if he'd done it himself. I wondered if Pastor Shay would mention his great-nephew's unfortunate demise, or gloss over it on his next trip to the pulpit.

After school that day, I walked home through another bone-chilling drizzle. Dad had to stay for a staff meeting, and Mom was tied up with Corbin's soccer game, so instead of waiting, I had struck out for home on foot. I wasn't too upset. Tyson and Denny had wanted me to stay through for the varsity soccer game, but I'd found myself wanting more and more alone time in the months since the tumultuous summer had drawn to a close.

I entered Pete's card shop and was happy to see his familiar face. I hadn't visited him for a long time. As I walked up to the counter, I noticed all Mandy's signs were gone. The spots where they'd hung were empty, a faint outline of dust around the spaces the only clue something had ever even been displayed there. He walked out from the back and greeted me.

"How's the collection going, Dav? Ever finish your complete set of '87 Topps?" he asked.

"Not exactly," I replied. I cringed as I recalled watching my valued collection floating on choppy brown swells. It reminded me once again that despite the toil and focus we put into things, nothing tangible ever really lasts. "When are you getting in the '88s?"

"You'll be the first to know," he winked. "Say, that reminds me." He walked into the back room, and through a crack in the wall I saw him kneel down and open a large safe. He pulled an object out from underneath a stack of papers.

I could tell immediately that it was one of Mandy's signs. He brought it out and showed it to me. The wood was painted dark blue, and the letters affixed to it spelled *REDONDO*. Each letter was blue, on a bright white metal background, and each had tell-tale traces of being issued by the state of California.

Redondo Beach. She'd mentioned the place before, I remembered. Number 8 on her list crept back into my mind: *MTRB*. I cringed as I recalled that I'd once worried it had stood for *Move The Rotting Body*. I wondered now if it had in fact stood for *Move To Redondo Beach*. I had absolutely no way of confirming my theory, and I found it frustrating.

"After Mandy left, I found this in the back. I couldn't bring myself to sell it. Something told me you might like to have it." Pete's eyes gleamed as he handed it to me. I thanked him, and as I turned to leave, I thought of one last question.

"Your safe... Do the numbers '50-25-50' mean anything to you?" I asked. I remembered I had seen those numbers jotted down on Mandy's journal page. He looked at me oddly.

"Yes. Funny you should ask. That's the default combination setting on safes like these. Anyone with half a brain knows to change it as soon as they get it out of the box." I nodded. Enrique's arrogance had been complete. He had never altered the initial combination, and Mandy had used his pride against him with devastating results.

I still hadn't heard from Mandy since the church sleepover, and I missed her. The only thing I had to remember her by was the package she'd mailed to my house, and the cassette single that had been inside it.

When I arrived at home, I unlocked the front door and went inside. The stillness was comforting, and I made myself a snack and turned on the television. Transformers was on, and I knew that Punky Brewster would follow half an hour after, if my parents didn't demand it be shut off first. I got comfortable under a woven blanket on the big reclining chair and settled in.

A knock at the door startled me for a second. My nerves had been shot ever since the harrowing experience with Asperat, but they had finally nearly returned to normal. Fourteen-year-olds are more resilient than most people realize. I got up, and was greeted at the door by a middle-aged woman.

"Hello," she said to me hesitantly through the glass. I opened the door, and she stepped in quickly before I could invite her to do so.

"Are you Dav by chance?" she asked, and after a brief consideration, I confirmed it. She finally managed a weak smile. "Oh, good! We just bought the nice big house over on Paris street. We moved in today. In the garage, we found something very interesting—something I've never seen before. It's big, but I managed to get it in the car somehow." She motioned for me to come out with her to the porch to see.

I was amazed to find our finished map of the United States in license plates propped up against the wall. Mandy had completed it without me.

"The girl who lived there before us left this note next to it. It told us to make sure you got it. It's an amazing piece of work! She must have thought a lot of you to leave you such a gift," she said, looking at it admiringly.

"You'd have to have met her to really understand," I said sadly. I thanked her for her trouble, and after a bit more small talk, she departed. She came running back up to the door seconds later, and handed me a small object.

"I almost forgot. This was in a pile of trash the real estate company gathered when they cleaned out the house for us. It seemed like something you might like to see as well, since it has notes and sketches about the map project inside." I looked down to see that it was Mandy's infamous sketch book, damp and smeared, but still readable nonetheless.

Not long after, I sat studying the map piece down in my room. I had hauled it down there myself, wanting to cherish the secret of its existence as long as possible, just as I had done with Mandy herself.

My eyes stopped abruptly on the mitten shape of Michigan's lower peninsula. The girl had nerves of steel and a sense of humor to boot: The first three embossed letters of Enrique's missing XANADU vanity plate stood out from the intricately-cut blue metal chunk as clear as day.

I removed the tape from the manila envelope she'd mailed to me anonymously from Ann Arbor back in August and inserted it into the stereo tray, and—as I had so often whenever I was lucky enough to be alone in the house—I pressed play.

Michael Jackson's single Billie Jean began, with the familiar words

I'd heard Denny croon out on the picnic table months earlier.

As it played, I noticed that every nail we'd used for the entire map project had a brushed silver head. Hundreds of the nails were all the same, scattered around to attach all the fifty states—except for one that I noticed in that moment. It was brass, and it had been driven into the far left edge of California. *Redondo Beach again*, I whispered to myself, recognizing its location. She had left me a final hidden message about her ultimate destination with a wire nail.

I opened her soiled sketch book and flipped through the sticky pages until I reached her checklist, and scanned down to the final two items on it. I held my breath in anticipation of what they might be. Number 9 was *Open My Own Shop*. And Number 10 was simply *Find Dad*.

I pictured Mandy at that very moment, wading into the surf of the Pacific, before walking back up to join her father in the recycled art gift shop she'd opened with all of Enrique's money. She had made it there after all. Every bone in my body knew it to be a fact. Her dreams had finally come true, and I was happy for her.

I grabbed a pen from my desk and carefully checked off all the items on the list for her. Tears and laughter both hit me at once. I closed my eyes and repeated the words of the song from memory as it played loudly from the stereo, the sounds carrying into the farthest reaches of my empty house:

For forty days and forty nights
The law was on her side
But who can stand when she's in demand
Her schemes and plans.

THE END

the Storage garages *why?*

Mom and Me '75

THY WORD IS TRUTH
JOHN 17:17

an important Reminder

sunset Acres

Dav birthday '85

mandy's Map

Made in the USA
Middletown, DE
19 September 2023